DIE VOLUME 2.
SPLIT THE PARTY

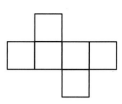

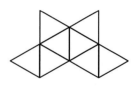

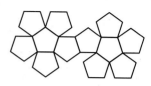

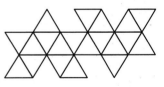

DIE VOLUME 2:
SPLIT THE PARTY

KIERON GILLEN
Writer

STEPHANIE HANS
Artist

CLAYTON COWLES
Letterer

RIAN HUGHES
Designer

CHRISSY WILLIAMS
Editor

with

ELVIRE DE COCK
Guest Colour Artist
Issue 9, pages 8-18

IMAGE COMICS, INC.
Robert Kirkman: Chief Operating Officer
Erik Larsen: Chief Financial Officer
Todd McFarlane: President
Marc Silvestri: Chief Executive Officer
Jim Valentino: Vice President
Eric Stephenson: Publisher / Chief Creative Officer
Jeff Boison: Director of Publishing Planning, Book Trade Sales
Chris Ross: Director of Digital Services
Jeff Stang: Director of Direct Market Sales
Kat Salazar: Director of PR & Marketing
Drew Gill: Cover Editor
Heather Doornink: Production Director
Nicole Lapalme: Controller
imagecomics.com

ISBN, Standard Edition: 978-1-5343-1497-9
ISBN, Newbury Exclusive: 978-1-5343-1665-2

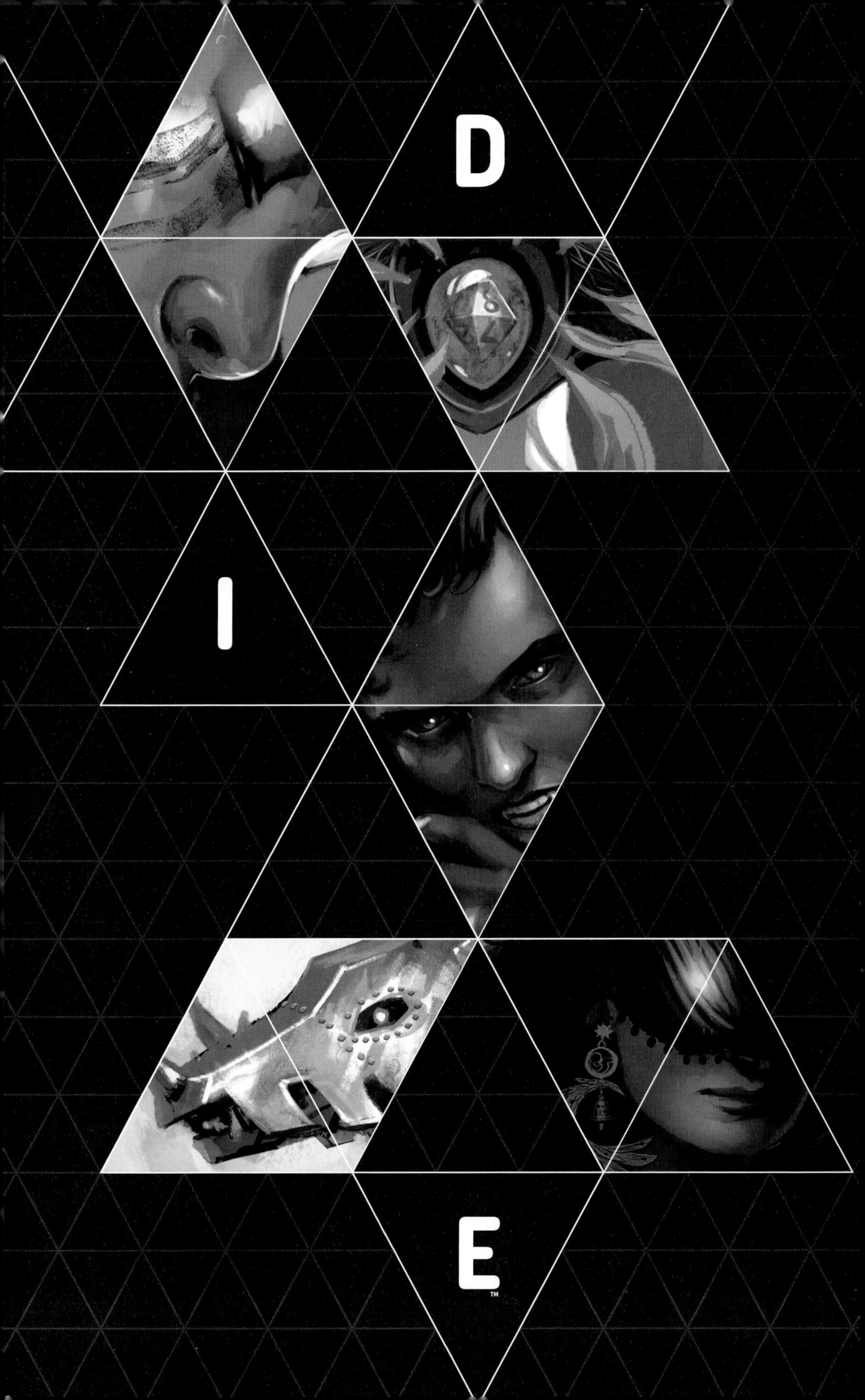
D
I
E™

In 1991, six teenagers disappeared into a fantasy role-playing game. Only five returned.

In 2018, they're all dragged back in. They can't go home until six agree. They don't. The Party splits.

D4

ASH
Dictator

Dominic Ash in the real world, Ash in the world of Die. Married. In marketing. Sol's best friend.

D6

CHUCK
Fool

Fantasy novelist with multiple ex-wives, no tact, and a film franchise.

D8

MATT
Grief Knight

Parent and husband. Statistics professor at the local university.

D10

ANGELA
Neo

Coder and parent on the outside, going through an ugly divorce. Ash's sister.

D12

ISABELLE
Godbinder

Divorced school-teacher with aggressively bilingual intelligence.

D20

SOL
Grandmaster

Solomon made the game but never made it out. Murdered by Ash and is now one of the Fallen.

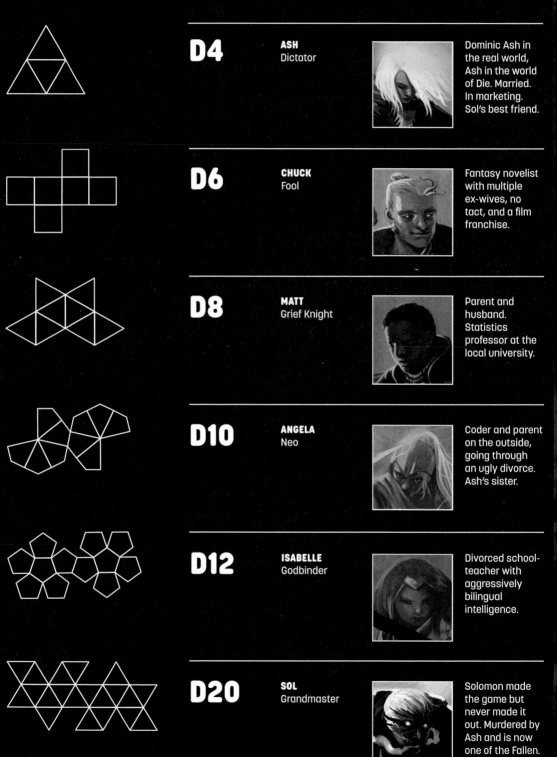

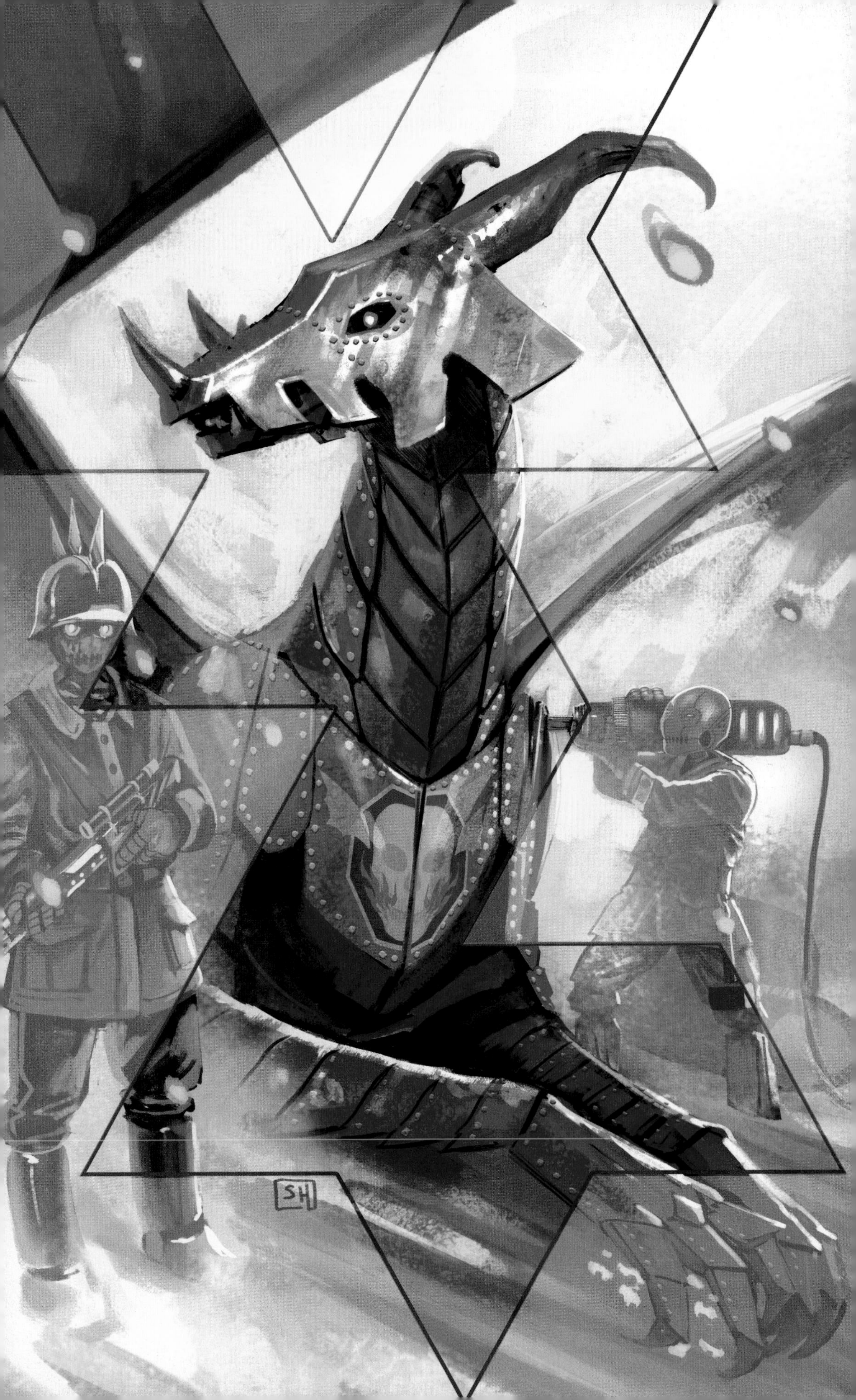

6:
THE GRIND

"'There's a tendency among the press to attribute the creation of a game to a single person,' says Warren Spector, creator of *Thief* and *Deus Ex*."
– *IGN*

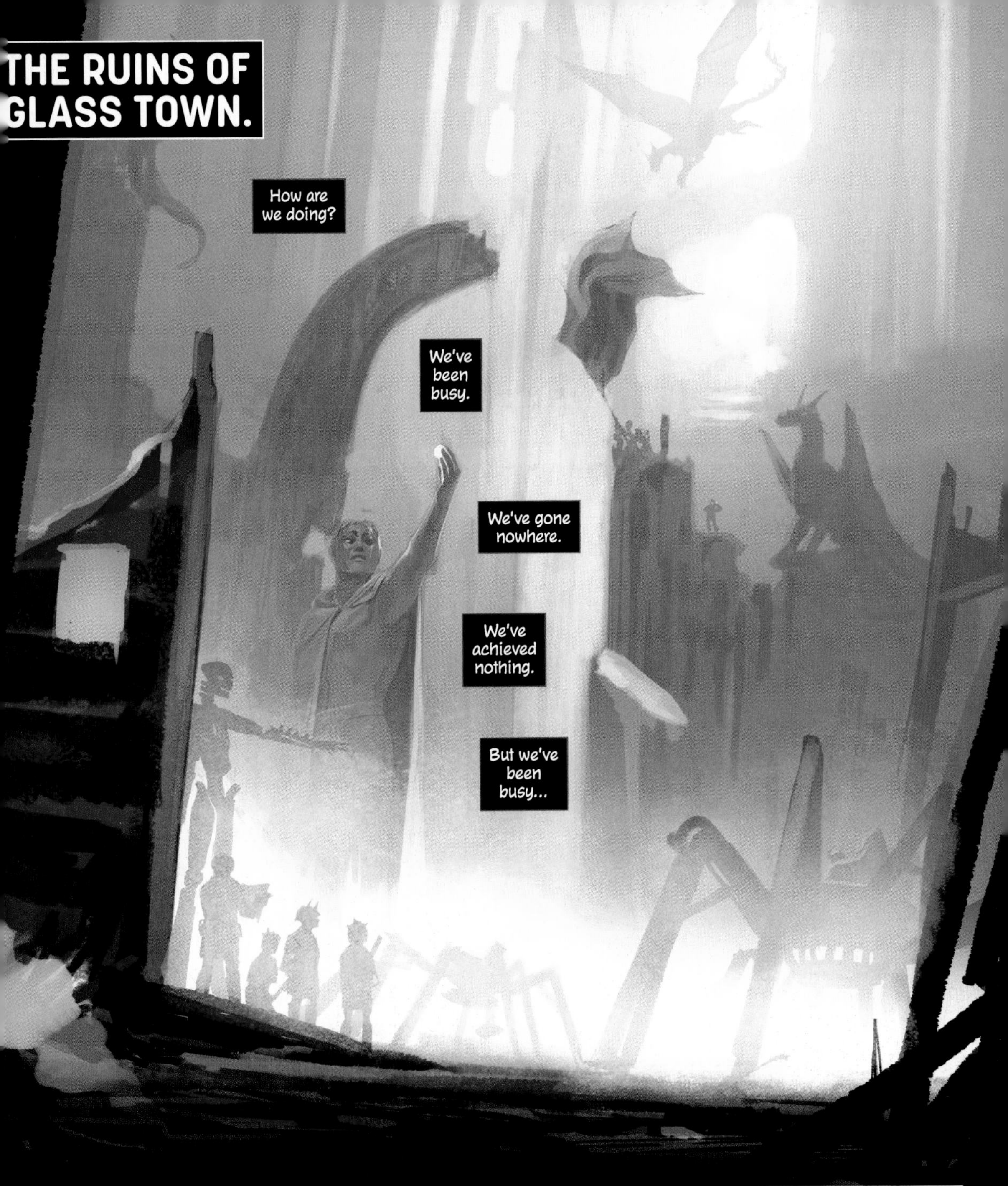
THE RUINS OF GLASS TOWN.
How are we doing?
We've been busy.
We've gone nowhere.
We've achieved nothing.
But we've been busy...

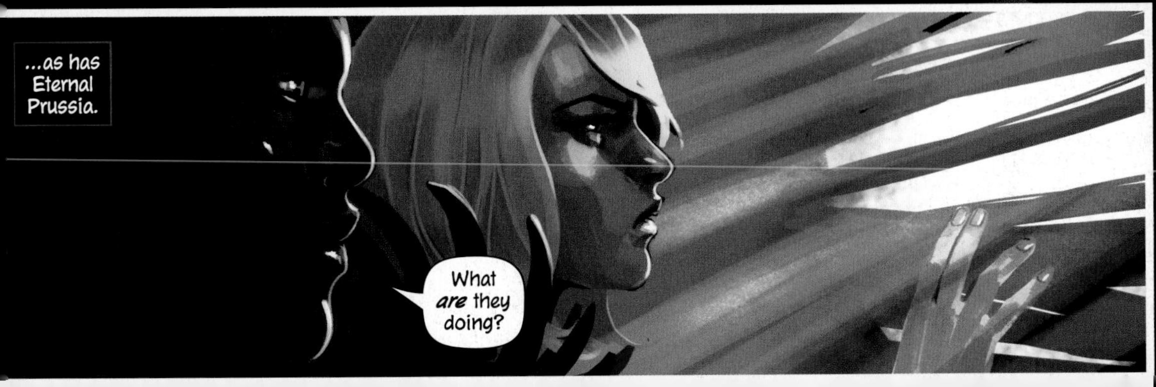
...as has Eternal Prussia.
What *are* they doing?

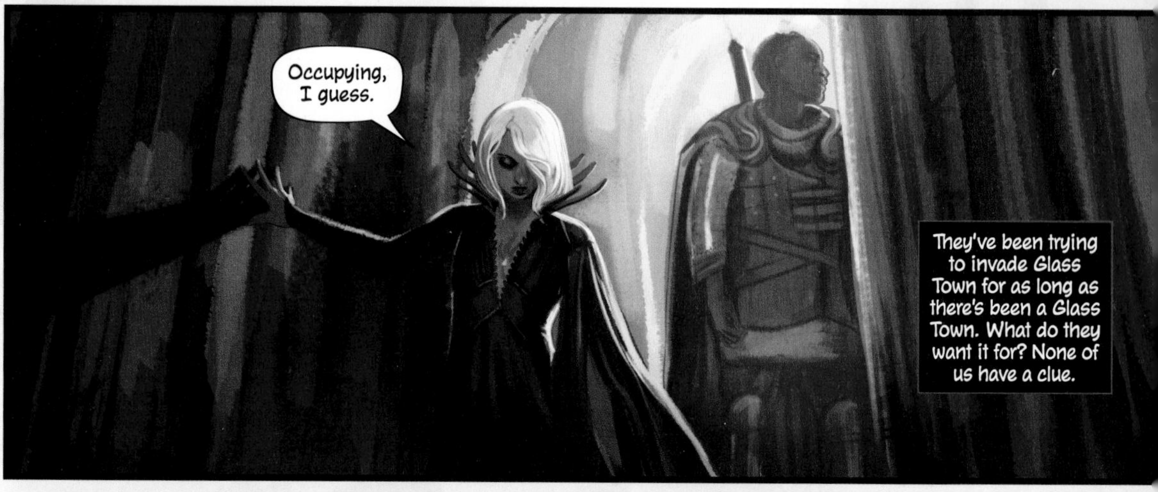
Occupying, I guess.
They've been trying to invade Glass Town for as long as there's been a Glass Town. What do they want it for? None of us have a clue.

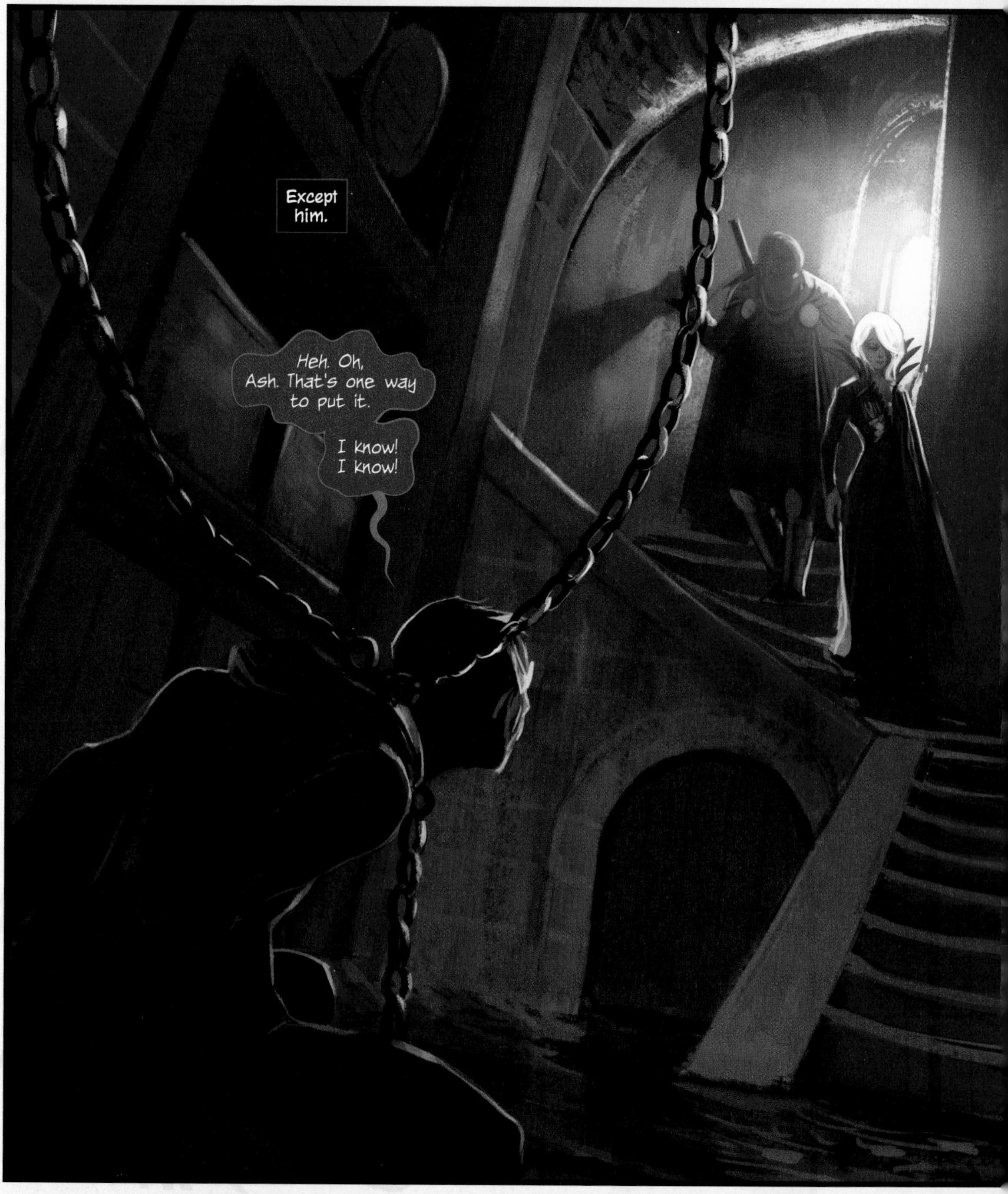
Except him.
Heh. Oh, Ash. That's one way to put it.
I know! I know!

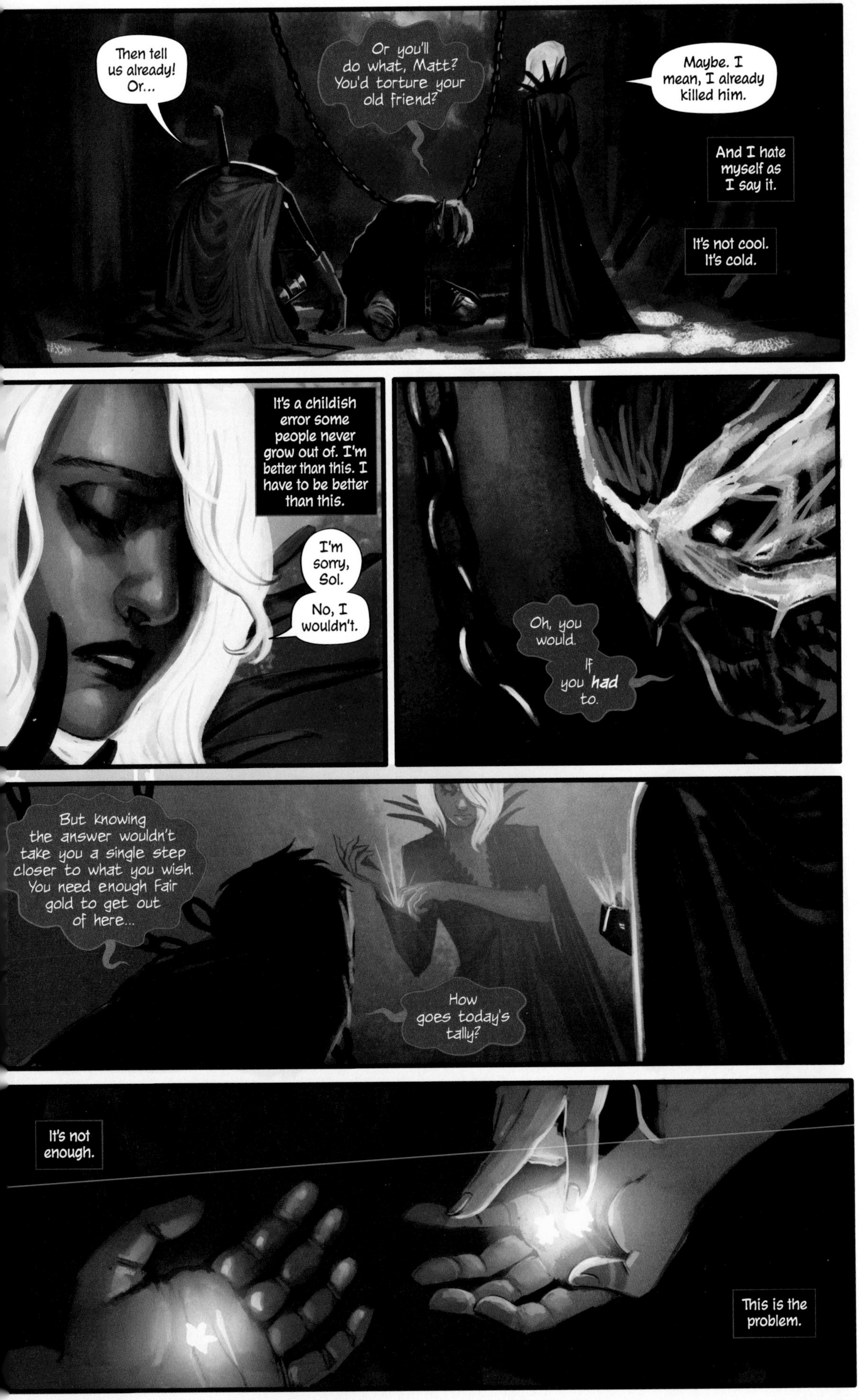
Then tell us already! Or...
Or you'll do what, Matt? You'd torture your old friend?
Maybe. I mean, I already killed him.
And I hate myself as I say it.
It's not cool. It's cold.
It's a childish error some people never grow out of. I'm better than this. I have to be better than this.
I'm sorry, Sol.
No, I wouldn't.
Oh, you would.
If you had to.
But knowing the answer wouldn't take you a single step closer to what you wish. You need enough Fair gold to get out of here...
How goes today's tally?
It's not enough.
This is the problem.

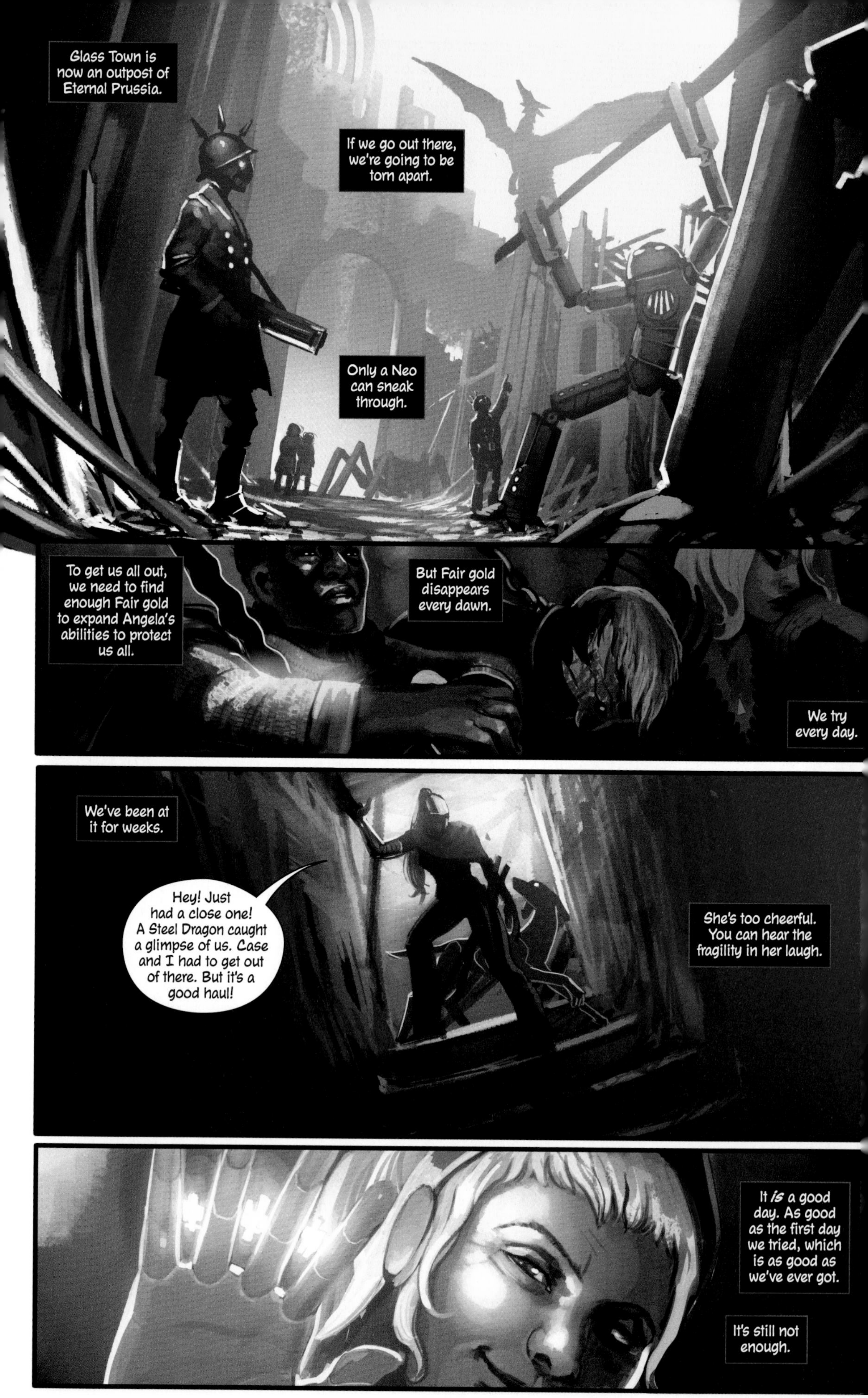
Glass Town is now an outpost of Eternal Prussia.
If we go out there, we're going to be torn apart.
Only a Neo can sneak through.
To get us all out, we need to find enough Fair gold to expand Angela's abilities to protect us all.
But Fair gold disappears every dawn.
We try every day.
We've been at it for weeks.
Hey! Just had a close one! A Steel Dragon caught a glimpse of us. Case and I had to get out of there. But it's a good haul!
She's too cheerful. You can hear the fragility in her laugh.
It *is* a good day. As good as the first day we tried, which is as good as we've ever got.
It's still not enough.

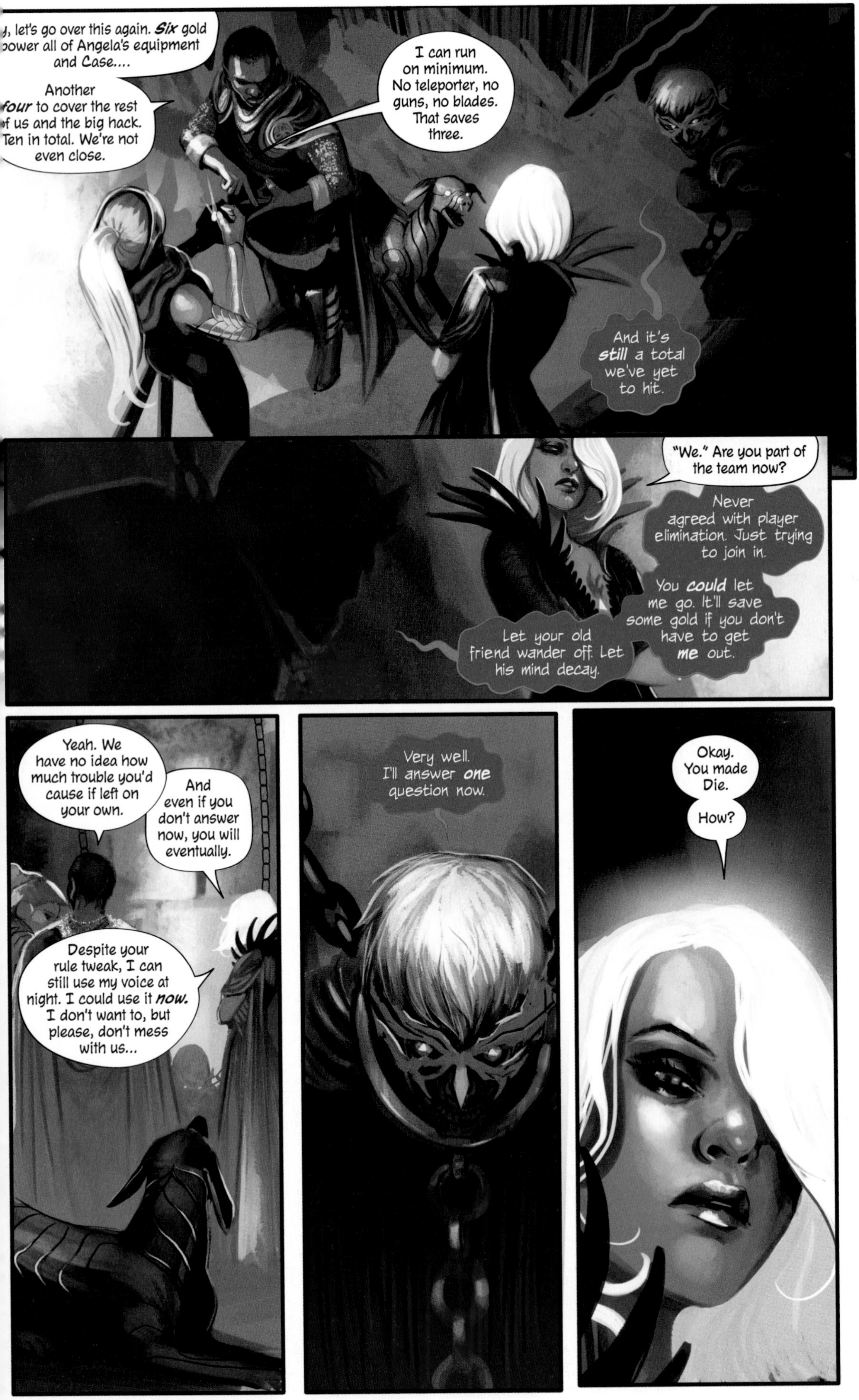
let's go over this again. Six gold
power all of Angela's equipment and Case....
Another four to cover the rest of us and the big hack. Ten in total. We're not even close.
I can run on minimum. No teleporter, no guns, no blades. That saves three.
And it's still a total we've yet to hit.
"We." Are you part of the team now?
Never agreed with player elimination. Just trying to join in.
You could let me go. It'll save some gold if you don't have to get me out.
Let your old friend wander off. Let his mind decay.
Yeah. We have no idea how much trouble you'd cause if left on your own.
And even if you don't answer now, you will eventually.
Despite your rule tweak, I can still use my voice at night. I could use it now. I don't want to, but please, don't mess with us...
Very well. I'll answer one question now.
Okay. You made Die.
How?

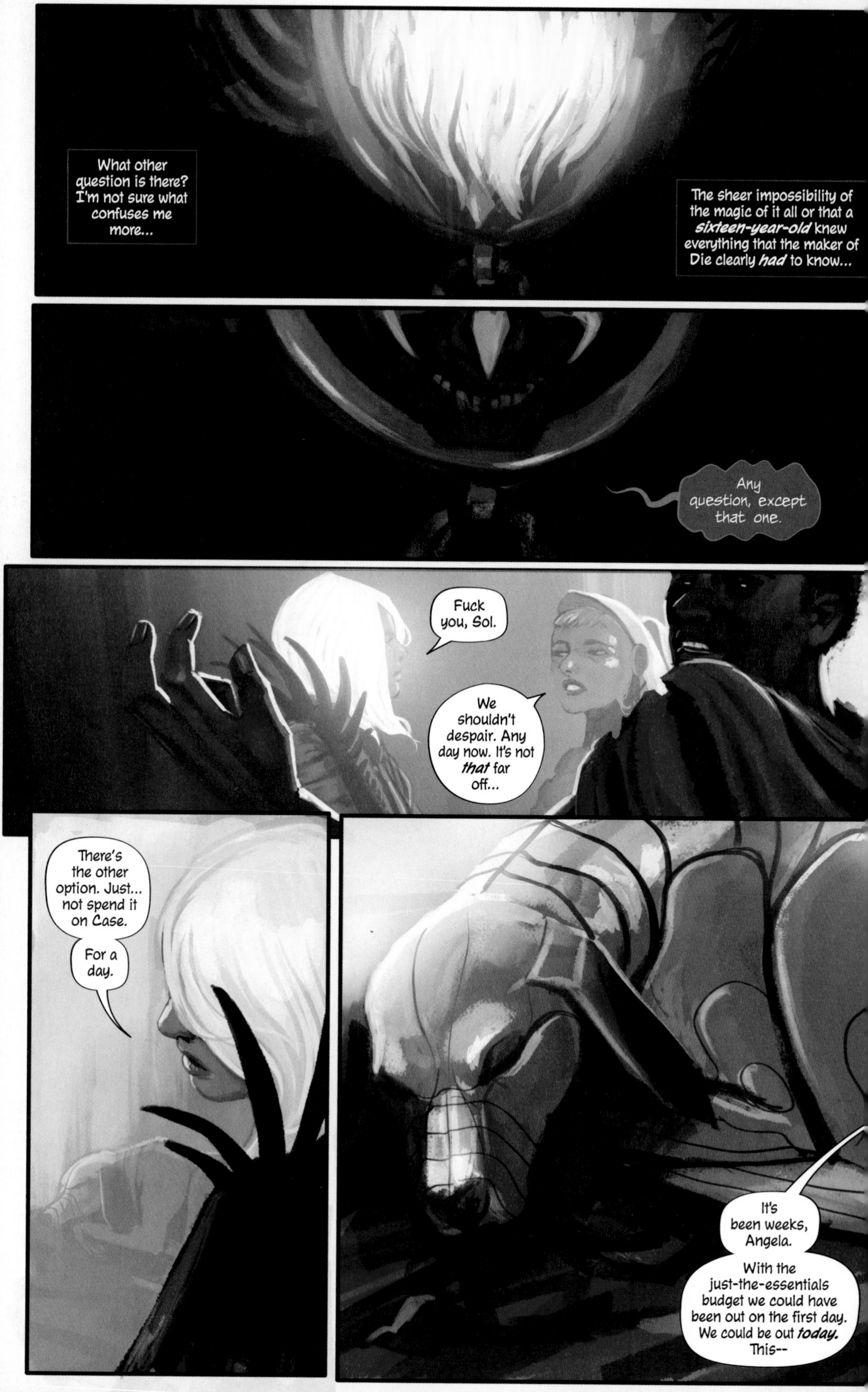
What other question is there? I'm not sure what confuses me more...
The sheer impossibility of the magic of it all or that a *sixteen-year-old* knew everything that the maker of Die clearly *had* to know...
Any question, except that one.
Fuck you, Sol.
We shouldn't despair. Any day now. It's not *that* far off...
There's the other option. Just... not spend it on Case.
For a day.
It's been weeks, Angela.
With the just-the-essentials budget we could have been out on the first day. We could be out *today.* This--

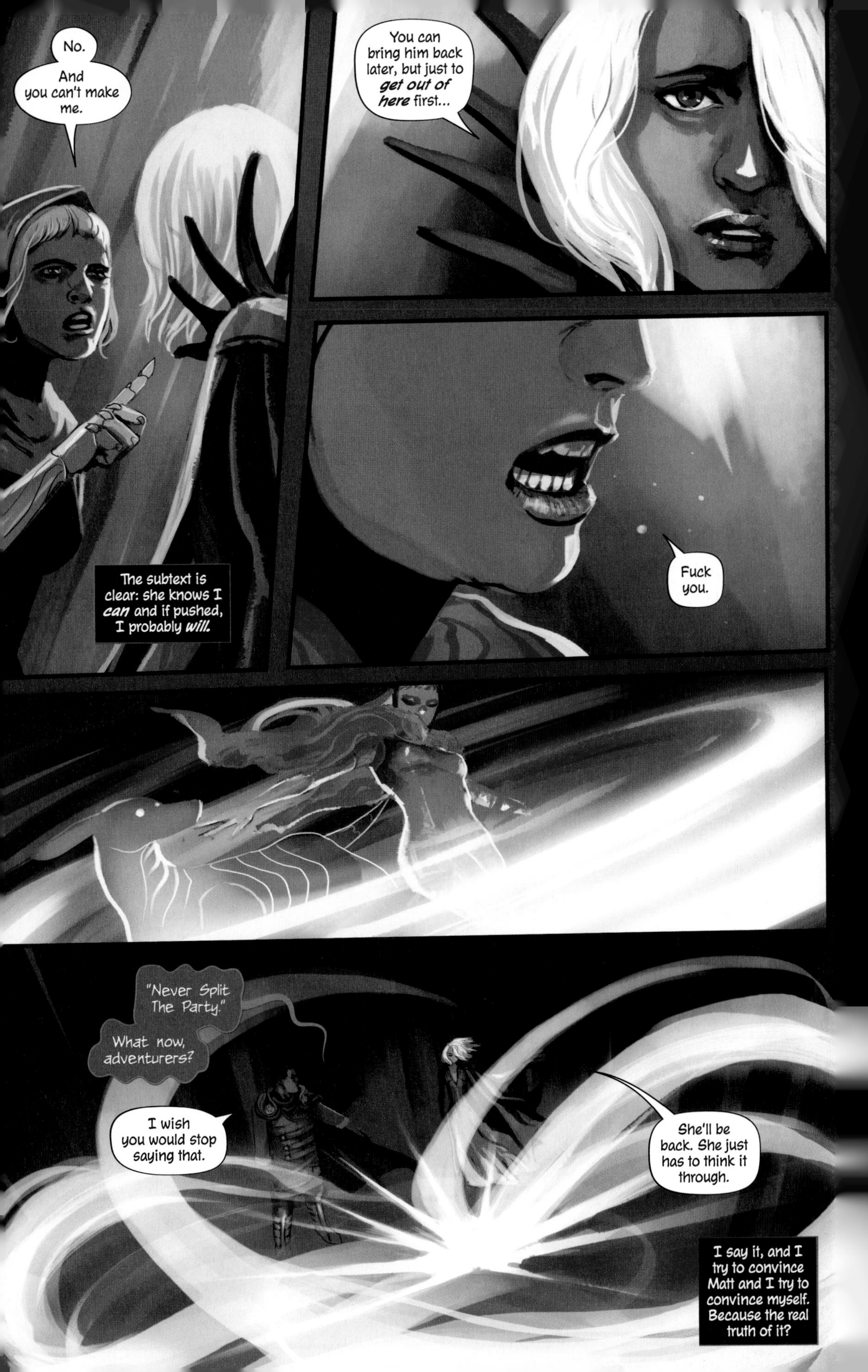

No.
And you can't make me.
You can bring him back later, but just to *get out of here* first...
The subtext is clear: she knows I *can* and if pushed, I probably *will.*
Fuck you.
"Never Split The Party."
What now, adventurers?
I wish you would stop saying that.
She'll be back. She just has to think it through.
I say it, and I try to convince Matt and I try to convince myself. Because the real truth of it?

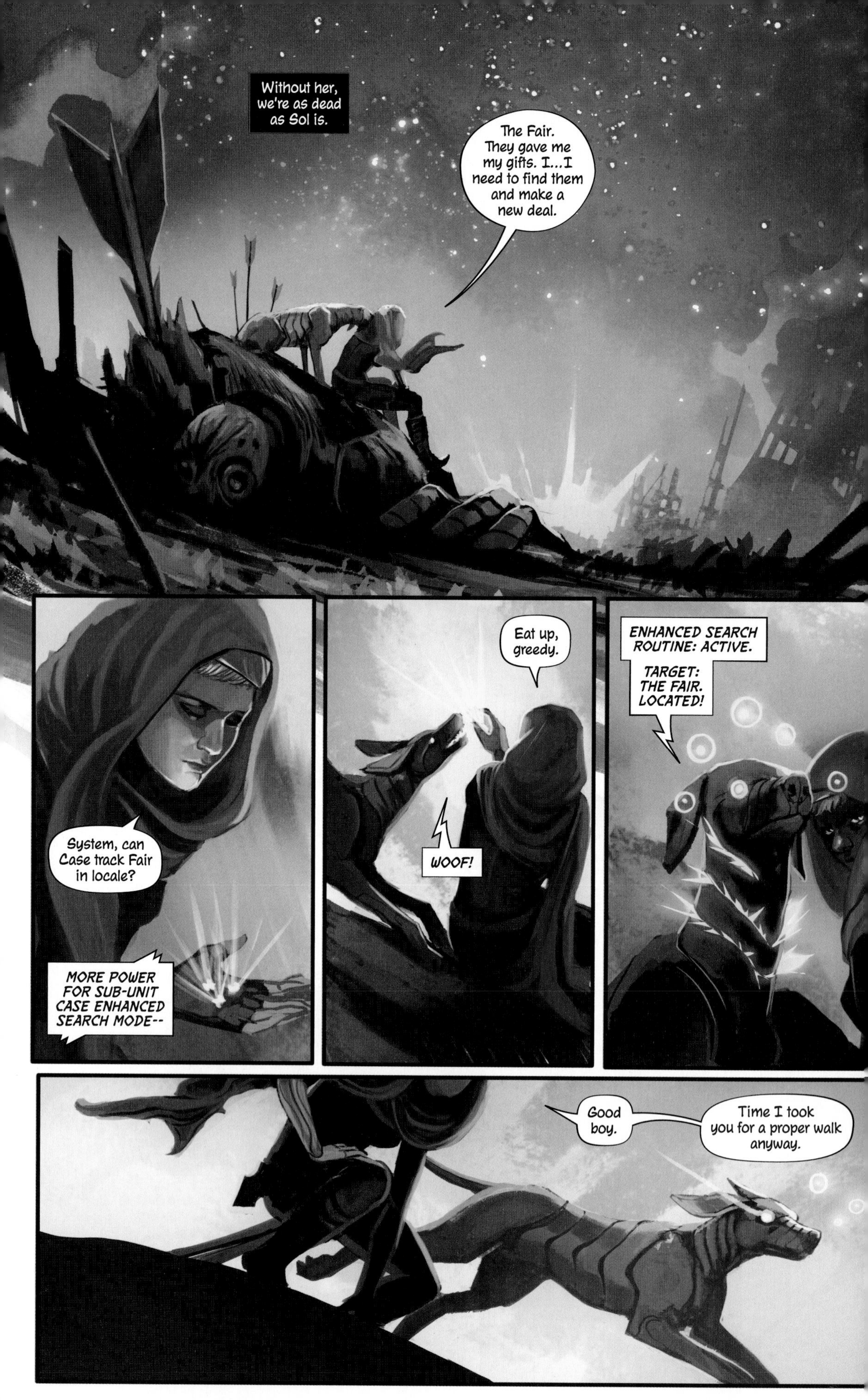
Without her, we're as dead as Sol is.
The Fair. They gave me my gifts. I...I need to find them and make a new deal.
System, can Case track Fair in locale?
MORE POWER FOR SUB-UNIT CASE ENHANCED SEARCH MODE--
Eat up, greedy.
WOOF!
ENHANCED SEARCH ROUTINE: ACTIVE.
TARGET: THE FAIR. LOCATED!
Good boy.
Time I took you for a proper walk anyway.

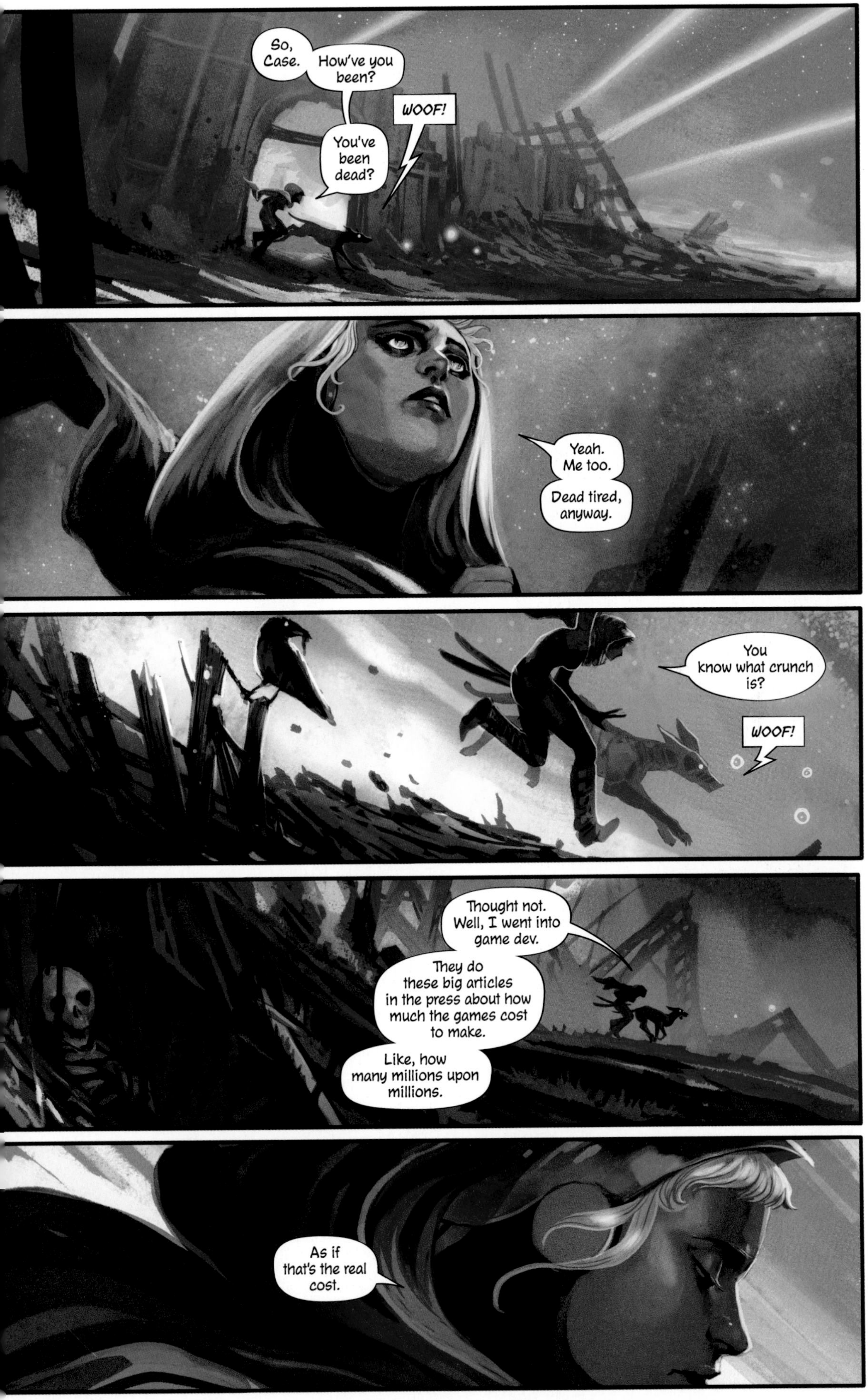
So, Case.
How've you been?
You've been dead?
WOOF!
Yeah. Me too.
Dead tired, anyway.
You know what crunch is?
WOOF!
Thought not. Well, I went into game dev.
They do these big articles in the press about how much the games cost to make.
Like, how many millions upon millions.
As if that's the real cost.

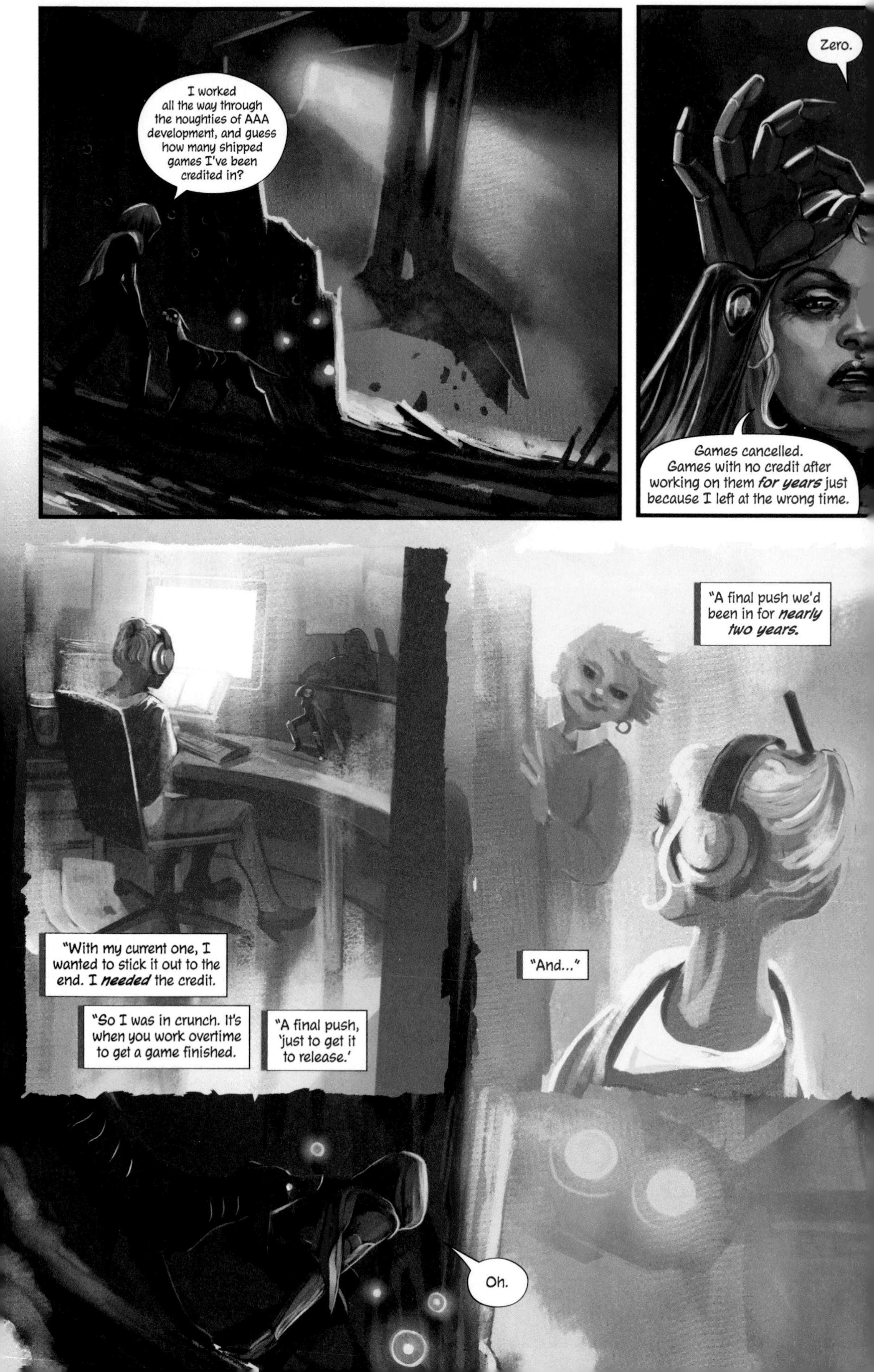

I worked all the way through the noughties of AAA development, and guess how many shipped games I've been credited in?
Zero.
Games cancelled. Games with no credit after working on them *for years* just because I left at the wrong time.
"With my current one, I wanted to stick it out to the end. I *needed* the credit.
"So I was in crunch. It's when you work overtime to get a game finished.
"A final push, 'just to get it to release.'
"A final push we'd been in for *nearly two years.*
"And..."
Oh.

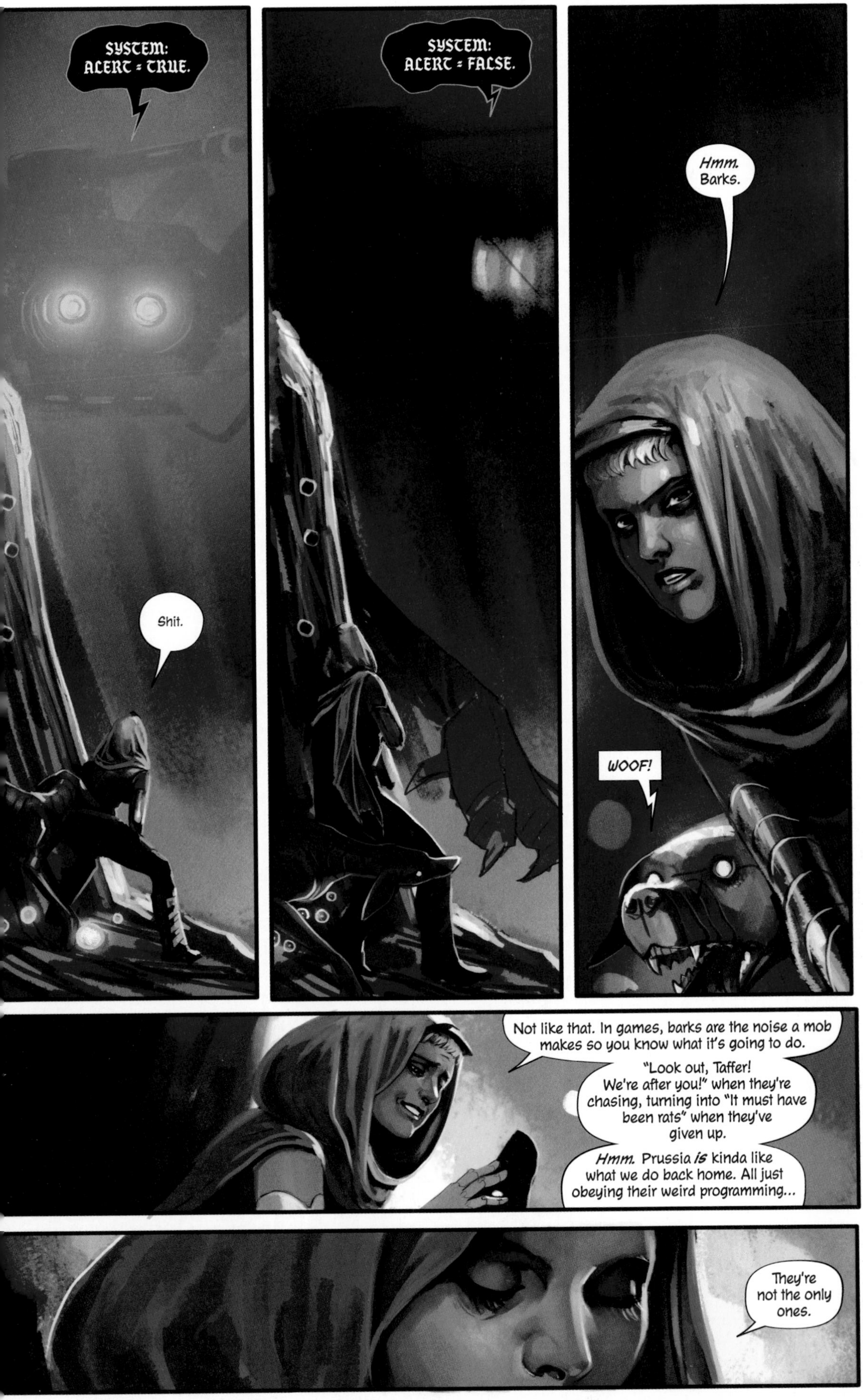
SYSTEM: ALERT = TRUE.
Shit.
SYSTEM: ALERT = FALSE.
Hmm. Barks.
WOOF!
Not like that. In games, barks are the noise a mob makes so you know what it's going to do.
"Look out, Taffer! We're after you!" when they're chasing, turning into "It must have been rats" when they've given up.
Hmm. Prussia *is* kinda like what we do back home. All just obeying their weird programming...
They're not the only ones.

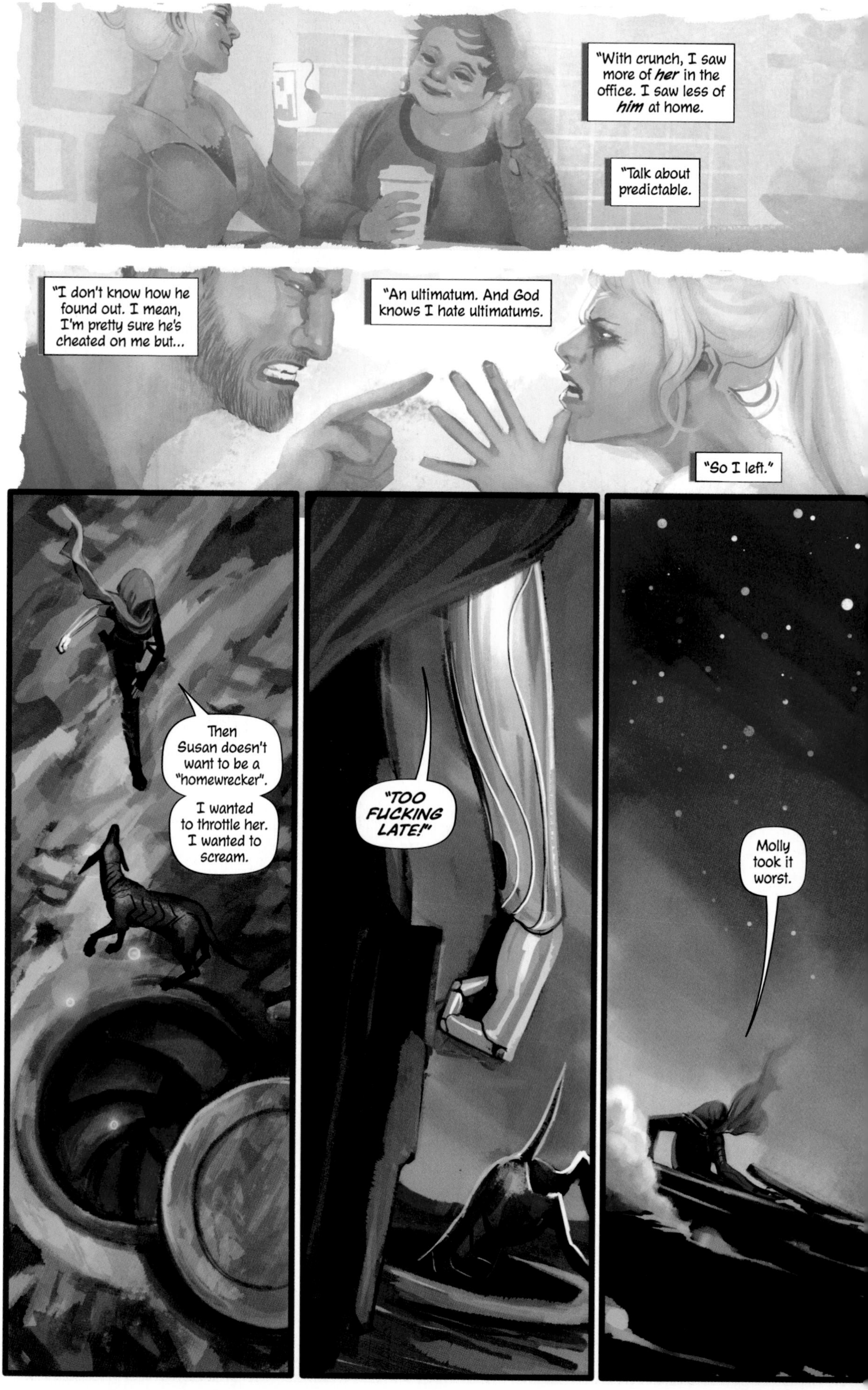
"With crunch, I saw more of *her* in the office. I saw less of *him* at home.
"Talk about predictable.
"I don't know how he found out. I mean, I'm pretty sure he's cheated on me but...
"An ultimatum. And God knows I hate ultimatums.
"So I left."
Then Susan doesn't want to be a "homewrecker".
I wanted to throttle her. I wanted to scream.
"TOO FUCKING LATE!"
Molly took it worst.

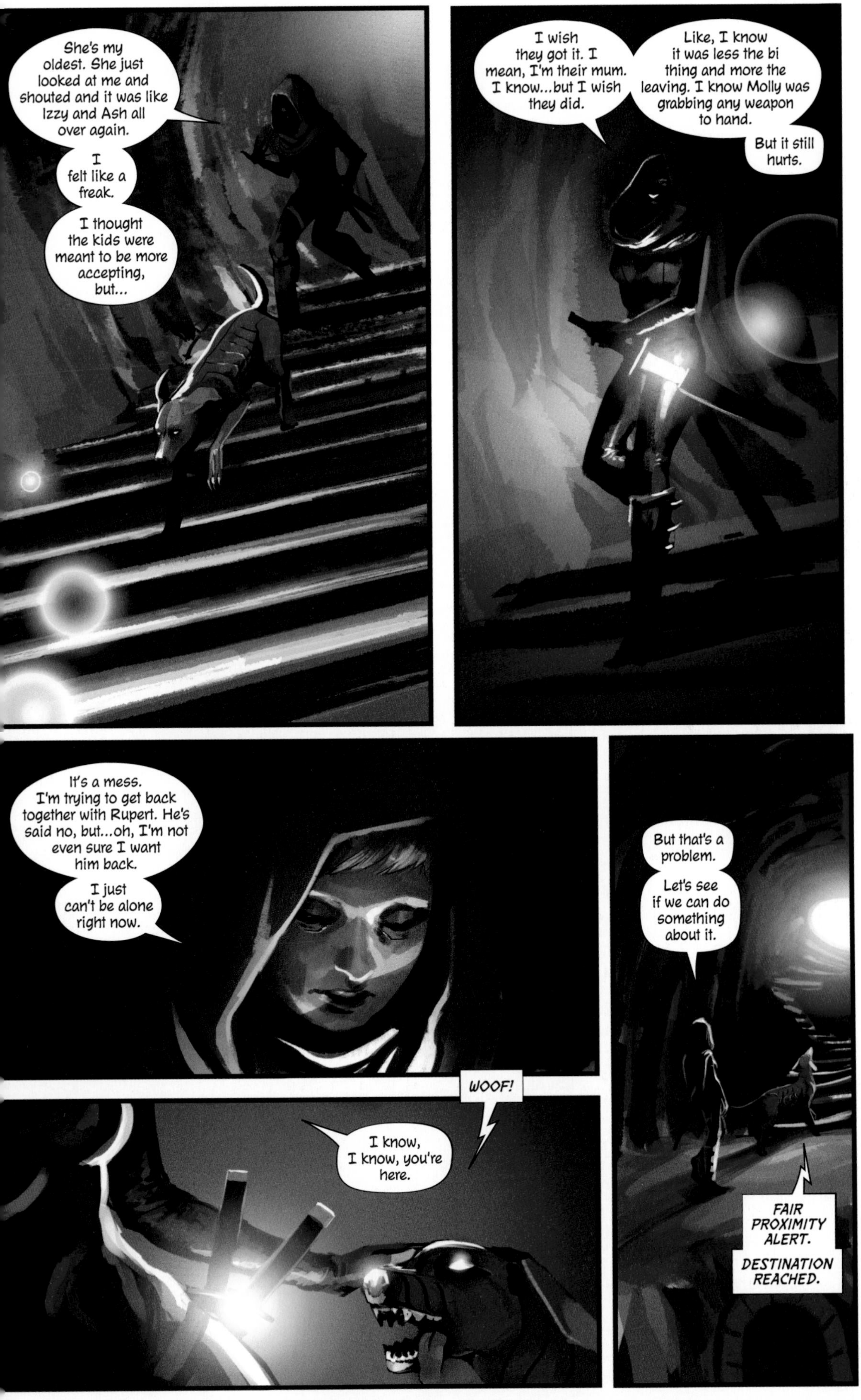

She's my oldest. She just looked at me and shouted and it was like Izzy and Ash all over again.
I felt like a freak.
I thought the kids were meant to be more accepting, but...
I wish they got it. I mean, I'm their mum. I know...but I wish they did.
Like, I know it was less the bi thing and more the leaving. I know Molly was grabbing any weapon to hand.
But it still hurts.
It's a mess. I'm trying to get back together with Rupert. He's said no, but...oh, I'm not even sure I want him back.
I just can't be alone right now.
But that's a problem.
Let's see if we can do something about it.
WOOF!
I know, I know, you're here.
FAIR PROXIMITY ALERT.
DESTINATION REACHED.

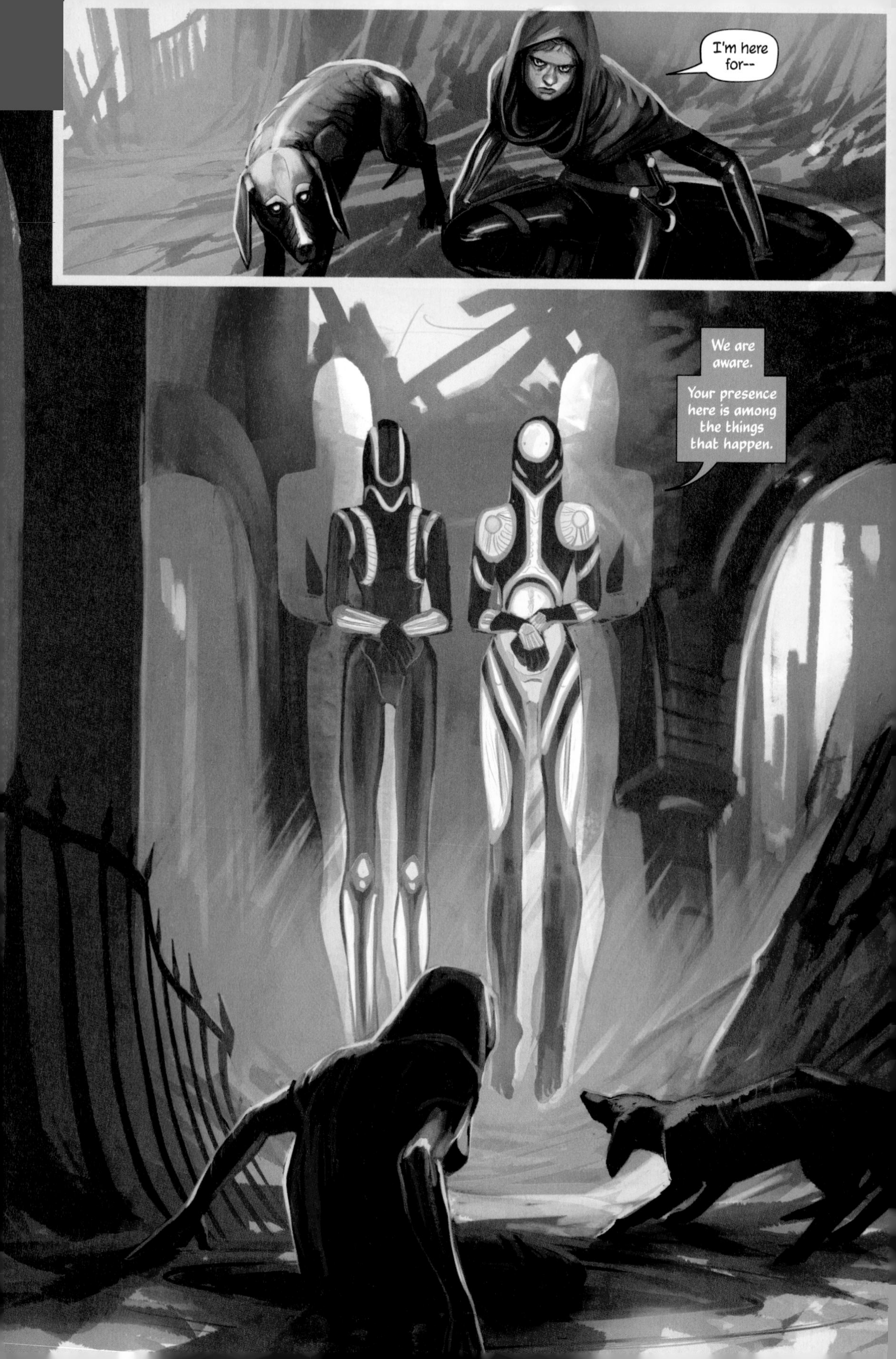

I'm here for--
We are aware.
Your presence here is among the things that happen.

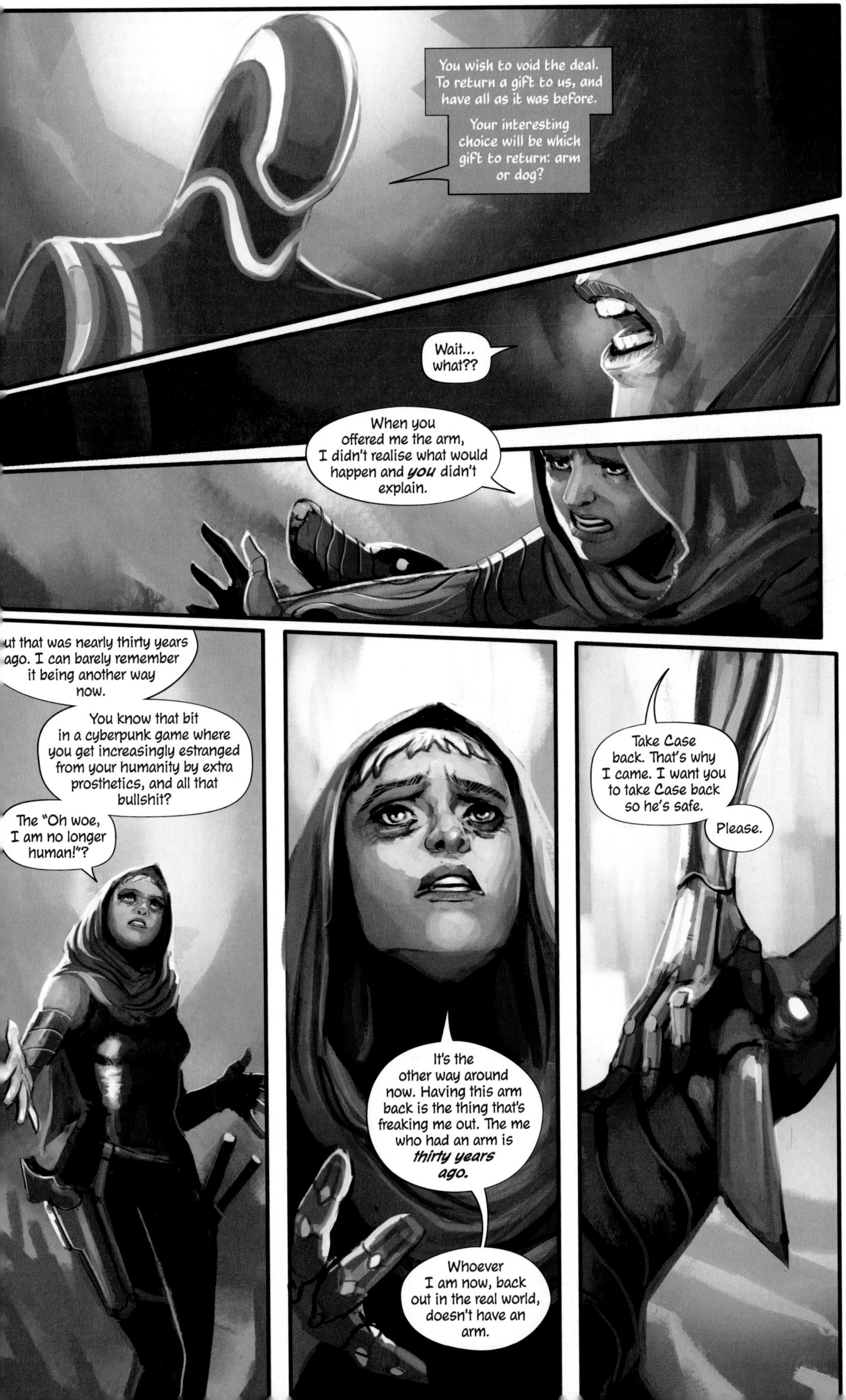
You wish to void the deal. To return a gift to us, and have all as it was before.
Your interesting choice will be which gift to return: arm or dog?
Wait... what??
When you offered me the arm, I didn't realise what would happen and *you* didn't explain.
ut that was nearly thirty years ago. I can barely remember it being another way now.
You know that bit in a cyberpunk game where you get increasingly estranged from your humanity by extra prosthetics, and all that bullshit?
The "Oh woe, I am no longer human!"?
It's the other way around now. Having this arm back is the thing that's freaking me out. The me who had an arm is ***thirty years ago.***
Whoever I am now, back out in the real world, doesn't have an arm.
Take Case back. That's why I came. I want you to take Case back so he's safe.
Please.

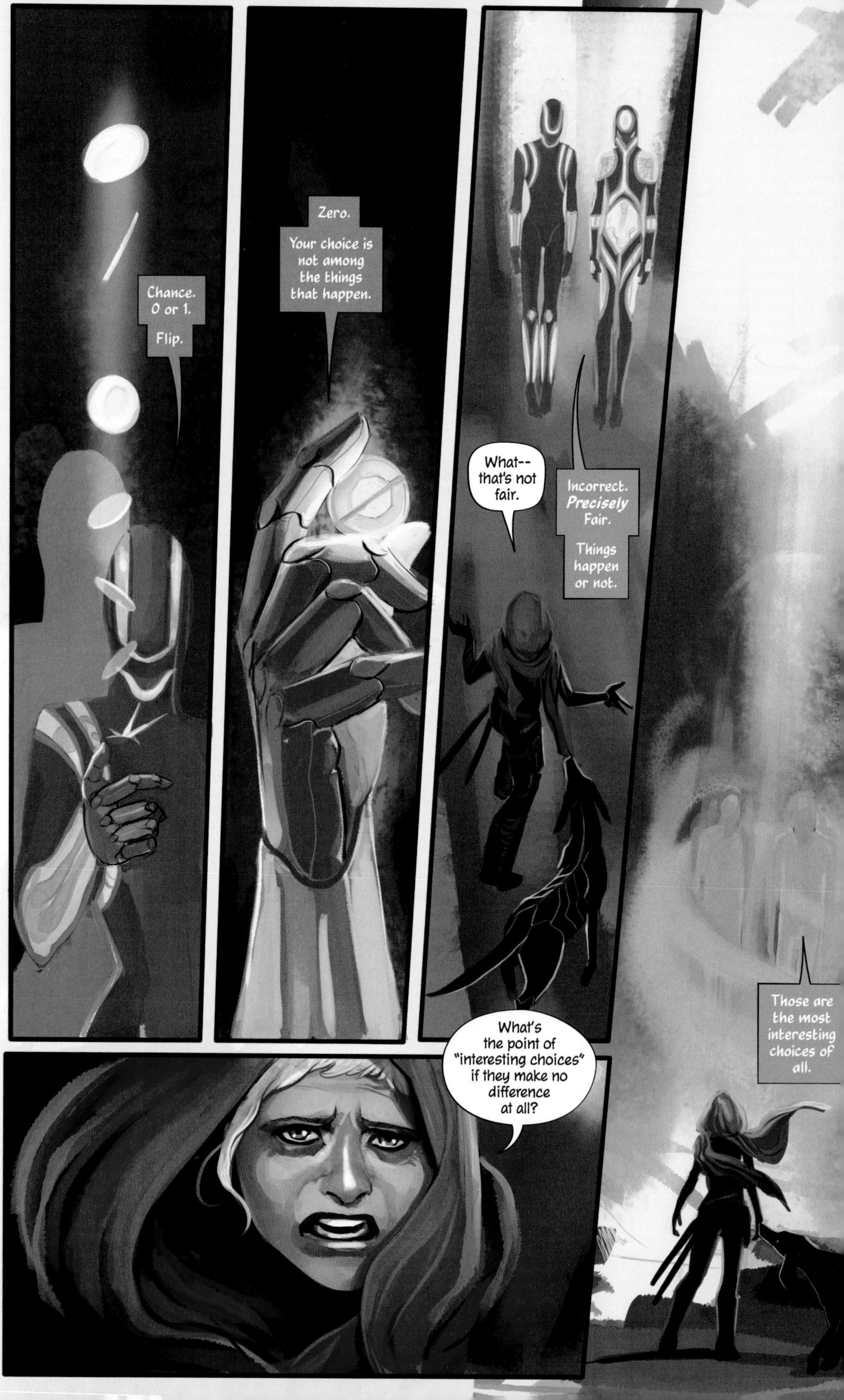
Chance.
0 or 1.
Flip.
Zero.
Your choice is not among the things that happen.
What-- that's not fair.
Incorrect. *Precisely* Fair.
Things happen or not.
Those are the most interesting choices of all.
What's the point of "interesting choices" if they make no difference at all?

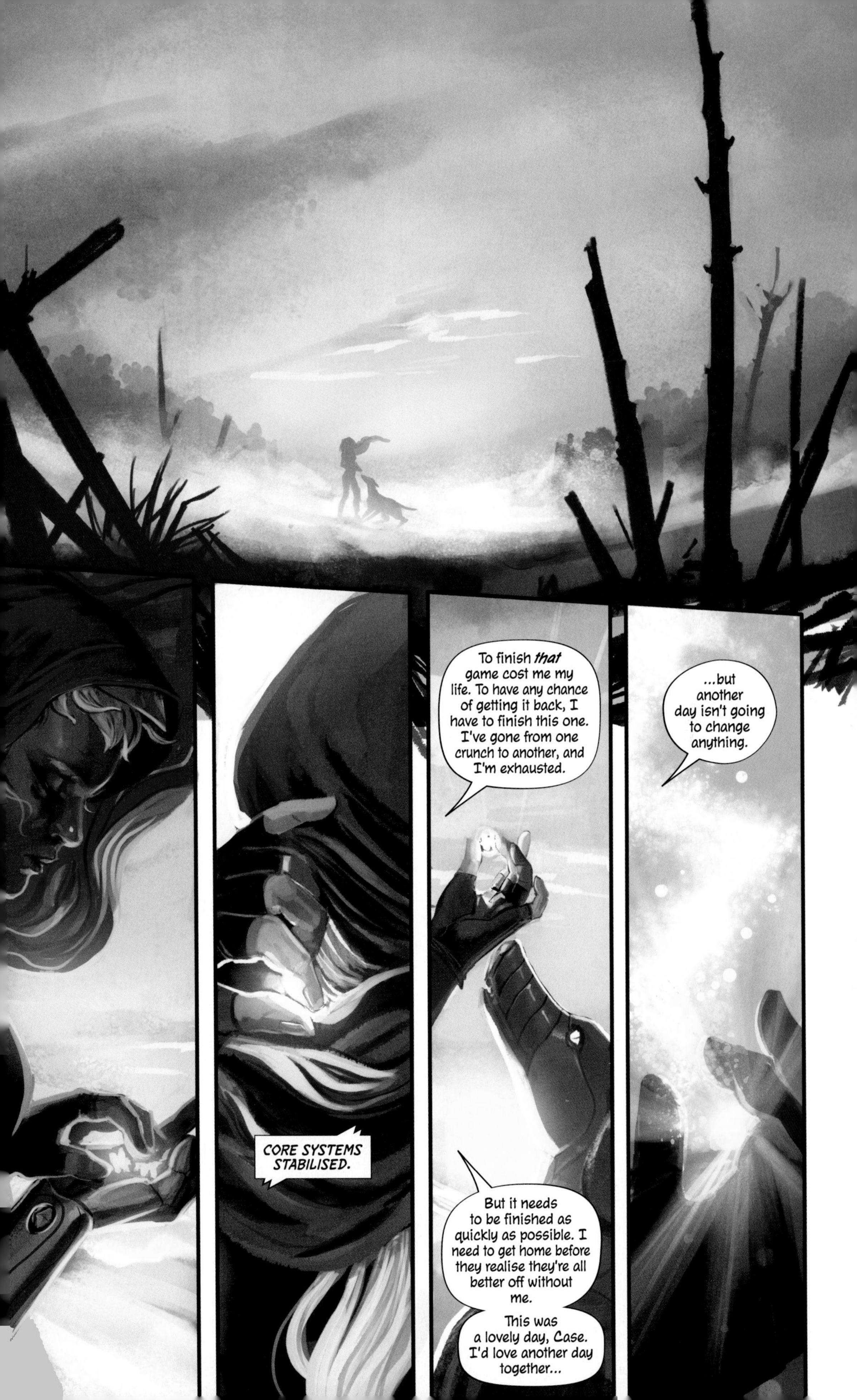
CORE SYSTEMS STABILISED.
To finish *that* game cost me my life. To have any chance of getting it back, I have to finish this one. I've gone from one crunch to another, and I'm exhausted.
But it needs to be finished as quickly as possible. I need to get home before they realise they're all better off without me.
This was a lovely day, Case. I'd love another day together...
...but another day isn't going to change anything.

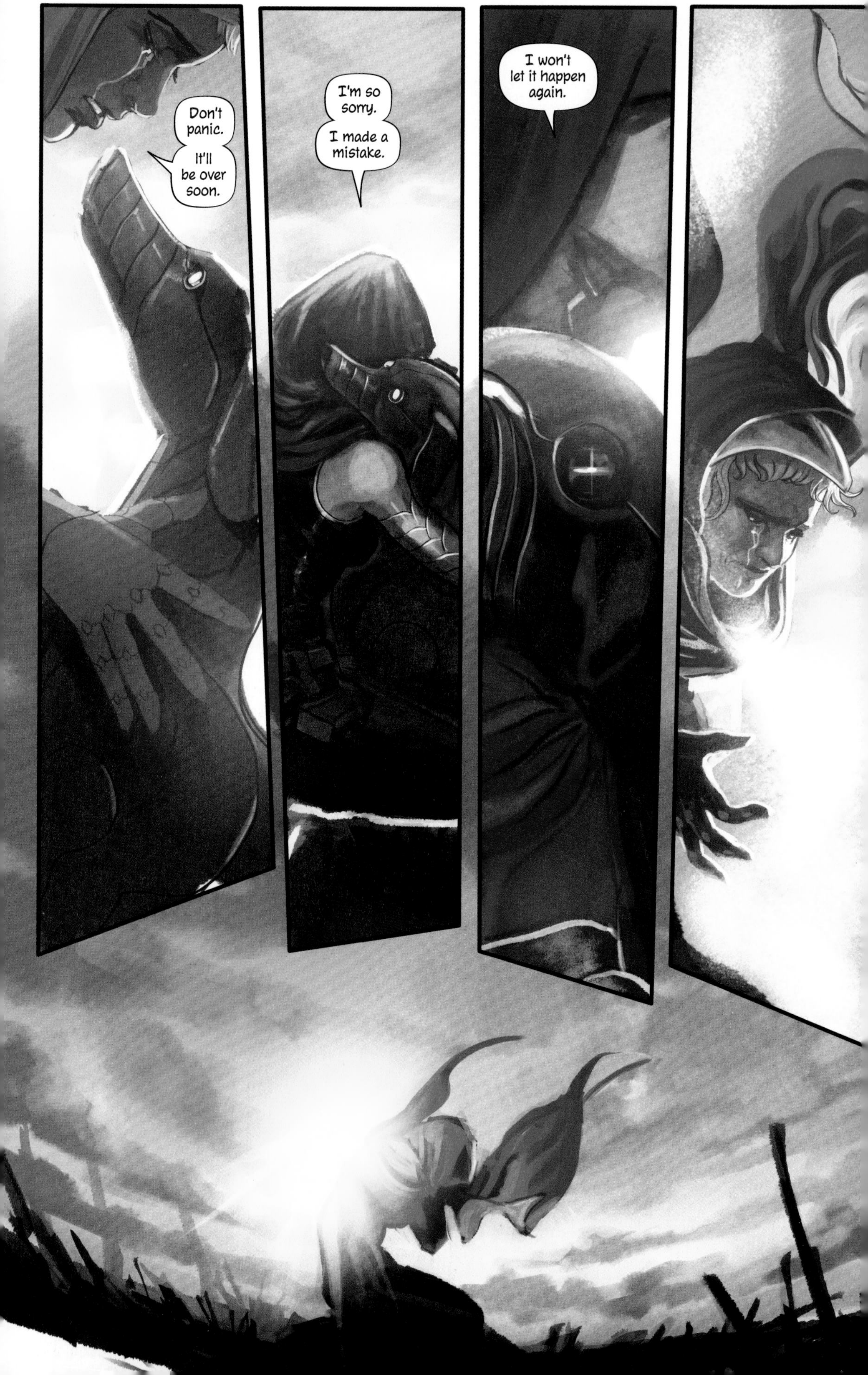
Don't panic.
It'll be over soon.
I'm so sorry.
I made a mistake.
I won't let it happen again.

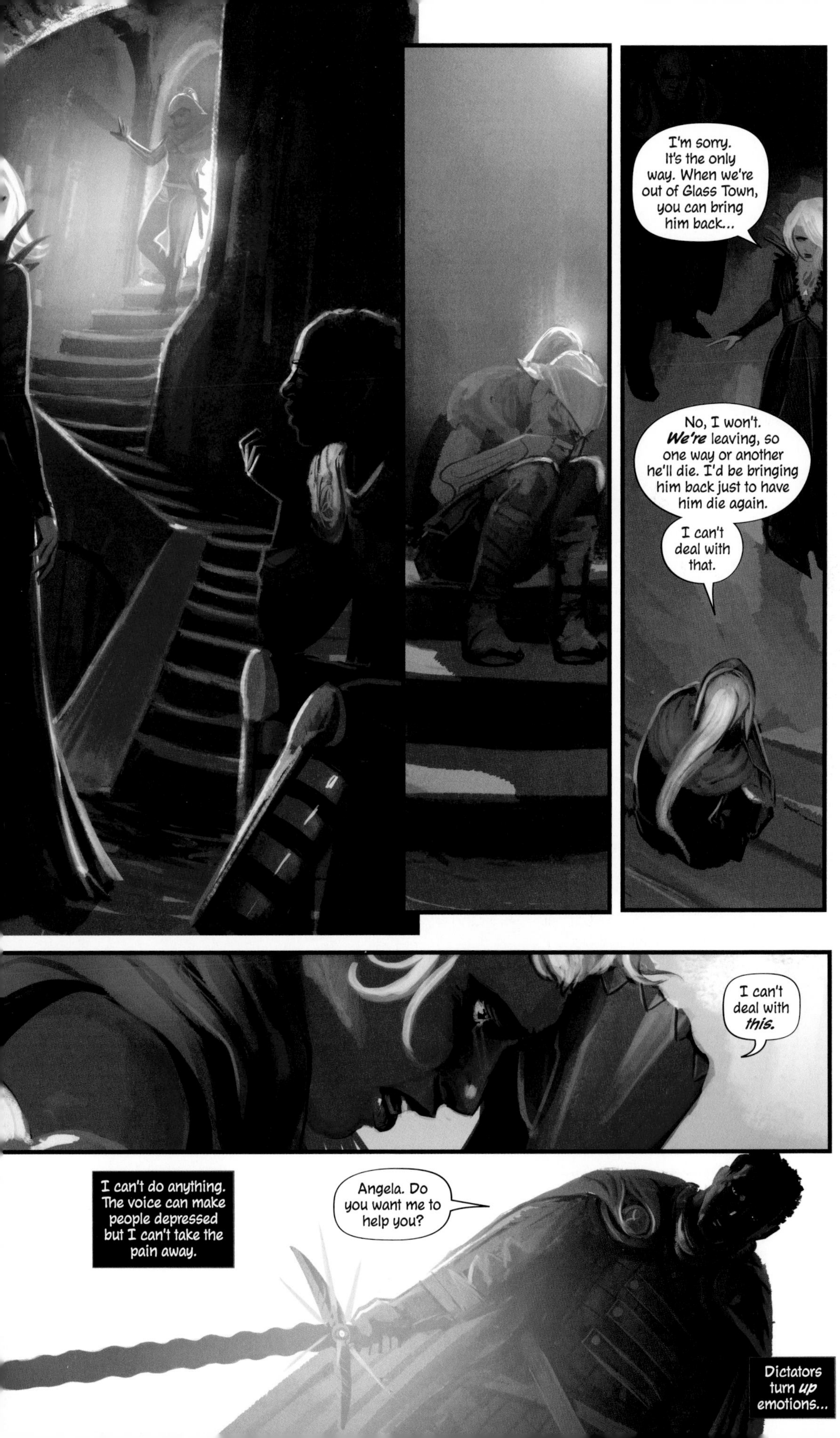
I'm sorry. It's the only way. When we're out of Glass Town, you can bring him back...
No, I won't. *We're* leaving, so one way or another he'll die. I'd be bringing him back just to have him die again.
I can't deal with that.
I can't deal with *this.*
I can't do anything. The voice can make people depressed but I can't take the pain away.
Angela. Do you want me to help you?
Dictators turn *up* emotions...

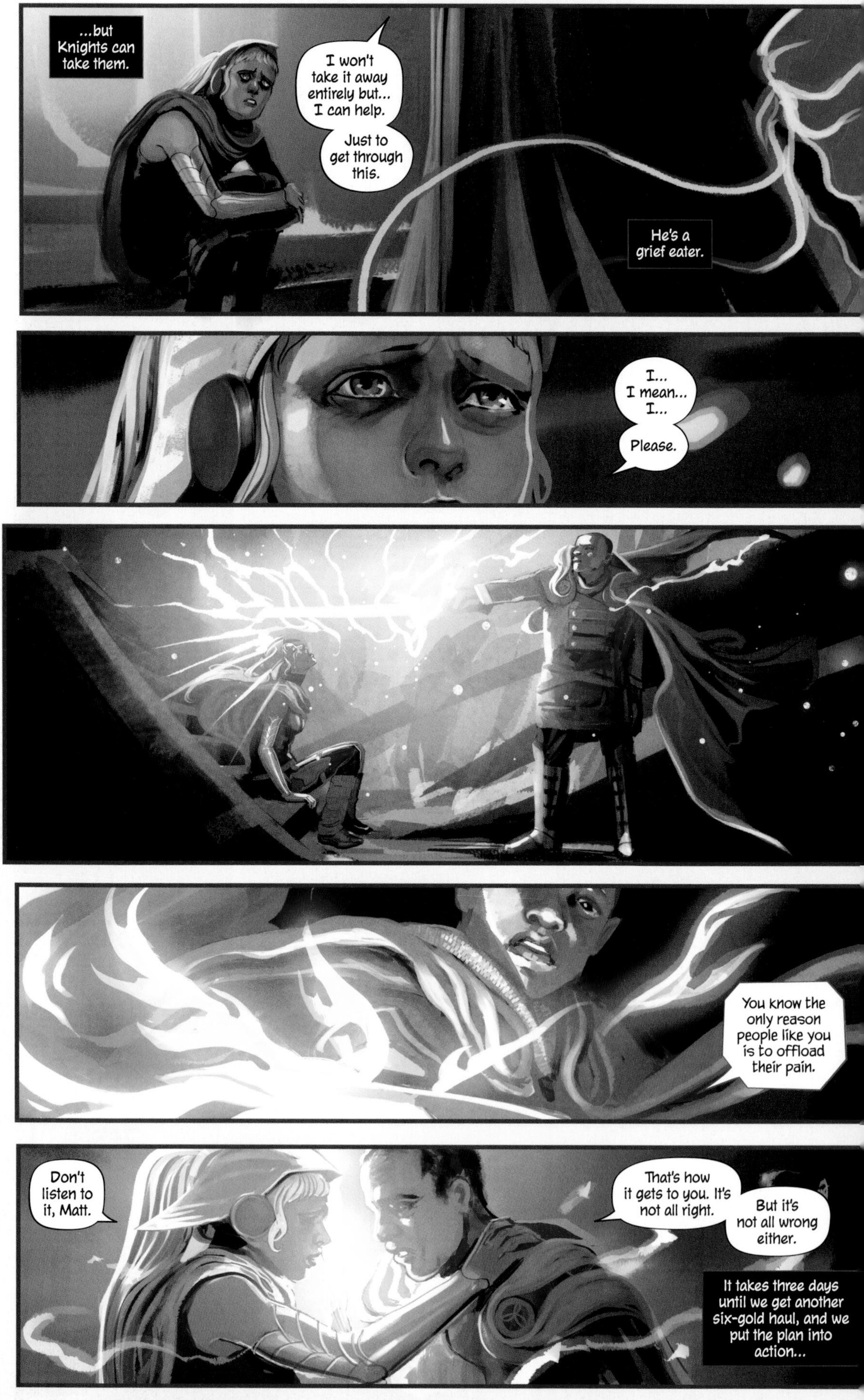

...but Knights can take them.
I won't take it away entirely but... I can help.
Just to get through this.
He's a grief eater.
I... I mean... I...
Please.
You know the only reason people like you is to offload their pain.
Don't listen to it, Matt.
That's how it gets to you. It's not all right.
But it's not all wrong either.
It takes three days until we get another six-gold haul, and we put the plan into action...

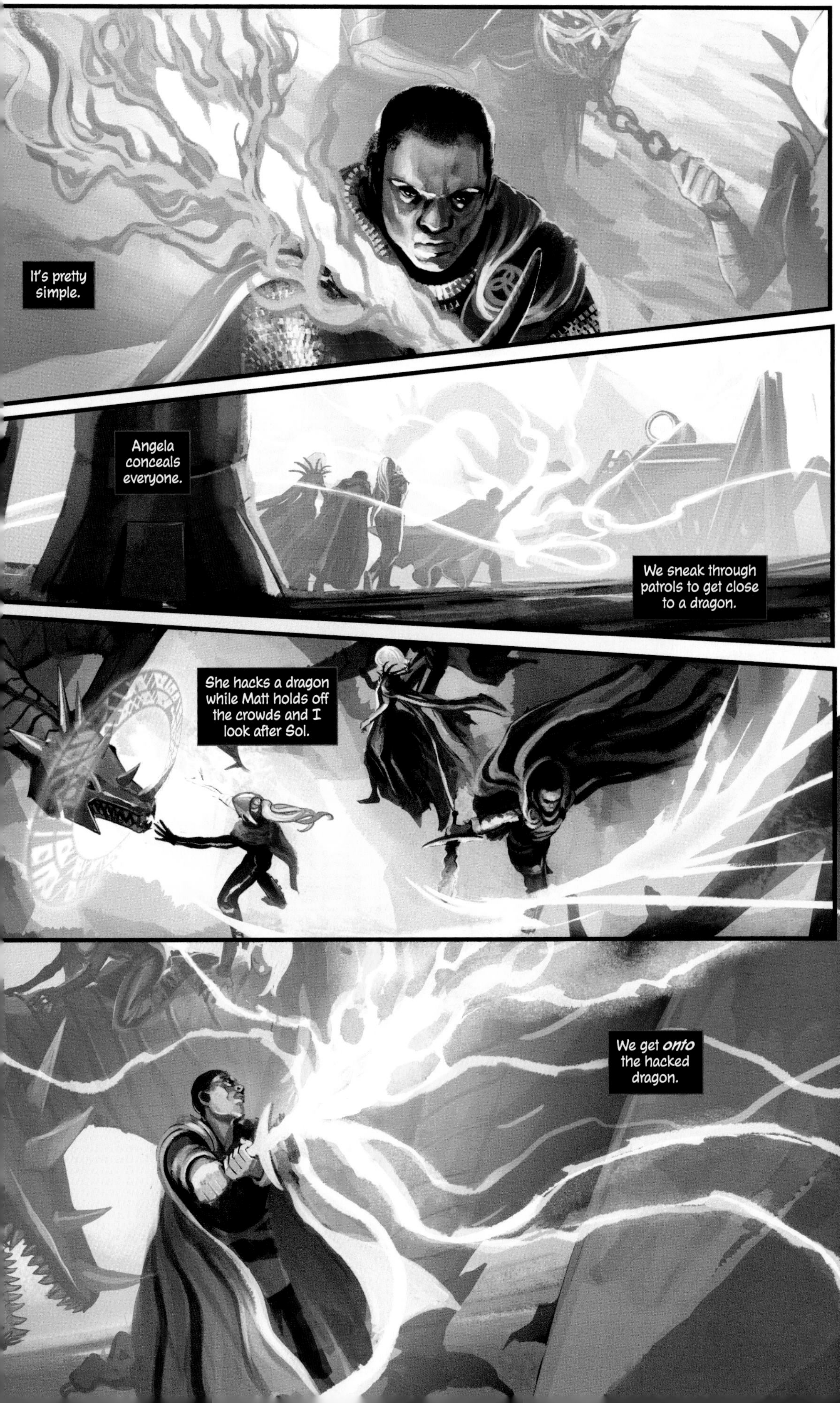
It's pretty simple.
Angela conceals everyone.
We sneak through patrols to get close to a dragon.
She hacks a dragon while Matt holds off the crowds and I look after Sol.
We get *onto* the hacked dragon.

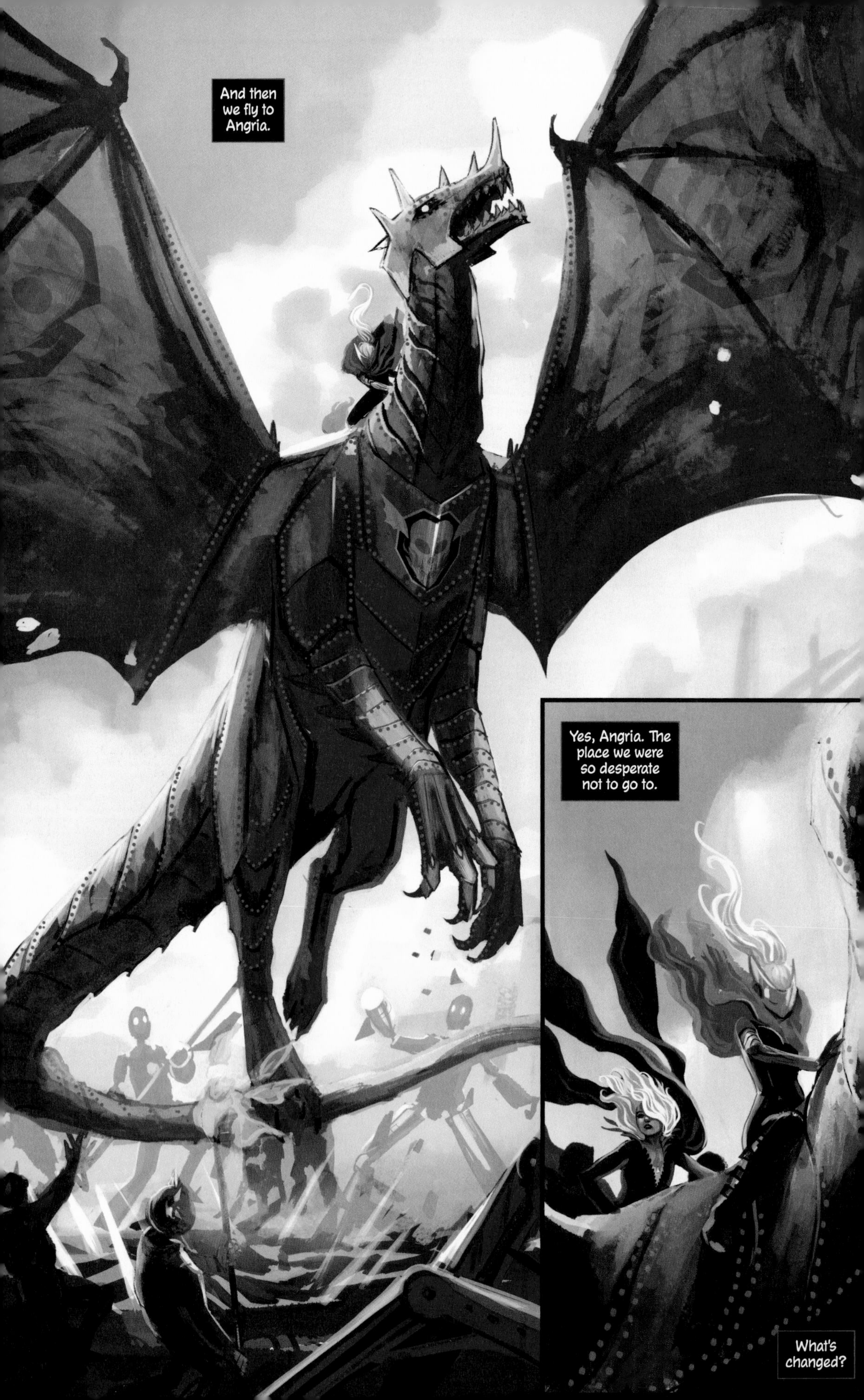

And then we fly to Angria.
Yes, Angria. The place we were so desperate not to go to.
What's changed?

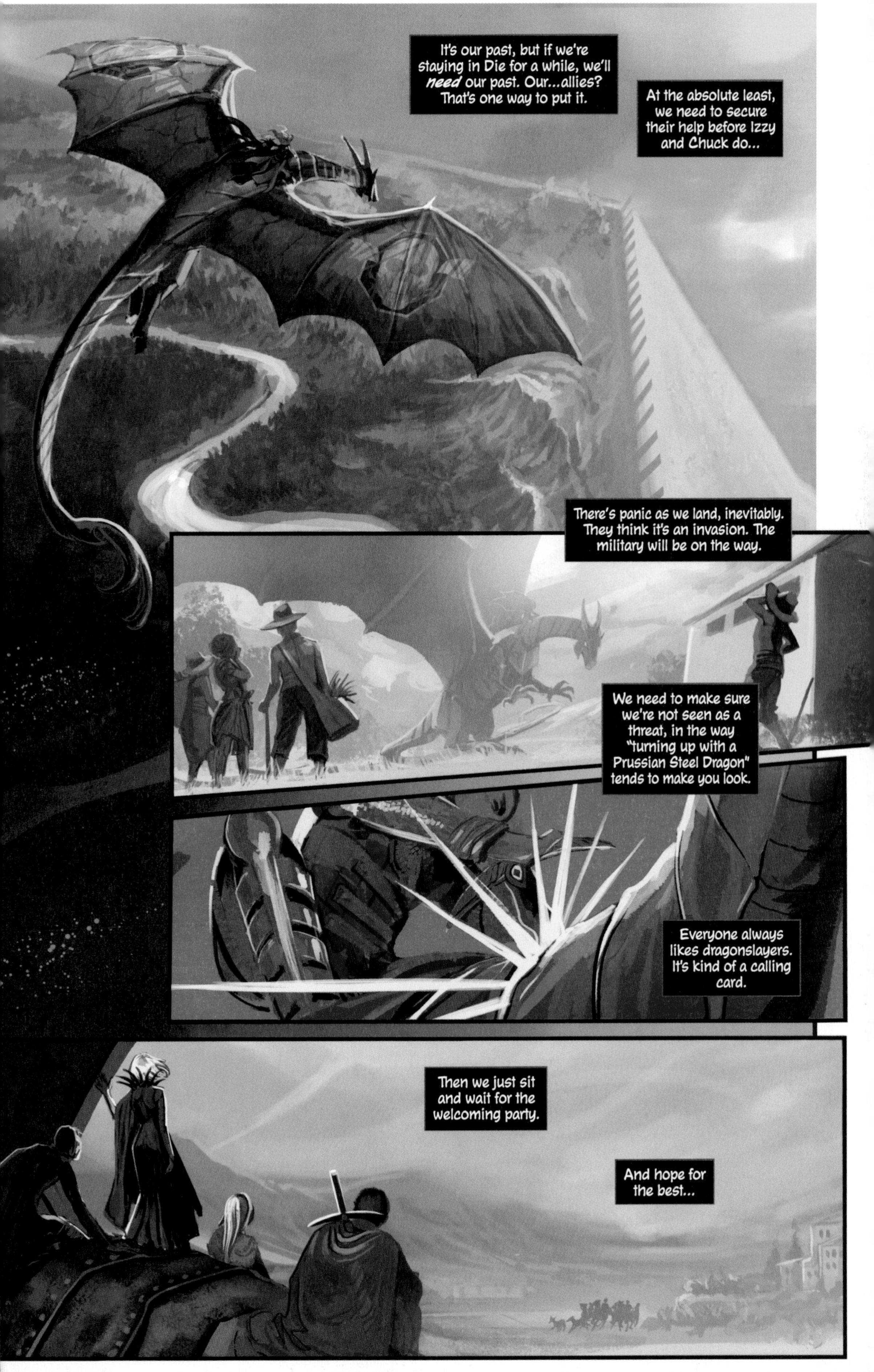
It's our past, but if we're staying in Die for a while, we'll *need* our past. Our...allies? That's one way to put it.
At the absolute least, we need to secure their help before Izzy and Chuck do...
There's panic as we land, inevitably. They think it's an invasion. The military will be on the way.
We need to make sure we're not seen as a threat, in the way "turning up with a Prussian Steel Dragon" tends to make you look.
Everyone always likes dragonslayers. It's kind of a calling card.
Then we just sit and wait for the welcoming party.
And hope for the best...

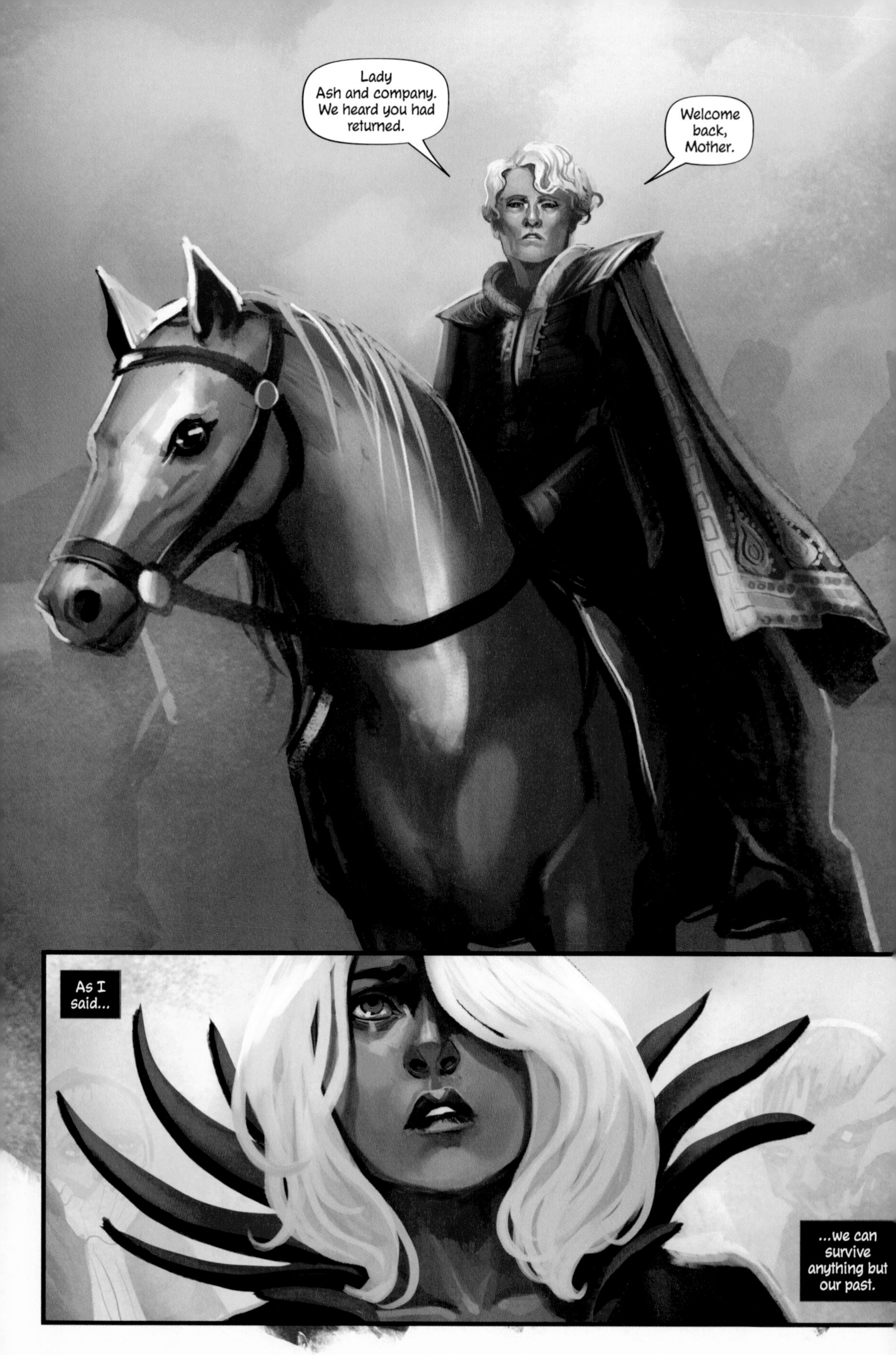
Lady Ash and company. We heard you had returned.
Welcome back, Mother.
As I said...
...we can survive anything but our past.

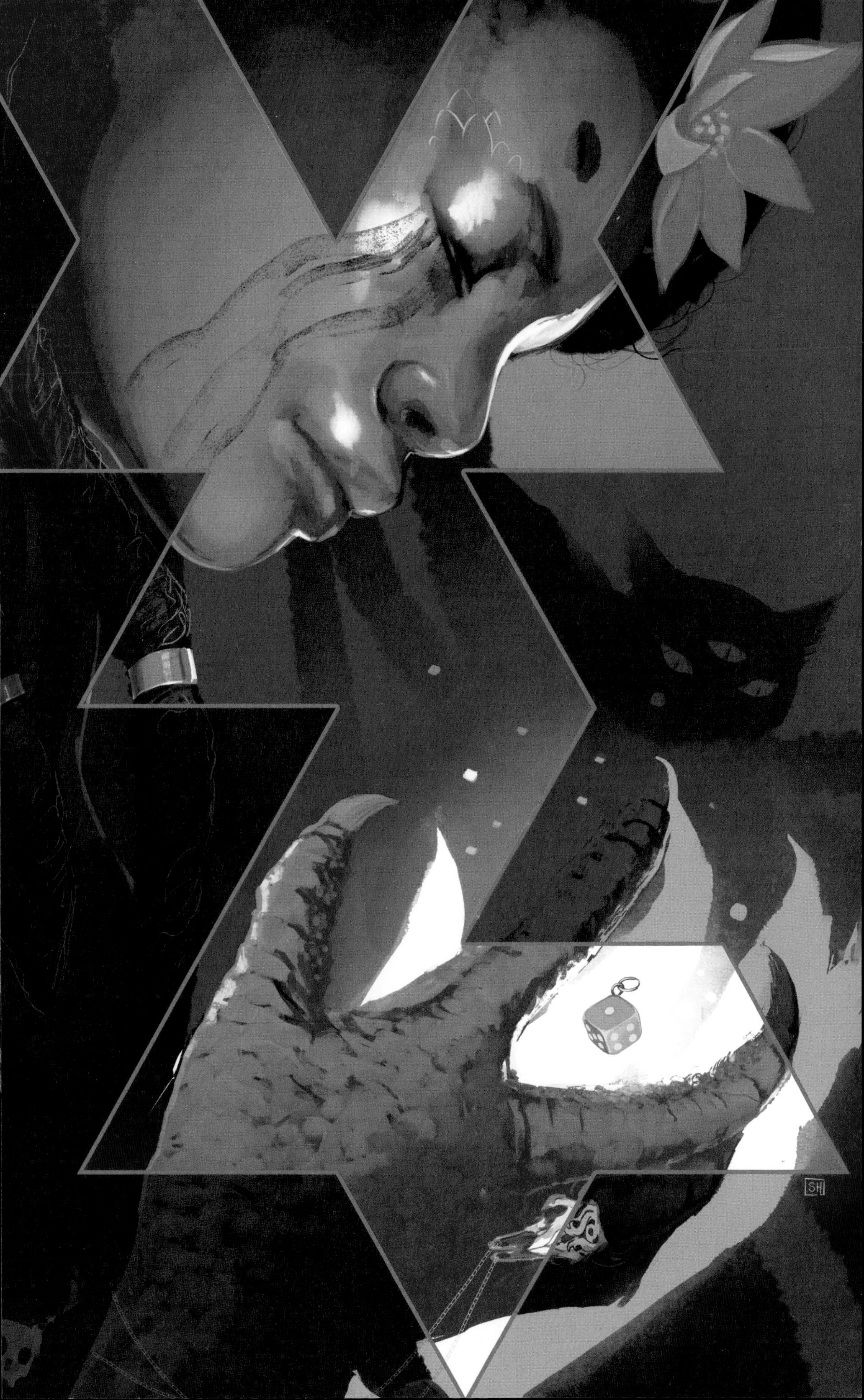
SH

7:
WISDOM
CHECK

"He longed to become Real, to know what it felt like; and yet the idea of growing shabby and losing his eyes and whiskers was rather sad. He wished that he could become it without these uncomfortable things happening to him."
– *Margery Williams,*
The Velveteen Rabbit

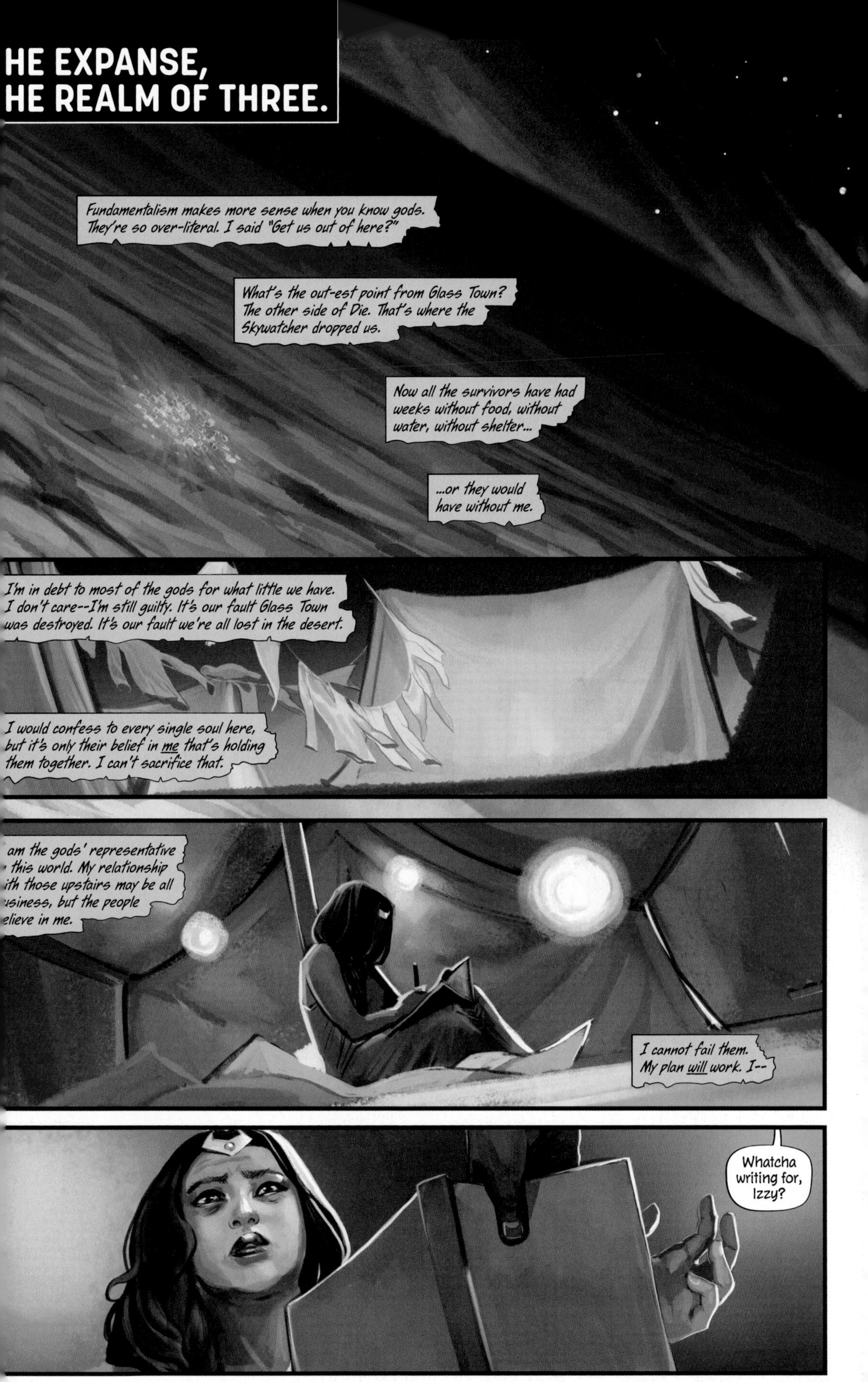
HE EXPANSE,
HE REALM OF THREE.
Fundamentalism makes more sense when you know gods. They're so over-literal. I said "Get us out of here?"
What's the out-est point from Glass Town? The other side of Die. That's where the Skywatcher dropped us.
Now all the survivors have had weeks without food, without water, without shelter...
...or they would have without me.
I'm in debt to most of the gods for what little we have. I don't care--I'm still guilty. It's our fault Glass Town was destroyed. It's our fault we're all lost in the desert.
I would confess to every single soul here, but it's only their belief in me that's holding them together. I can't sacrifice that.
am the gods' representative this world. My relationship ith those upstairs may be all usiness, but the people elieve in me.
I cannot fail them. My plan will work. I--
Whatcha writing for, Izzy?

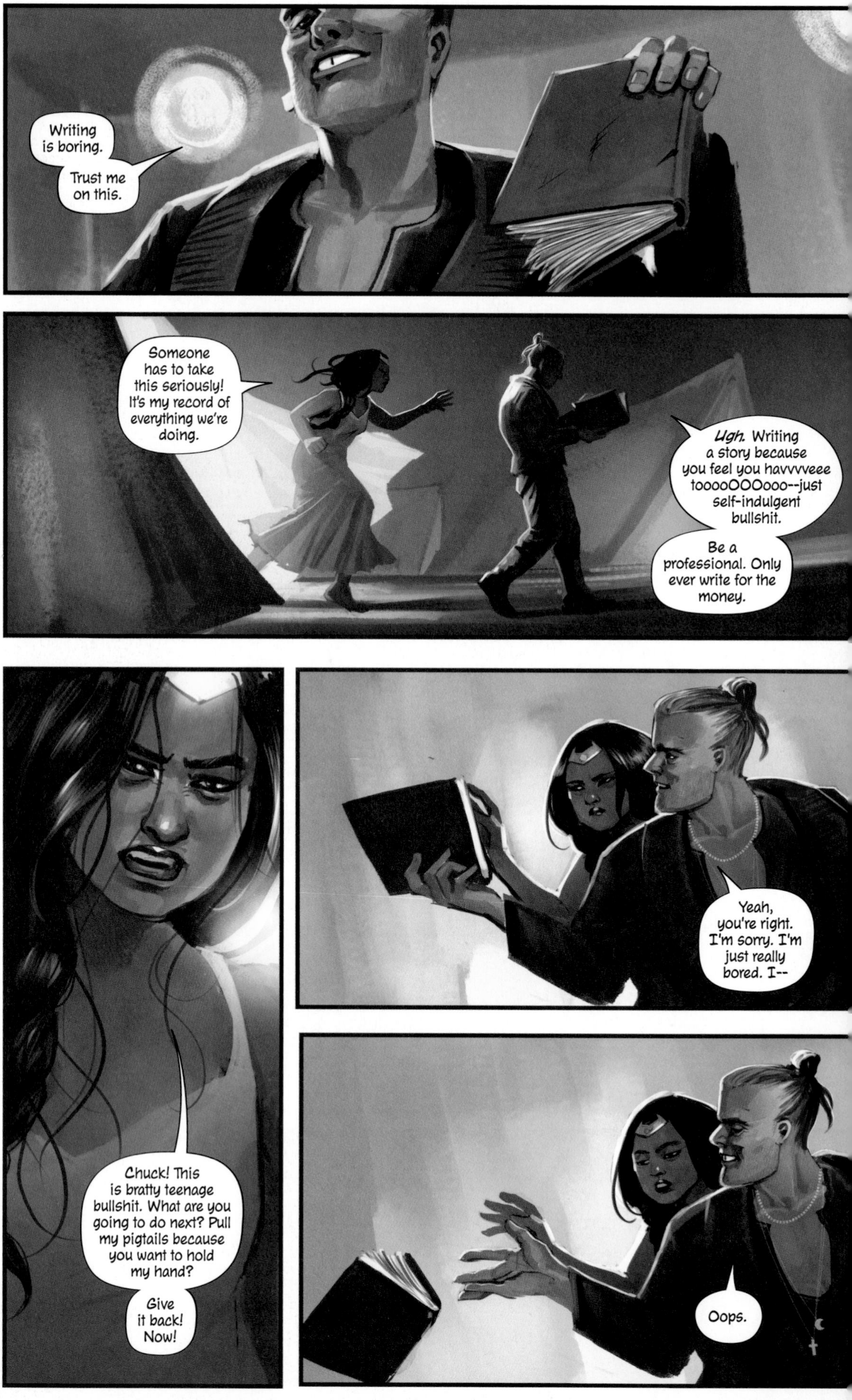
Writing is boring.
Trust me on this.
Someone has to take this seriously! It's my record of everything we're doing.
Ugh. Writing a story because you feel you havvvveee toooOOOooo--just self-indulgent bullshit.
Be a professional. Only ever write for the money.
Chuck! This is bratty teenage bullshit. What are you going to do next? Pull my pigtails because you want to hold my hand?
Give it back! Now!
Yeah, you're right. I'm sorry. I'm just really bored. I--
Oops.

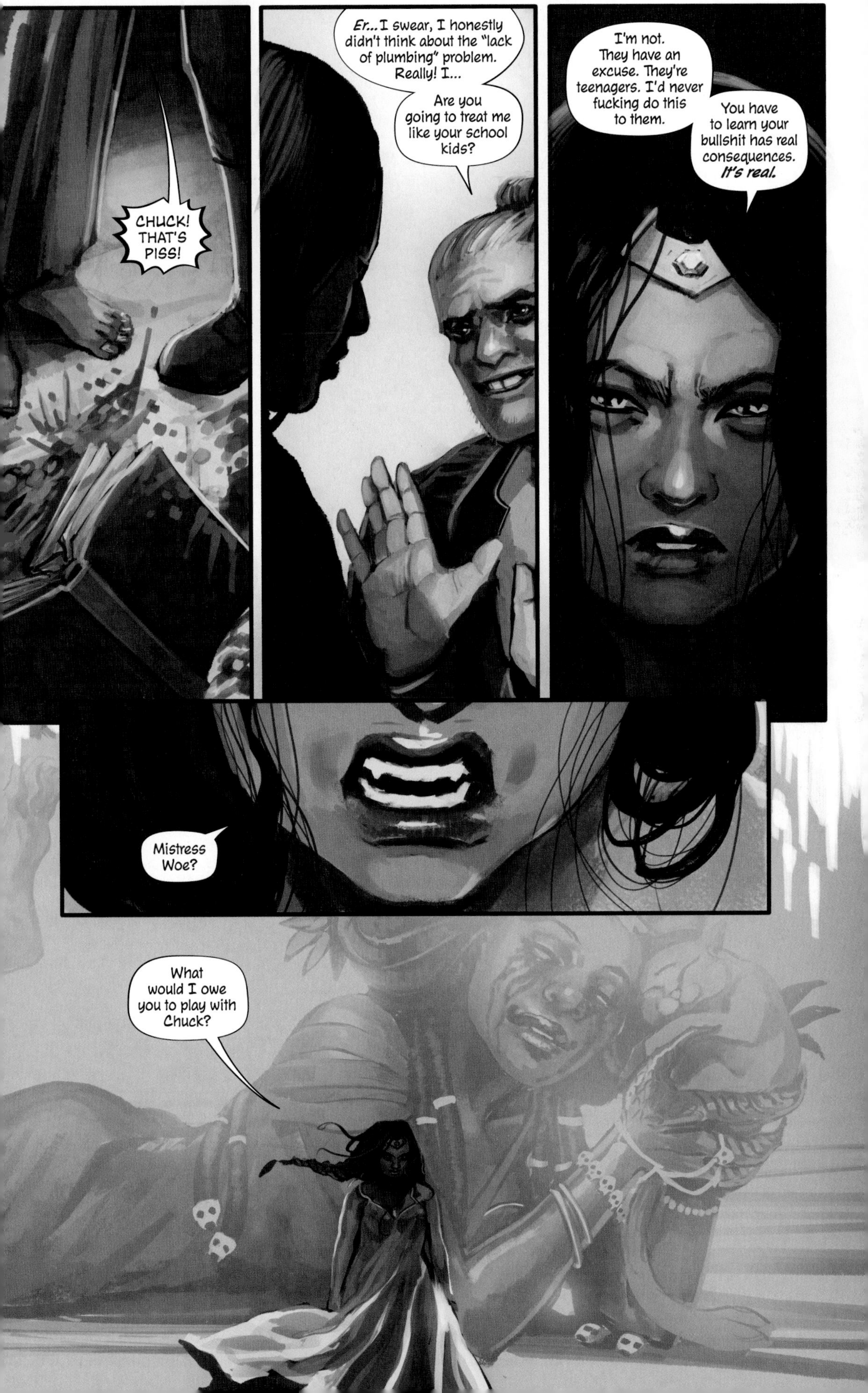
CHUCK! THAT'S PISS!
Er... I swear, I honestly didn't think about the "lack of plumbing" problem. Really! I...
Are you going to treat me like your school kids?
I'm not. They have an excuse. They're teenagers. I'd never fucking do this to them.
You have to learn your bullshit has real consequences. ***It's real.***
Mistress Woe?
What would I owe you to play with Chuck?

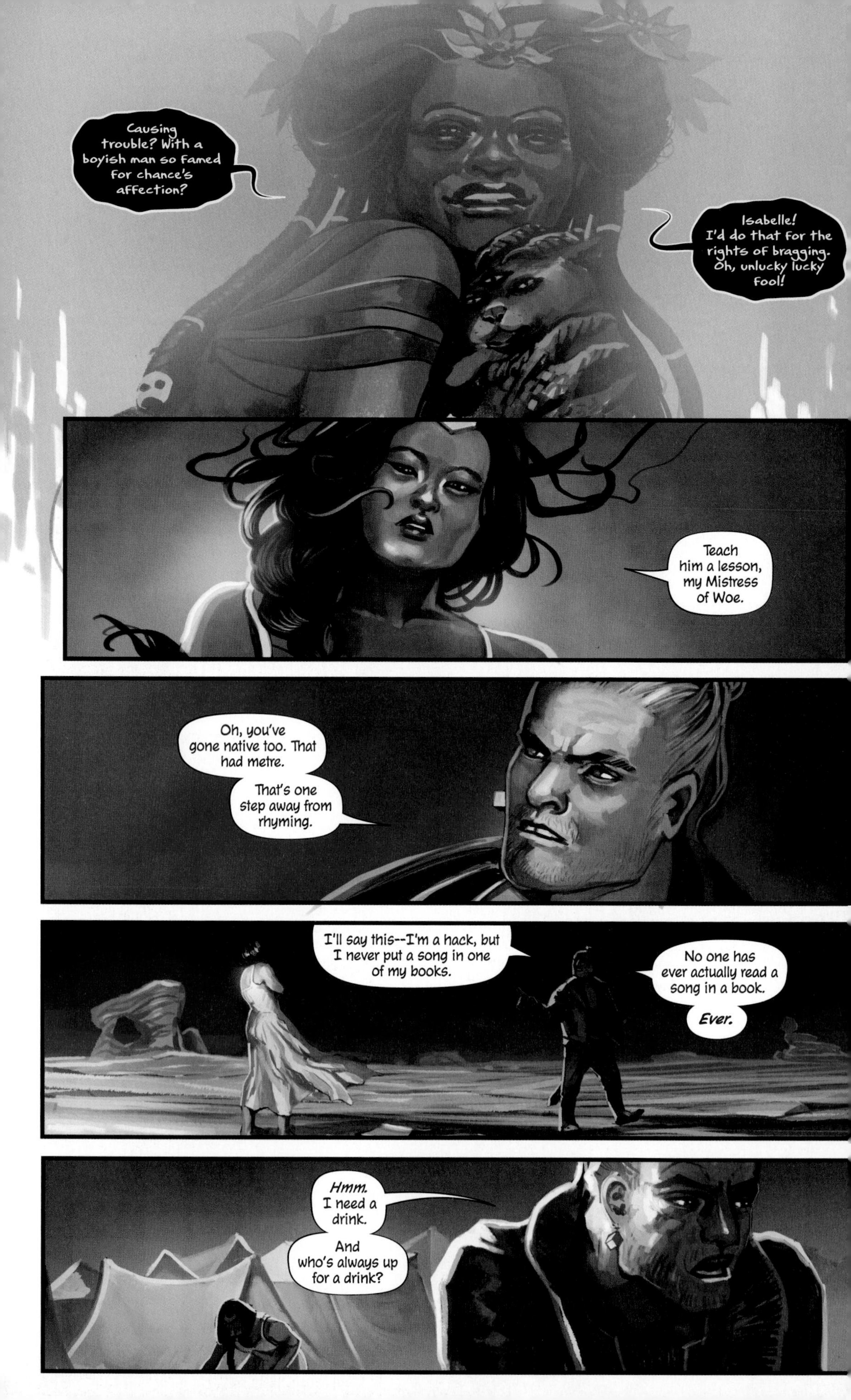
Causing trouble? With a boyish man so famed for chance's affection?
Isabelle! I'd do that for the rights of bragging. Oh, unlucky lucky fool!
Teach him a lesson, my Mistress of Woe.
Oh, you've gone native too. That had metre.
That's one step away from rhyming.
I'll say this--I'm a hack, but I never put a song in one of my books.
No one has ever actually read a song in a book.
Ever.
Hmm. I need a drink.
And who's always up for a drink?

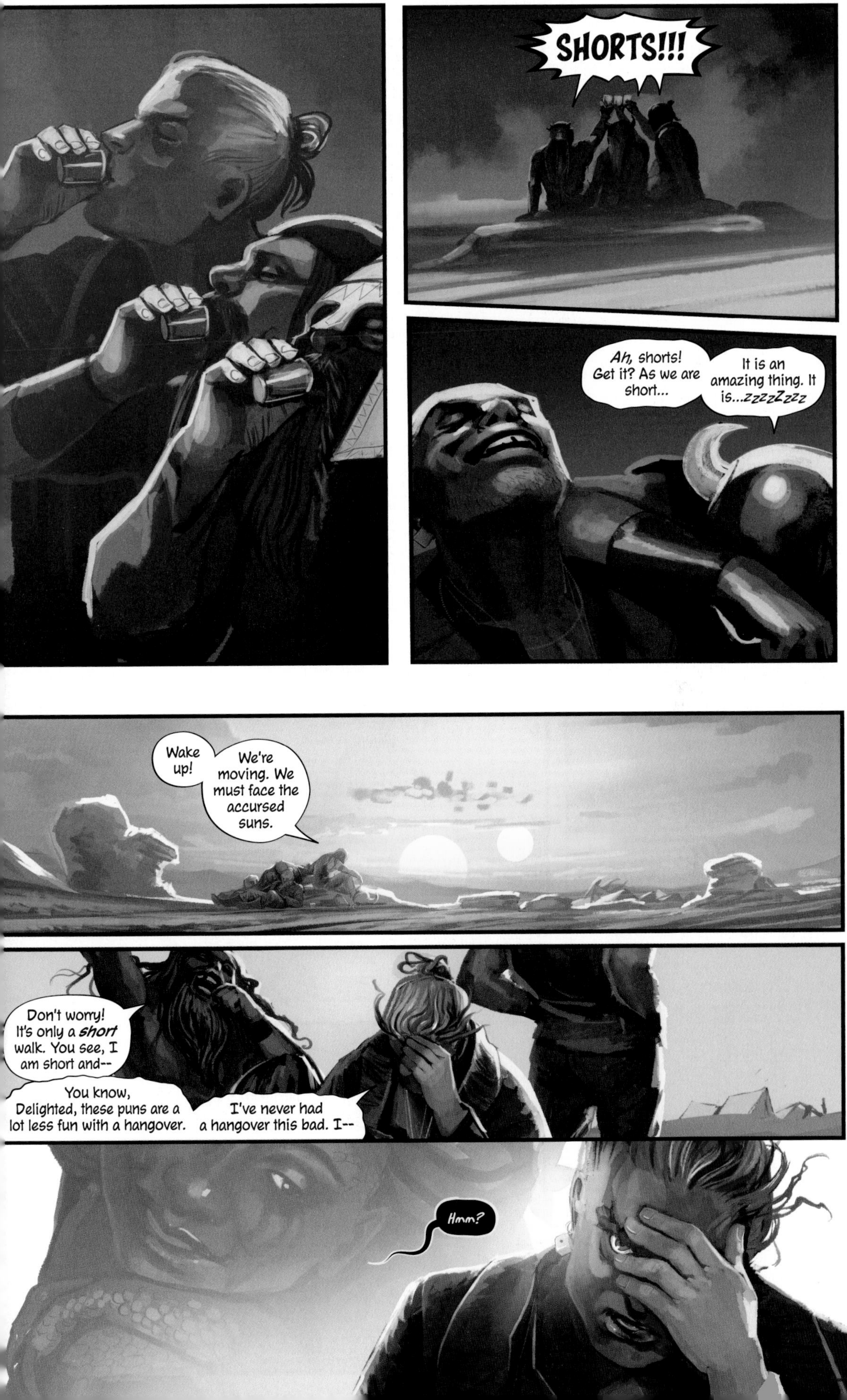

SHORTS!!!
Ah, shorts! Get it? As we are short...
It is an amazing thing. It is...zzzzZzzz
Wake up!
We're moving. We must face the accursed suns.
Don't worry! It's only a short walk. You see, I am short and--
You know, Delighted, these puns are a lot less fun with a hangover.
I've never had a hangover this bad. I--
Hmm?

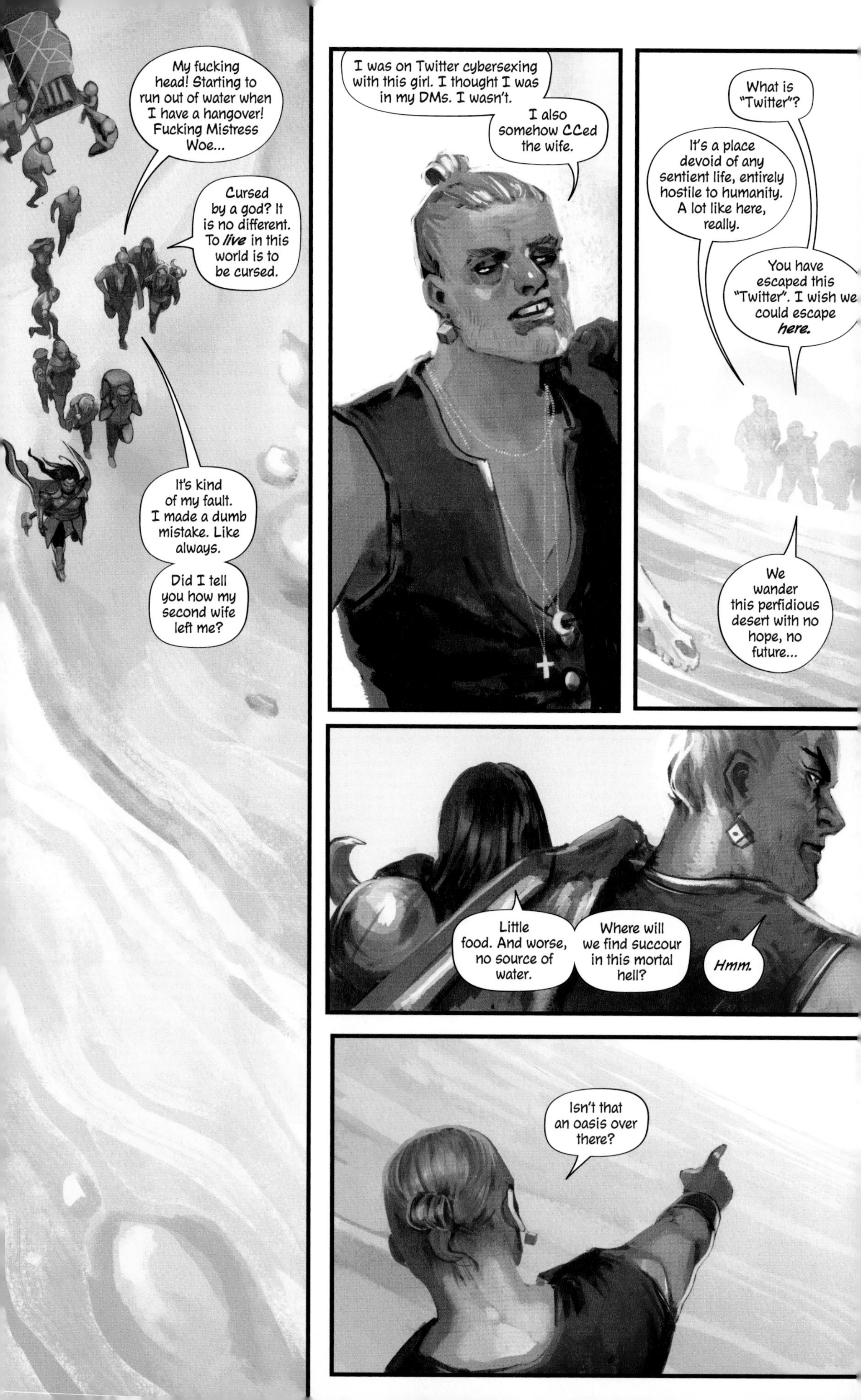
My fucking head! Starting to run out of water when I have a hangover! Fucking Mistress Woe...
Cursed by a god? It is no different. To *live* in this world is to be cursed.
It's kind of my fault. I made a dumb mistake. Like always.
Did I tell you how my second wife left me?
I was on Twitter cybersexing with this girl. I thought I was in my DMs. I wasn't.
I also somehow CCed the wife.
What is "Twitter"?
It's a place devoid of any sentient life, entirely hostile to humanity. A lot like here, really.
You have escaped this "Twitter". I wish we could escape ***here.***
We wander this perfidious desert with no hope, no future...
Little food. And worse, no source of water.
Where will we find succour in this mortal hell?
Hmm.
Isn't that an oasis over there?

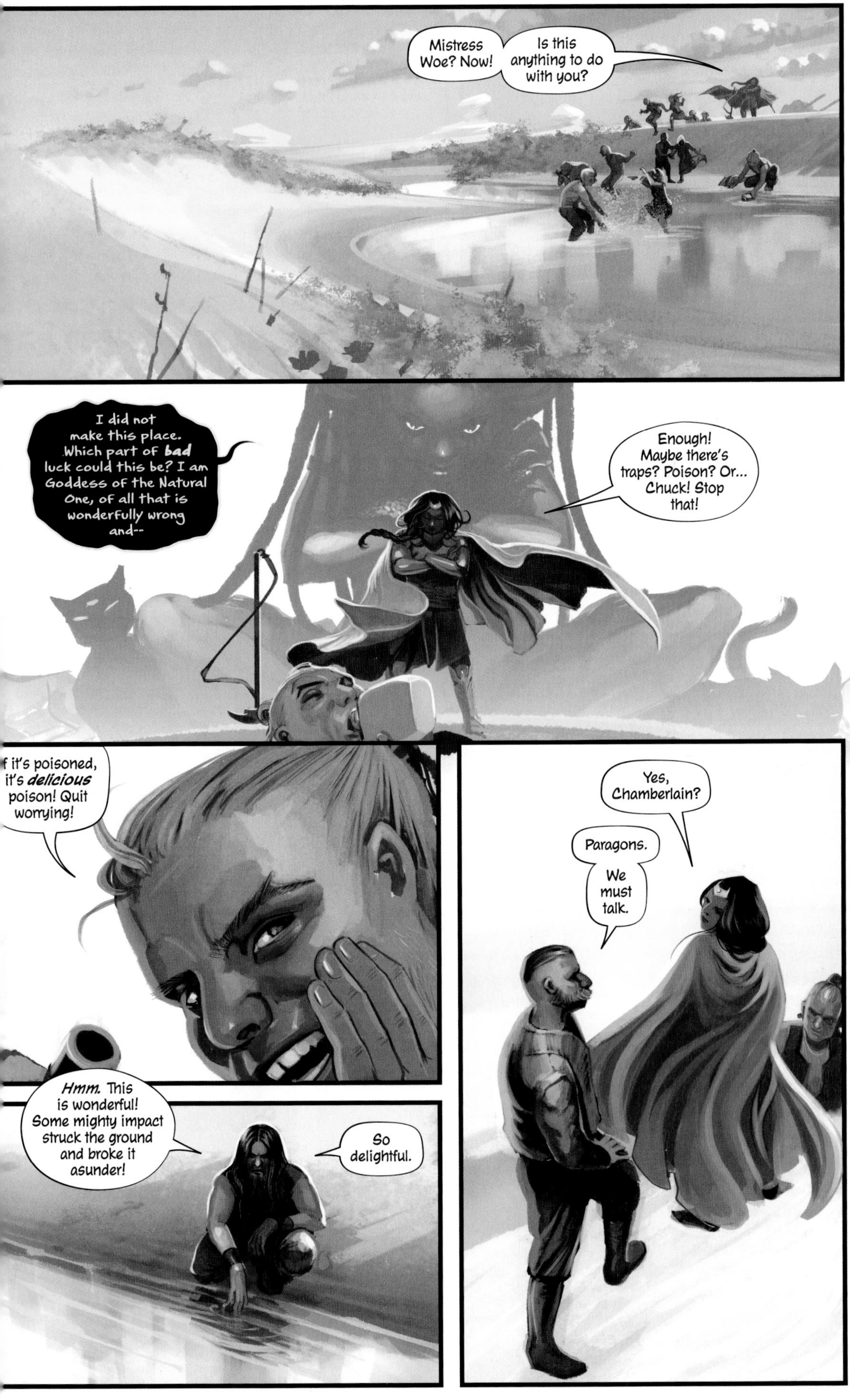
Mistress Woe? Now!
Is this anything to do with you?
I did not make this place. Which part of **bad** luck could this be? I am Goddess of the Natural One, of all that is wonderfully wrong and--
Enough! Maybe there's traps? Poison? Or... Chuck! Stop that!
f it's poisoned, it's *delicious* poison! Quit worrying!
Hmm. This is wonderful! Some mighty impact struck the ground and broke it asunder!
So delightful.
Yes, Chamberlain?
Paragons.
We must talk.

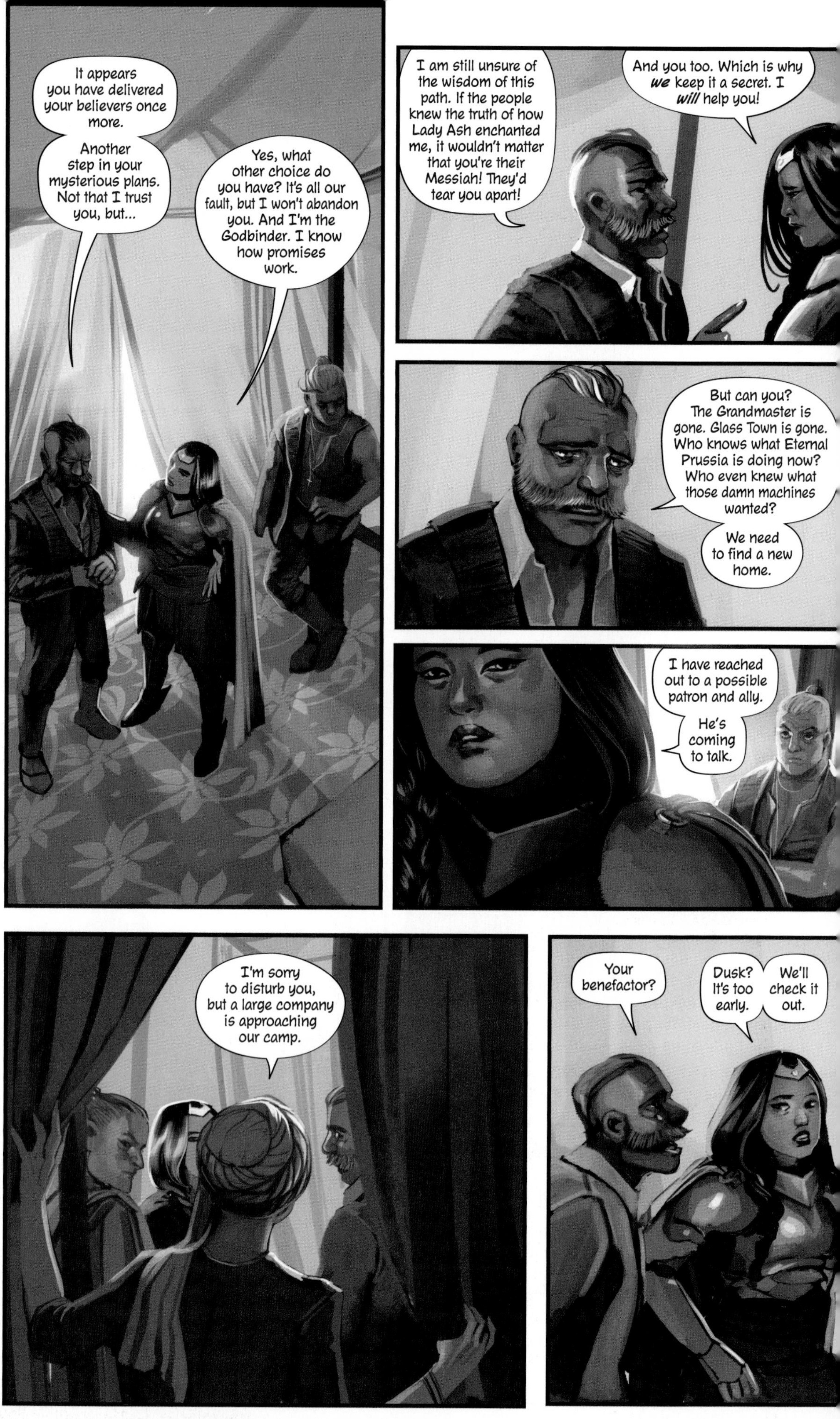
It appears you have delivered your believers once more.
Another step in your mysterious plans. Not that I trust you, but...
Yes, what other choice do you have? It's all our fault, but I won't abandon you. And I'm the Godbinder. I know how promises work.
I am still unsure of the wisdom of this path. If the people knew the truth of how Lady Ash enchanted me, it wouldn't matter that you're their Messiah! They'd tear you apart!
And you too. Which is why *we* keep it a secret. I *will* help you!
But can you? The Grandmaster is gone. Glass Town is gone. Who knows what Eternal Prussia is doing now? Who even knew what those damn machines wanted?
We need to find a new home.
I have reached out to a possible patron and ally.
He's coming to talk.
I'm sorry to disturb you, but a large company is approaching our camp.
Your benefactor?
Dusk? It's too early.
We'll check it out.

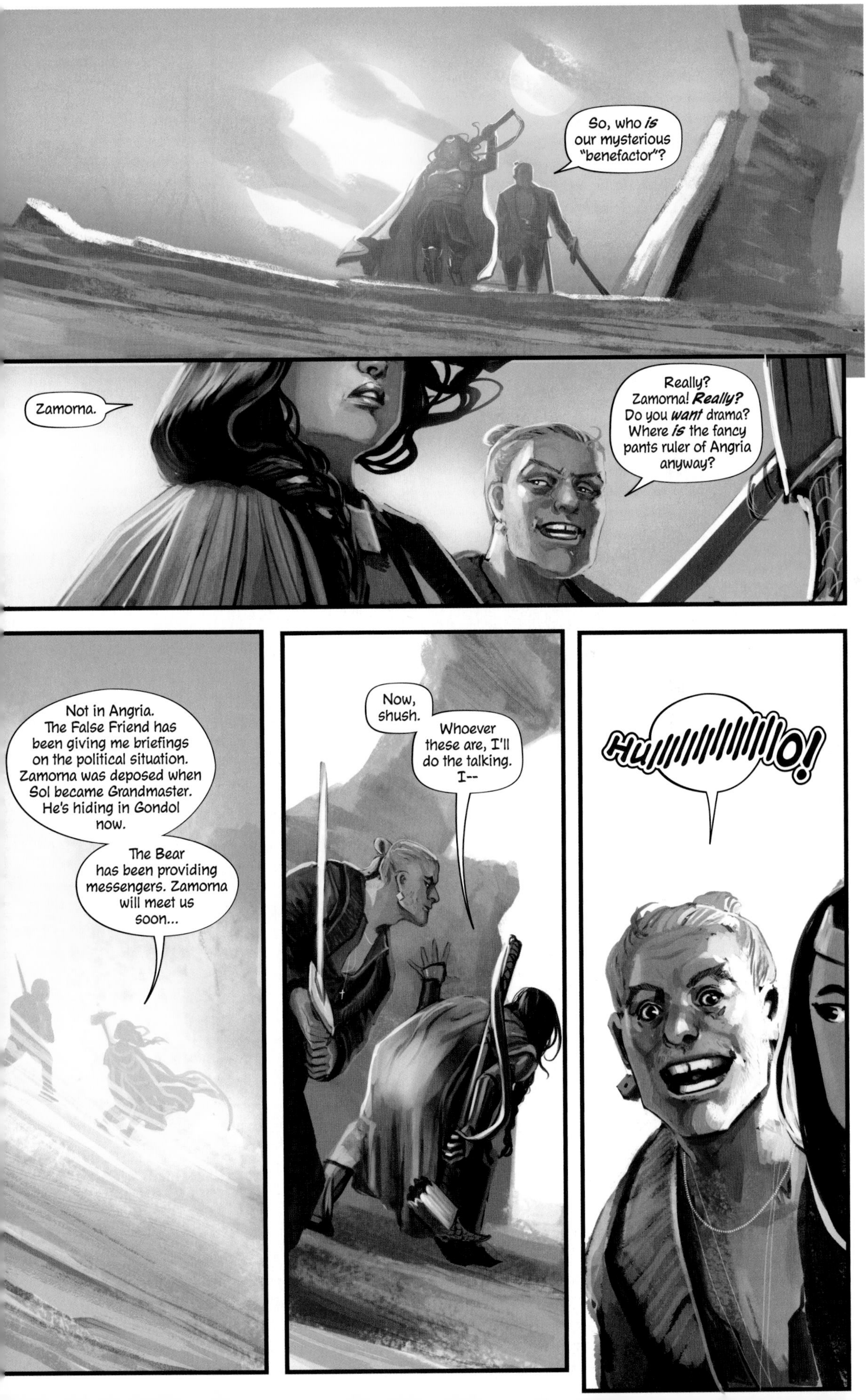

So, who *is* our mysterious "benefactor"?
Zamorna.
Really? Zamorna! ***Really?*** Do you *want* drama? Where *is* the fancy pants ruler of Angria anyway?
Not in Angria. The False Friend has been giving me briefings on the political situation. Zamorna was deposed when Sol became Grandmaster. He's hiding in Gondol now.
The Bear has been providing messengers. Zamorna will meet us soon...
Now, shush.
Whoever these are, I'll do the talking. I--
HU/////////////O!

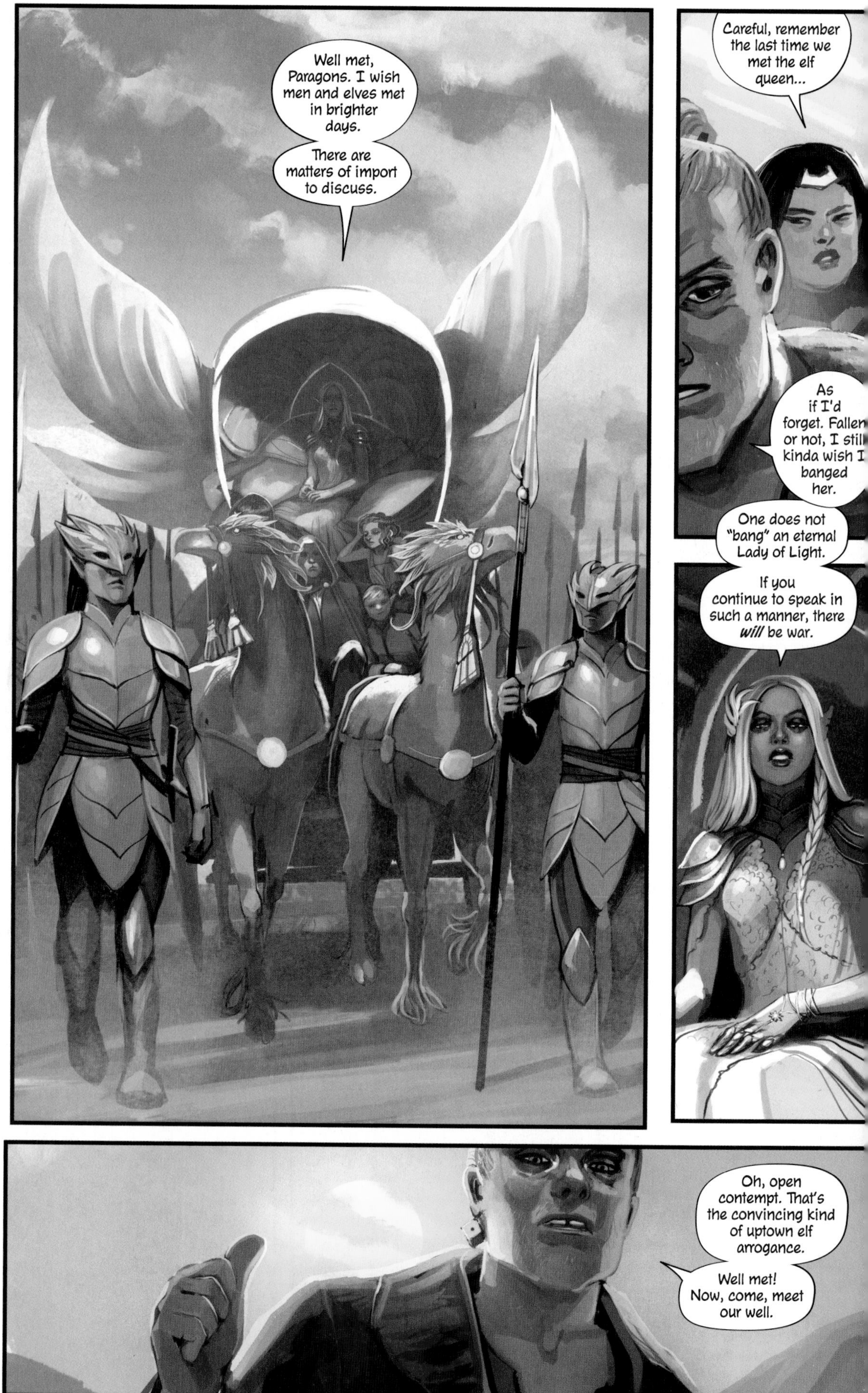
Well met, Paragons. I wish men and elves met in brighter days.
There are matters of import to discuss.
Careful, remember the last time we met the elf queen...
As if I'd forget. Fallen or not, I stil kinda wish I banged her.
One does not "bang" an eternal Lady of Light.
If you continue to speak in such a manner, there *will* be war.
Oh, open contempt. That's the convincing kind of uptown elf arrogance.
Well met! Now, come, meet our well.

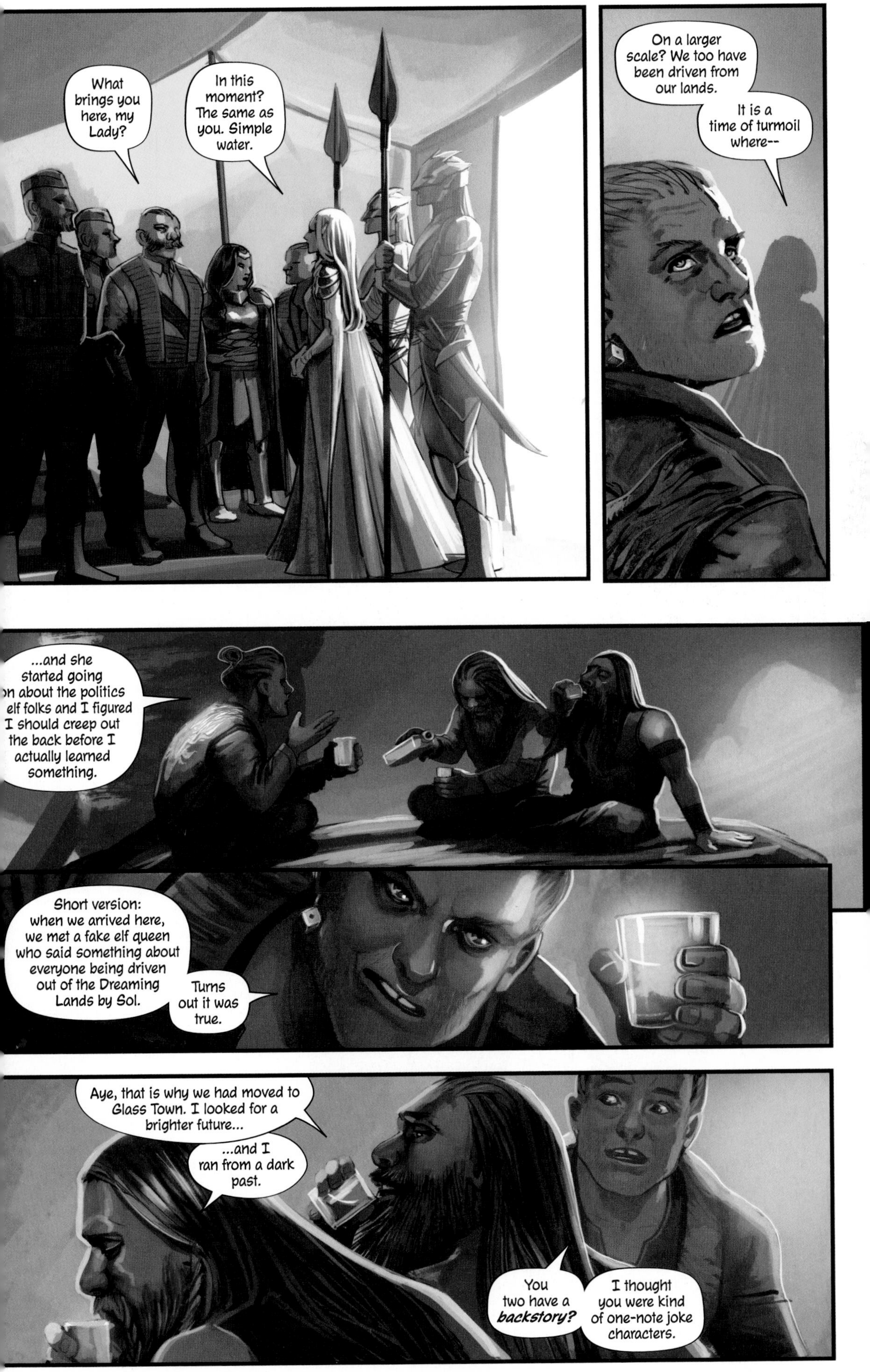
What brings you here, my Lady?
In this moment? The same as you. Simple water.
On a larger scale? We too have been driven from our lands.
It is a time of turmoil where--
...and she started going on about the politics elf folks and I figured I should creep out the back before I actually learned something.
Short version: when we arrived here, we met a fake elf queen who said something about everyone being driven out of the Dreaming Lands by Sol.
Turns out it was true.
Aye, that is why we had moved to Glass Town. I looked for a brighter future...
...and I ran from a dark past.
You two have a *backstory?*
I thought you were kind of one-note joke characters.

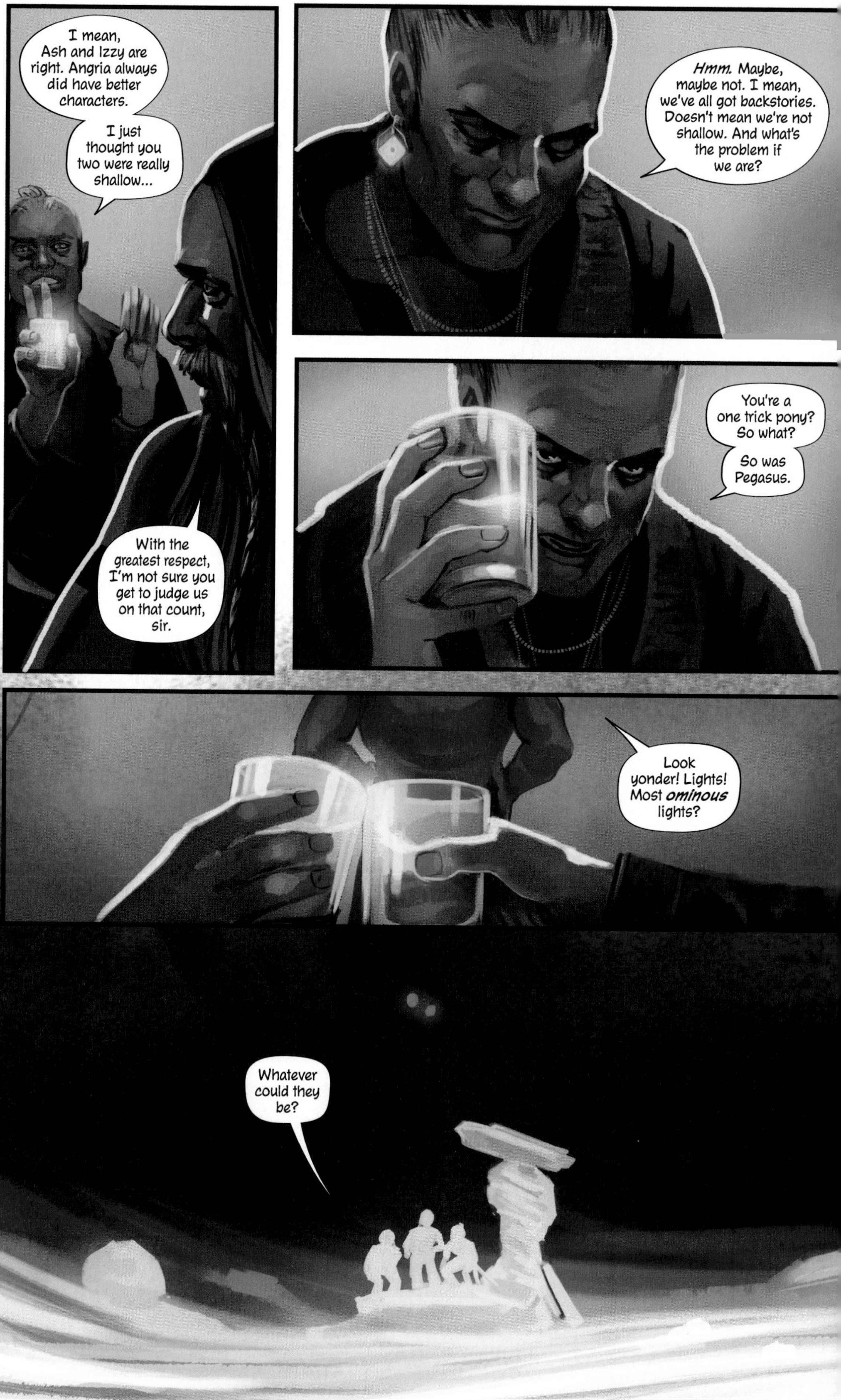
I mean, Ash and Izzy are right. Angria always did have better characters.
I just thought you two were really shallow...
With the greatest respect, I'm not sure you get to judge us on that count, sir.
Hmm. Maybe, maybe not. I mean, we've all got backstories. Doesn't mean we're not shallow. And what's the problem if we are?
You're a one trick pony? So what?
So was Pegasus.
Look yonder! Lights! Most *ominous* lights?
Whatever could they be?

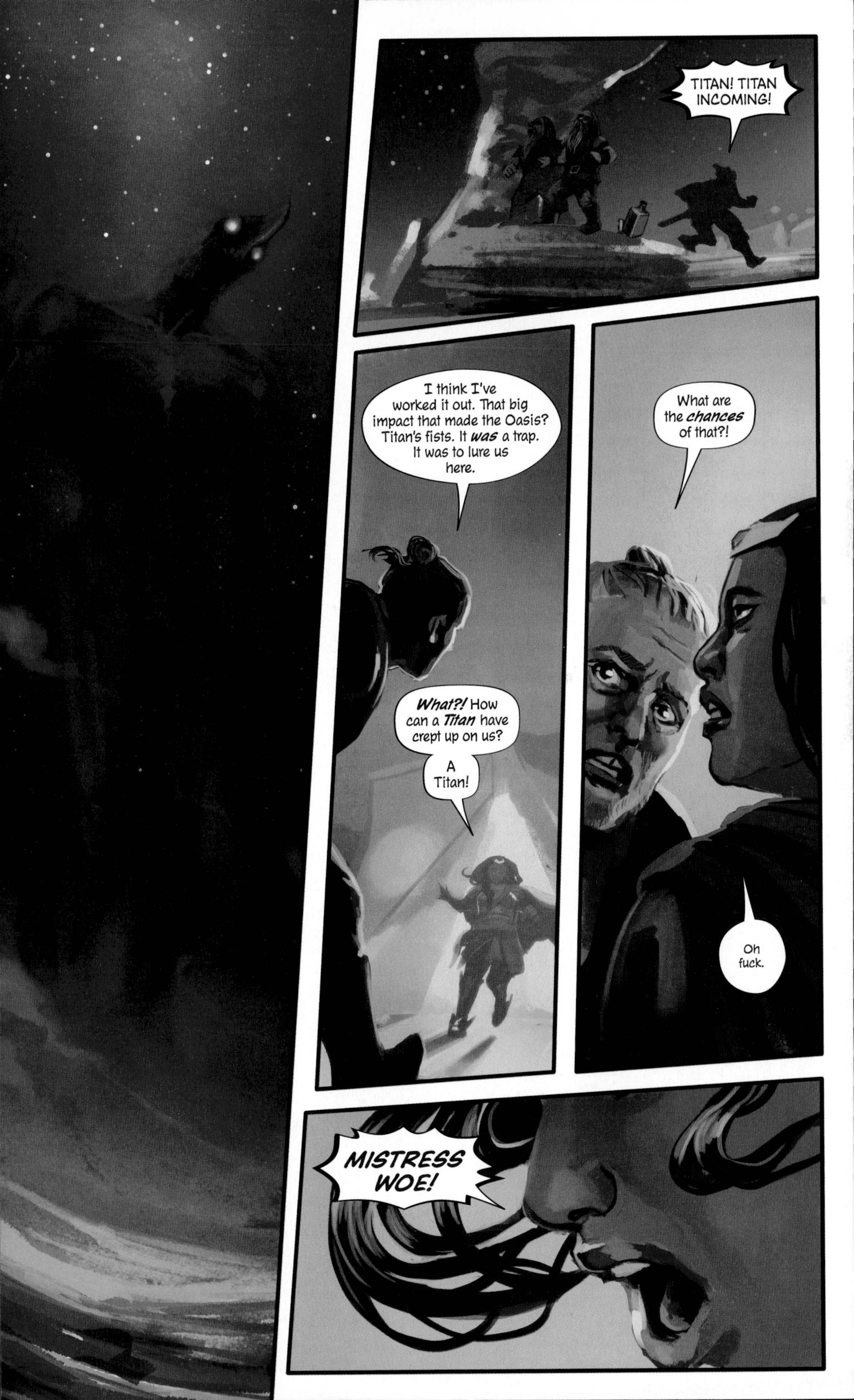

TITAN! TITAN INCOMING!
I think I've worked it out. That big impact that made the Oasis? Titan's fists. It *was* a trap. It was to lure us here.
What?! How can a *Titan* have crept up on us?
A Titan!
What are the *chances* of that?!
Oh fuck.
MISTRESS WOE!

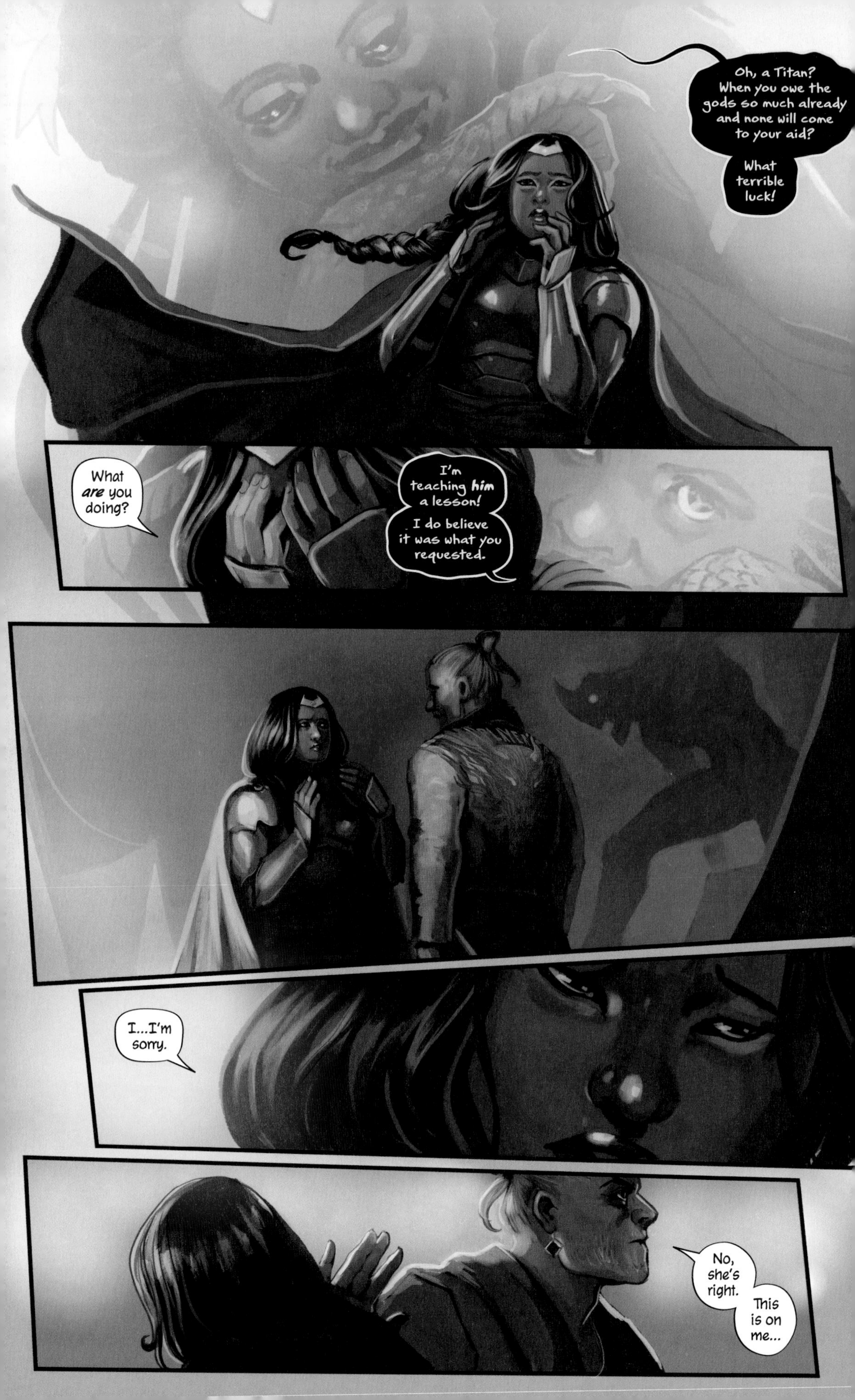
Oh, a Titan? When you owe the gods so much already and none will come to your aid?
What terrible luck!
What *are* you doing?
I'm teaching *him* a lesson!
I do believe it was what you requested.
I...I'm sorry.
No, she's right.
This is on me...

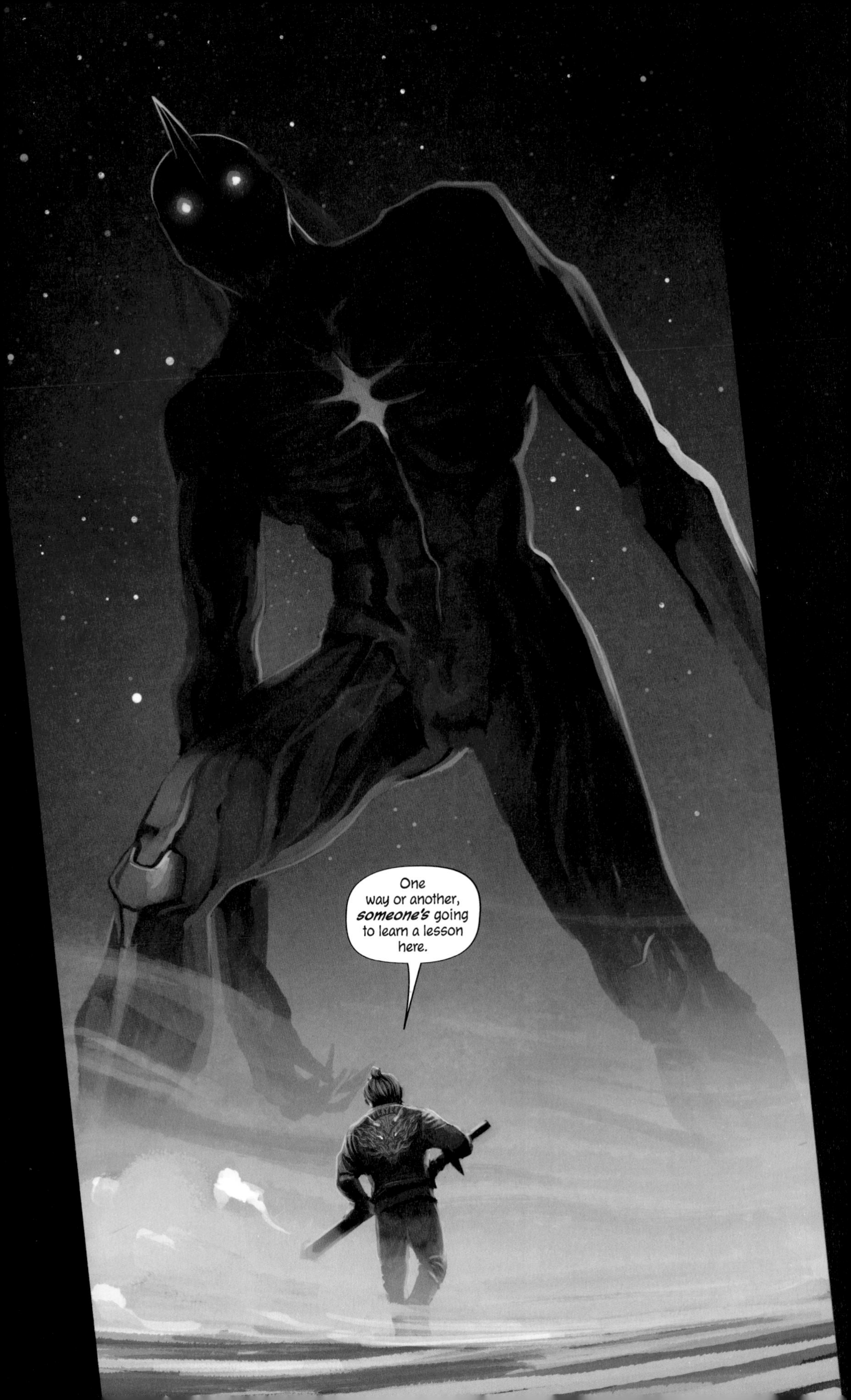
One way or another, ***someone's*** going to learn a lesson here.

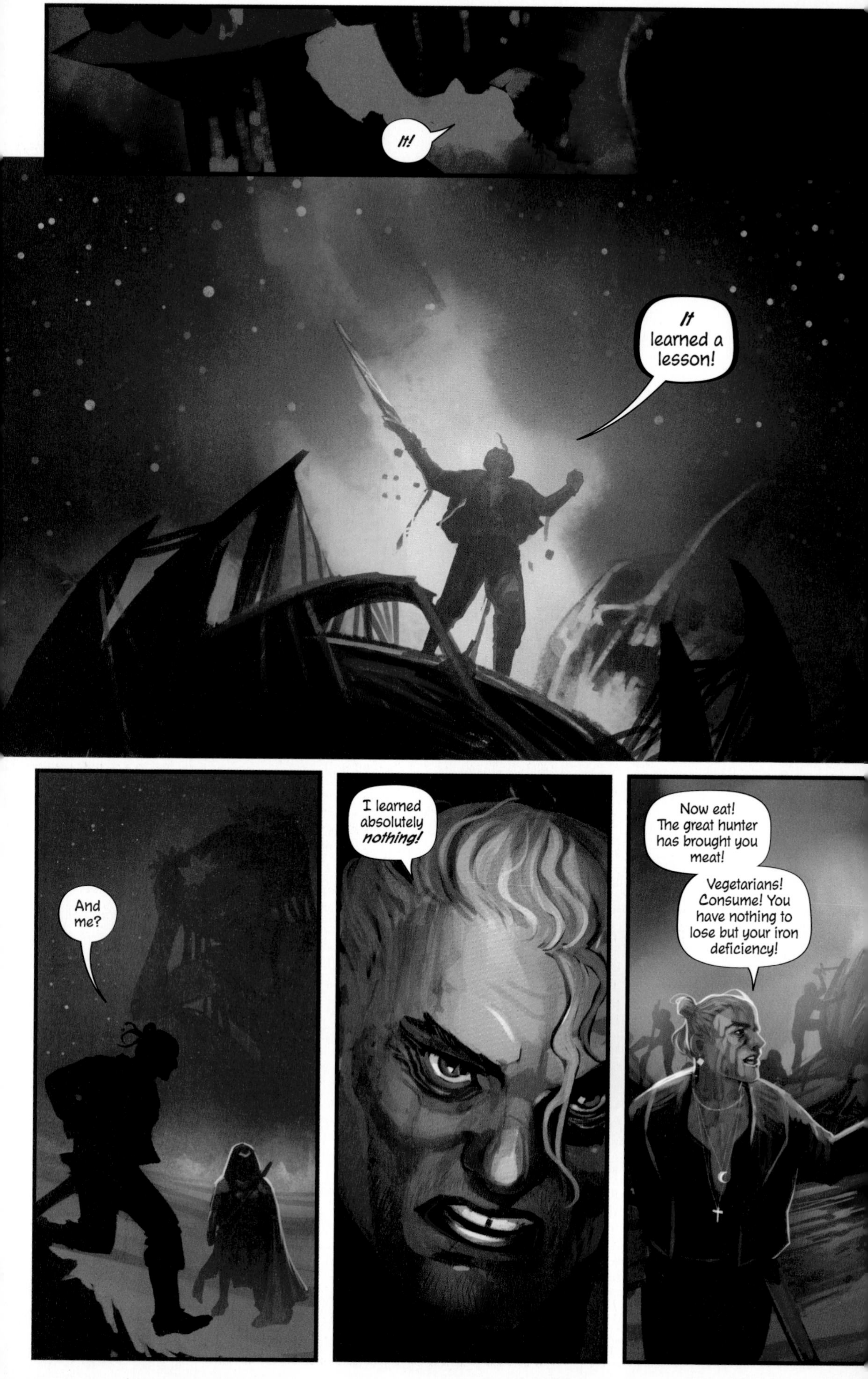
It!
It learned a lesson!
And me?
I learned absolutely nothing!
Now eat! The great hunter has brought you meat!
Vegetarians! Consume! You have nothing to lose but your iron deficiency!

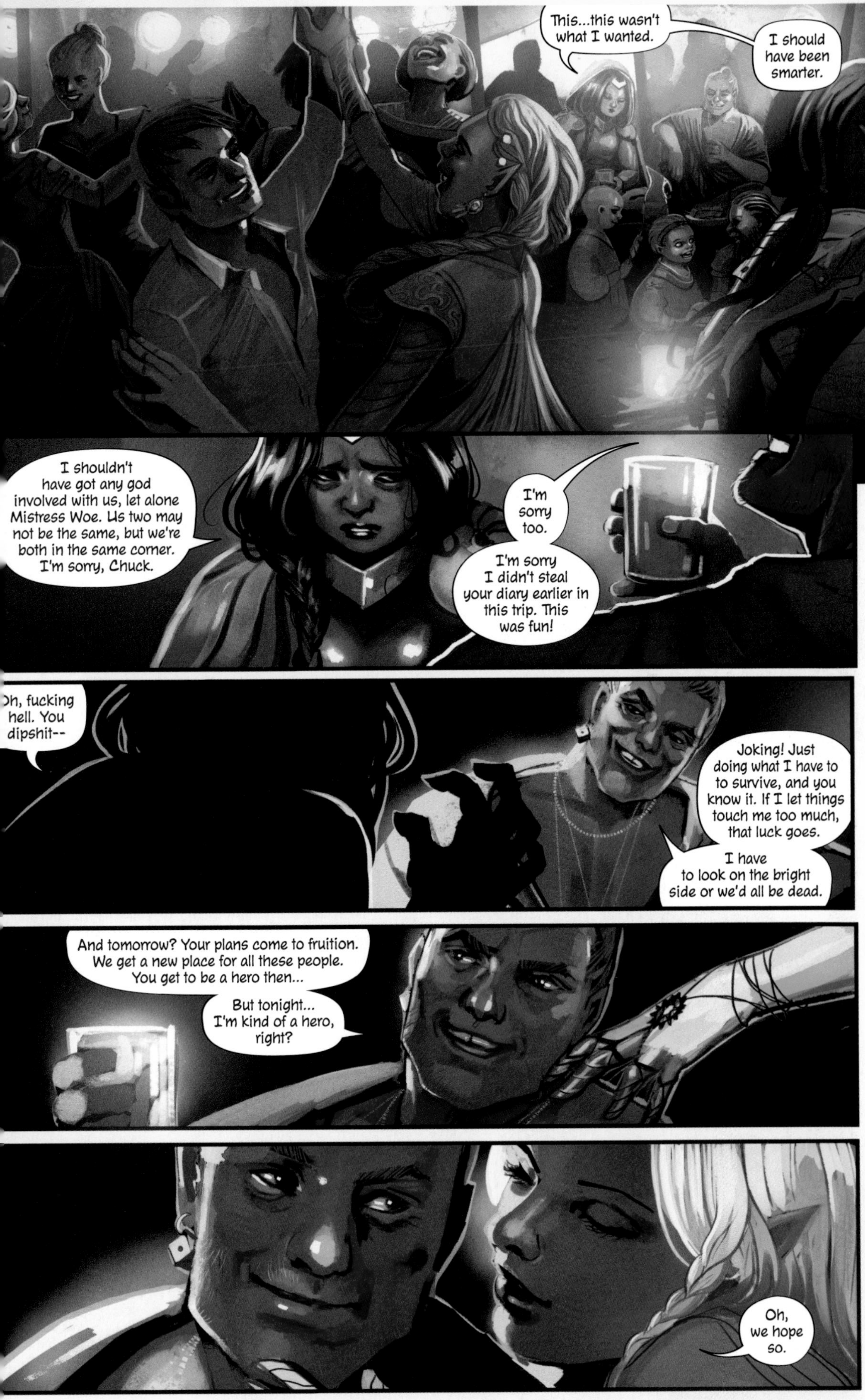
This...this wasn't what I wanted.
I should have been smarter.
I shouldn't have got any god involved with us, let alone Mistress Woe. Us two may not be the same, but we're both in the same corner. I'm sorry, Chuck.
I'm sorry too.
I'm sorry I didn't steal your diary earlier in this trip. This was fun!
Oh, fucking hell. You dipshit--
Joking! Just doing what I have to to survive, and you know it. If I let things touch me too much, that luck goes.
I have to look on the bright side or we'd all be dead.
And tomorrow? Your plans come to fruition. We get a new place for all these people. You get to be a hero then...
But tonight... I'm kind of a hero, right?
Oh, we hope so.

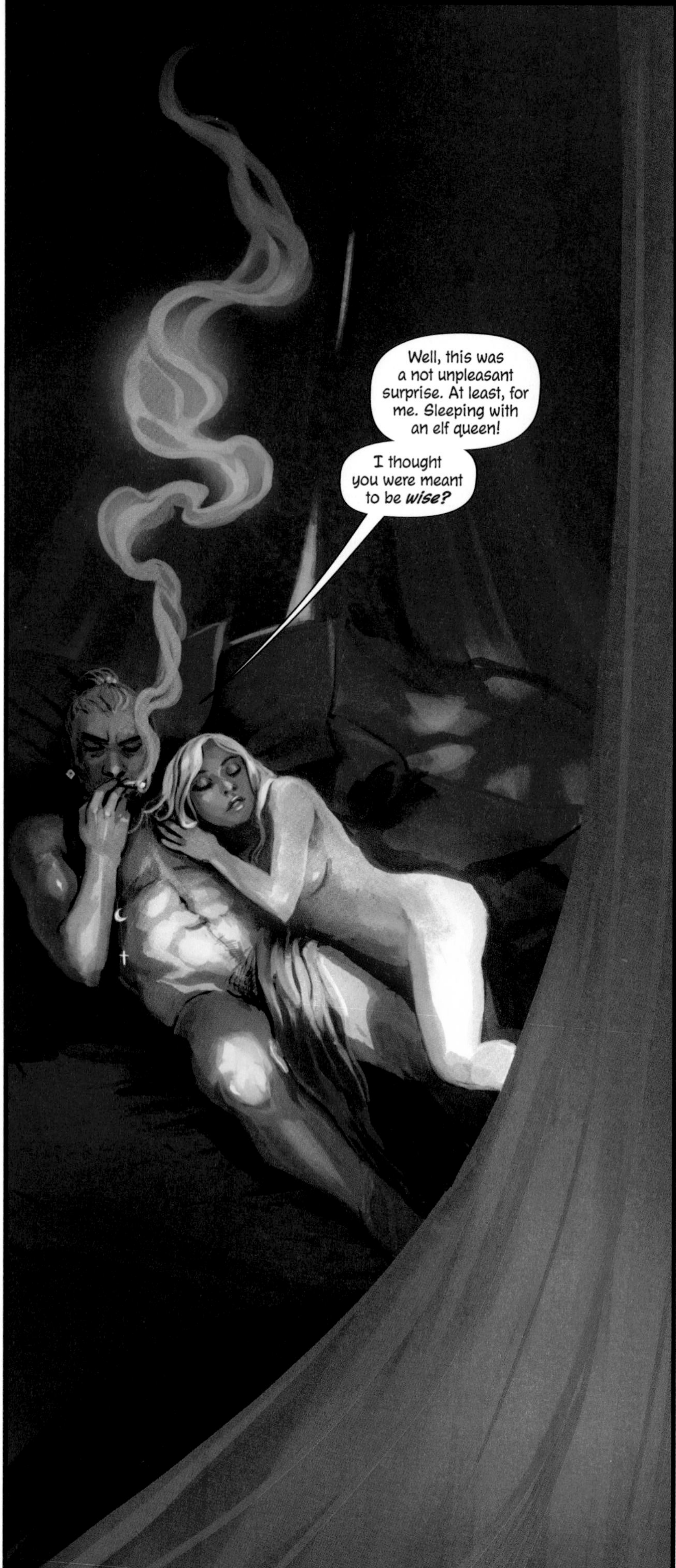
Well, this was a not unpleasant surprise. At least, for me. Sleeping with an elf queen!
I thought you were meant to be ***wise?***

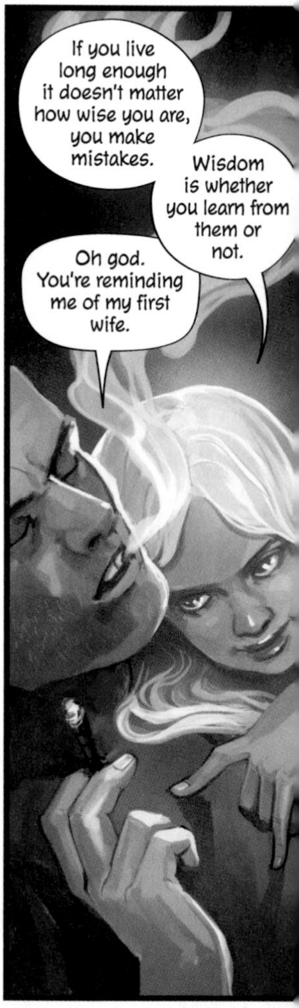
If you live long enough it doesn't matter how wise you are, you make mistakes.
Wisdom is whether you learn from them or not.
Oh god. You're reminding me of my first wife.

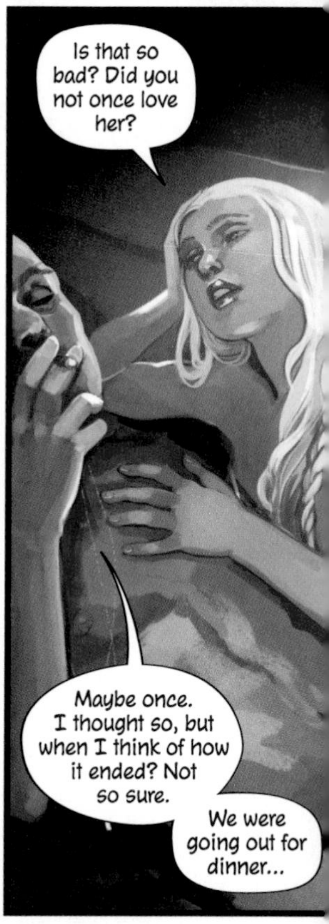
Is that so bad? Did you not once love her?
Maybe once. I thought so, but when I think of how it ended? Not so sure.
We were going out for dinner...

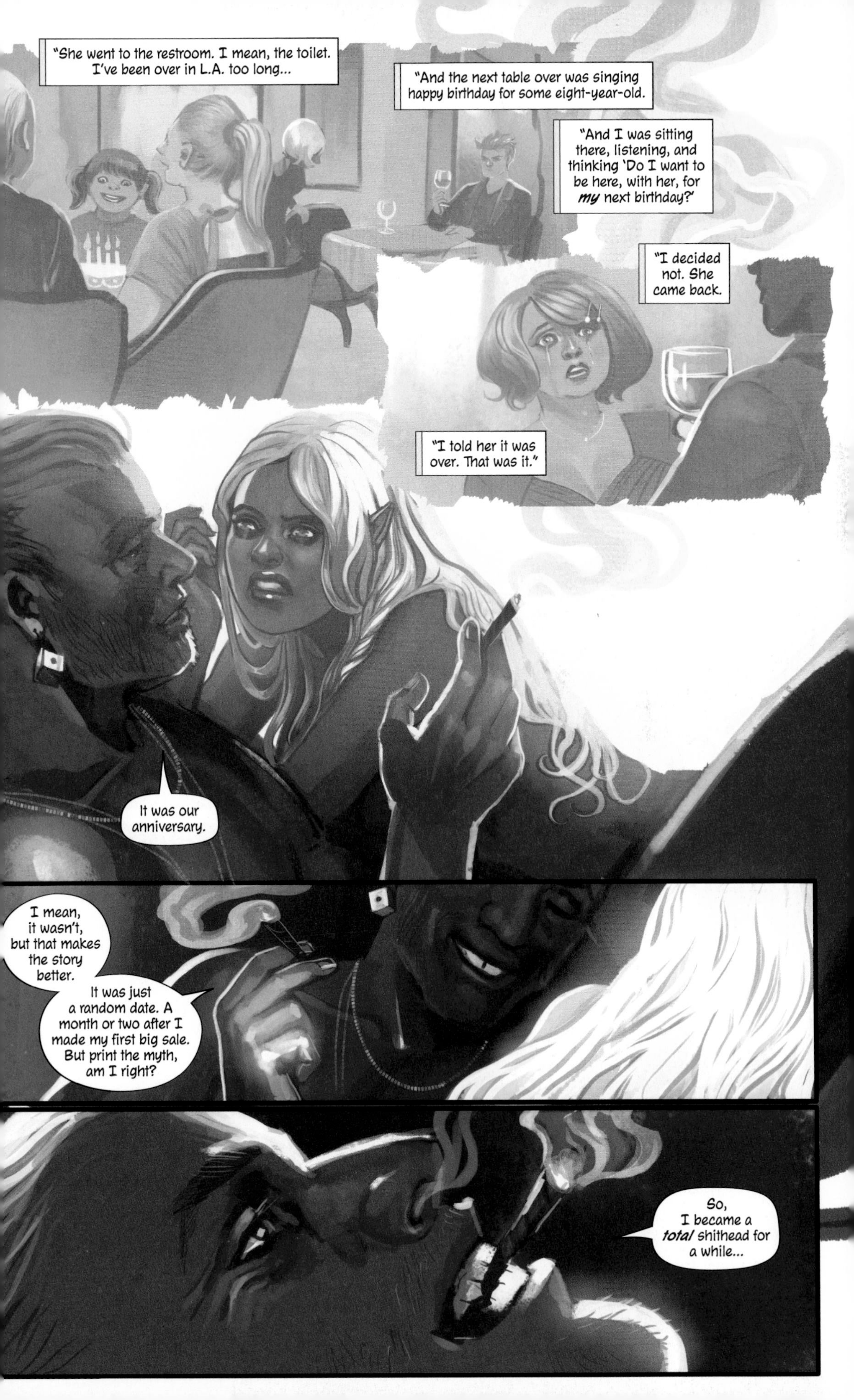
"She went to the restroom. I mean, the toilet. I've been over in L.A. too long...
"And the next table over was singing happy birthday for some eight-year-old.
"And I was sitting there, listening, and thinking 'Do I want to be here, with her, for *my* next birthday?'
"I decided not. She came back.
"I told her it was over. That was it."
It was our anniversary.
I mean, it wasn't, but that makes the story better.
It was just a random date. A month or two after I made my first big sale. But print the myth, am I right?
So, I became a *total* shithead for a while...

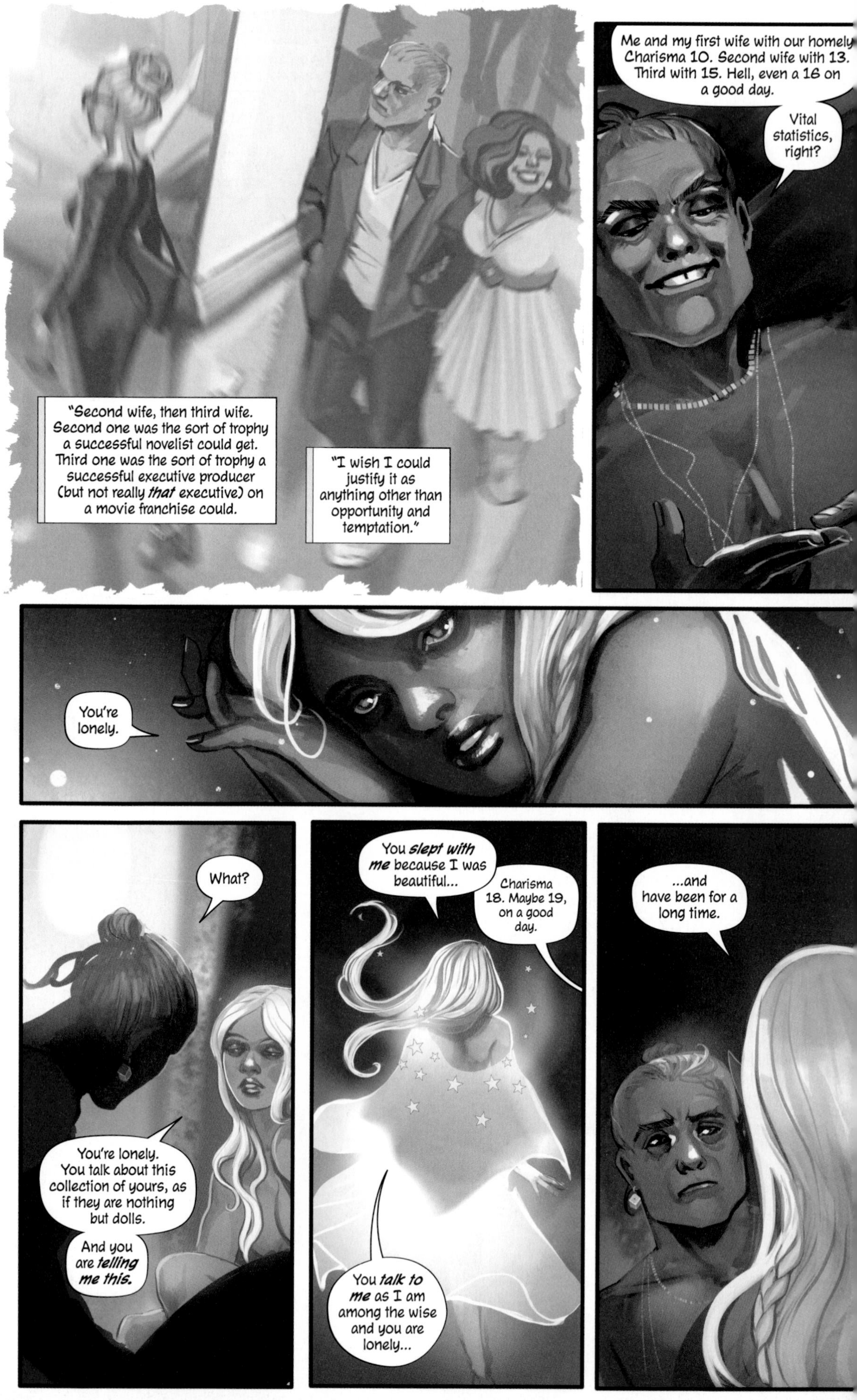
"Second wife, then third wife. Second one was the sort of trophy a successful novelist could get. Third one was the sort of trophy a successful executive producer (but not really *that* executive) on a movie franchise could.
"I wish I could justify it as anything other than opportunity and temptation."
Me and my first wife with our homely Charisma 10. Second wife with 13. Third with 15. Hell, even a 16 on a good day.
Vital statistics, right?
You're lonely.
What?
You're lonely. You talk about this collection of yours, as if they are nothing but dolls.
And you are ***telling me this.***
You ***slept with me*** because I was beautiful...
Charisma 18. Maybe 19, on a good day.
You ***talk to me*** as I am among the wise and you are lonely...
...and have been for a long time.

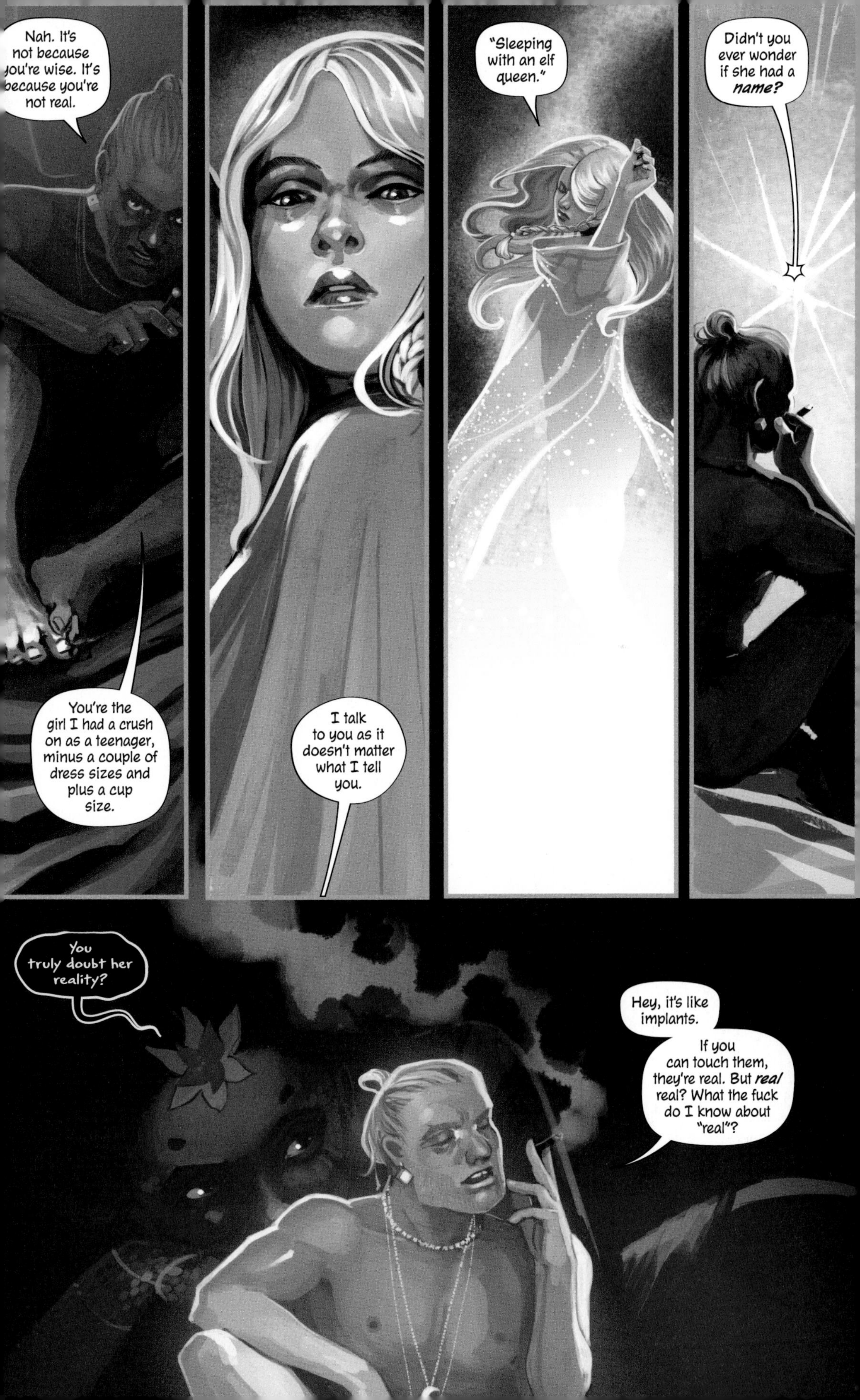
Nah. It's not because you're wise. It's because you're not real.
You're the girl I had a crush on as a teenager, minus a couple of dress sizes and plus a cup size.
I talk to you as it doesn't matter what I tell you.
"Sleeping with an elf queen."
Didn't you ever wonder if she had a ***name?***
You truly doubt her reality?
Hey, it's like implants.
If you can touch them, they're real. But *real* real? What the fuck do I know about "real"?

"I mean...that time I turned up to some drinks in London. And the party was on. It was a great night. A sort of real human connection evening.

"And I leave, and a friend texts me the next day...

"...says 'It's so funny. The second you left, everyone went home.'

"So none of it was real."

How can I know what's real, right? I haven't known what real was since my first book started selling.

I'm not sure if anything or *anyone* is real.

And so, a lesson is learned.

I'm sure you would recognise real if you had to...

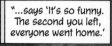

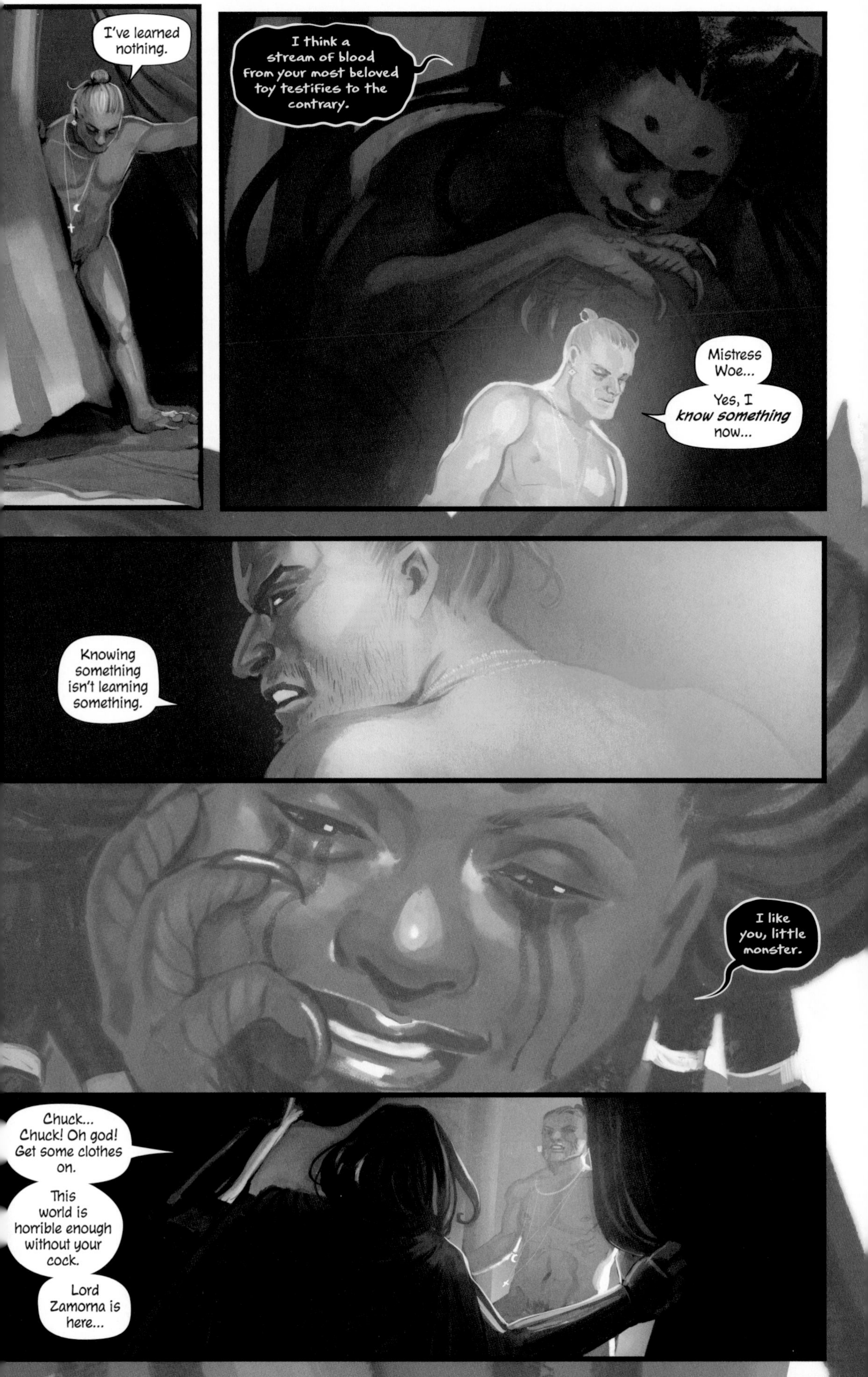
I've learned nothing.
I think a stream of blood from your most beloved toy testifies to the contrary.
Mistress Woe...
Yes, I *know something* now...
Knowing something isn't learning something.
I like you, little monster.
Chuck... Chuck! Oh god! Get some clothes on.
This world is horrible enough without your cock.
Lord Zamorna is here...

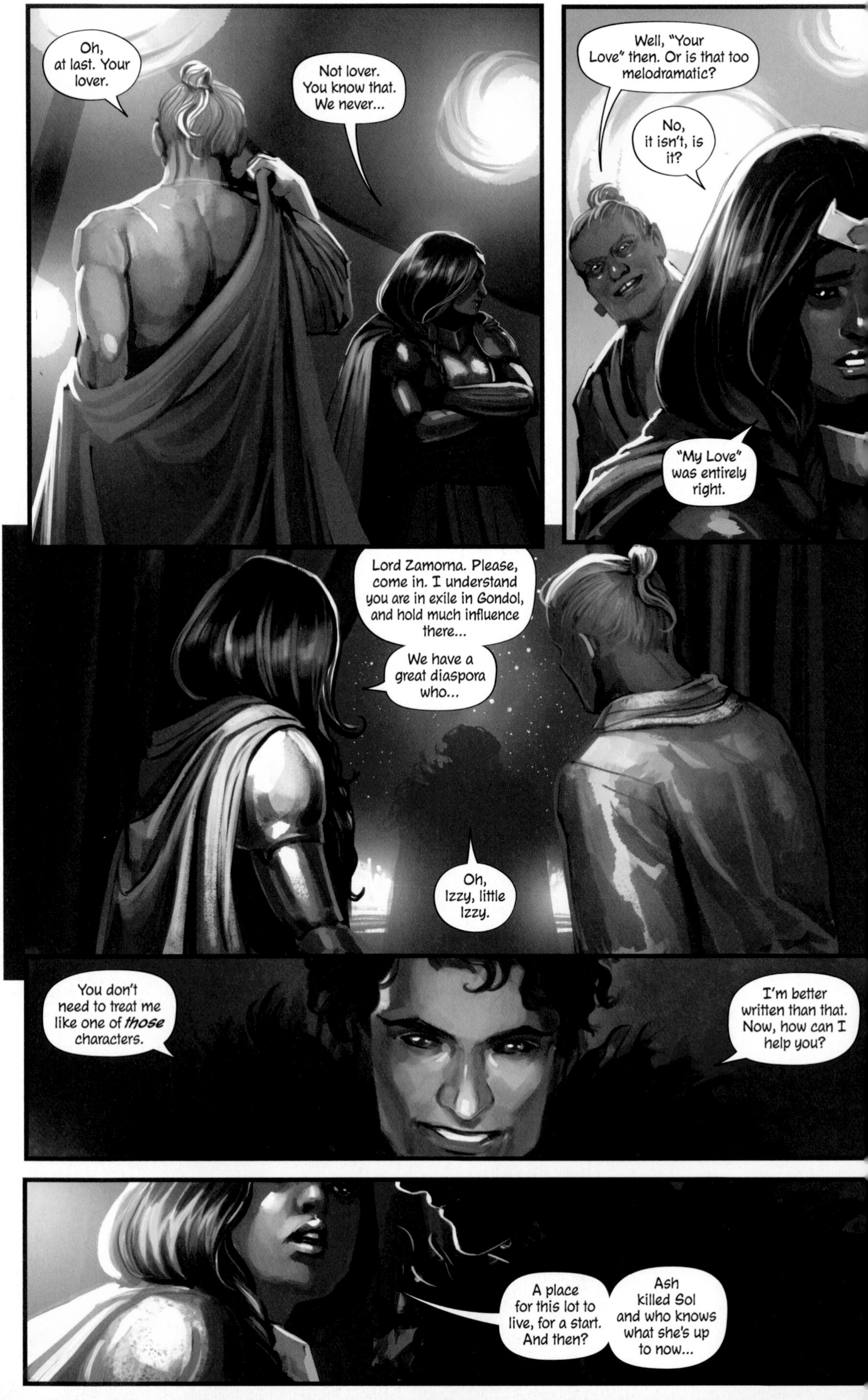
Oh, at last. Your lover.
Not lover. You know that. We never...
Well, "Your Love" then. Or is that too melodramatic?
No, it isn't, is it?
"My Love" was entirely right.
Lord Zamorna. Please, come in. I understand you are in exile in Gondol, and hold much influence there...
We have a great diaspora who...
Oh, Izzy, little Izzy.
You don't need to treat me like one of *those* characters.
I'm better written than that. Now, how can I help you?
A place for this lot to live, for a start. And then?
Ash killed Sol and who knows what she's up to now...

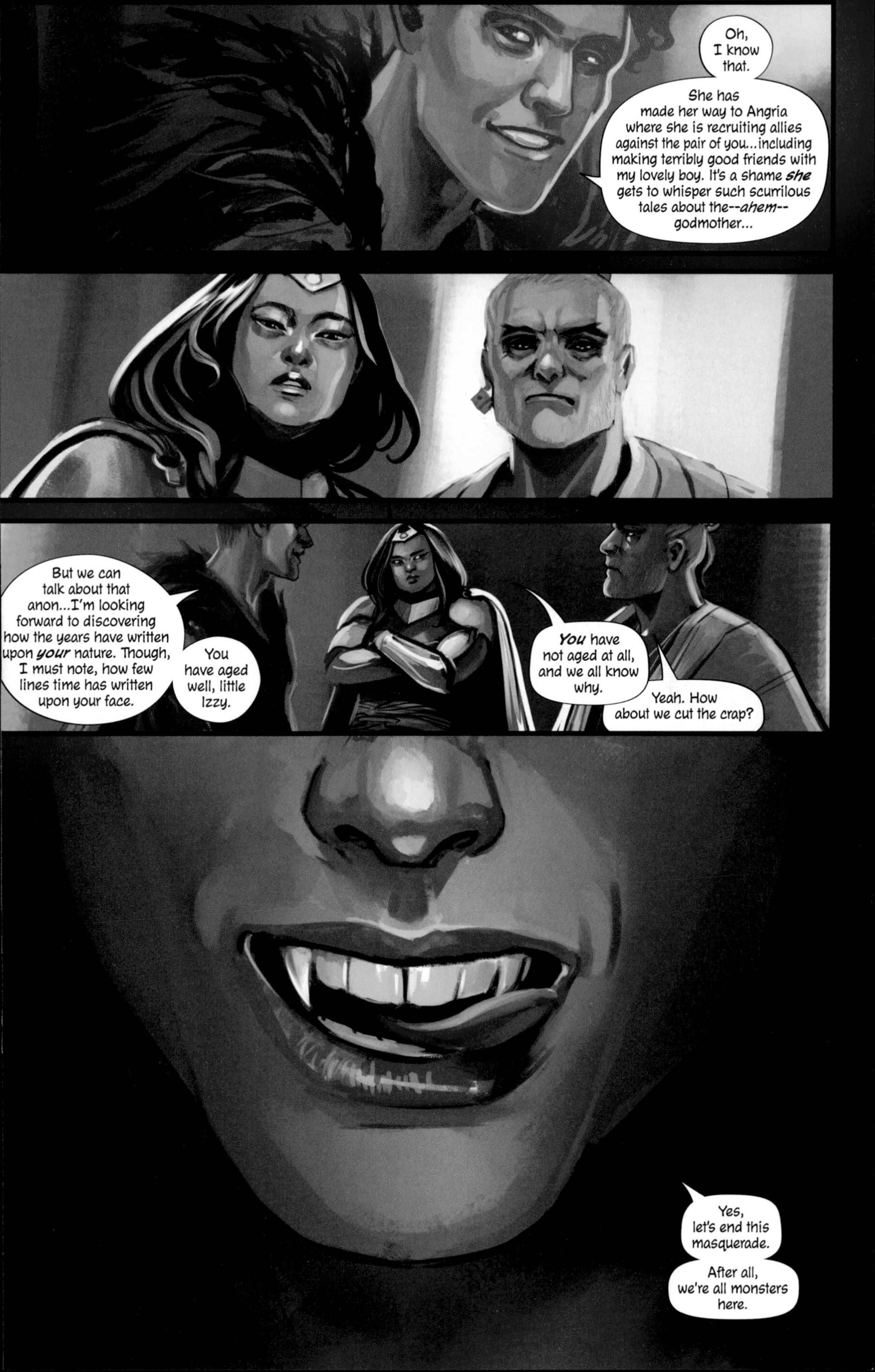

Oh, I know that.
She has made her way to Angria where she is recruiting allies against the pair of you...including making terribly good friends with my lovely boy. It's a shame ***she*** gets to whisper such scurrilous tales about the--*ahem*--godmother...
But we can talk about that anon...I'm looking forward to discovering how the years have written upon ***your*** nature. Though, I must note, how few lines time has written upon your face.
You have aged well, little Izzy.
You have not aged at all, and we all know why.
Yeah. How about we cut the crap?
Yes, let's end this masquerade.
After all, we're all monsters here.

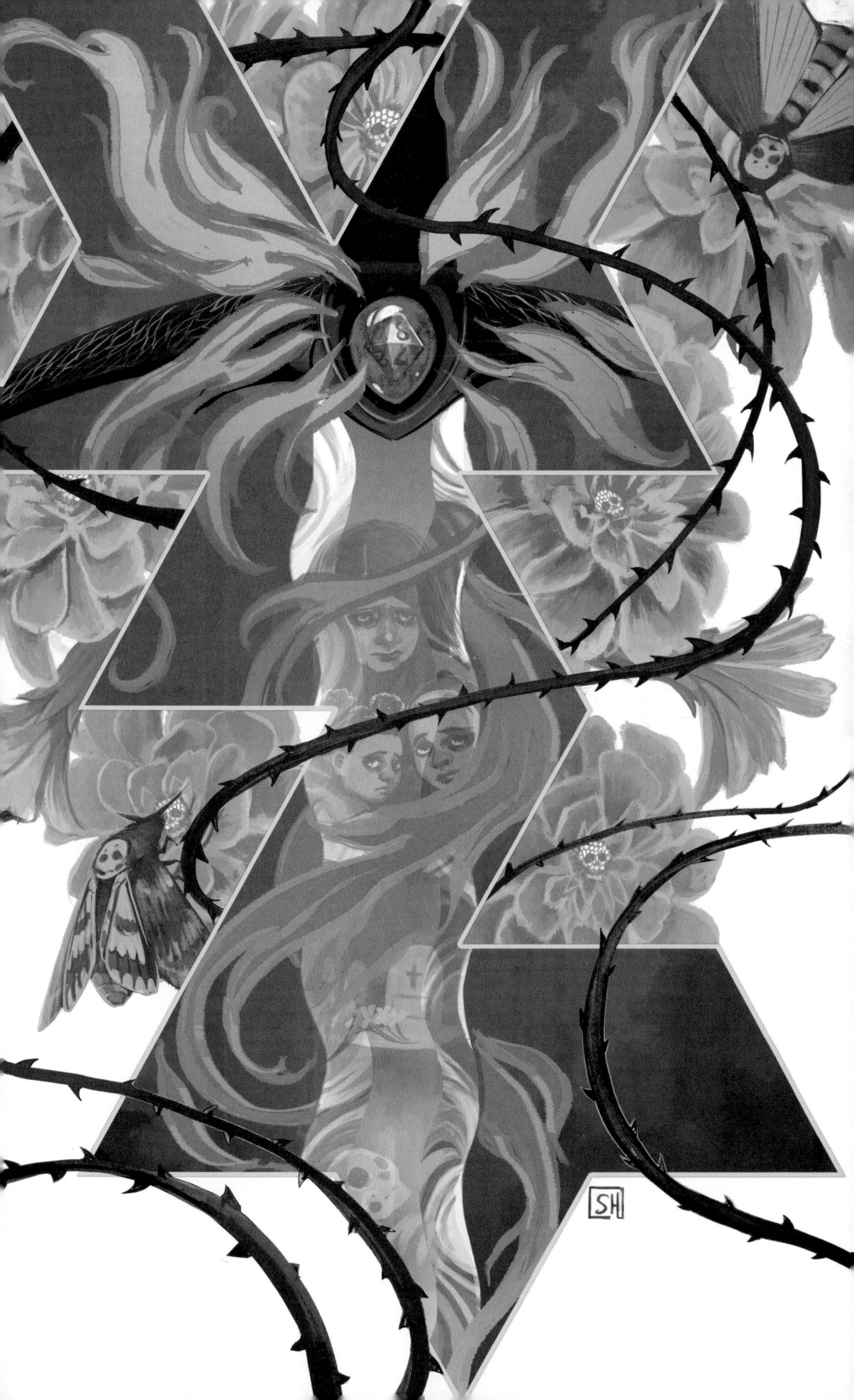
SH

8:
LEGACY HEROES

"I've watched thee every hour –
I know my mighty sway –
I know my magic power
To drive thy griefs away –"
– *Emily Brontë,*
'Shall earth no more inspire thee'

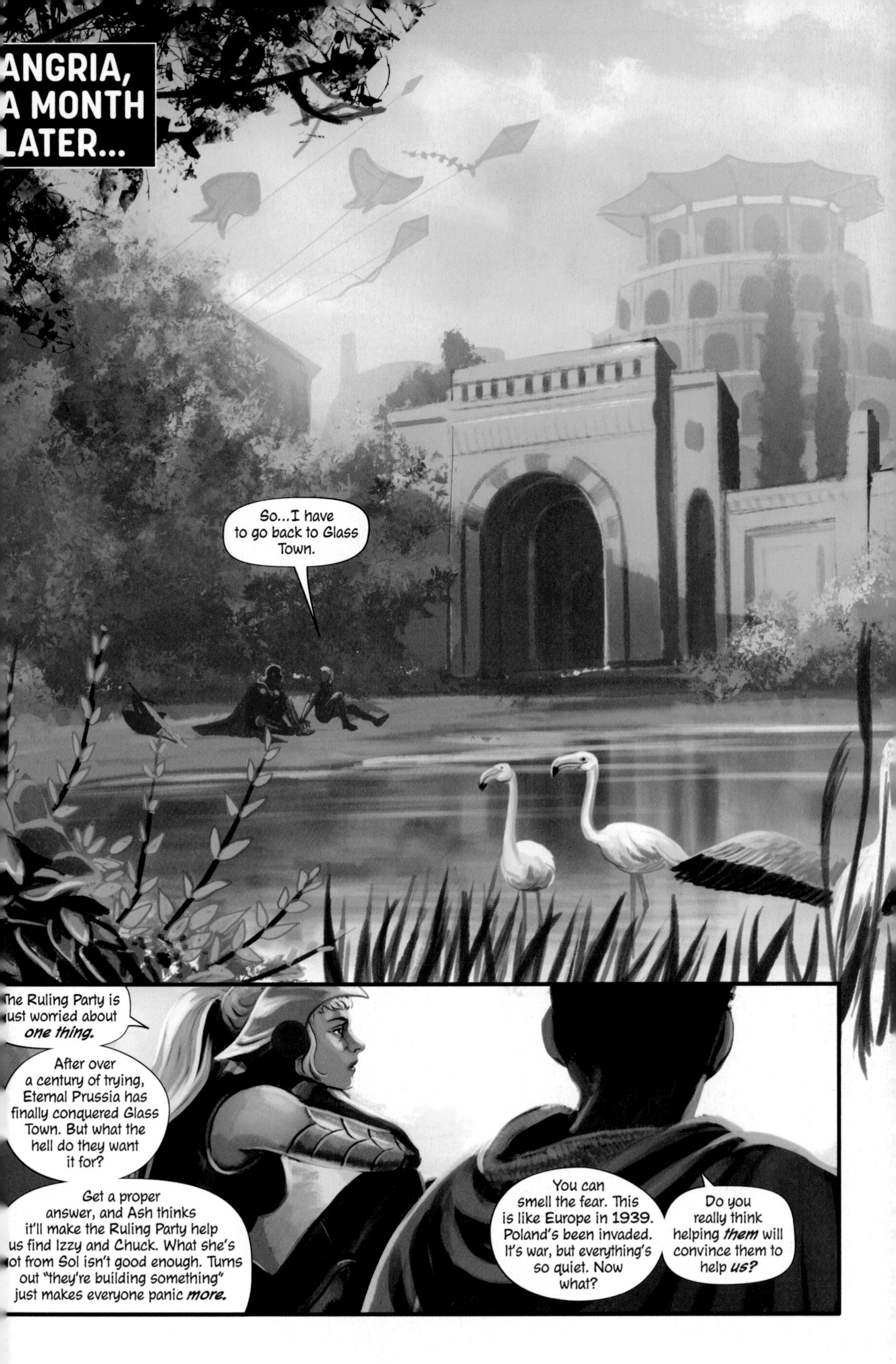
ANGRIA, A MONTH LATER...
So...I have to go back to Glass Town.
he Ruling Party is ust worried about *one thing.*
After over a century of trying, Eternal Prussia has finally conquered Glass Town. But what the hell do they want it for?
Get a proper answer, and Ash thinks it'll make the Ruling Party help us find Izzy and Chuck. What she's ot from Sol isn't good enough. Turns out "they're building something" just makes everyone panic *more.*
You can smell the fear. This is like Europe in 1939. Poland's been invaded. It's war, but everything's so quiet. Now what?
Do you really think helping *them* will convince them to help *us?*

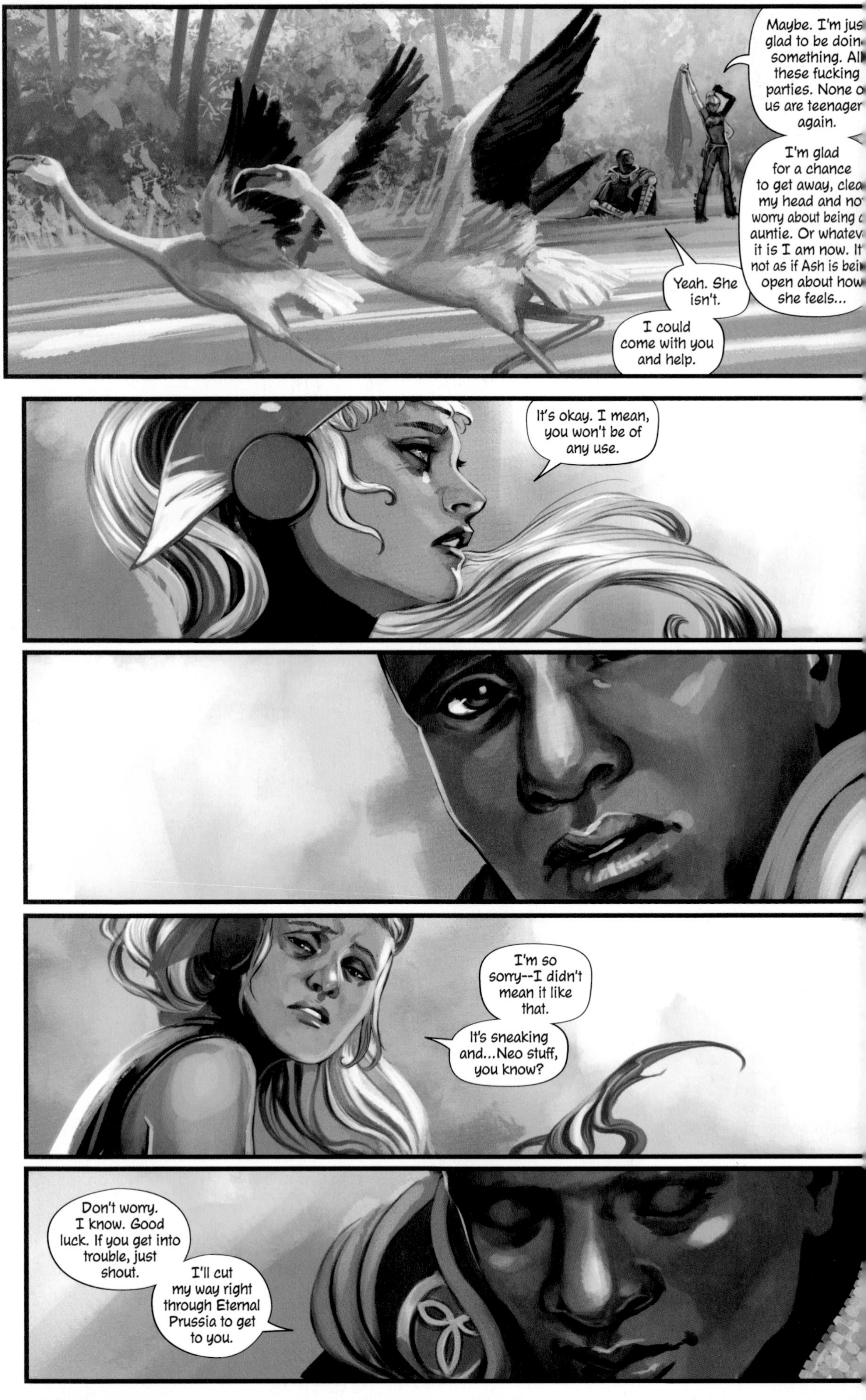
Maybe. I'm jus glad to be doin something. Al these fucking parties. None o us are teenager again.
I'm glad for a chance to get away, clea my head and no worry about being auntie. Or whatev it is I am now. It not as if Ash is bei open about how she feels...
Yeah. She isn't.
I could come with you and help.
It's okay. I mean, you won't be of any use.
I'm so sorry--I didn't mean it like that.
It's sneaking and...Neo stuff, you know?
Don't worry. I know. Good luck. If you get into trouble, just shout.
I'll cut my way right through Eternal Prussia to get to you.

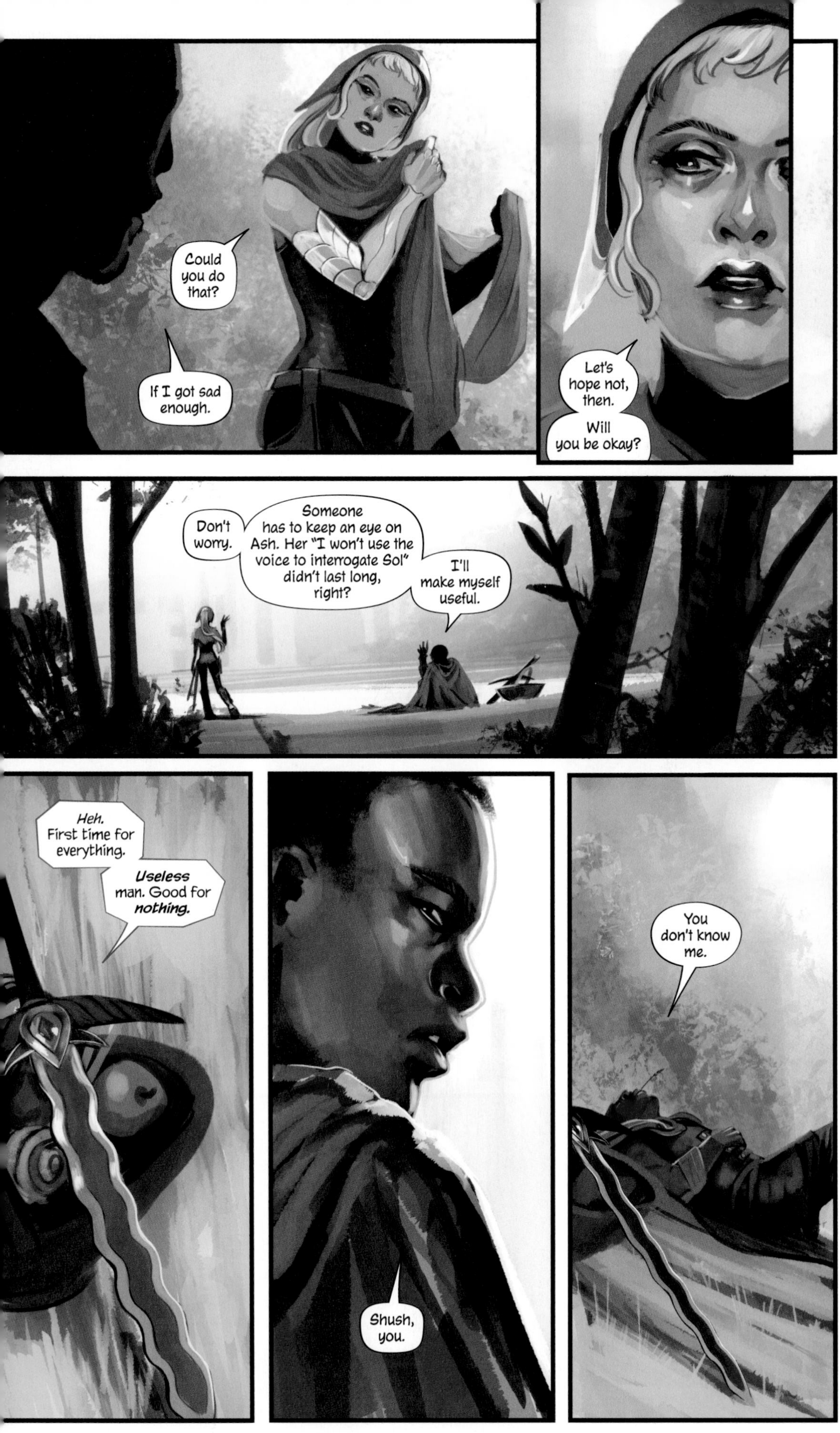
Could you do that?
If I got sad enough.
Let's hope not, then.
Will you be okay?
Don't worry.
Someone has to keep an eye on Ash. Her "I won't use the voice to interrogate Sol" didn't last long, right?
I'll make myself useful.
Heh. First time for everything.
Useless man. Good for ***nothing.***
Shush, you.
You don't know me.

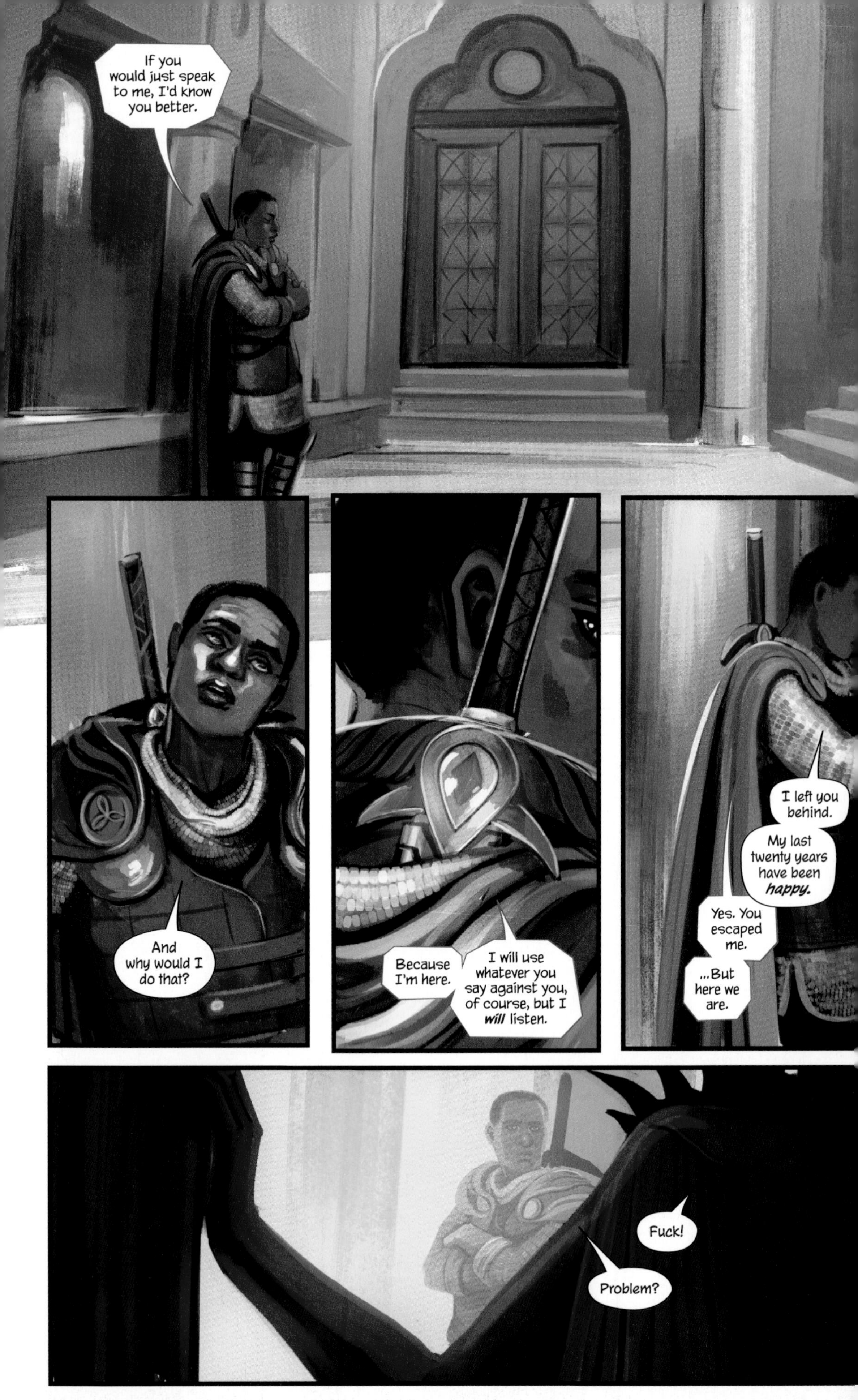
If you would just speak to me, I'd know you better.
And why would I do that?
Because I'm here.
I will use whatever you say against you, of course, but I *will* listen.
I left you behind.
My last twenty years have been ***happy.***
Yes. You escaped me.
...But here we are.
Fuck!
Problem?

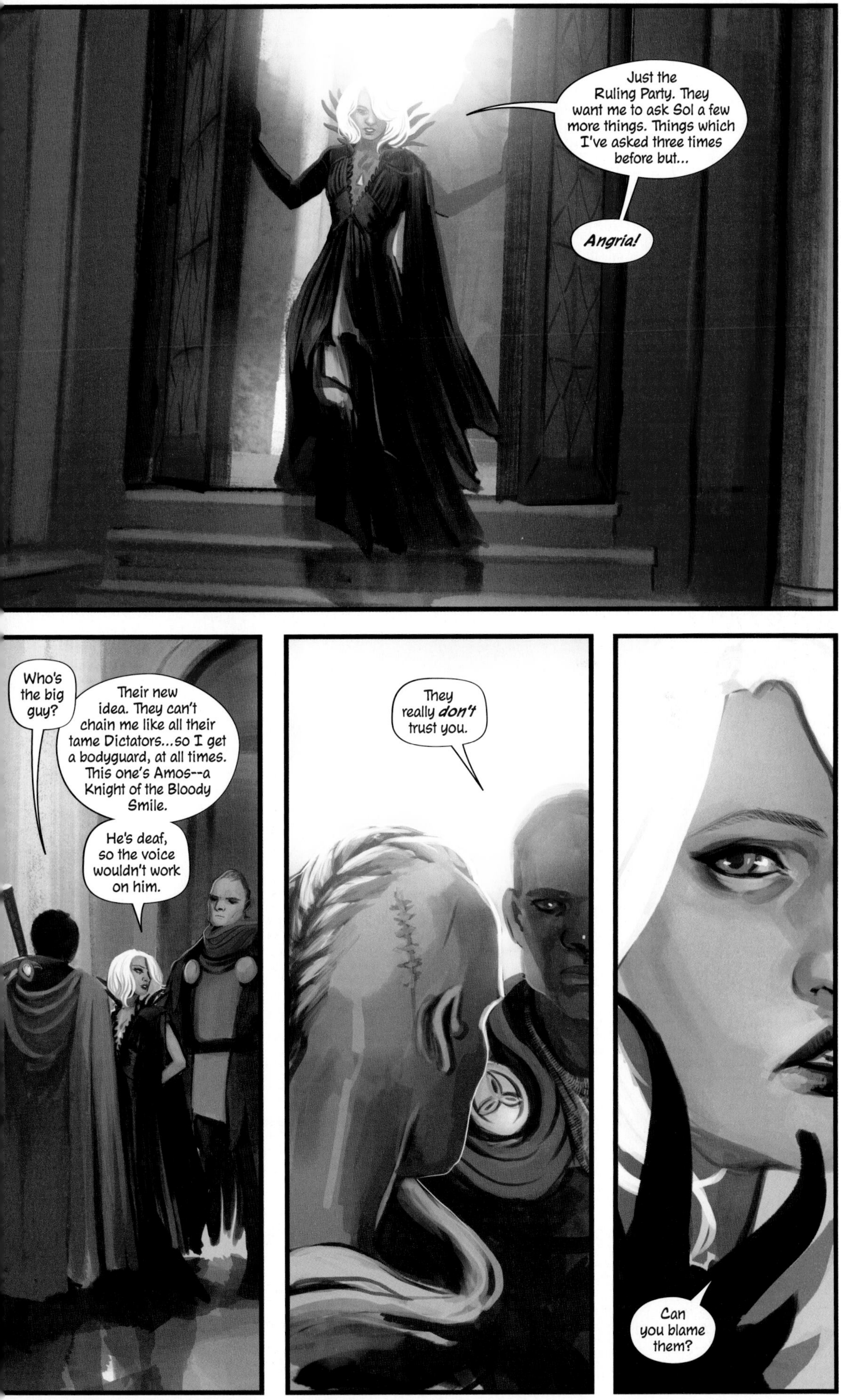
Just the Ruling Party. They want me to ask Sol a few more things. Things which I've asked three times before but...
Angria!
Who's the big guy?
Their new idea. They can't chain me like all their tame Dictators...so I get a bodyguard, at all times. This one's Amos--a Knight of the Bloody Smile.
He's deaf, so the voice wouldn't work on him.
They really *don't* trust you.
Can you blame them?

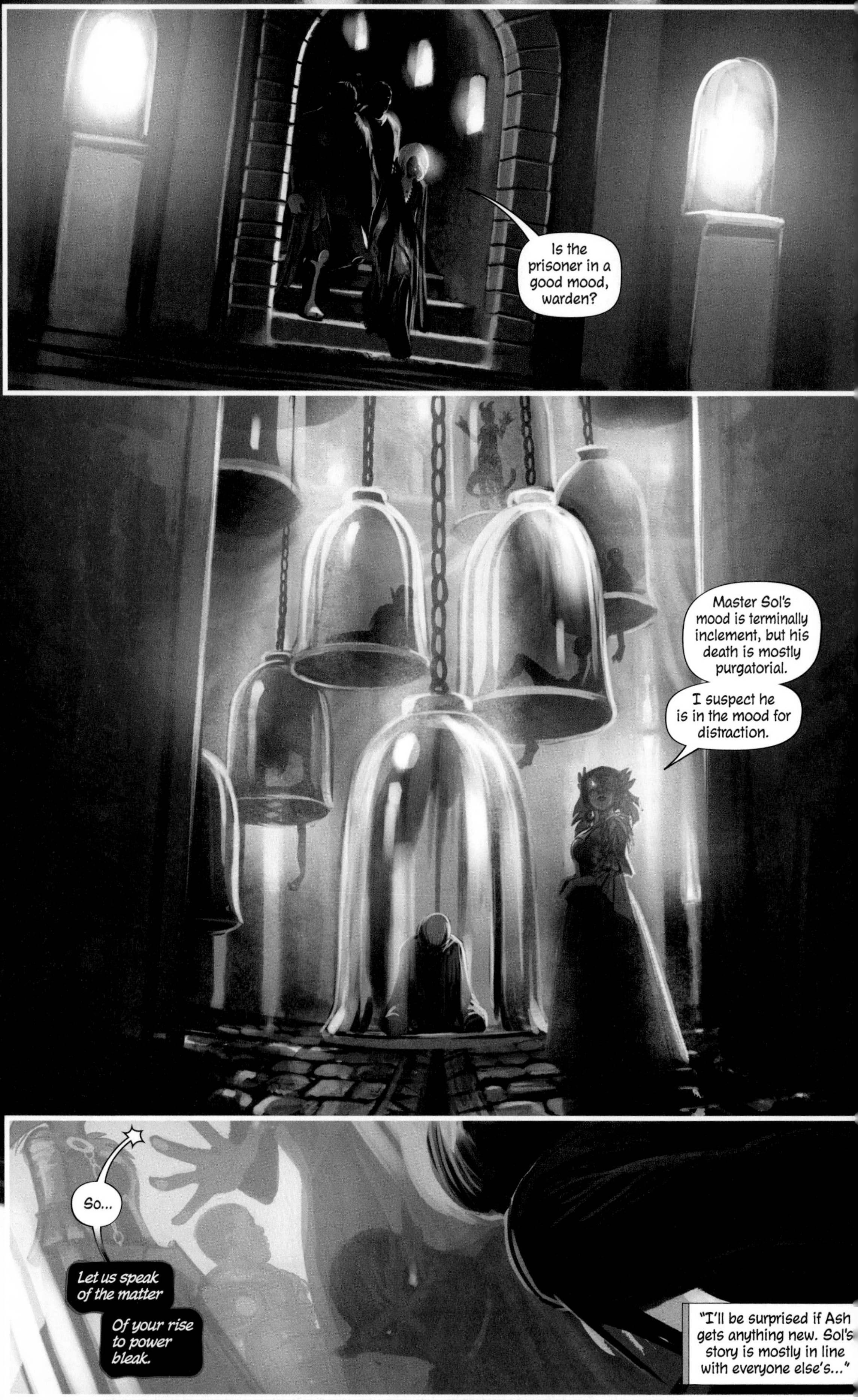
Is the prisoner in a good mood, warden?
Master Sol's mood is terminally inclement, but his death is mostly purgatorial.
I suspect he is in the mood for distraction.
So...
Let us speak of the matter
Of your rise to power bleak.
"I'll be surprised if Ash gets anything new. Sol's story is mostly in line with everyone else's..."

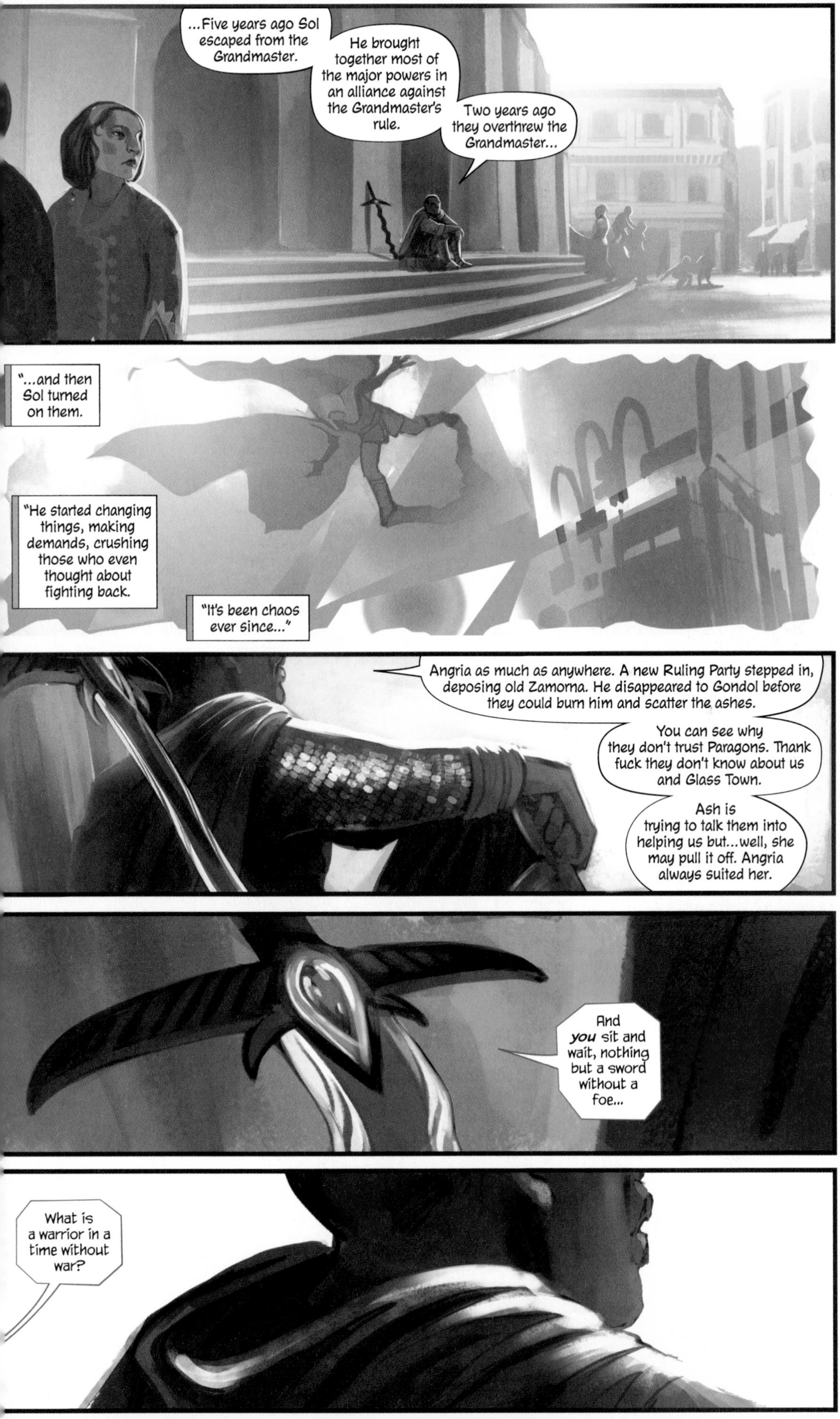
...Five years ago Sol escaped from the Grandmaster.
He brought together most of the major powers in an alliance against the Grandmaster's rule.
Two years ago they overthrew the Grandmaster...
"...and then Sol turned on them.
"He started changing things, making demands, crushing those who even thought about fighting back.
"It's been chaos ever since..."
Angria as much as anywhere. A new Ruling Party stepped in, deposing old Zamorna. He disappeared to Gondol before they could burn him and scatter the ashes.
You can see why they don't trust Paragons. Thank fuck they don't know about us and Glass Town.
Ash is trying to talk them into helping us but...well, she may pull it off. Angria always suited her.
And *you* sit and wait, nothing but a sword without a foe...
What is a warrior in a time without war?

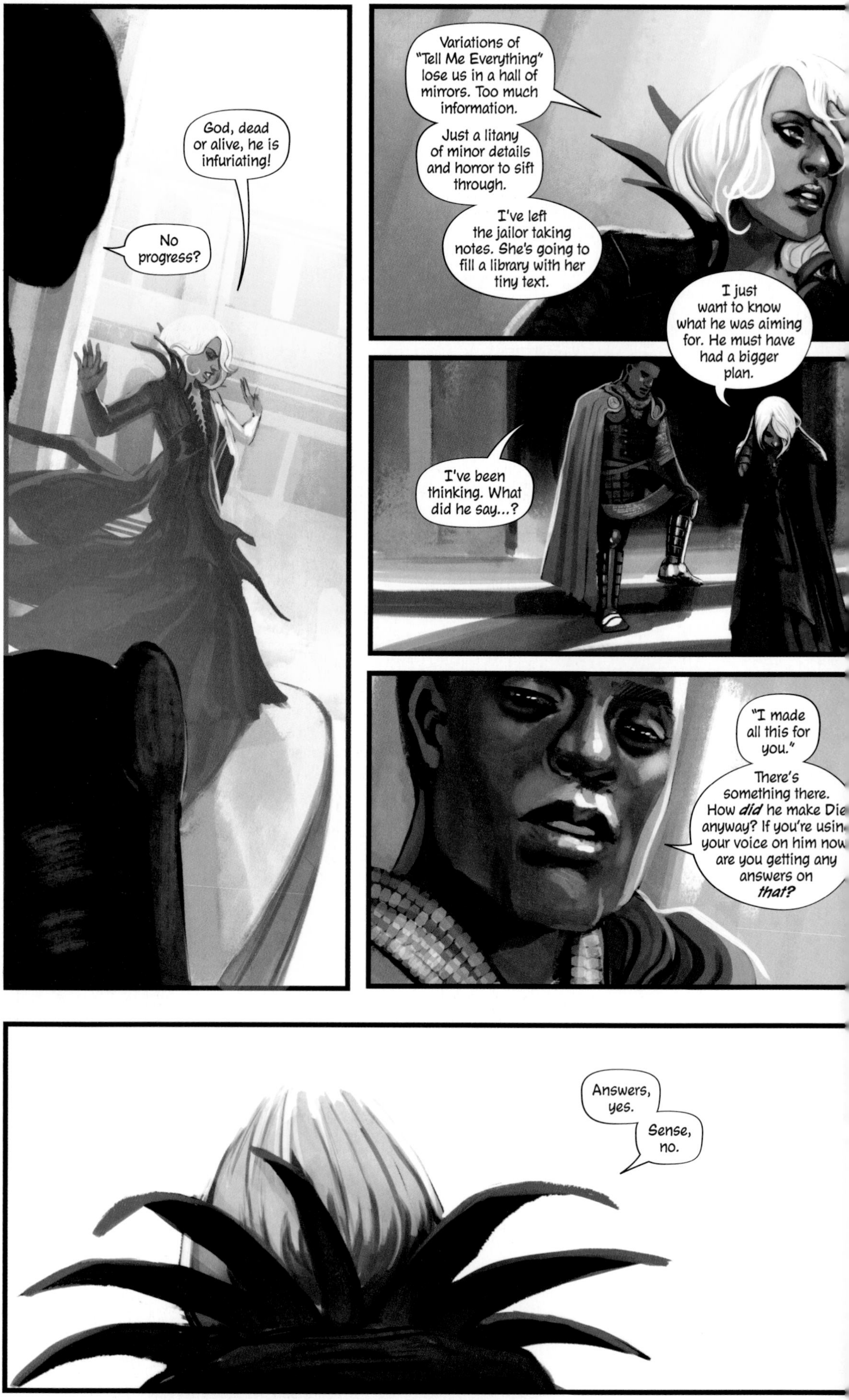
God, dead or alive, he is infuriating!
No progress?
Variations of "Tell Me Everything" lose us in a hall of mirrors. Too much information.
Just a litany of minor details and horror to sift through.
I've left the jailor taking notes. She's going to fill a library with her tiny text.
I just want to know what he was aiming for. He must have had a bigger plan.
I've been thinking. What did he say...?
"I made all this for you."
There's something there. How *did* he make Die anyway? If you're usin your voice on him now are you getting any answers on *that?*
Answers, yes.
Sense, no.

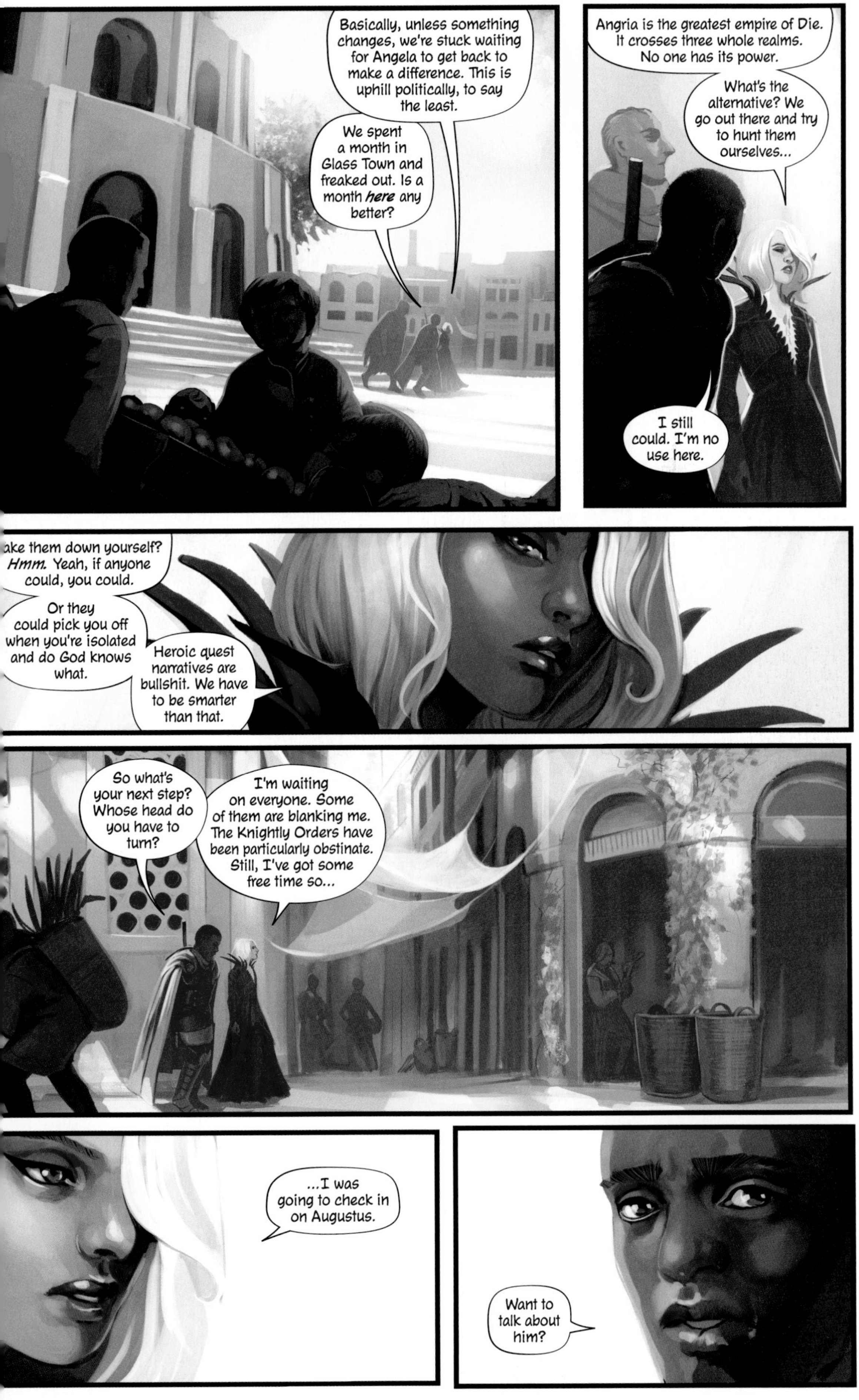

Basically, unless something changes, we're stuck waiting for Angela to get back to make a difference. This is uphill politically, to say the least.
We spent a month in Glass Town and freaked out. Is a month *here* any better?
Angria is the greatest empire of Die. It crosses three whole realms. No one has its power.
What's the alternative? We go out there and try to hunt them ourselves...
I still could. I'm no use here.
ake them down yourself? *Hmm.* Yeah, if anyone could, you could.
Or they could pick you off when you're isolated and do God knows what.
Heroic quest narratives are bullshit. We have to be smarter than that.
So what's your next step? Whose head do you have to turn?
I'm waiting on everyone. Some of them are blanking me. The Knightly Orders have been particularly obstinate. Still, I've got some free time so...
...I was going to check in on Augustus.
Want to talk about him?

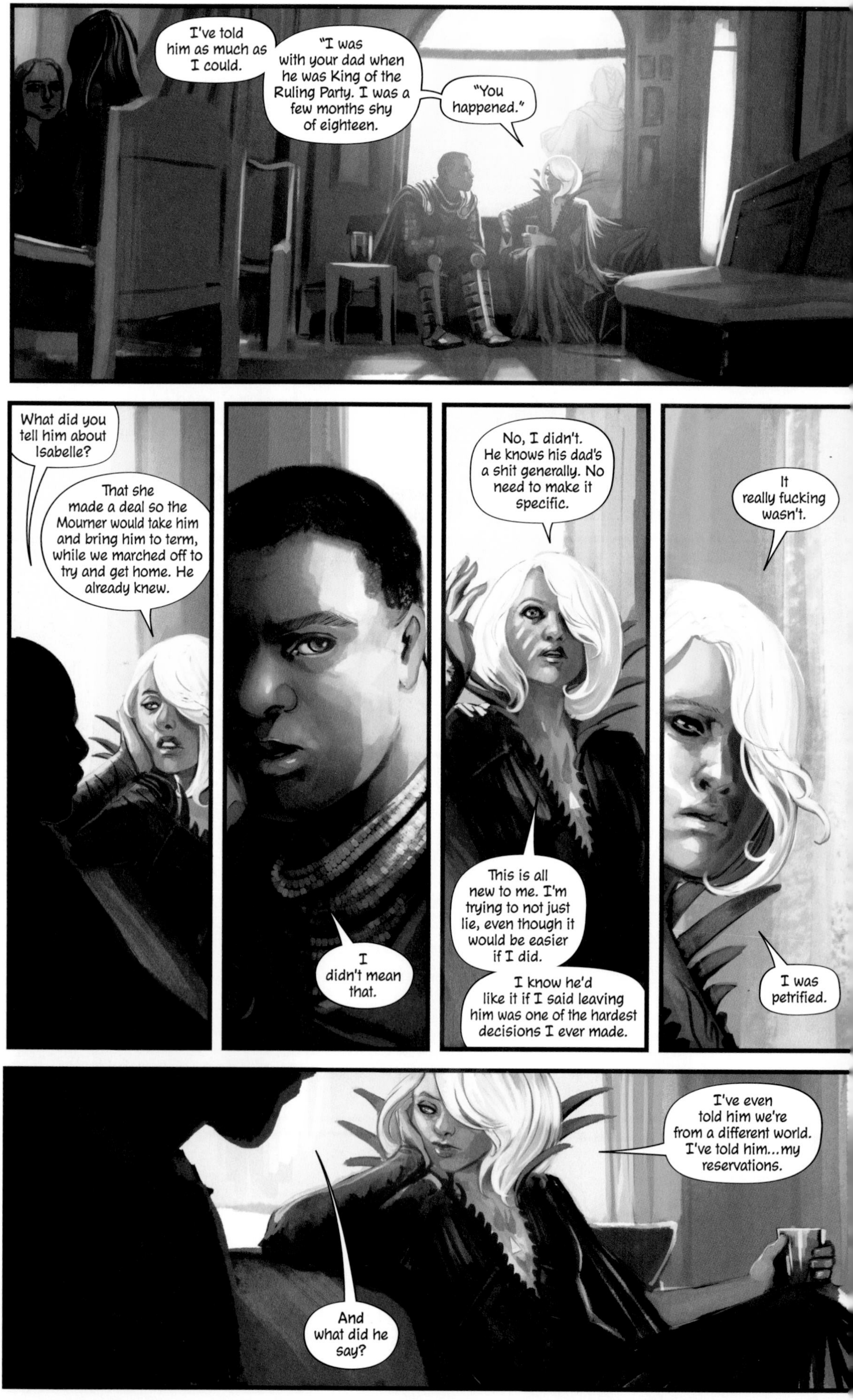
I've told him as much as I could.
"I was with your dad when he was King of the Ruling Party. I was a few months shy of eighteen.
"You happened."
What did you tell him about Isabelle?
That she made a deal so the Mourner would take him and bring him to term, while we marched off to try and get home. He already knew.
I didn't mean that.
No, I didn't. He knows his dad's a shit generally. No need to make it specific.
This is all new to me. I'm trying to not just lie, even though it would be easier if I did.
I know he'd like it if I said leaving him was one of the hardest decisions I ever made.
It really fucking wasn't.
I was petrified.
I've even told him we're from a different world. I've told him...my reservations.
And what did he say?

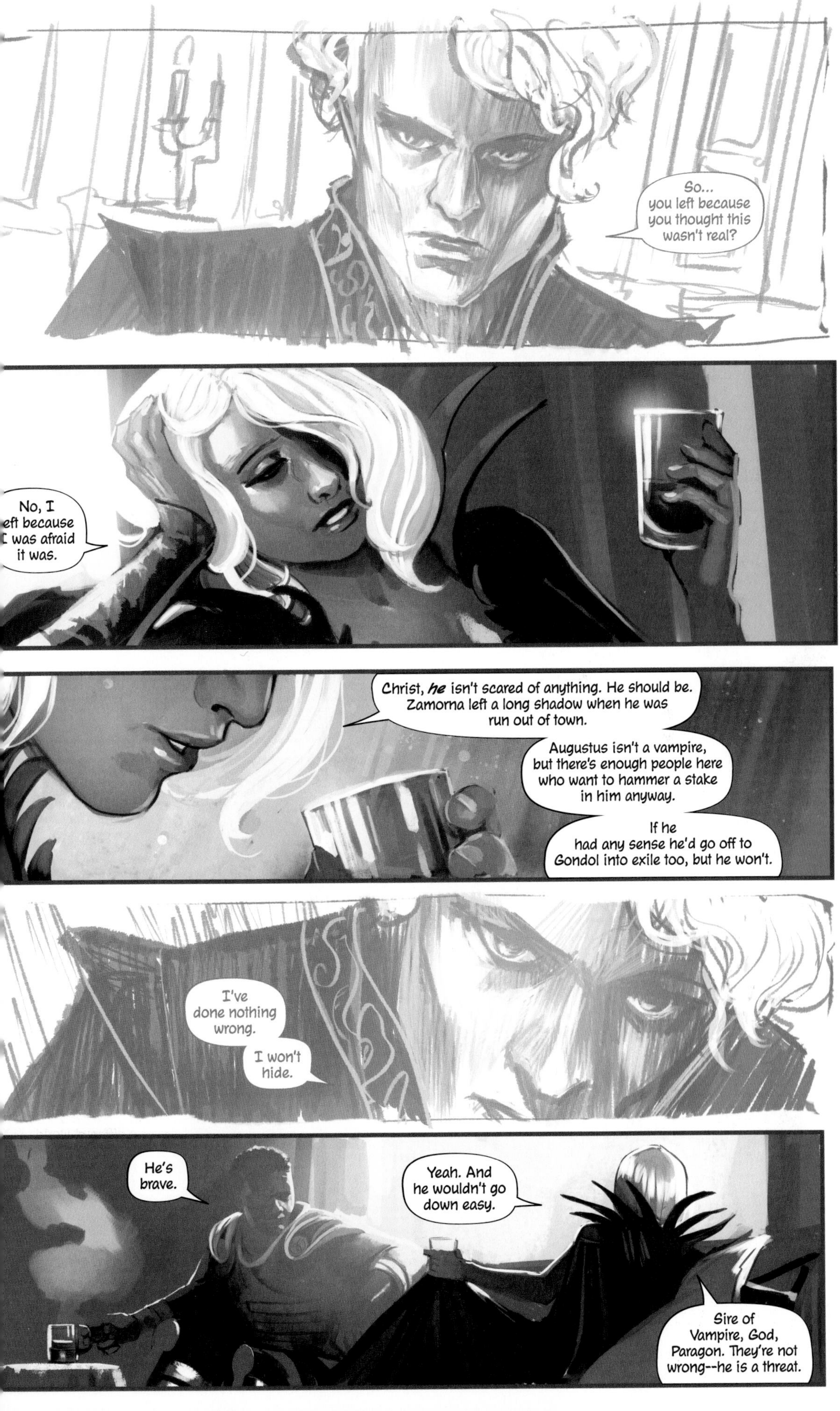

So... you left because you thought this wasn't real?
No, I eft because I was afraid it was.
Christ, ***he*** isn't scared of anything. He should be. Zamorna left a long shadow when he was run out of town.
Augustus isn't a vampire, but there's enough people here who want to hammer a stake in him anyway.
If he had any sense he'd go off to Gondol into exile too, but he won't.
I've done nothing wrong.
I won't hide.
He's brave.
Yeah. And he wouldn't go down easy.
Sire of Vampire, God, Paragon. They're not wrong--he is a threat.

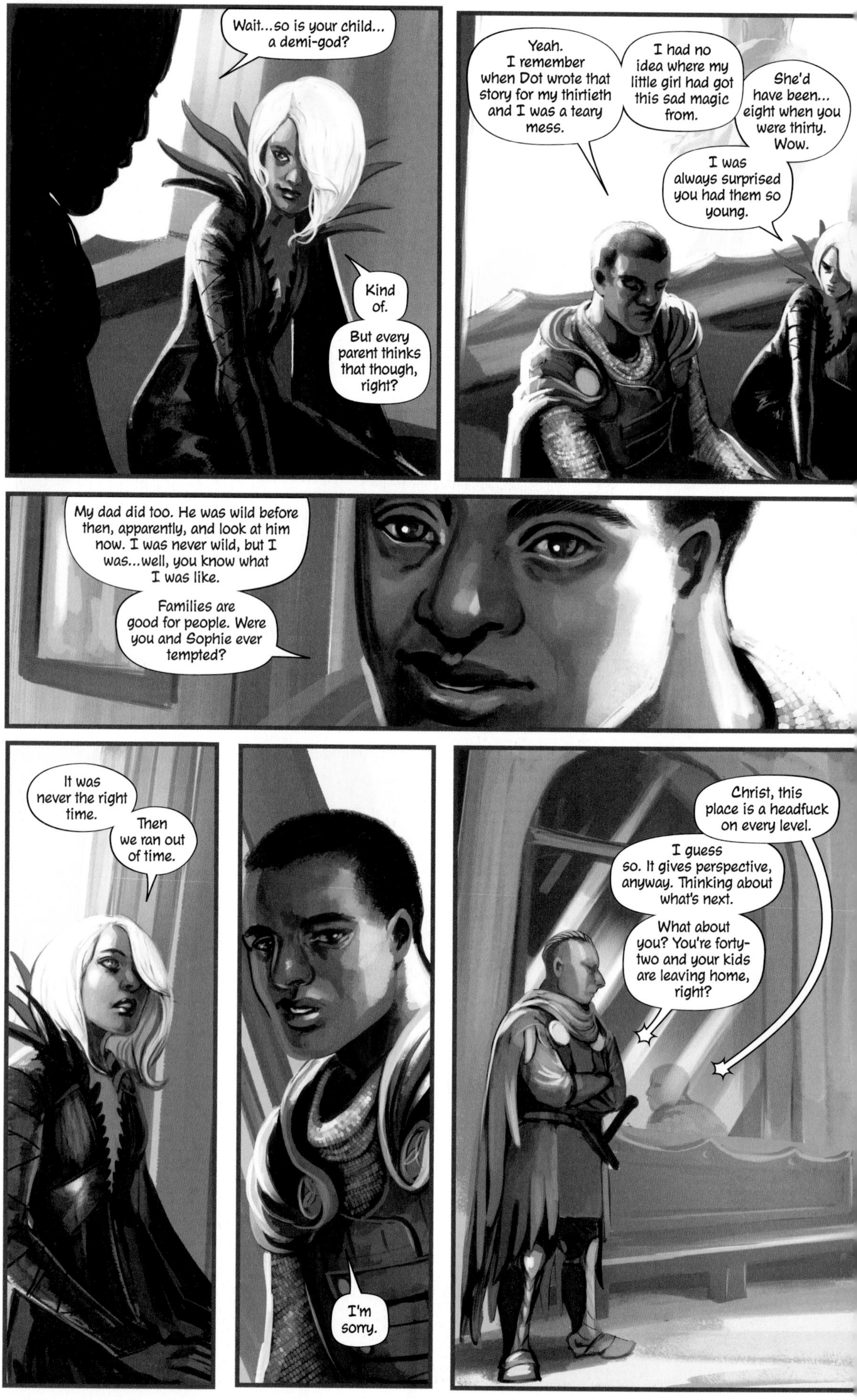

Wait...so is your child... a demi-god?
Kind of.
But every parent thinks that though, right?
Yeah. I remember when Dot wrote that story for my thirtieth and I was a teary mess.
I had no idea where my little girl had got this sad magic from.
She'd have been... eight when you were thirty. Wow.
I was always surprised you had them so young.
My dad did too. He was wild before then, apparently, and look at him now. I was never wild, but I was...well, you know what I was like.
Families are good for people. Were you and Sophie ever tempted?
It was never the right time.
Then we ran out of time.
I'm sorry.
Christ, this place is a headfuck on every level.
I guess so. It gives perspective, anyway. Thinking about what's next.
What about you? You're forty-two and your kids are leaving home, right?

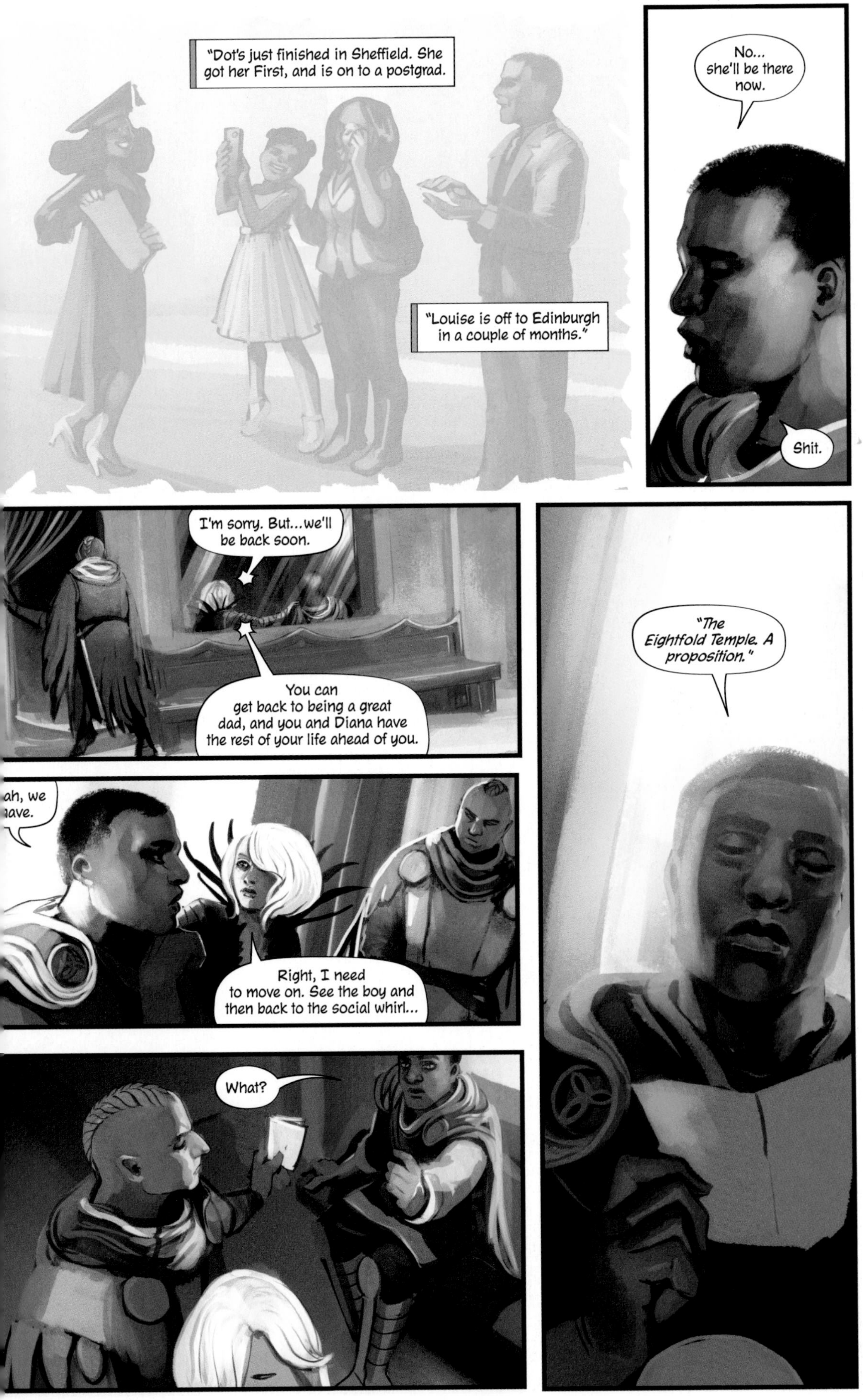
"Dot's just finished in Sheffield. She got her First, and is on to a postgrad.
"Louise is off to Edinburgh in a couple of months."
No... she'll be there now.
Shit.
I'm sorry. But...we'll be back soon.
You can get back to being a great dad, and you and Diana have the rest of your life ahead of you.
ah, we
ave.
Right, I need to move on. See the boy and then back to the social whirl...
What?
"The Eightfold Temple. A proposition."

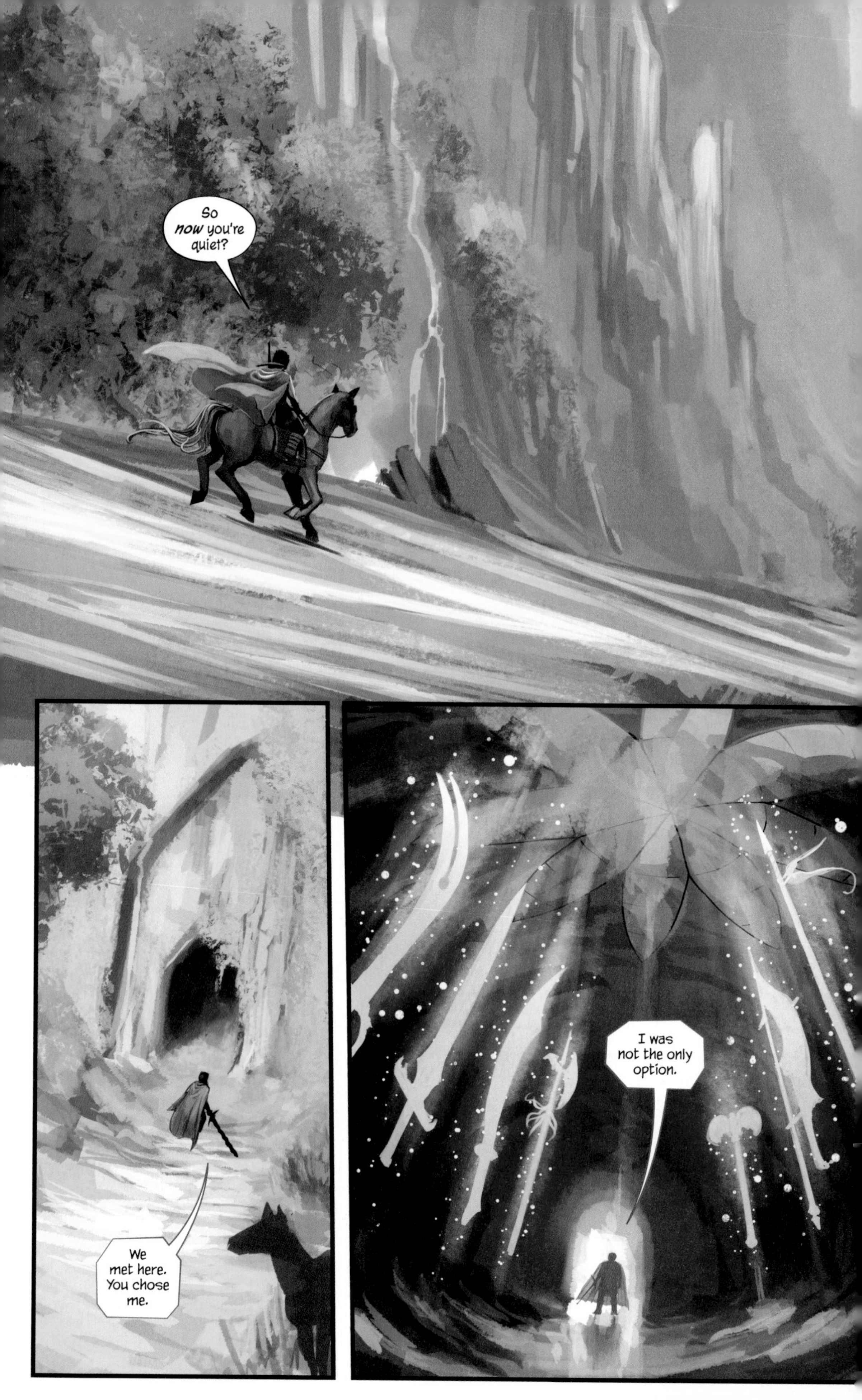
So *now* you're quiet?
We met here. You chose me.
I was not the only option.

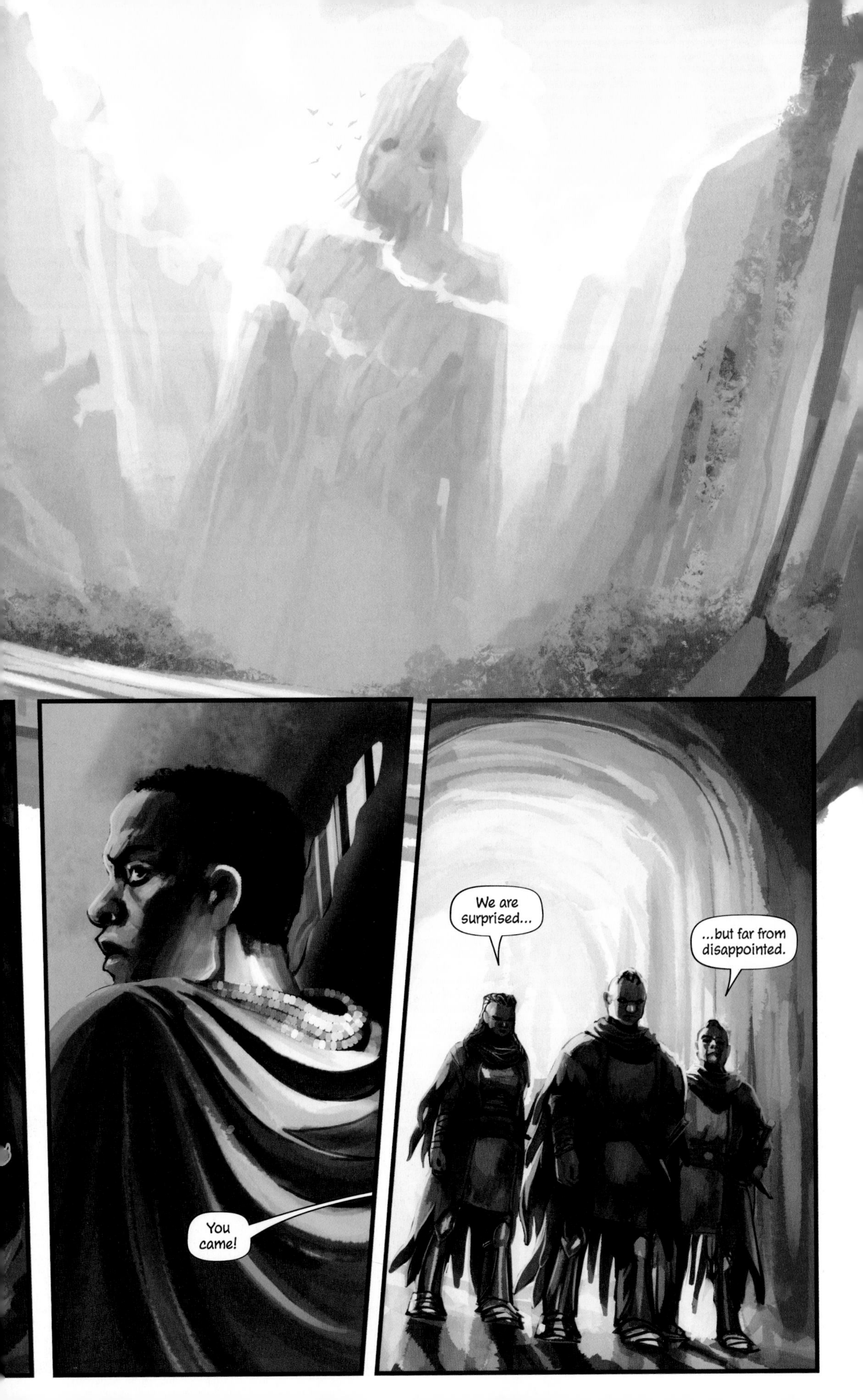
You came!
We are surprised...
...but far from disappointed.

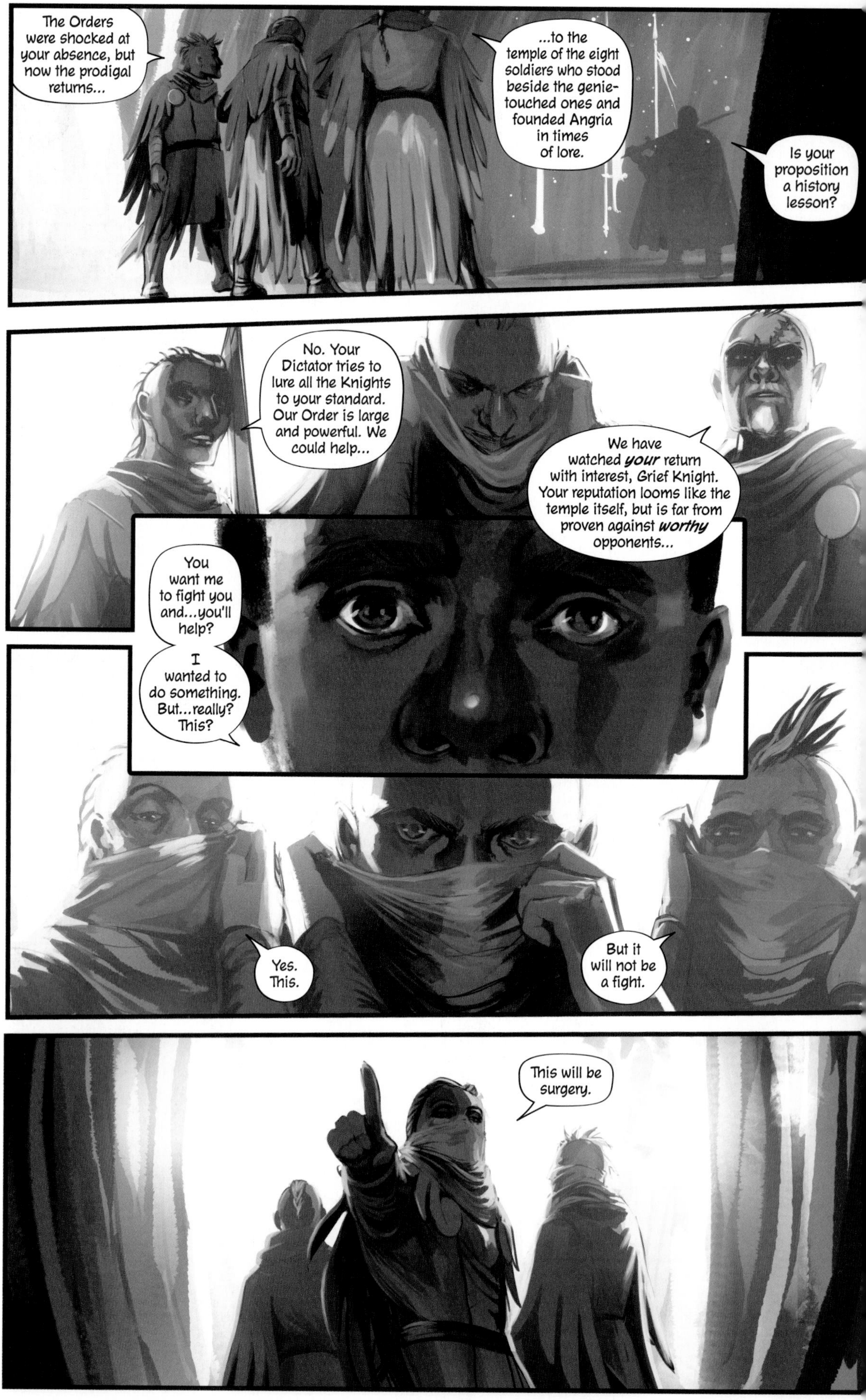

The Orders were shocked at your absence, but now the prodigal returns...
...to the temple of the eight soldiers who stood beside the genie-touched ones and founded Angria in times of lore.
Is your proposition a history lesson?
No. Your Dictator tries to lure all the Knights to your standard. Our Order is large and powerful. We could help...
We have watched *your* return with interest, Grief Knight. Your reputation looms like the temple itself, but is far from proven against *worthy* opponents...
You want me to fight you and...you'll help?
I wanted to do something. But...really? This?
Yes. This.
But it will not be a fight.
This will be surgery.

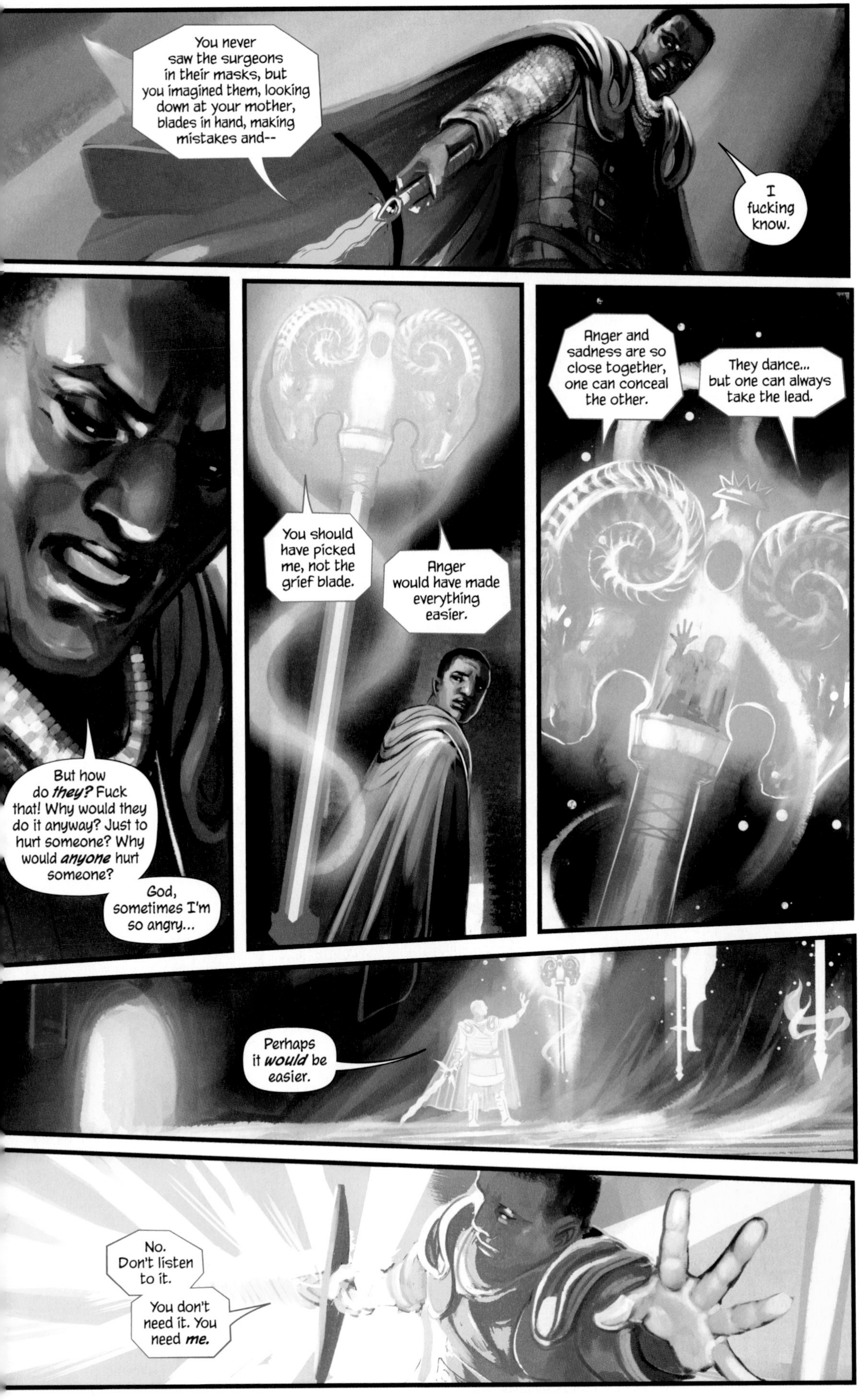
You never saw the surgeons in their masks, but you imagined them, looking down at your mother, blades in hand, making mistakes and--
I fucking know.
But how do *they?* Fuck that! Why would they do it anyway? Just to hurt someone? Why would *anyone* hurt someone?
God, sometimes I'm so angry...
You should have picked me, not the grief blade.
Anger would have made everything easier.
Anger and sadness are so close together, one can conceal the other.
They dance... but one can always take the lead.
Perhaps it *would* be easier.
No. Don't listen to it.
You don't need it. You need *me.*

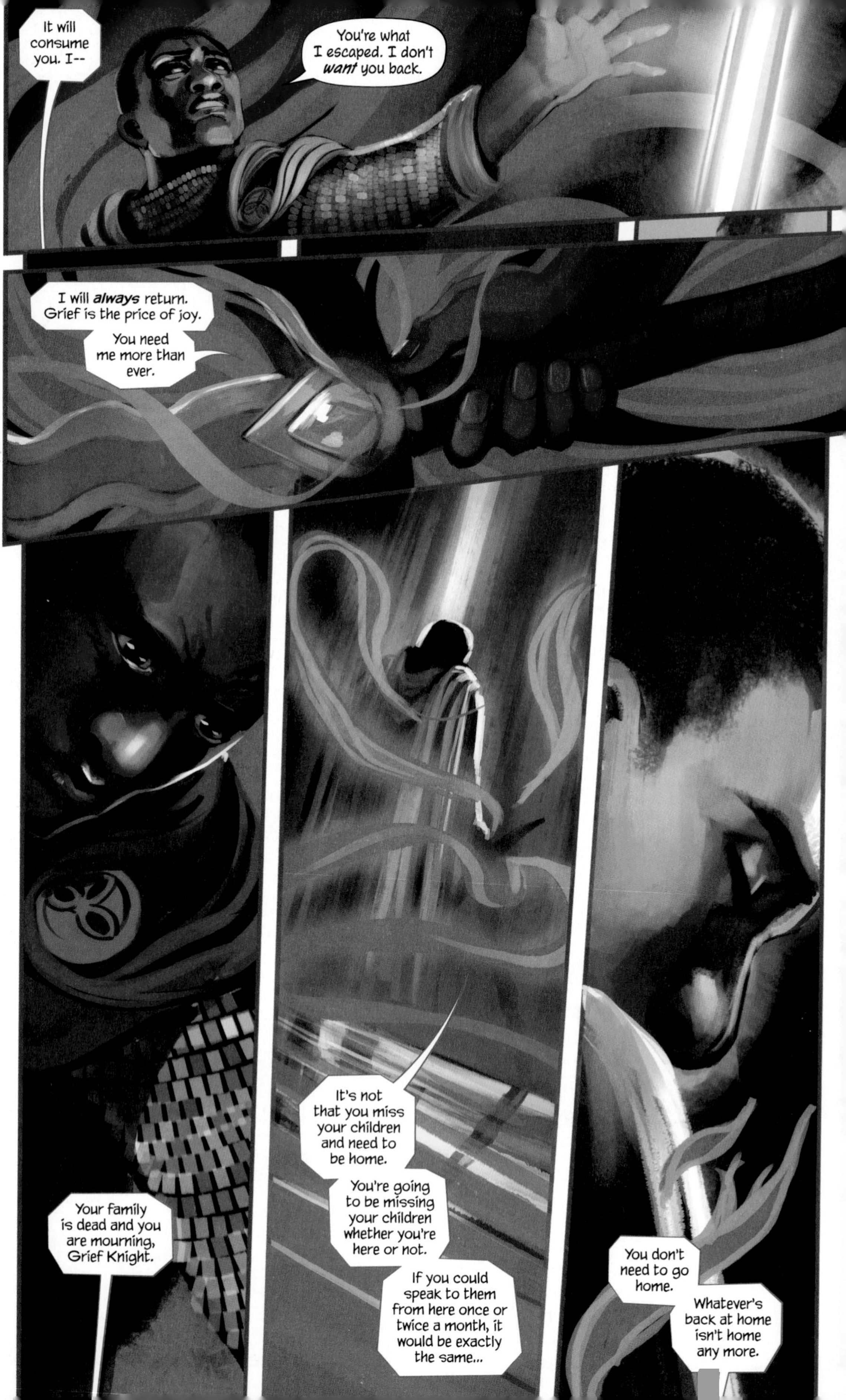
It will consume you. I--
You're what I escaped. I don't *want* you back.
I will *always* return. Grief is the price of joy.
You need me more than ever.
Your family is dead and you are mourning, Grief Knight.
It's not that you miss your children and need to be home.
You're going to be missing your children whether you're here or not.
If you could speak to them from here once or twice a month, it would be exactly the same...
You don't need to go home.
Whatever's back at home isn't home any more.

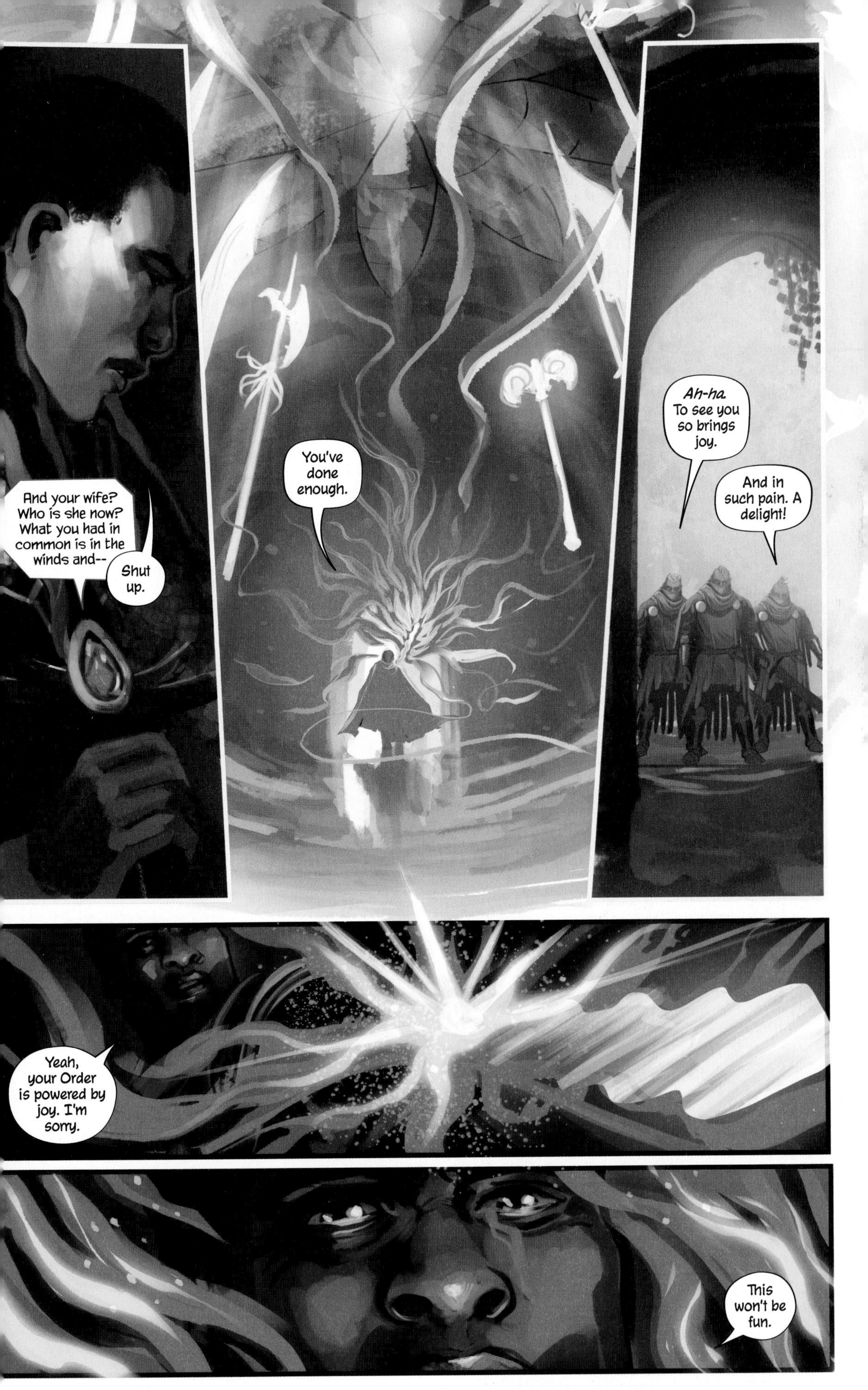
And your wife? Who is she now? What you had in common is in the winds and--
Shut up.
You've done enough.
Ah-ha To see you so brings joy.
And in such pain. A delight!
Yeah, your Order is powered by joy. I'm sorry.
This won't be fun.

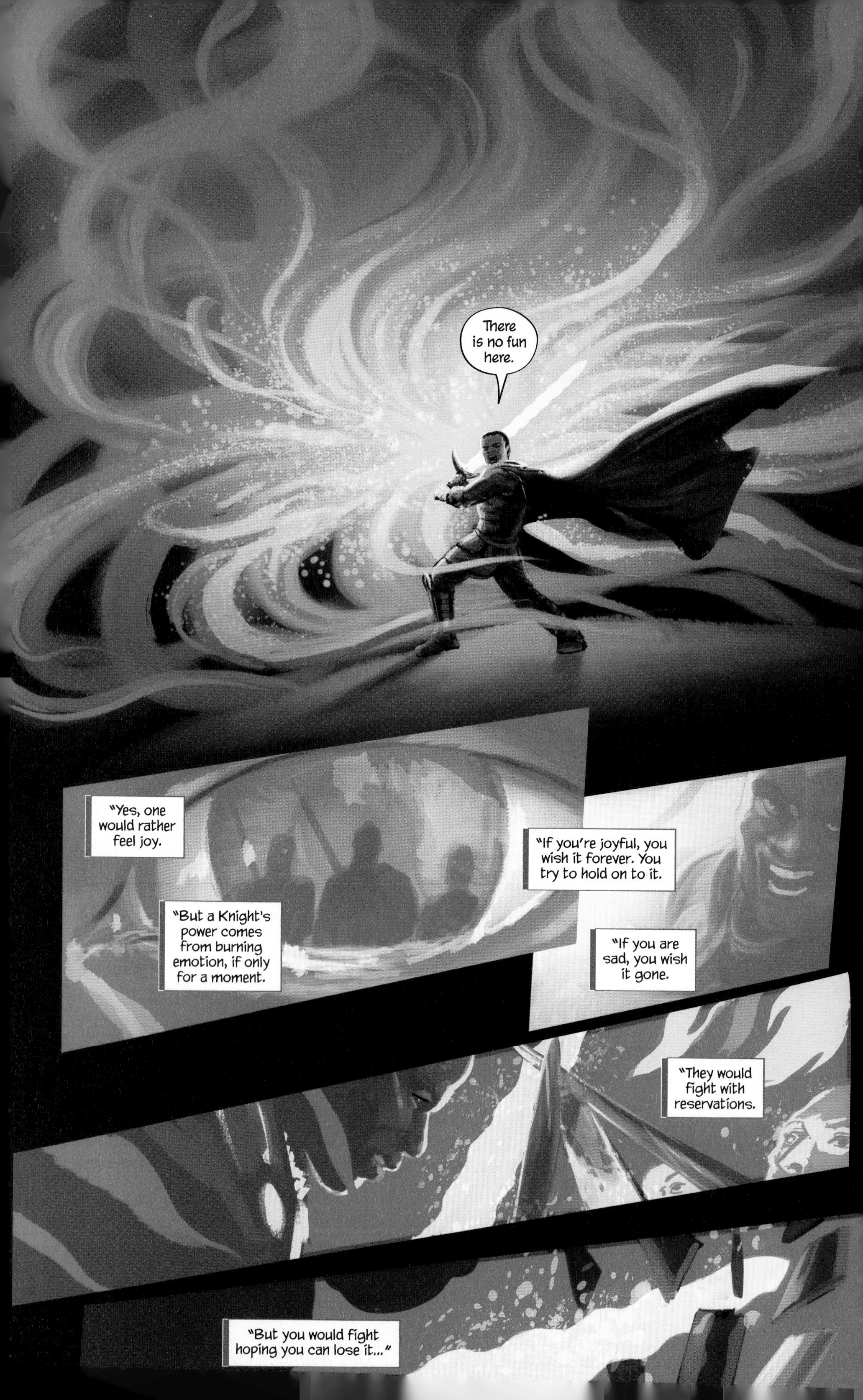
There is no fun here.
"Yes, one would rather feel joy.
"But a Knight's power comes from burning emotion, if only for a moment.
"If you're joyful, you wish it forever. You try to hold on to it.
"If you are sad, you wish it gone.
"They would fight with reservations.
"But you would fight hoping you can lose it..."

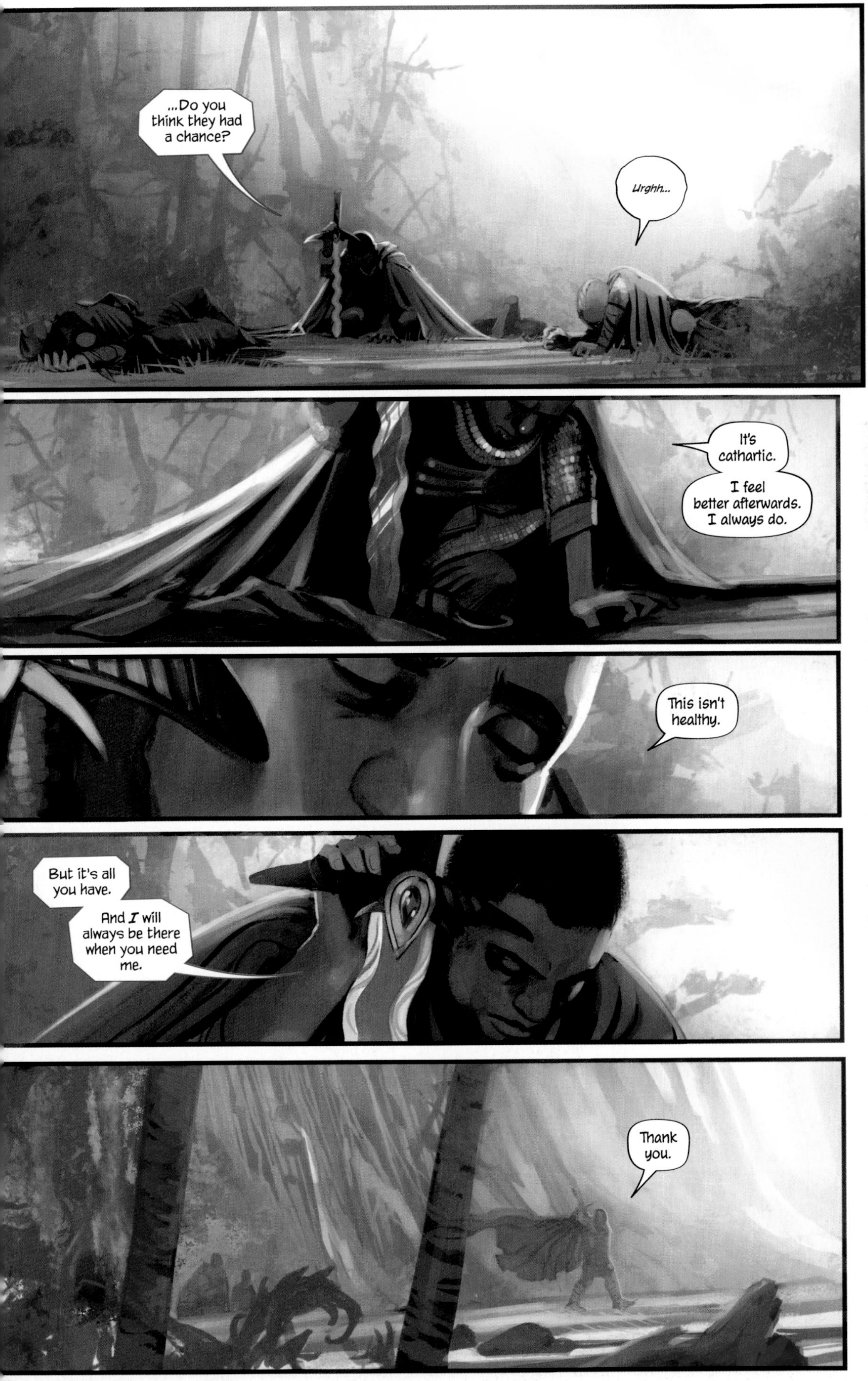
...Do you think they had a chance?
Urghh...
It's cathartic.
I feel better afterwards. I always do.
This isn't healthy.
But it's all you have.
And I will always be there when you need me.
Thank you.

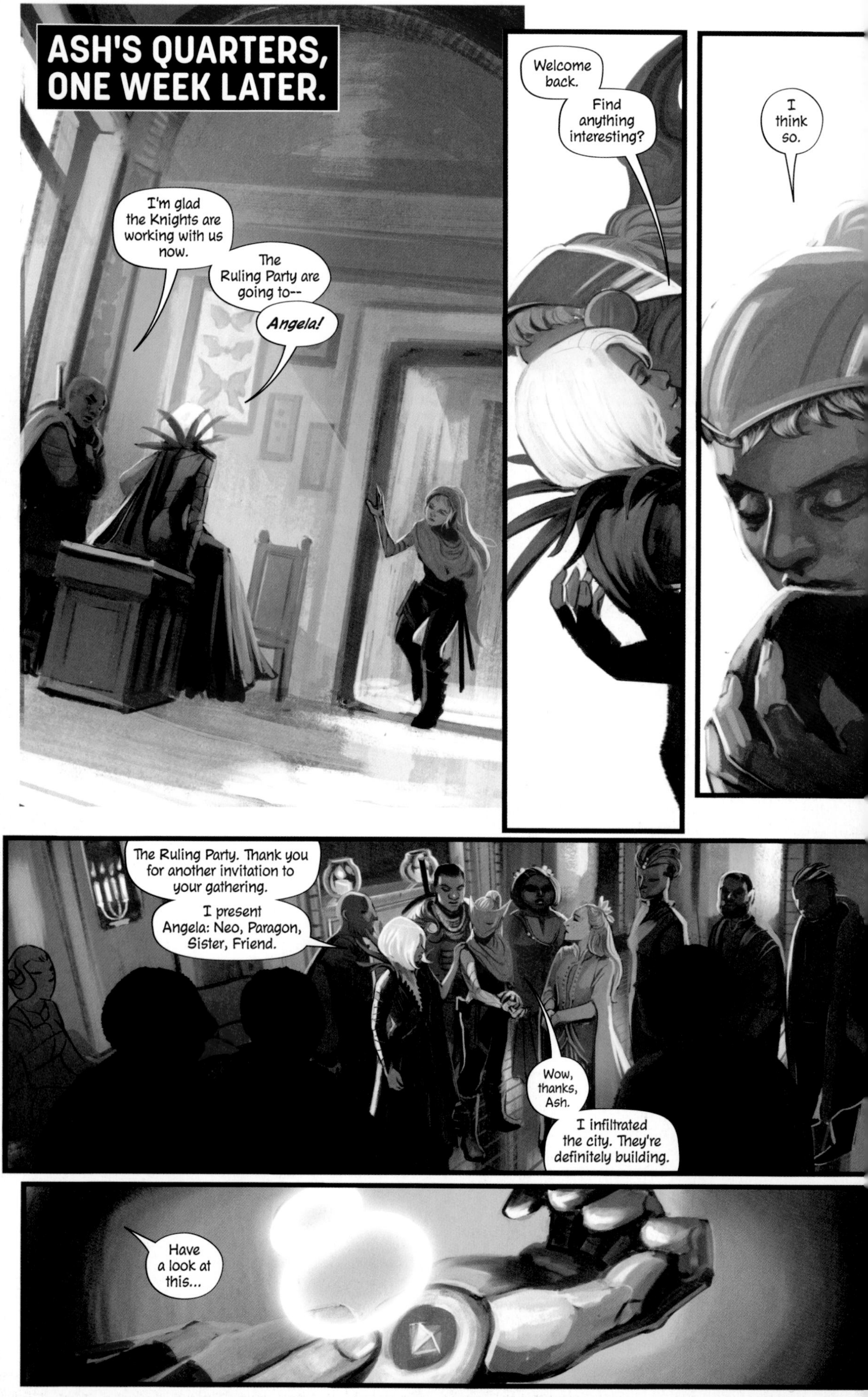
ASH'S QUARTERS, ONE WEEK LATER.
I'm glad the Knights are working with us now.
The Ruling Party are going to--
Angela!
Welcome back.
Find anything interesting?
I think so.
The Ruling Party. Thank you for another invitation to your gathering.
I present Angela: Neo, Paragon, Sister, Friend.
Wow, thanks, Ash.
I infiltrated the city. They're definitely building.
Have a look at this...

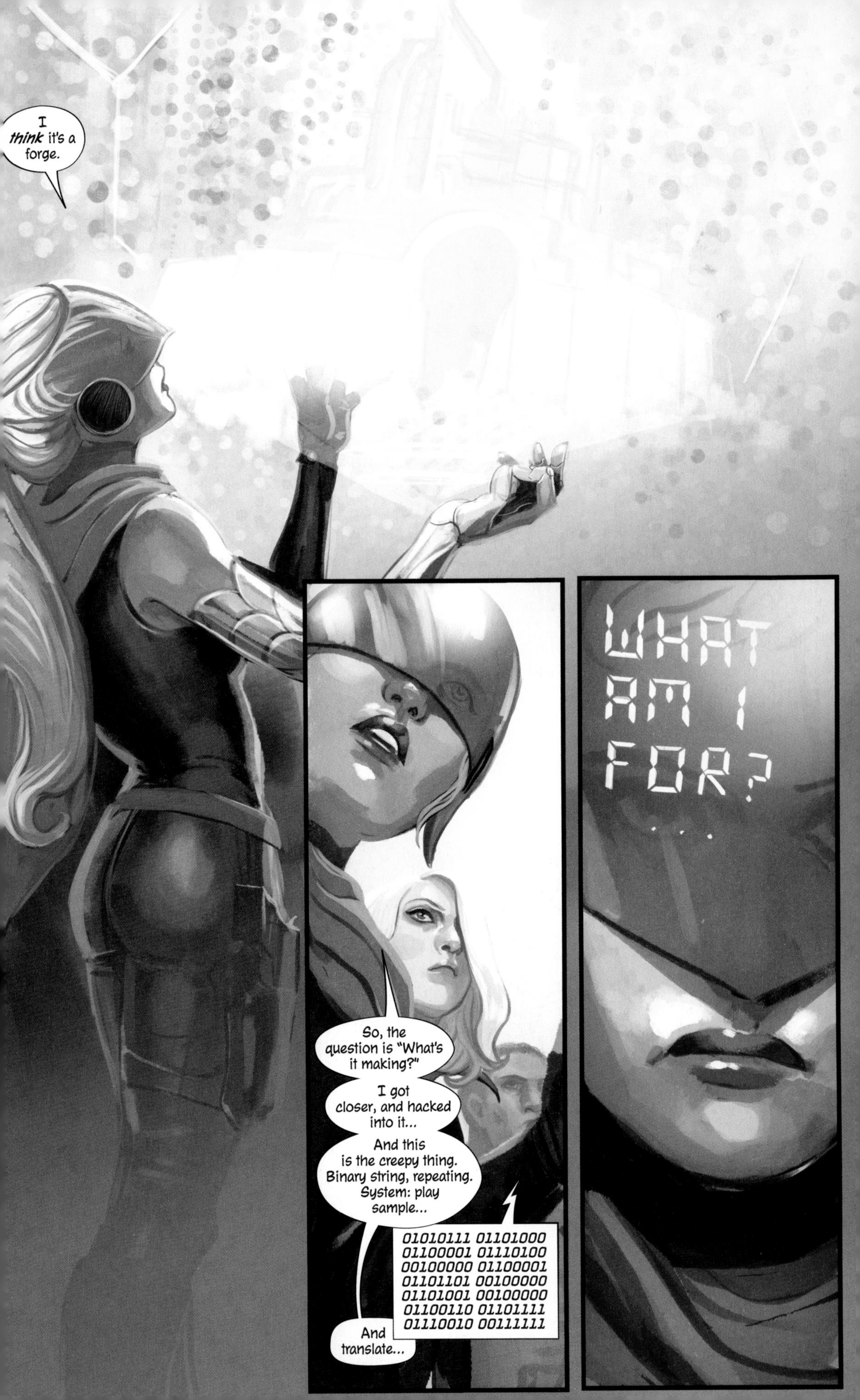
I *think* it's a forge.
So, the question is "What's it making?"
I got closer, and hacked into it...
And this is the creepy thing. Binary string, repeating. System: play sample...
01010111 01101000 01100001 01110100 00100000 01100001 01101101 00100000 01101001 00100000 01100110 01101111 01110010 00111111
And translate...
WHAT AM I FOR?

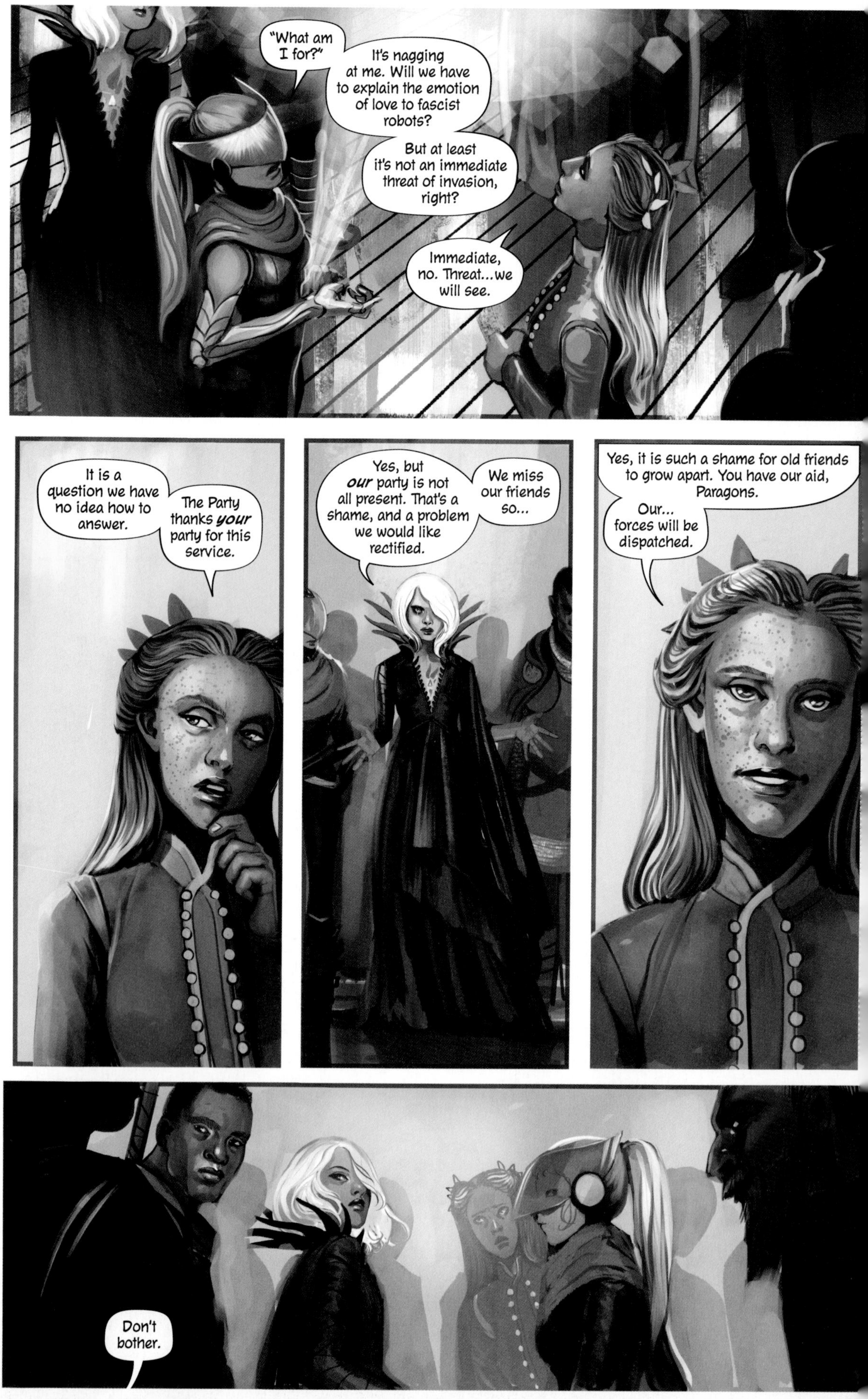
"What am I for?"
It's nagging at me. Will we have to explain the emotion of love to fascist robots?
But at least it's not an immediate threat of invasion, right?
Immediate, no. Threat...we will see.
It is a question we have no idea how to answer.
The Party thanks *your* party for this service.
Yes, but *our* party is not all present. That's a shame, and a problem we would like rectified.
We miss our friends so...
Yes, it is such a shame for old friends to grow apart. You have our aid, Paragons.
Our... forces will be dispatched.
Don't bother.

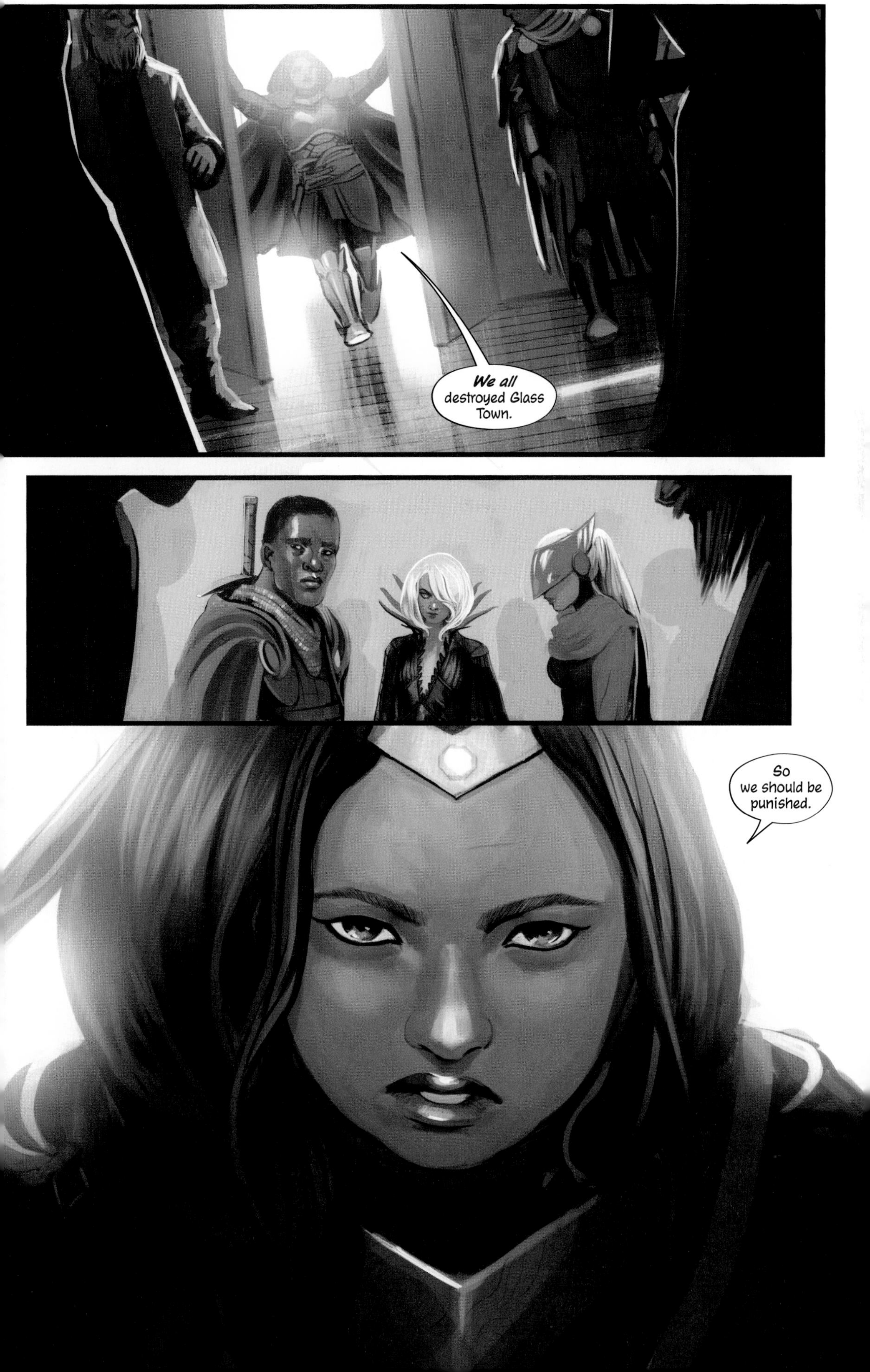
We all destroyed Glass Town.
So we should be punished.

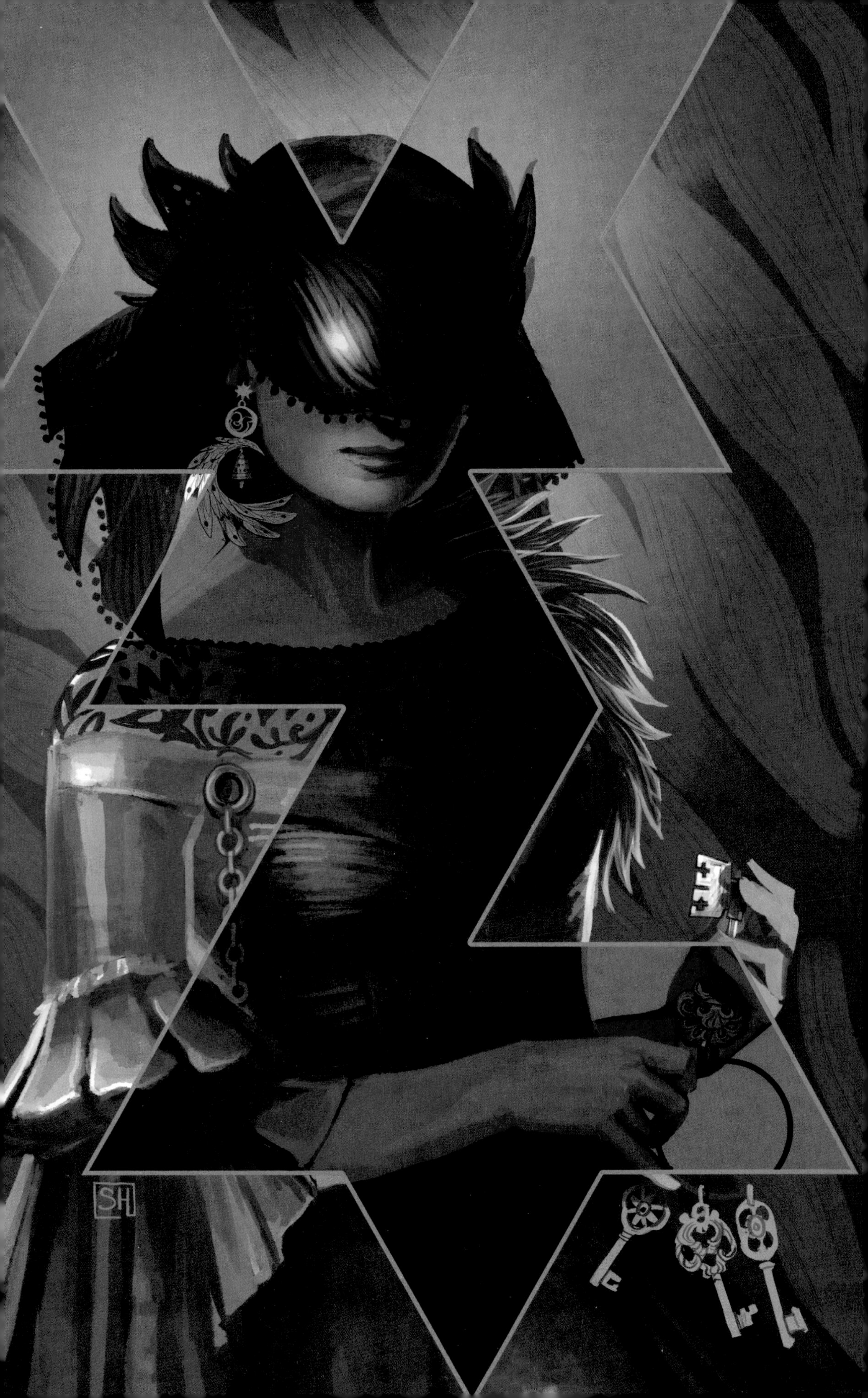

9:
SELF-INSERT

"It is very edifying and profitable to create a world out of one's brain and people it with inhabitants."
– *Charlotte Brontë*

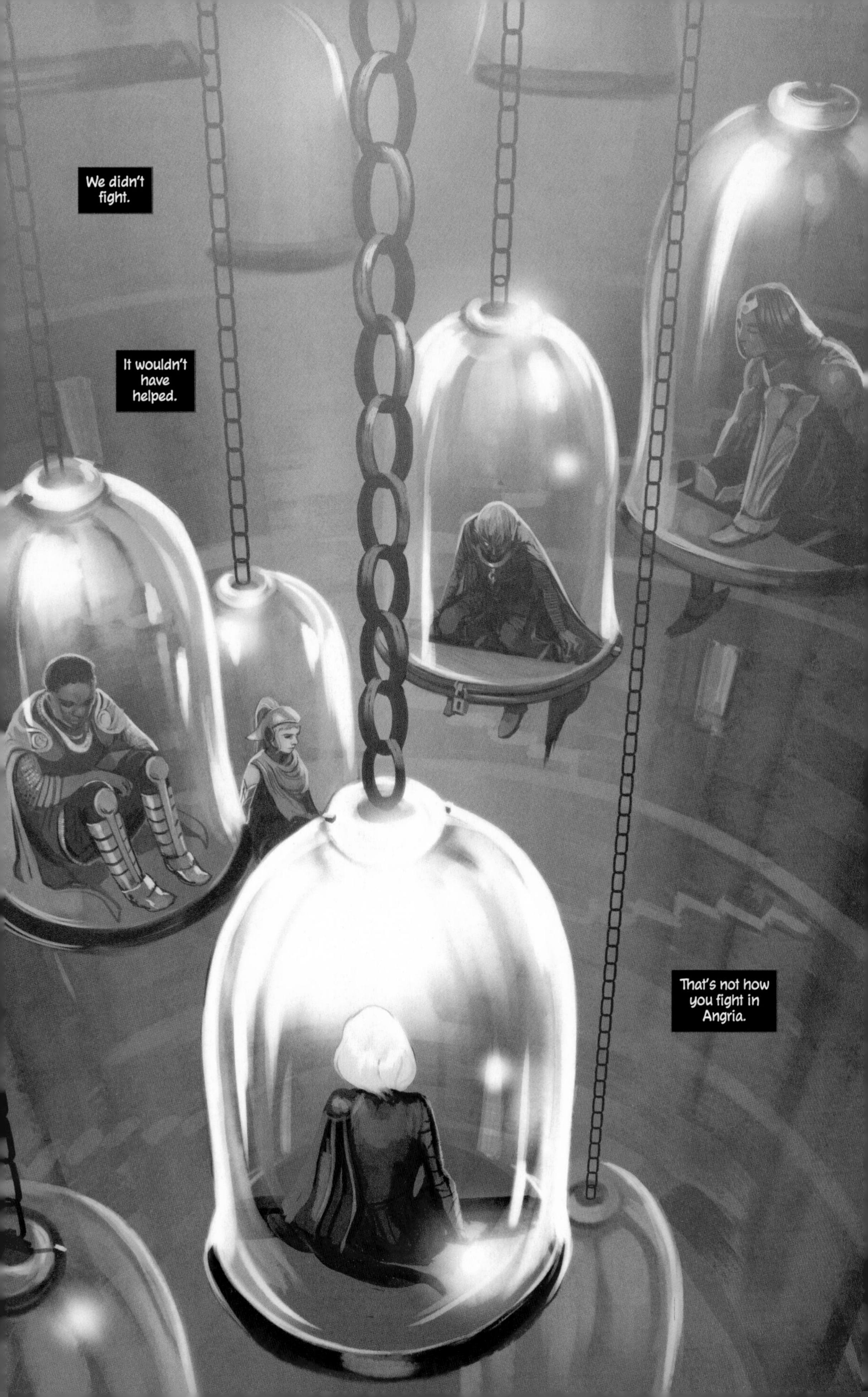
We didn't fight.
It wouldn't have helped.
That's not how you fight in Angria.

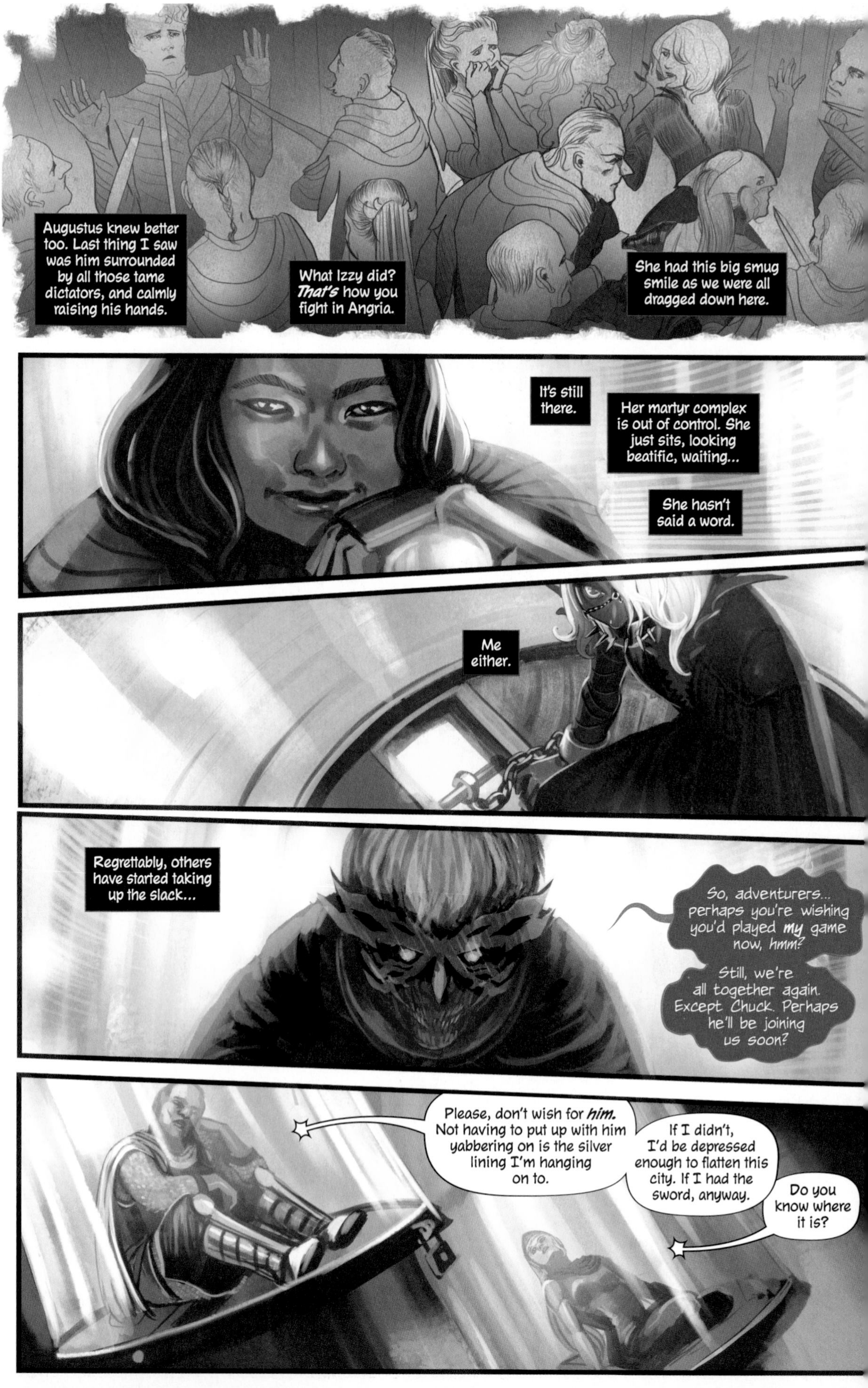
Augustus knew better too. Last thing I saw was him surrounded by all those tame dictators, and calmly raising his hands.
What Izzy did? *That's* how you fight in Angria.
She had this big smug smile as we were all dragged down here.
It's still there.
Her martyr complex is out of control. She just sits, looking beatific, waiting...
She hasn't said a word.
Me either.
Regrettably, others have started taking up the slack...
So, adventurers... perhaps you're wishing you'd played *my* game now, hmm?
Still, we're all together again. Except Chuck. Perhaps he'll be joining us soon?
Please, don't wish for *him.* Not having to put up with him yabbering on is the silver lining I'm hanging on to.
If I didn't, I'd be depressed enough to flatten this city. If I had the sword, anyway.
Do you know where it is?

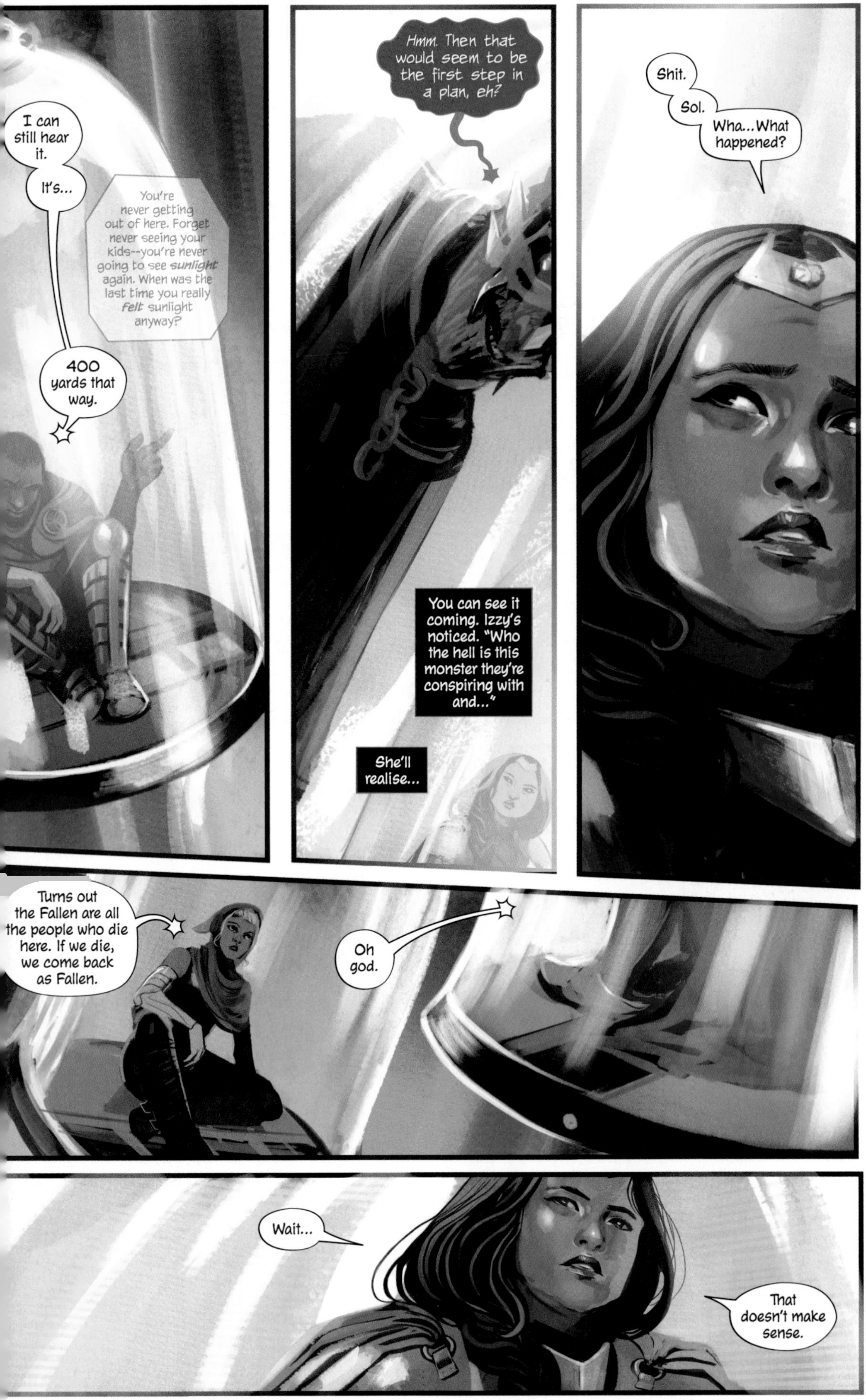
I can still hear it.
It's...
You're never getting out of here. Forget never seeing your kids--you're never going to see *sunlight* again. When was the last time you really *felt* sunlight anyway?
400 yards that way.
Hmm. Then that would seem to be the first step in a plan, eh?
You can see it coming. Izzy's noticed. "Who the hell is this monster they're conspiring with and..."
She'll realise...
Shit.
Sol.
Wha...What happened?
Turns out the Fallen are all the people who die here. If we die, we come back as Fallen.
Oh god.
Wait...
That doesn't make sense.

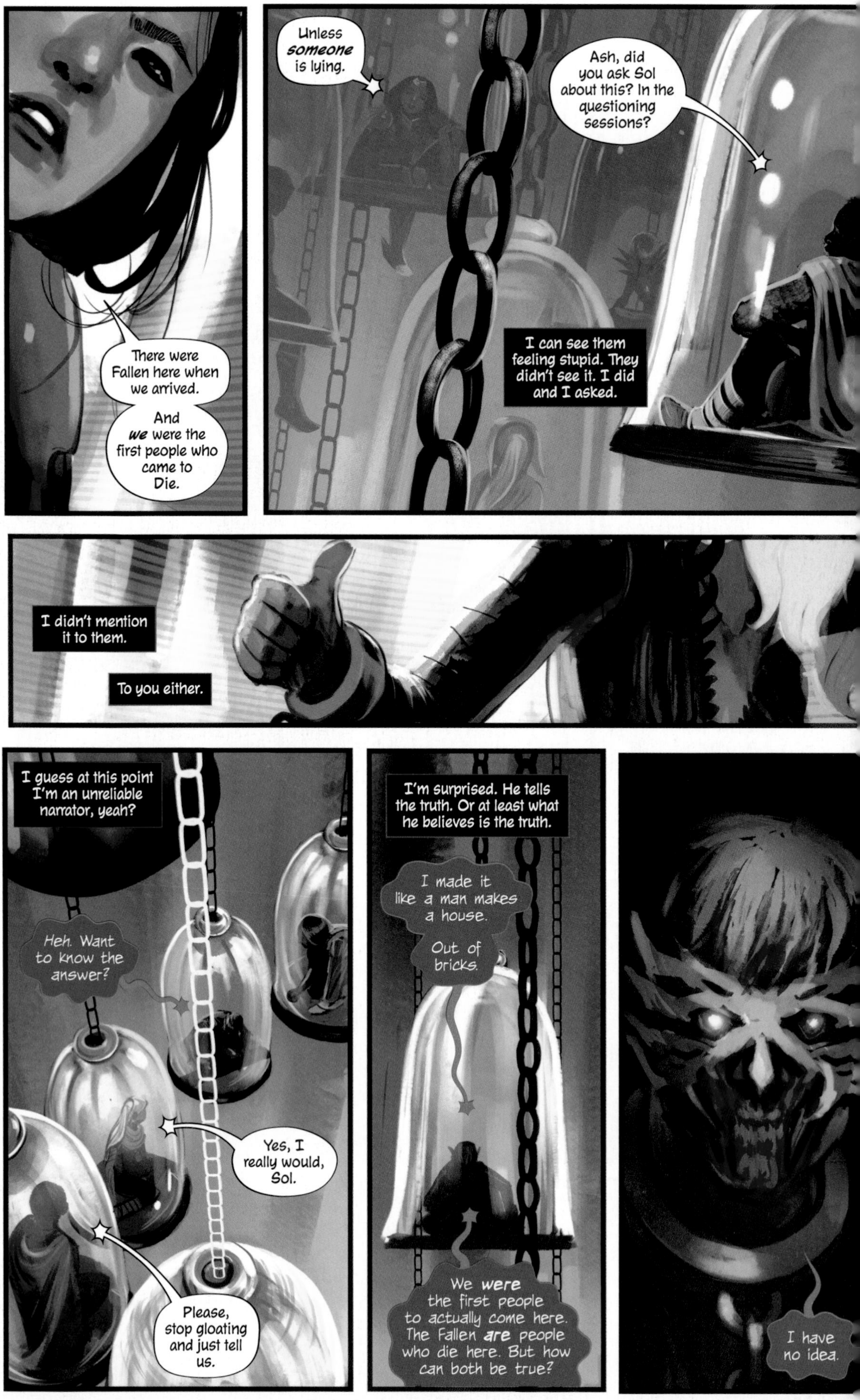
There were Fallen here when we arrived.
And *we* were the first people who came to Die.
Unless *someone* is lying.
Ash, did you ask Sol about this? In the questioning sessions?
I can see them feeling stupid. They didn't see it. I did and I asked.
I didn't mention it to them.
To you either.
I guess at this point I'm an unreliable narrator, yeah?
Heh. Want to know the answer?
Yes, I really would, Sol.
Please, stop gloating and just tell us.
I'm surprised. He tells the truth. Or at least what he believes is the truth.
I made it like a man makes a house.
Out of bricks.
We *were* the first people to actually come here. The Fallen *are* people who die here. But how can both be true?
I have no idea.

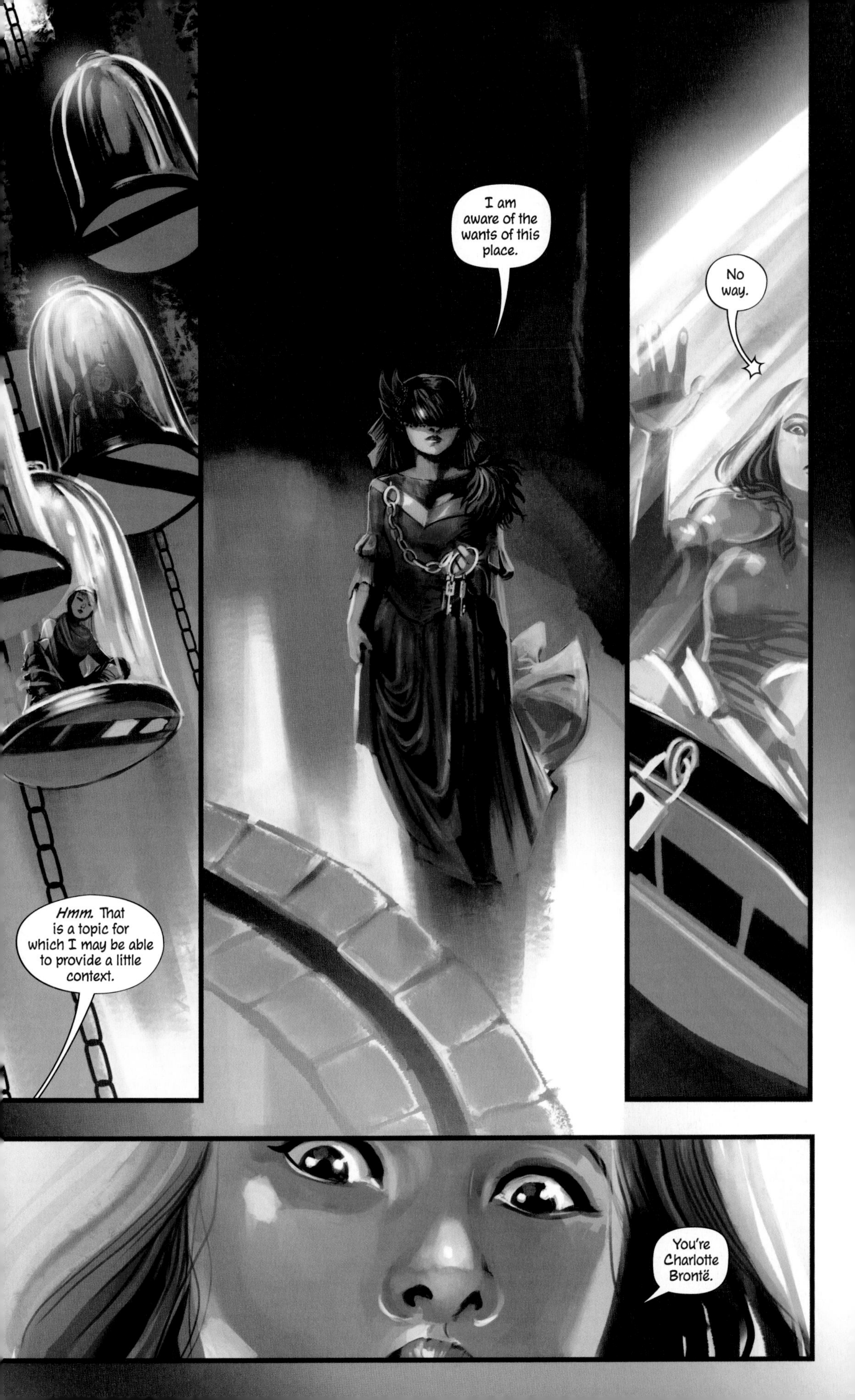
I am aware of the wants of this place.
No way.
Hmm. That is a topic for which I may be able to provide a little context.
You're Charlotte Brontë.

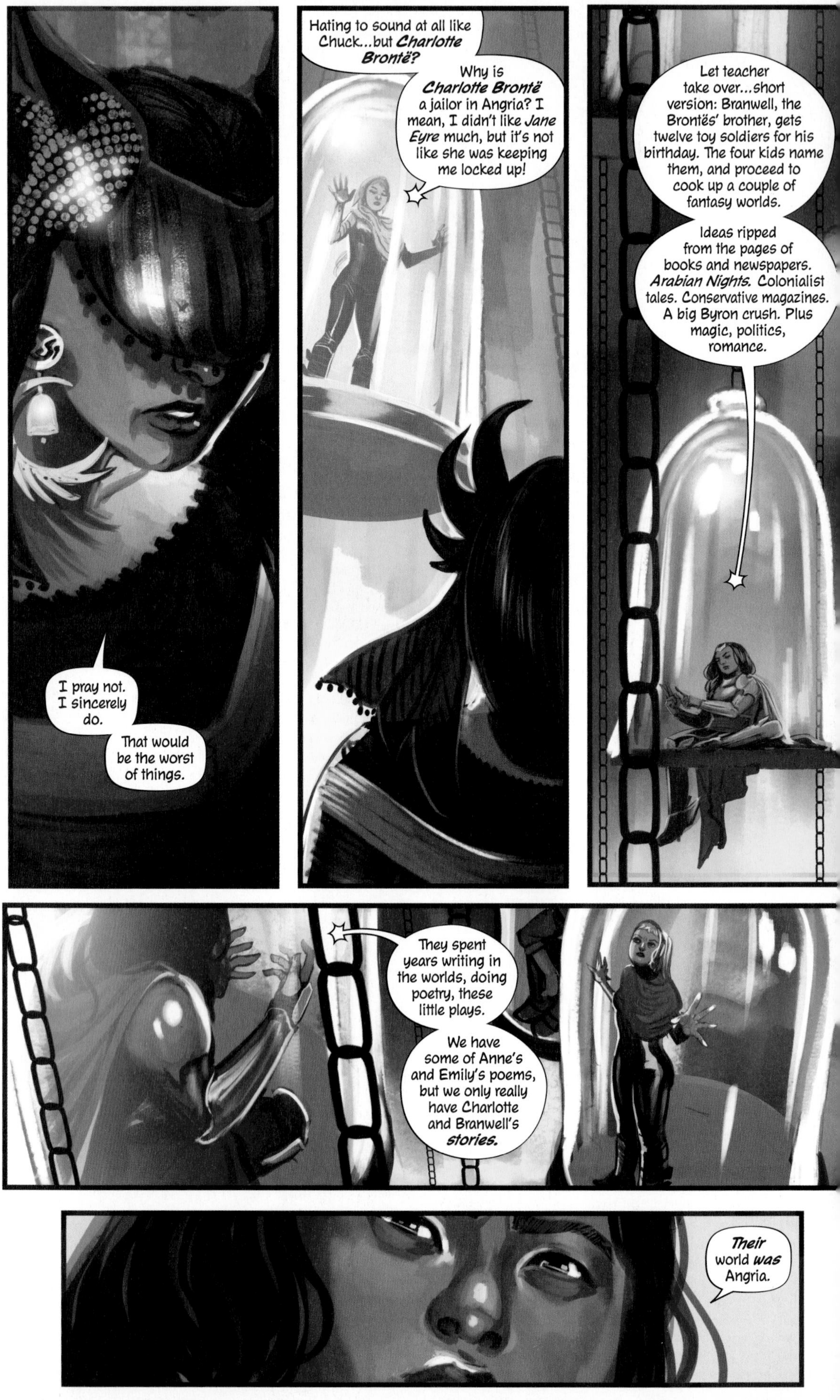

I pray not. I sincerely do.
That would be the worst of things.
Hating to sound at all like Chuck...but *Charlotte Brontë?*
Why is *Charlotte Brontë* a jailor in Angria? I mean, I didn't like *Jane Eyre* much, but it's not like she was keeping me locked up!
Let teacher take over...short version: Branwell, the Brontës' brother, gets twelve toy soldiers for his birthday. The four kids name them, and proceed to cook up a couple of fantasy worlds.
Ideas ripped from the pages of books and newspapers. *Arabian Nights.* Colonialist tales. Conservative magazines. A big Byron crush. Plus magic, politics, romance.
They spent years writing in the worlds, doing poetry, these little plays.
We have some of Anne's and Emily's poems, but we only really have Charlotte and Branwell's *stories.*
Their world *was* Angria.

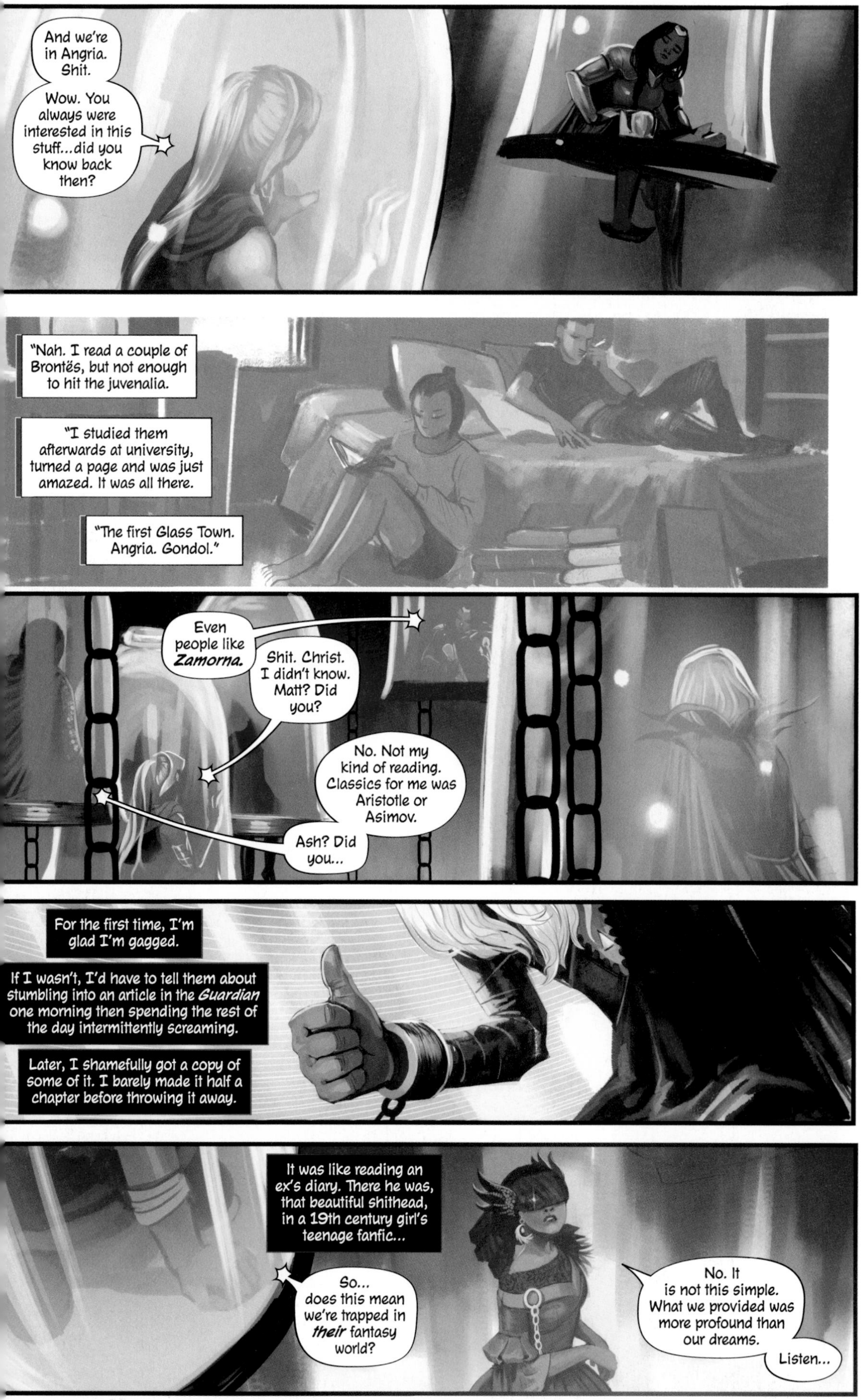

And we're in Angria. Shit.
Wow. You always were interested in this stuff...did you know back then?
"Nah. I read a couple of Brontës, but not enough to hit the juvenalia.
"I studied them afterwards at university, turned a page and was just amazed. It was all there.
"The first Glass Town. Angria. Gondol."
Even people like **Zamorna.**
Shit. Christ. I didn't know. Matt? Did you?
No. Not my kind of reading. Classics for me was Aristotle or Asimov.
Ash? Did you...
For the first time, I'm glad I'm gagged.
If I wasn't, I'd have to tell them about stumbling into an article in the *Guardian* one morning then spending the rest of the day intermittently screaming.
Later, I shamefully got a copy of some of it. I barely made it half a chapter before throwing it away.
It was like reading an ex's diary. There he was, that beautiful shithead, in a 19th century girl's teenage fanfic...
So... does this mean we're trapped in ***their*** fantasy world?
No. It is not this simple. What we provided was more profound than our dreams.
Listen...

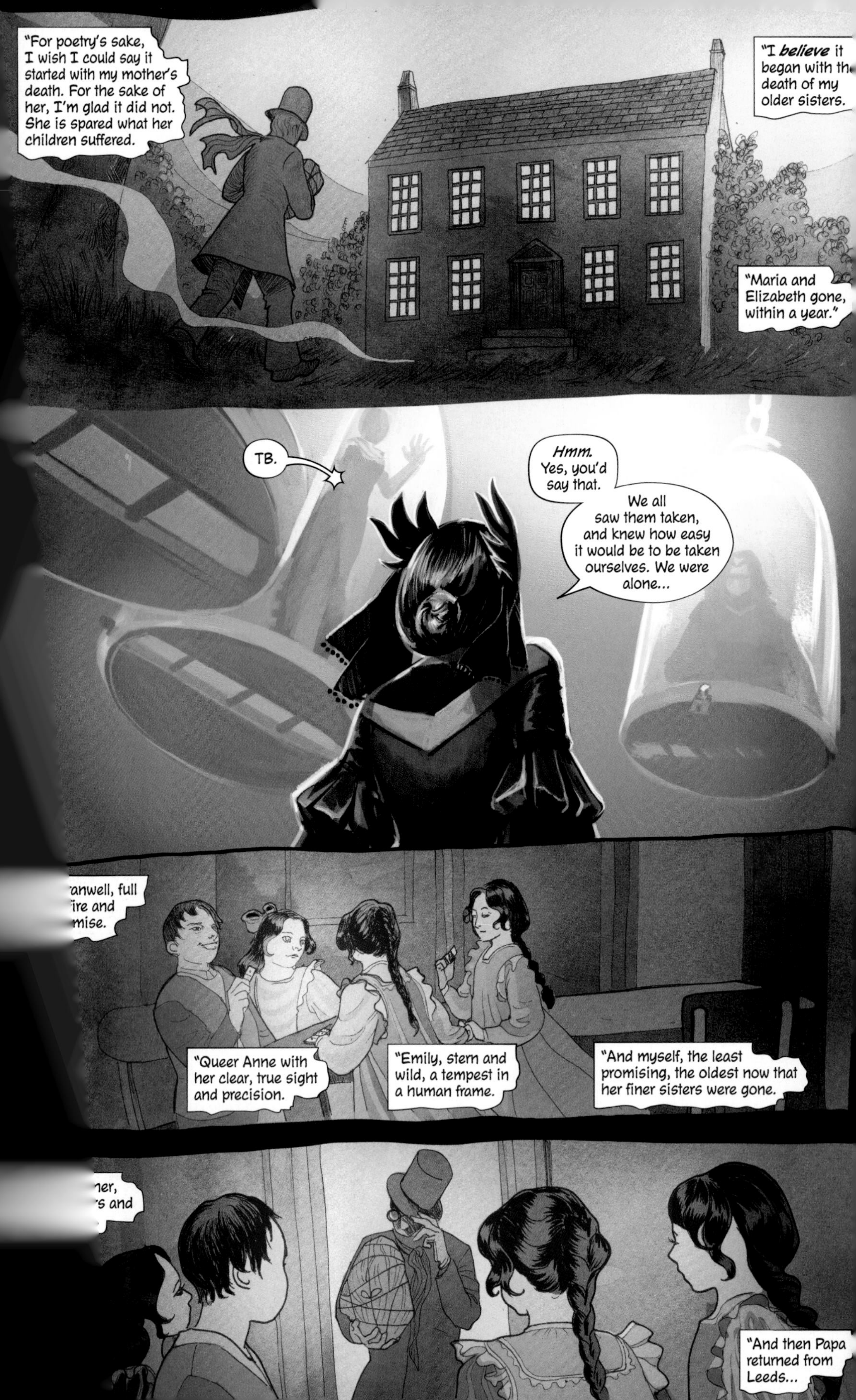
"For poetry's sake, I wish I could say it started with my mother's death. For the sake of her, I'm glad it did not. She is spared what her children suffered.
"I *believe* it began with th death of my older sisters.
"Maria and Elizabeth gone, within a year."
TB.
Hmm. Yes, you'd say that.
We all saw them taken, and knew how easy it would be to be taken ourselves. We were alone...
anwell, full ire and mise.
"Queer Anne with her clear, true sight and precision.
"Emily, stern and wild, a tempest in a human frame.
"And myself, the least promising, the oldest now that her finer sisters were gone.
ner, s and
"And then Papa returned from Leeds...

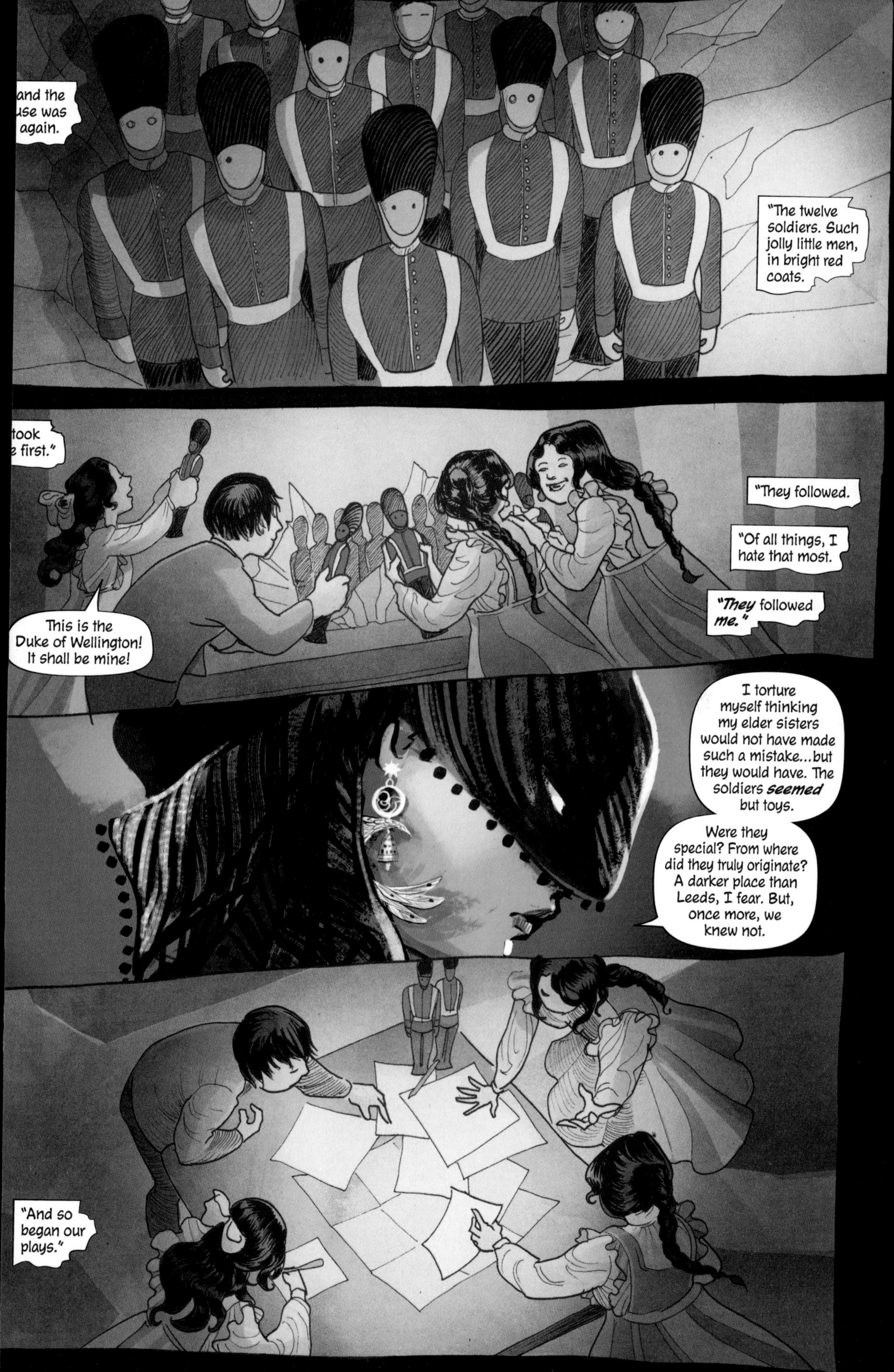
and the
use was
again.
"The twelve soldiers. Such jolly little men, in bright red coats.
took
first."
This is the Duke of Wellington! It shall be mine!
"They followed.
"Of all things, I hate that most.
"They** followed **me."
I torture myself thinking my elder sisters would not have made such a mistake...but they would have. The soldiers ***seemed*** but toys.
Were they special? From where did they truly originate? A darker place than Leeds, I fear. But, once more, we knew not.
"And so began our plays."

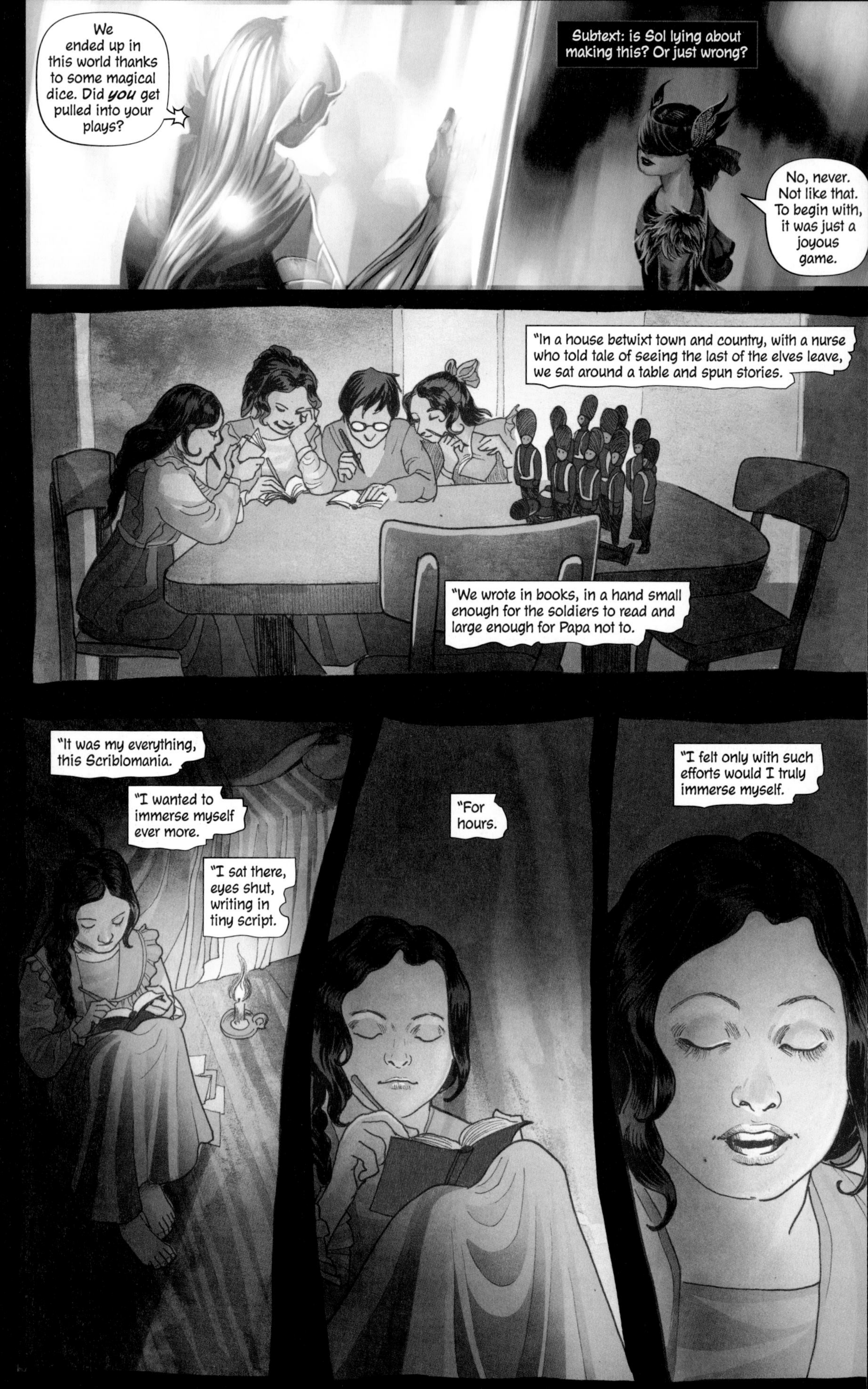
We ended up in this world thanks to some magical dice. Did *you* get pulled into your plays?
Subtext: is Sol lying about making this? Or just wrong?
No, never. Not like that. To begin with, it was just a joyous game.
"In a house betwixt town and country, with a nurse who told tale of seeing the last of the elves leave, we sat around a table and spun stories.
"We wrote in books, in a hand small enough for the soldiers to read and large enough for Papa not to.
"It was my everything, this Scriblomania.
"I wanted to immerse myself ever more.
"I sat there, eyes shut, writing in tiny script.
"For hours.
"I felt only with such efforts would I truly immerse myself.

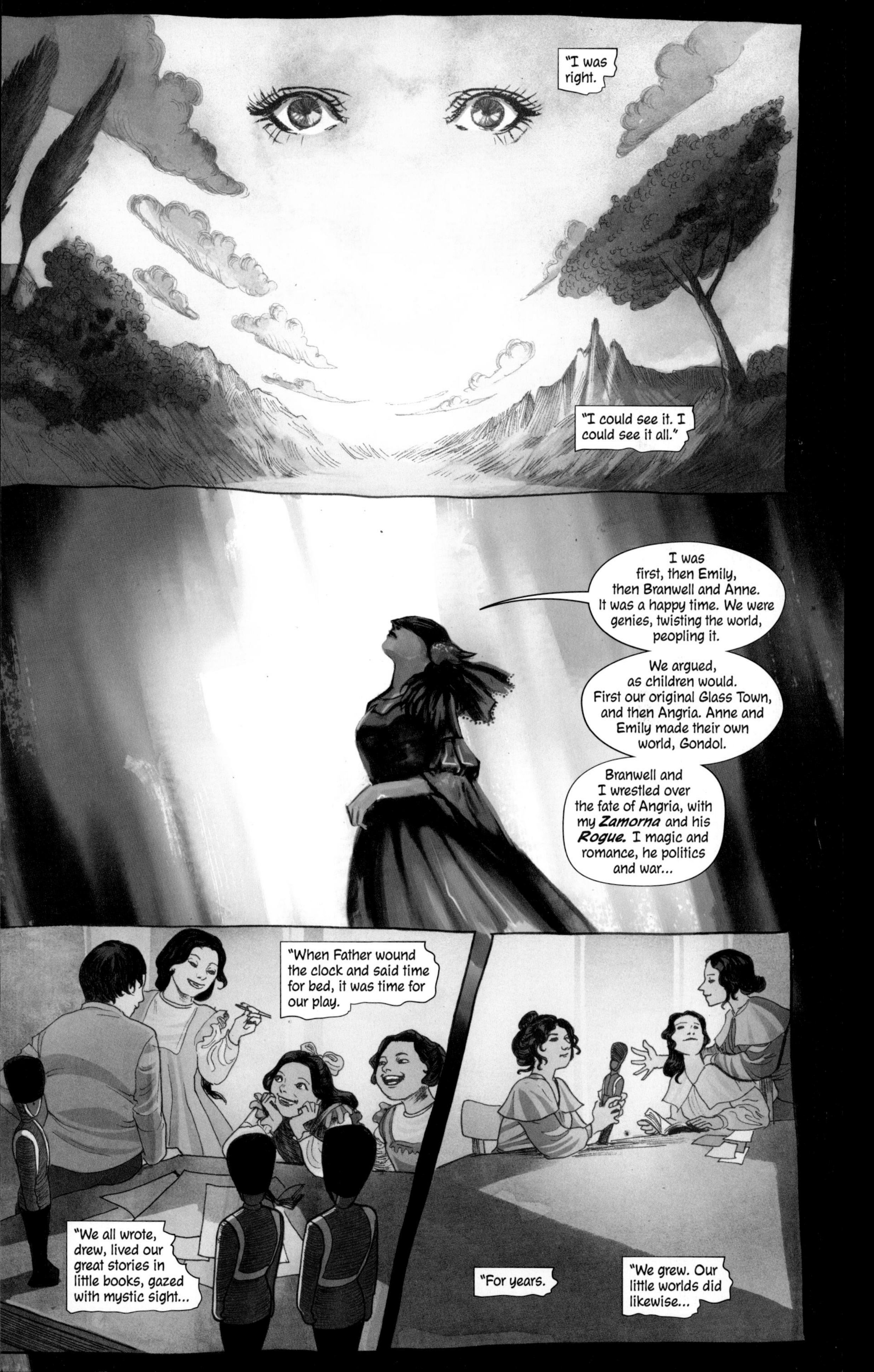
"I was right.
"I could see it. I could see it all."
I was first, then Emily, then Branwell and Anne. It was a happy time. We were genies, twisting the world, peopling it.
We argued, as children would. First our original Glass Town, and then Angria. Anne and Emily made their own world, Gondol.
Branwell and I wrestled over the fate of Angria, with my ***Zamorna*** and his ***Rogue.*** I magic and romance, he politics and war...
"When Father wound the clock and said time for bed, it was time for our play.
"We all wrote, drew, lived our great stories in little books, gazed with mystic sight...
"For years.
"We grew. Our little worlds did likewise...

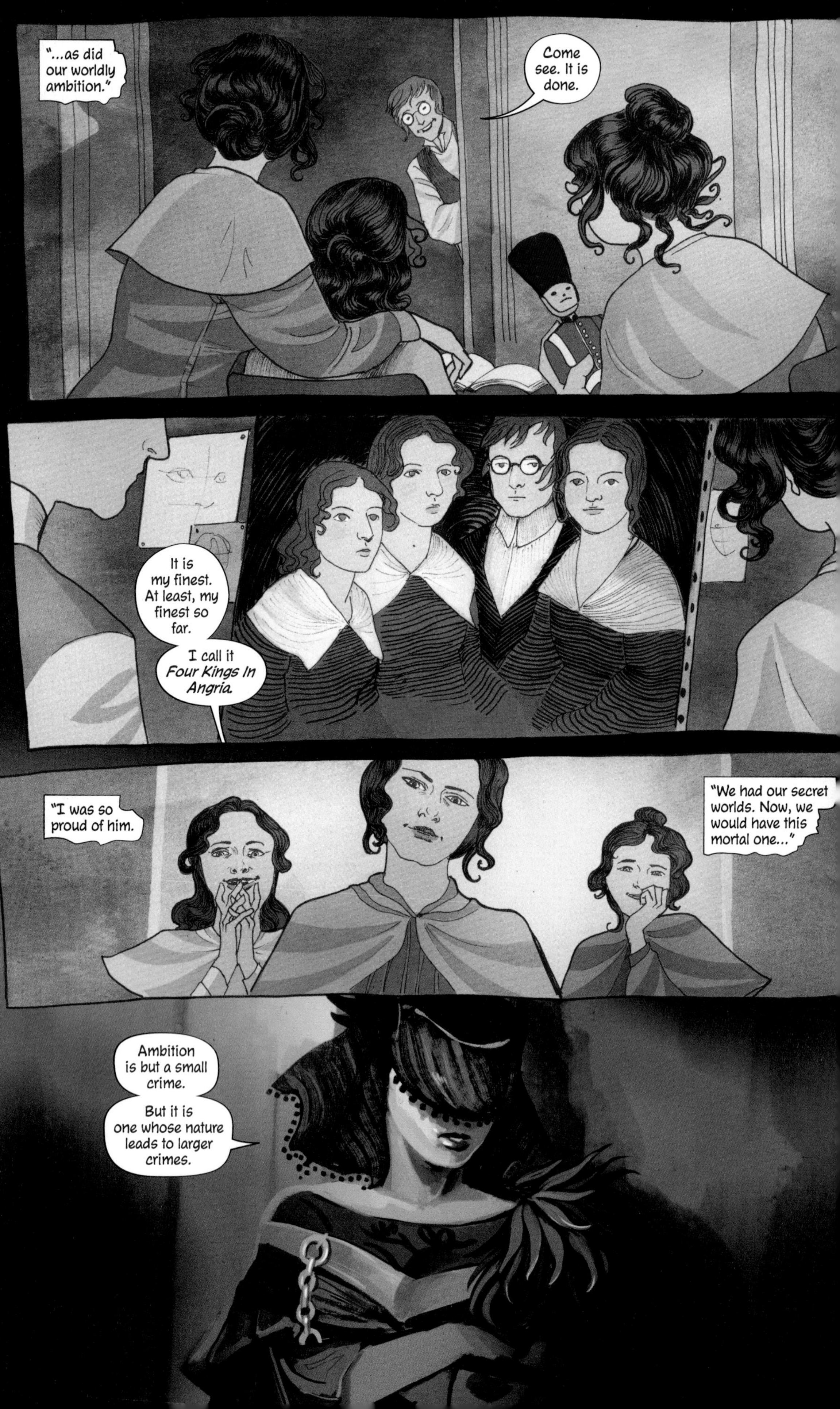
"...as did our worldly ambition."
Come see. It is done.
It is my finest. At least, my finest so far.
I call it *Four Kings In Angria.*
"I was so proud of him.
"We had our secret worlds. Now, we would have this mortal one..."
Ambition is but a small crime.
But it is one whose nature leads to larger crimes.

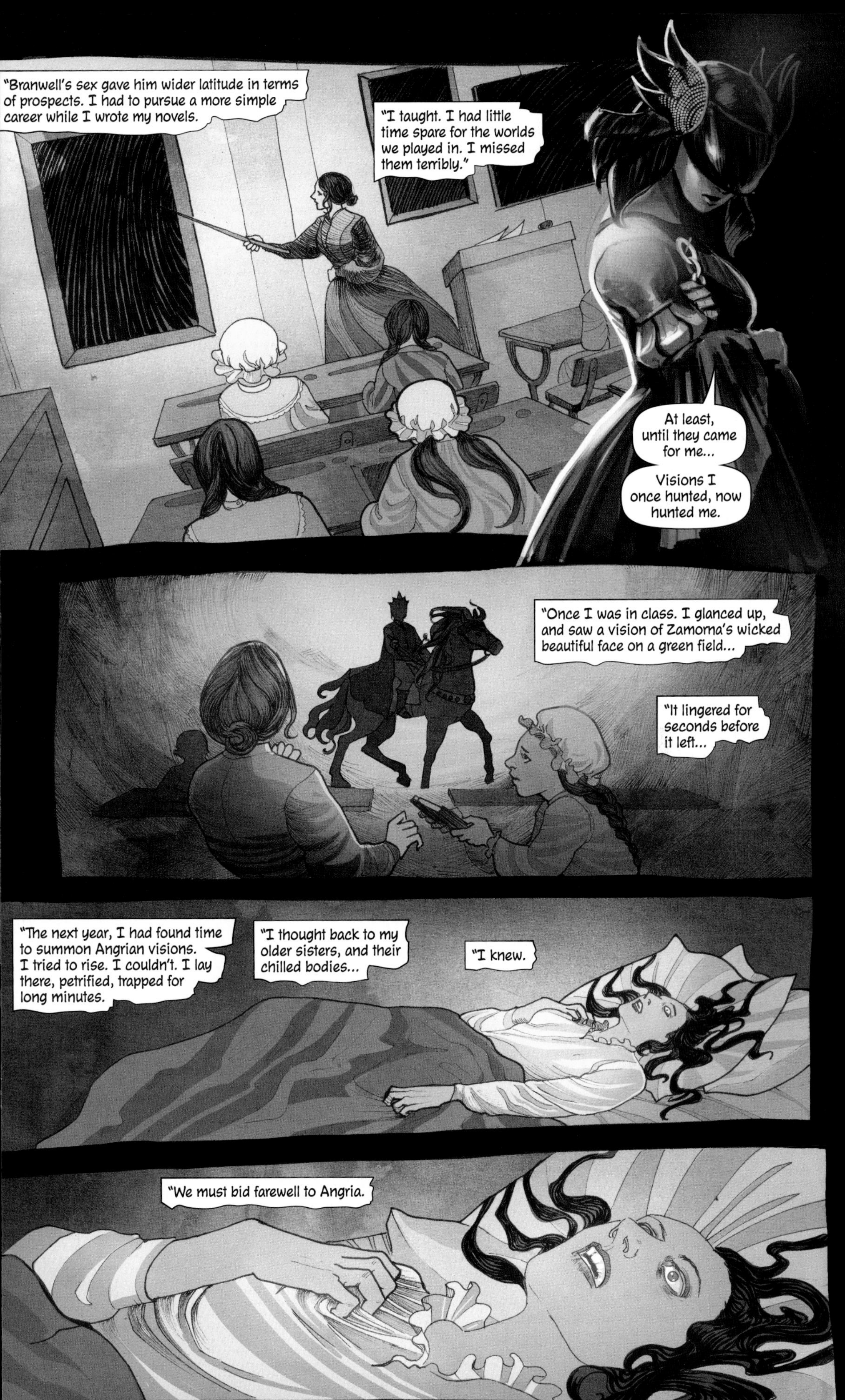
"Branwell's sex gave him wider latitude in terms of prospects. I had to pursue a more simple career while I wrote my novels.
"I taught. I had little time spare for the worlds we played in. I missed them terribly."
At least, until they came for me...
Visions I once hunted, now hunted me.
"Once I was in class. I glanced up, and saw a vision of Zamorna's wicked beautiful face on a green field...
"It lingered for seconds before it left...
"The next year, I had found time to summon Angrian visions. I tried to rise. I couldn't. I lay there, petrified, trapped for long minutes.
"I thought back to my older sisters, and their chilled bodies...
"I knew.
"We must bid farewell to Angria.

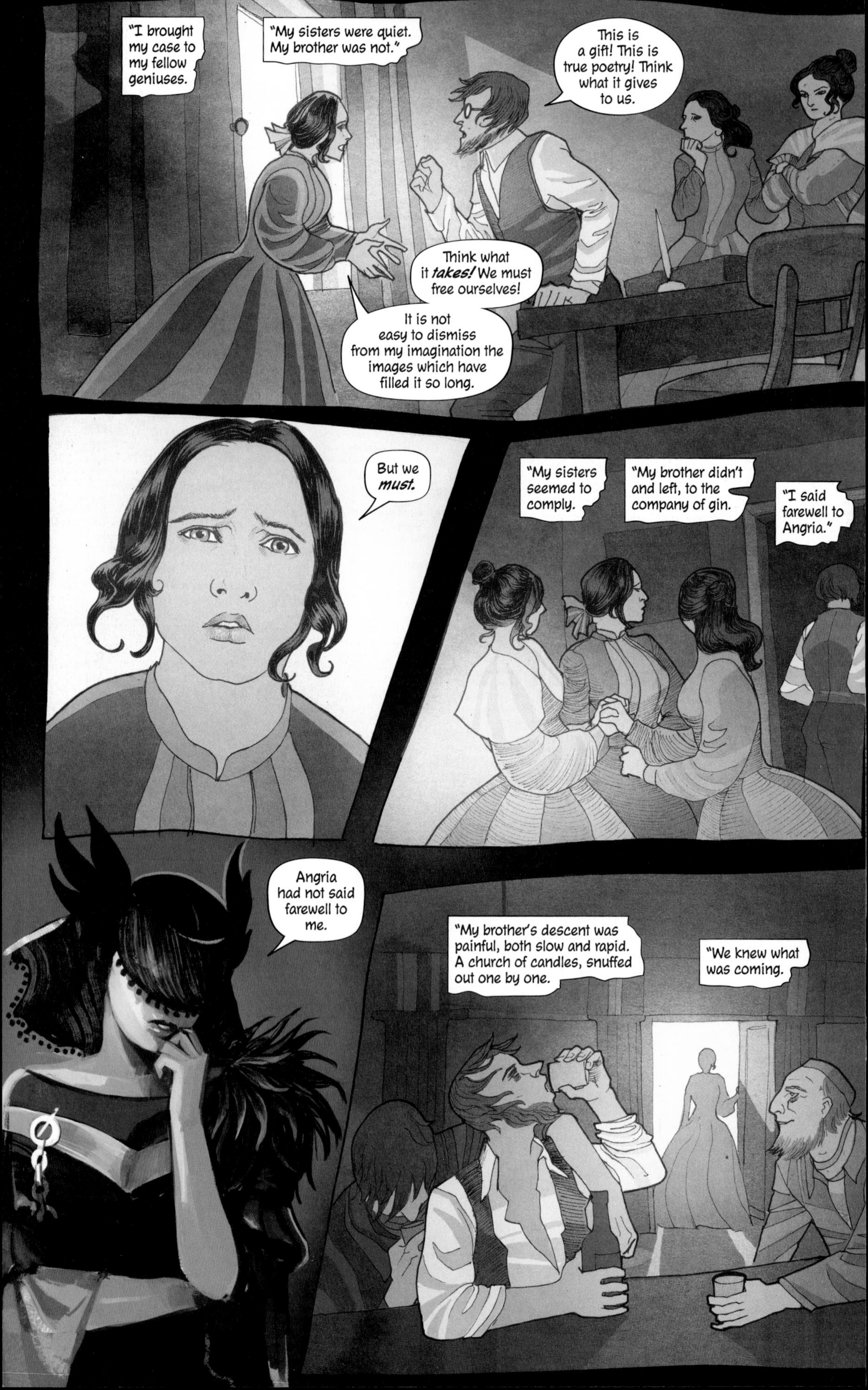
"I brought my case to my fellow geniuses.
"My sisters were quiet. My brother was not."
This is a gift! This is true poetry! Think what it gives to us.
Think what it *takes!* We must free ourselves!
It is not easy to dismiss from my imagination the images which have filled it so long.
But we *must.*
"My sisters seemed to comply.
"My brother didn't and left, to the company of gin.
"I said farewell to Angria."
Angria had not said farewell to me.
"My brother's descent was painful, both slow and rapid. A church of candles, snuffed out one by one.
"We knew what was coming.

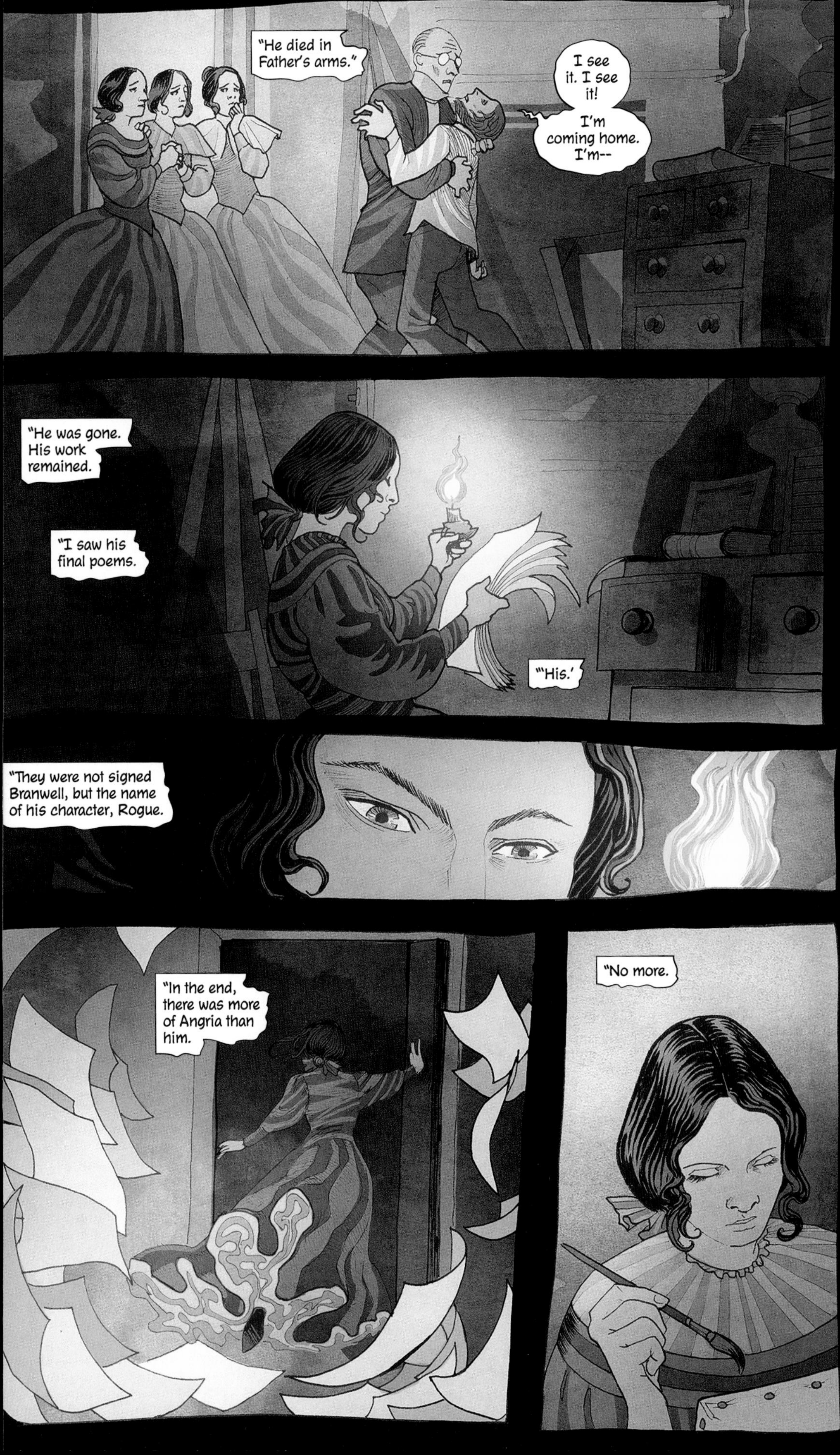
"He died in Father's arms."
I see it. I see it!
I'm coming home. I'm--
"He was gone. His work remained.
"I saw his final poems.
"'His.'
"They were not signed Branwell, but the name of his character, Rogue.
"In the end, there was more of Angria than him.
"No more.

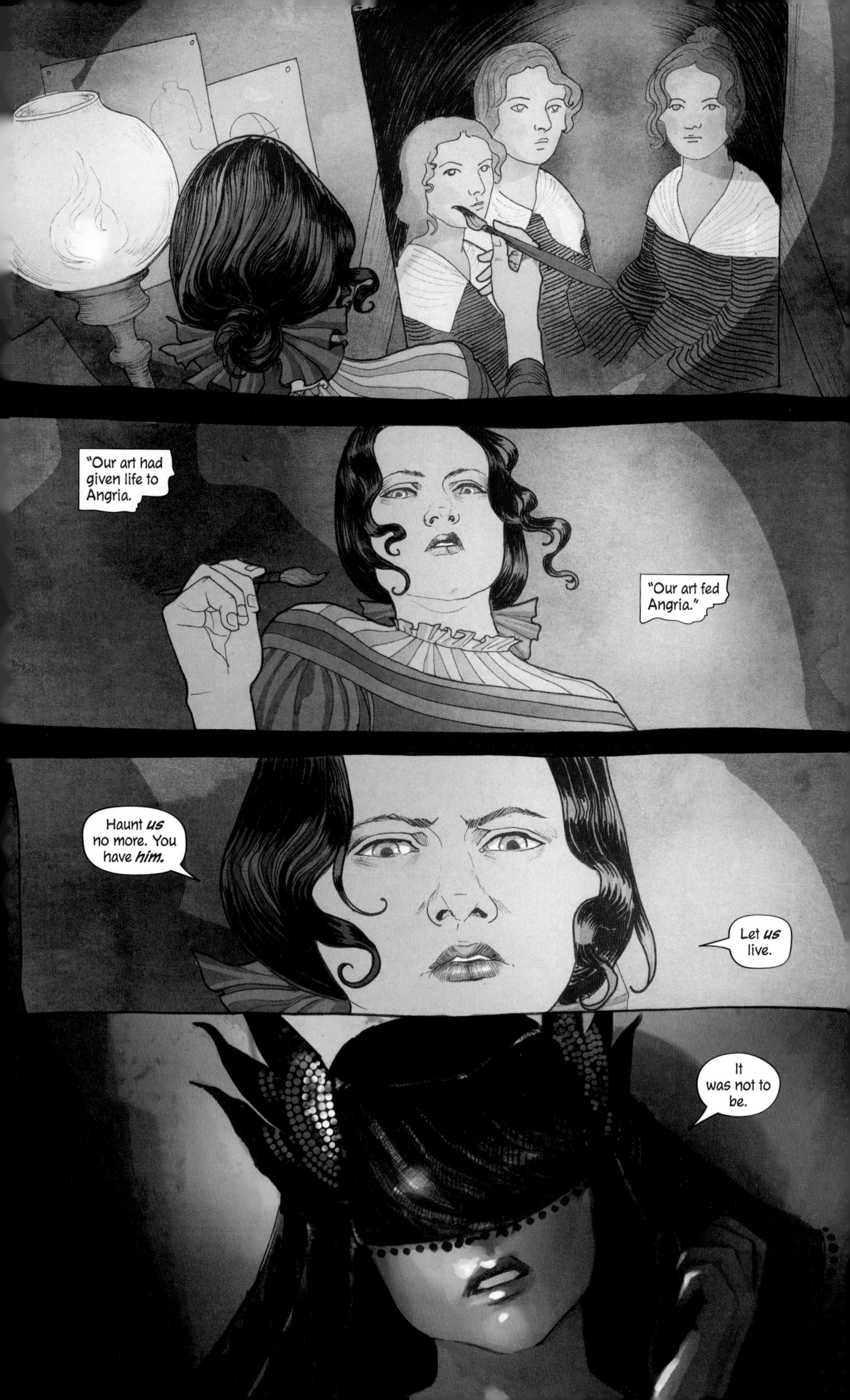

"Our art had given life to Angria.
"Our art fed Angria."
Haunt us no more. You have him.
Let us live.
It was not to be.

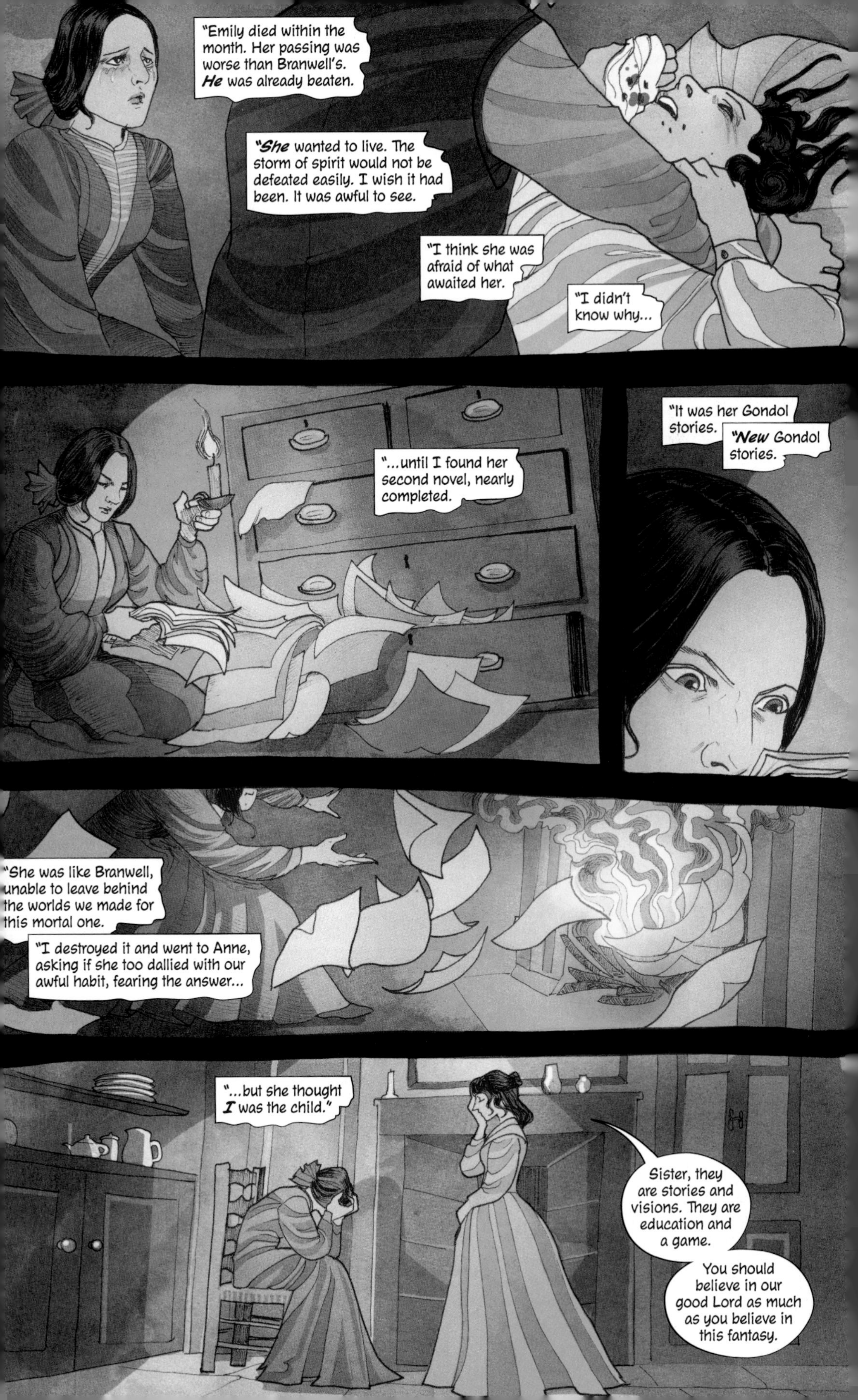
"Emily died within the month. Her passing was worse than Branwell's. *He* was already beaten.
"*She* wanted to live. The storm of spirit would not be defeated easily. I wish it had been. It was awful to see.
"I think she was afraid of what awaited her.
"I didn't know why...
"...until I found her second novel, nearly completed.
"It was her Gondol stories.
"*New* Gondol stories.
"She was like Branwell, unable to leave behind the worlds we made for this mortal one.
"I destroyed it and went to Anne, asking if she too dallied with our awful habit, fearing the answer...
"...but she thought *I* was the child."
Sister, they are stories and visions. They are education and a game.
You should believe in our good Lord as much as you believe in this fantasy.

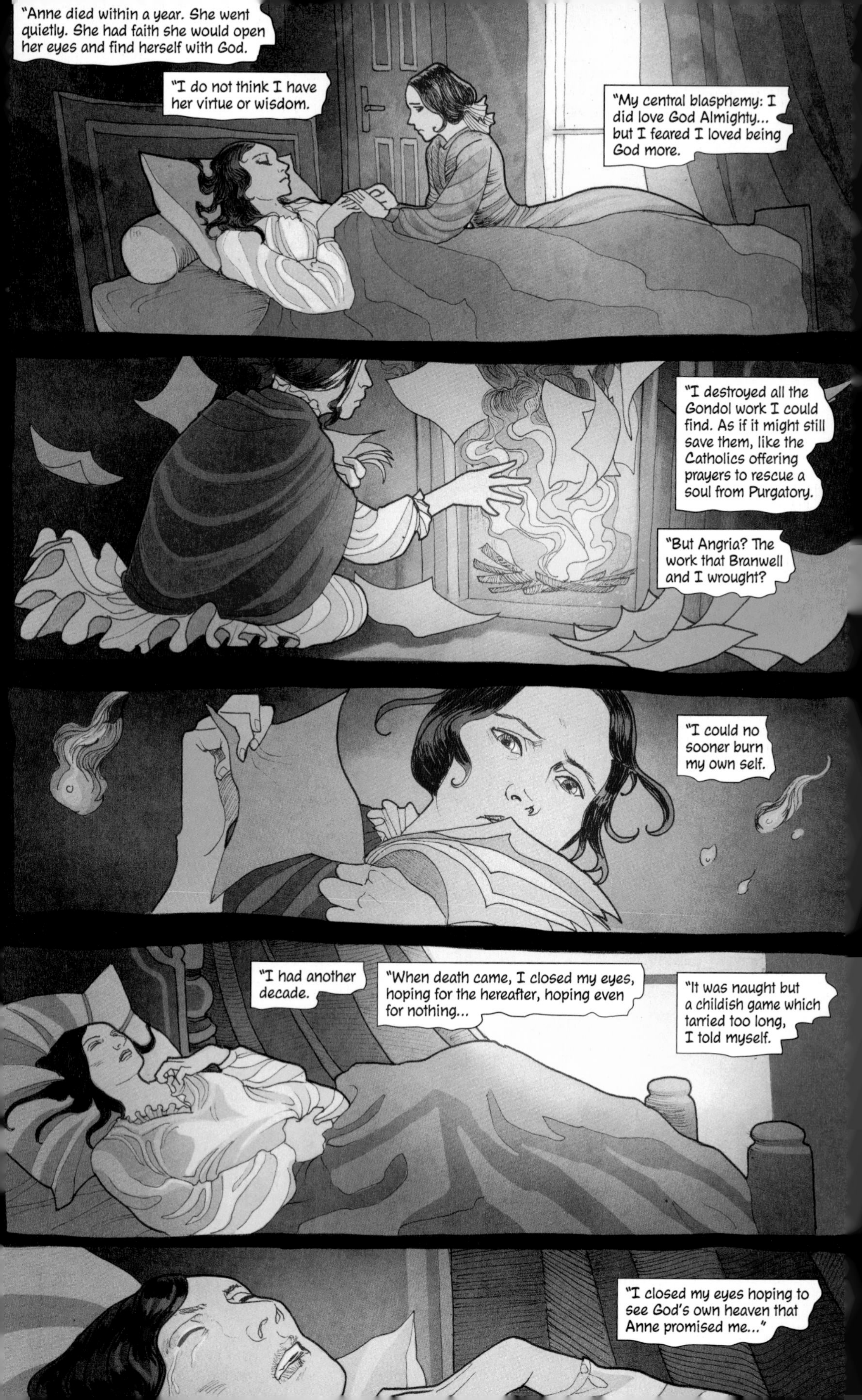
"Anne died within a year. She went quietly. She had faith she would open her eyes and find herself with God.
"I do not think I have her virtue or wisdom.
"My central blasphemy: I did love God Almighty... but I feared I loved being God more.
"I destroyed all the Gondol work I could find. As if it might still save them, like the Catholics offering prayers to rescue a soul from Purgatory.
"But Angria? The work that Branwell and I wrought?
"I could no sooner burn my own self.
"I had another decade.
"When death came, I closed my eyes, hoping for the hereafter, hoping even for nothing...
"It was naught but a childish game which tarried too long, I told myself.
"I closed my eyes hoping to see God's own heaven that Anne promised me..."

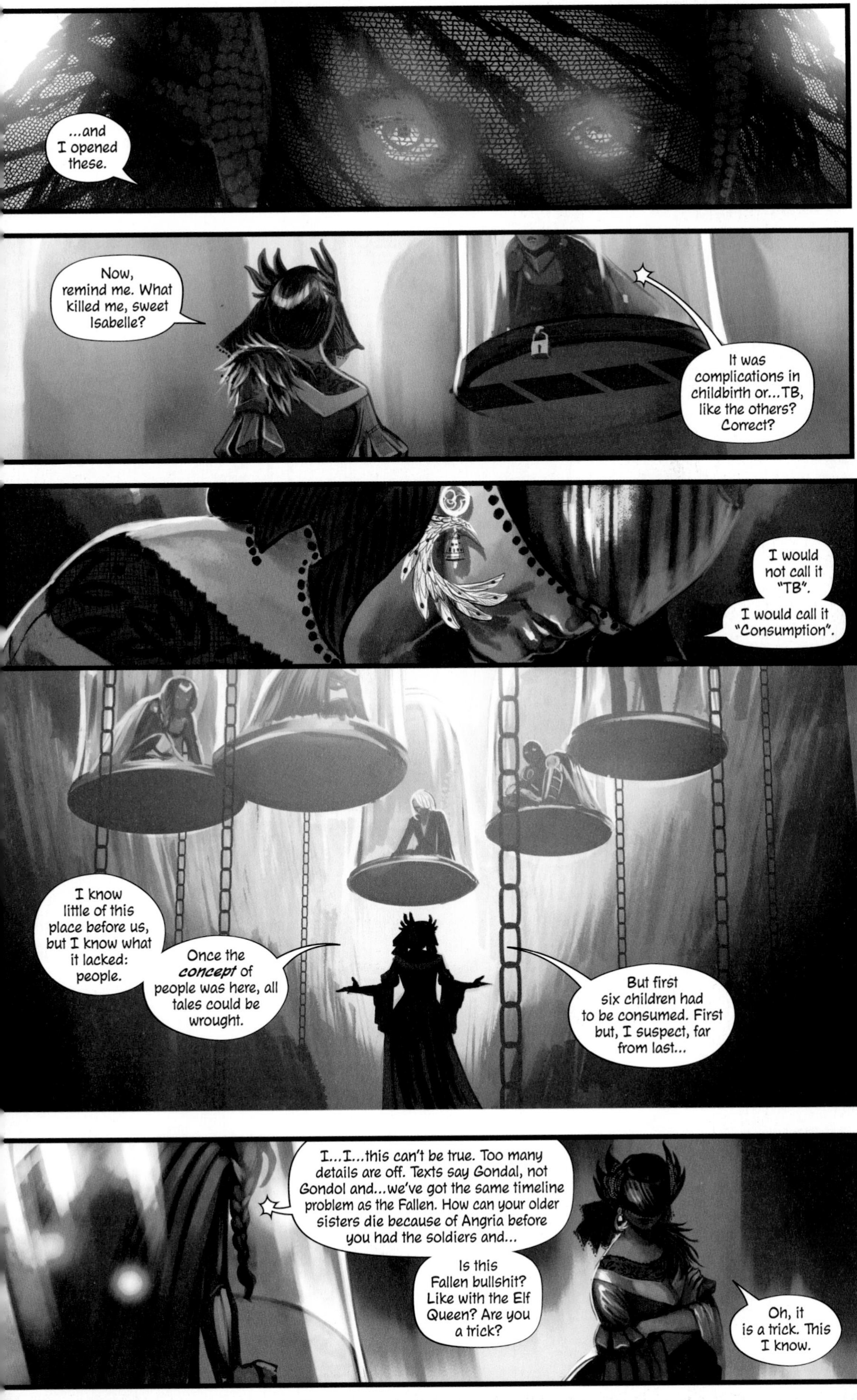
...and I opened these.
Now, remind me. What killed me, sweet Isabelle?
It was complications in childbirth or...TB, like the others? Correct?
I would not call it "TB".
I would call it "Consumption".
I know little of this place before us, but I know what it lacked: people.
Once the *concept* of people was here, all tales could be wrought.
But first six children had to be consumed. First but, I suspect, far from last...
I...I...this can't be true. Too many details are off. Texts say Gondal, not Gondol and...we've got the same timeline problem as the Fallen. How can your older sisters die because of Angria before you had the soldiers and...
Is this Fallen bullshit? Like with the Elf Queen? Are you a trick?
Oh, it is a trick. This I know.

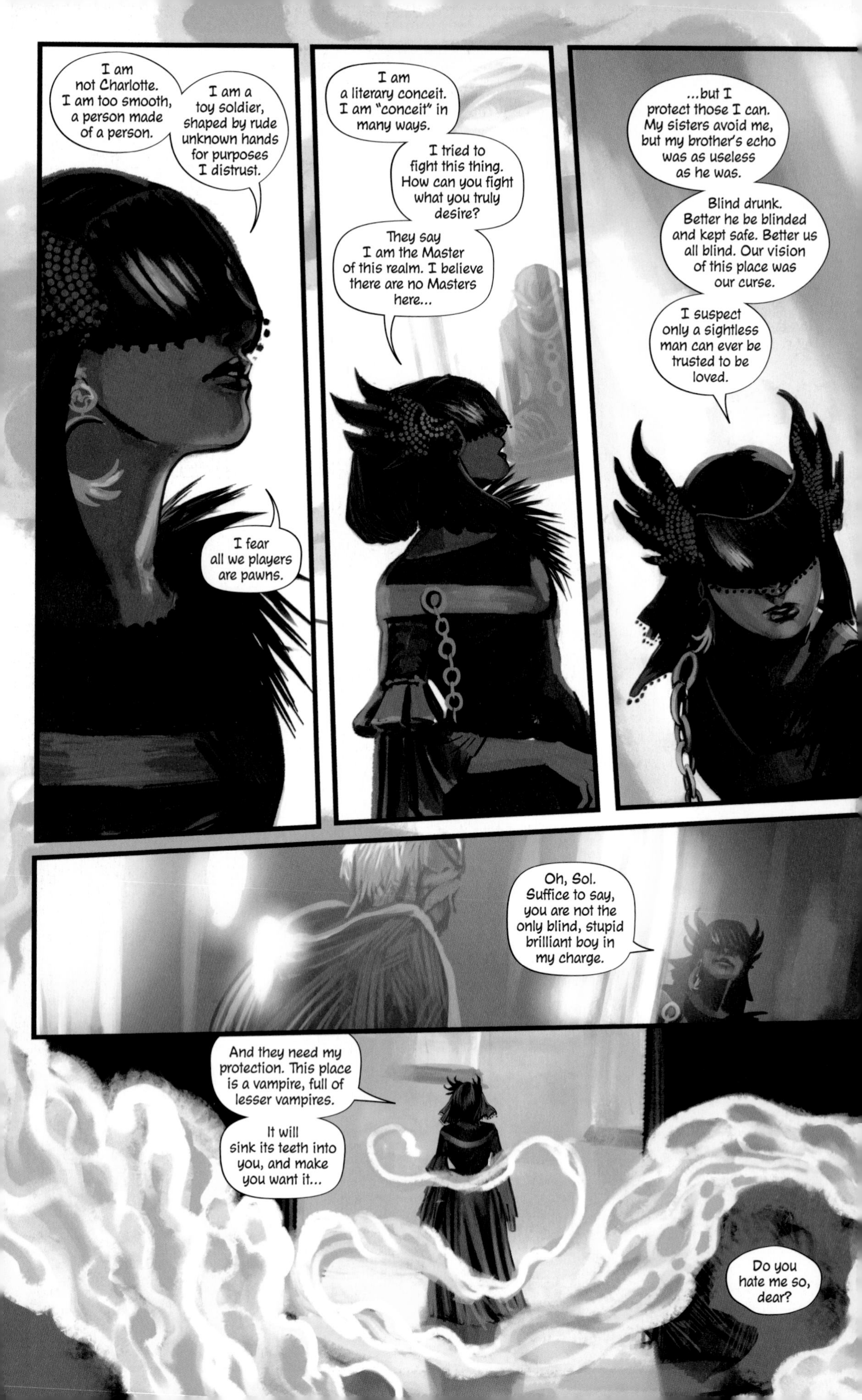
I am not Charlotte. I am too smooth, a person made of a person.
I am a toy soldier, shaped by rude unknown hands for purposes I distrust.
I fear all we players are pawns.
I am a literary conceit. I am "conceit" in many ways.
I tried to fight this thing. How can you fight what you truly desire?
They say I am the Master of this realm. I believe there are no Masters here...
...but I protect those I can. My sisters avoid me, but my brother's echo was as useless as he was.
Blind drunk. Better he be blinded and kept safe. Better us all blind. Our vision of this place was our curse.
I suspect only a sightless man can ever be trusted to be loved.
Oh, Sol. Suffice to say, you are not the only blind, stupid brilliant boy in my charge.
And they need my protection. This place is a vampire, full of lesser vampires.
It will sink its teeth into you, and make you want it...
Do you hate me so, dear?

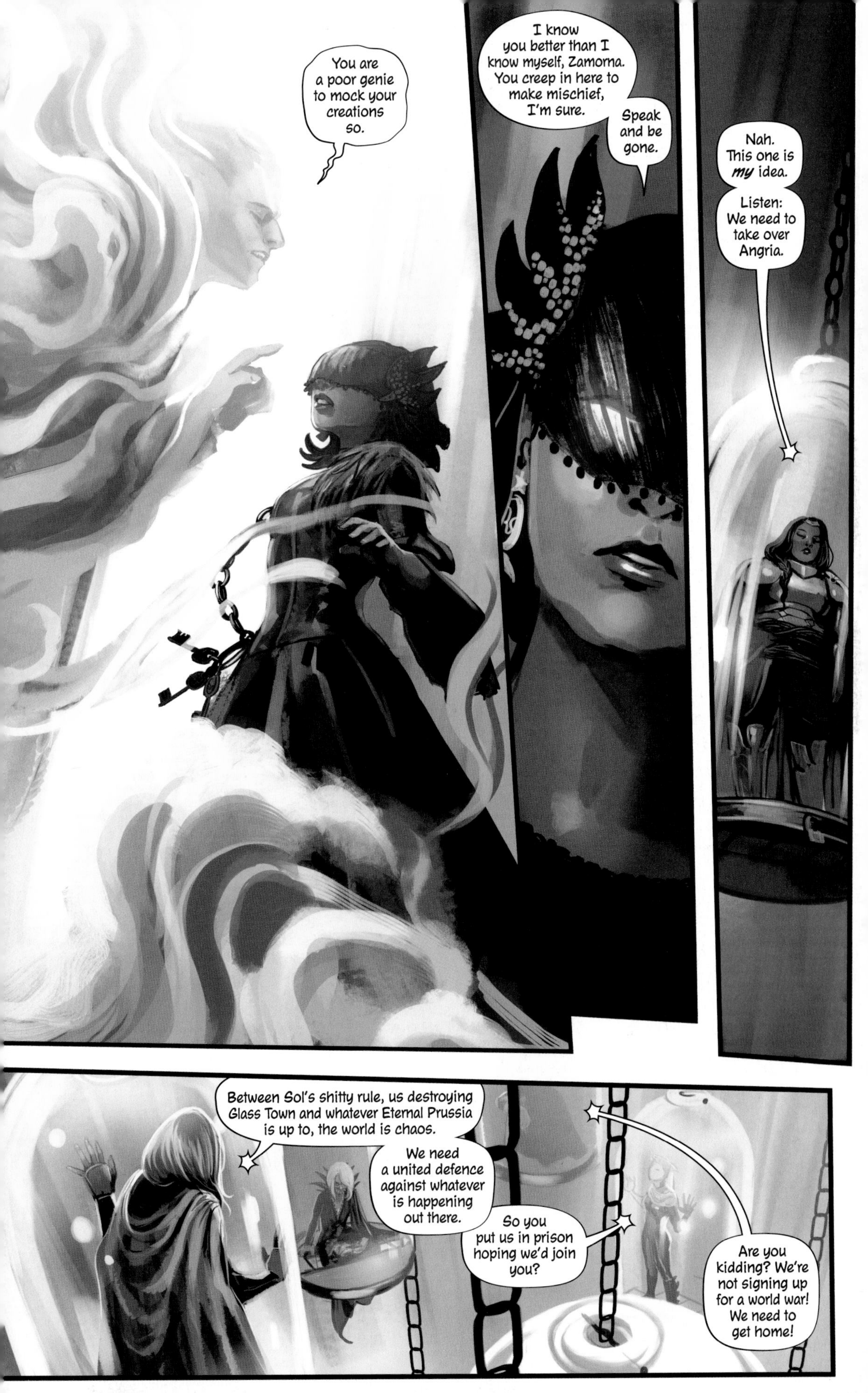
You are a poor genie to mock your creations so.
I know you better than I know myself, Zamorna. You creep in here to make mischief, I'm sure.
Speak and be gone.
Nah. This one is *my* idea.
Listen: We need to take over Angria.
Between Sol's shitty rule, us destroying Glass Town and whatever Eternal Prussia is up to, the world is chaos.
We need a united defence against whatever is happening out there.
So you put us in prison hoping we'd join you?
Are you kidding? We're not signing up for a world war! We need to get home!

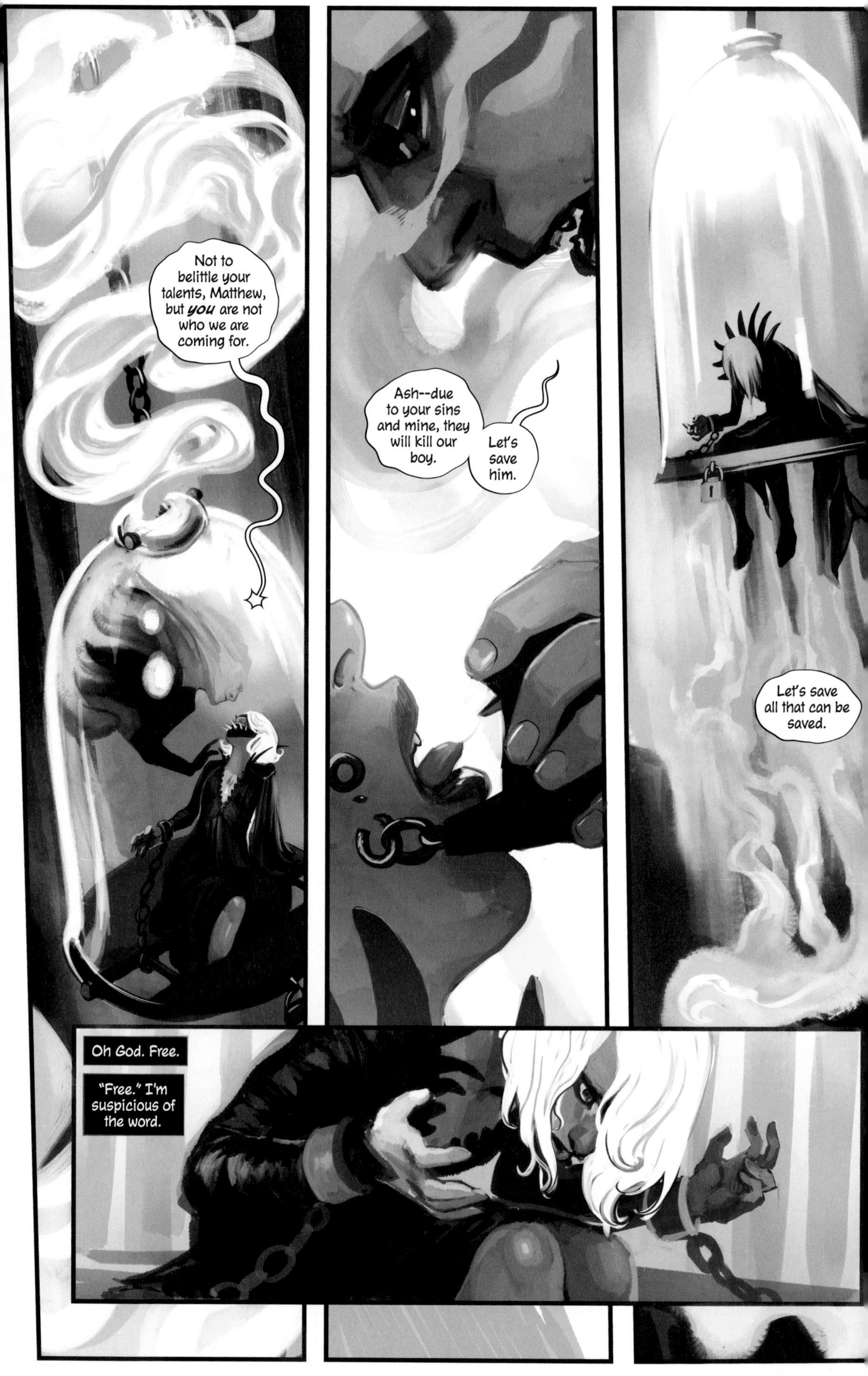
Not to belittle your talents, Matthew, but *you* are not who we are coming for.
Ash--due to your sins and mine, they will kill our boy.
Let's save him.
Let's save all that can be saved.
Oh God. Free.
"Free." I'm suspicious of the word.

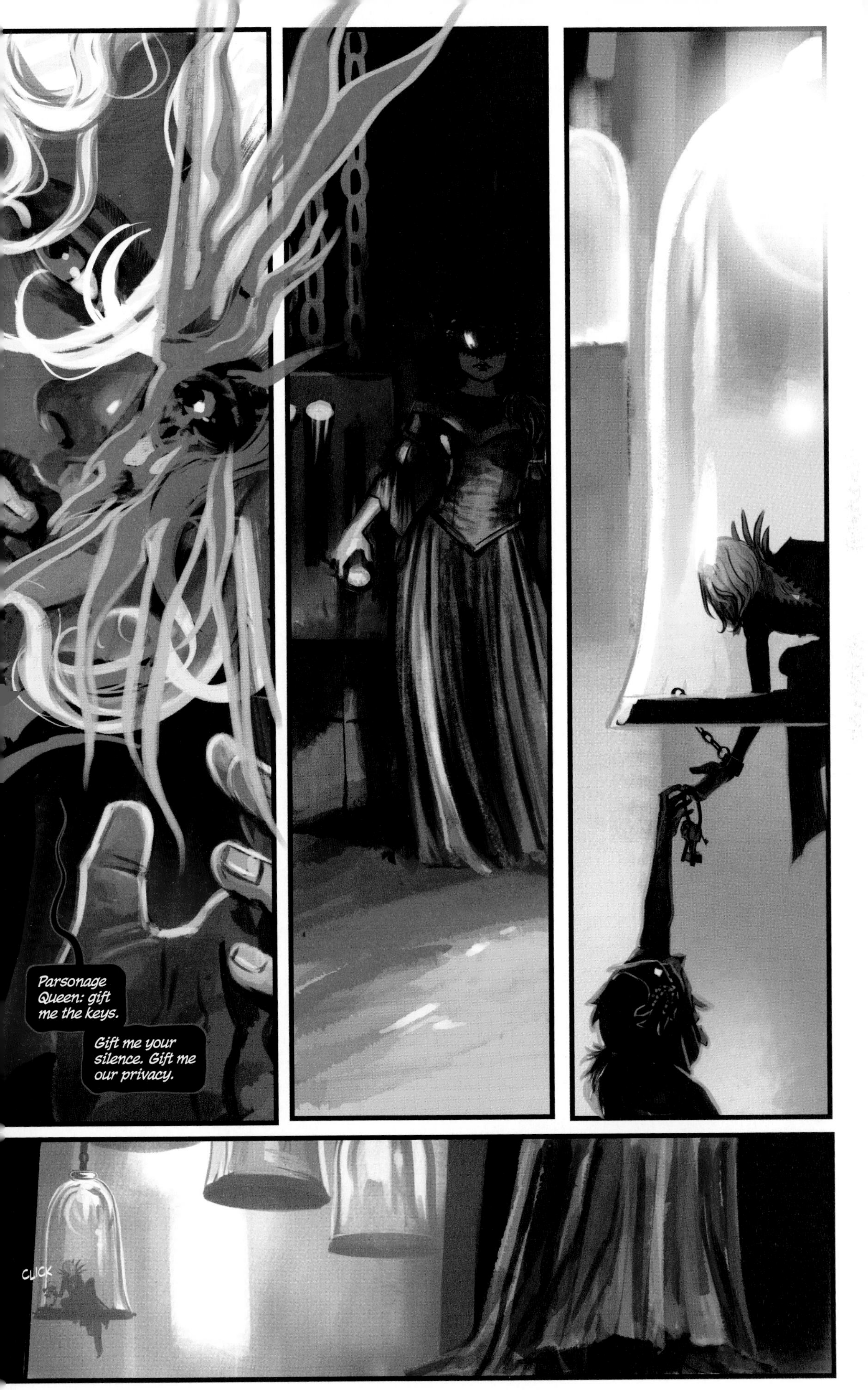
Parsonage Queen: gift me the keys.
Gift me your silence. Gift me our privacy.
CLICK

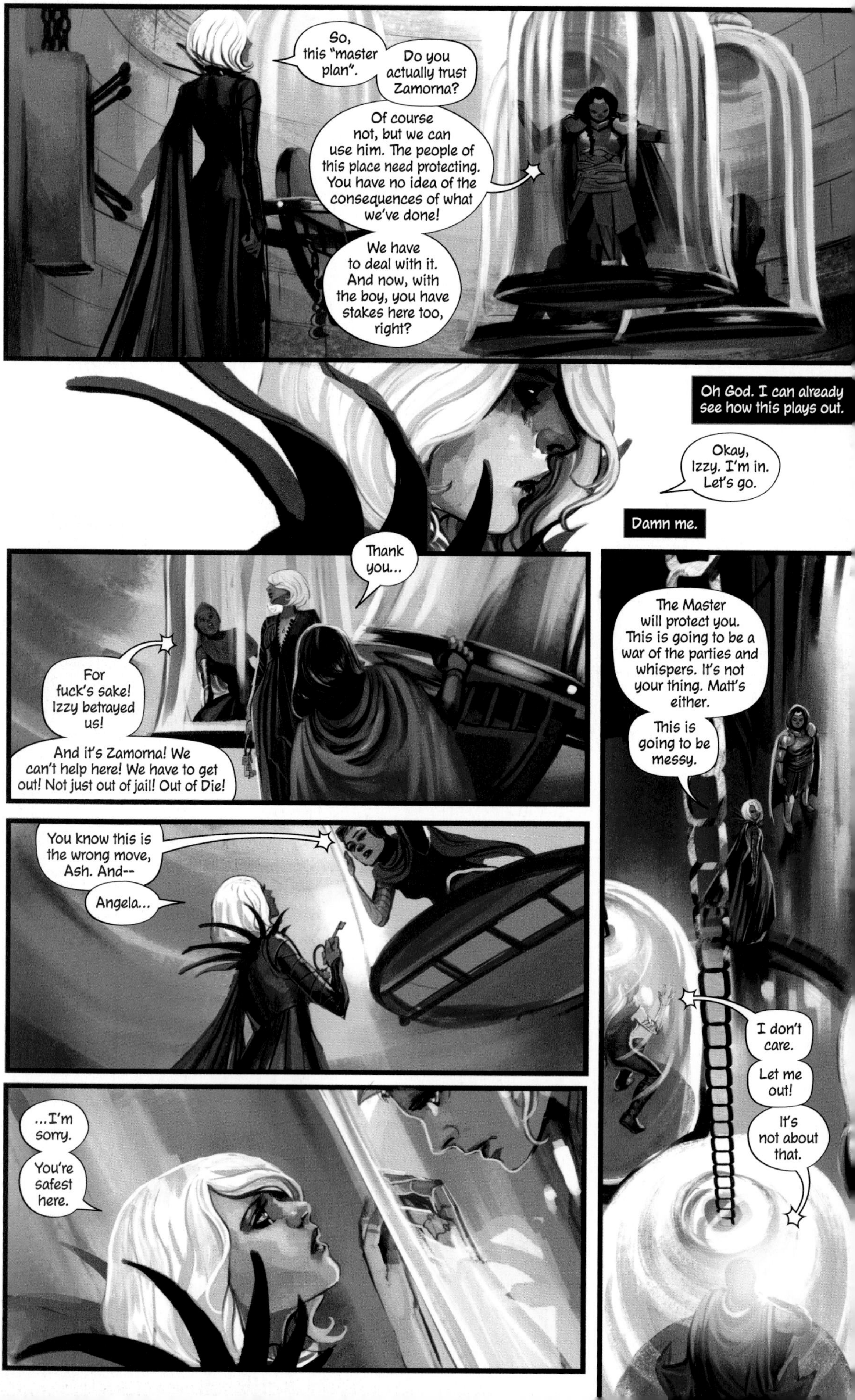
So, this "master plan".
Do you actually trust Zamorna?
Of course not, but we can use him. The people of this place need protecting. You have no idea of the consequences of what we've done!
We have to deal with it. And now, with the boy, you have stakes here too, right?
Oh God. I can already see how this plays out.
Okay, Izzy. I'm in. Let's go.
Damn me.
Thank you...
For fuck's sake! Izzy betrayed us!
And it's Zamorna! We can't help here! We have to get out! Not just out of jail! Out of Die!
You know this is the wrong move, Ash. And--
Angela...
...I'm sorry.
You're safest here.
The Master will protect you. This is going to be a war of the parties and whispers. It's not your thing. Matt's either.
This is going to be messy.
I don't care.
Let me out!
It's not about that.

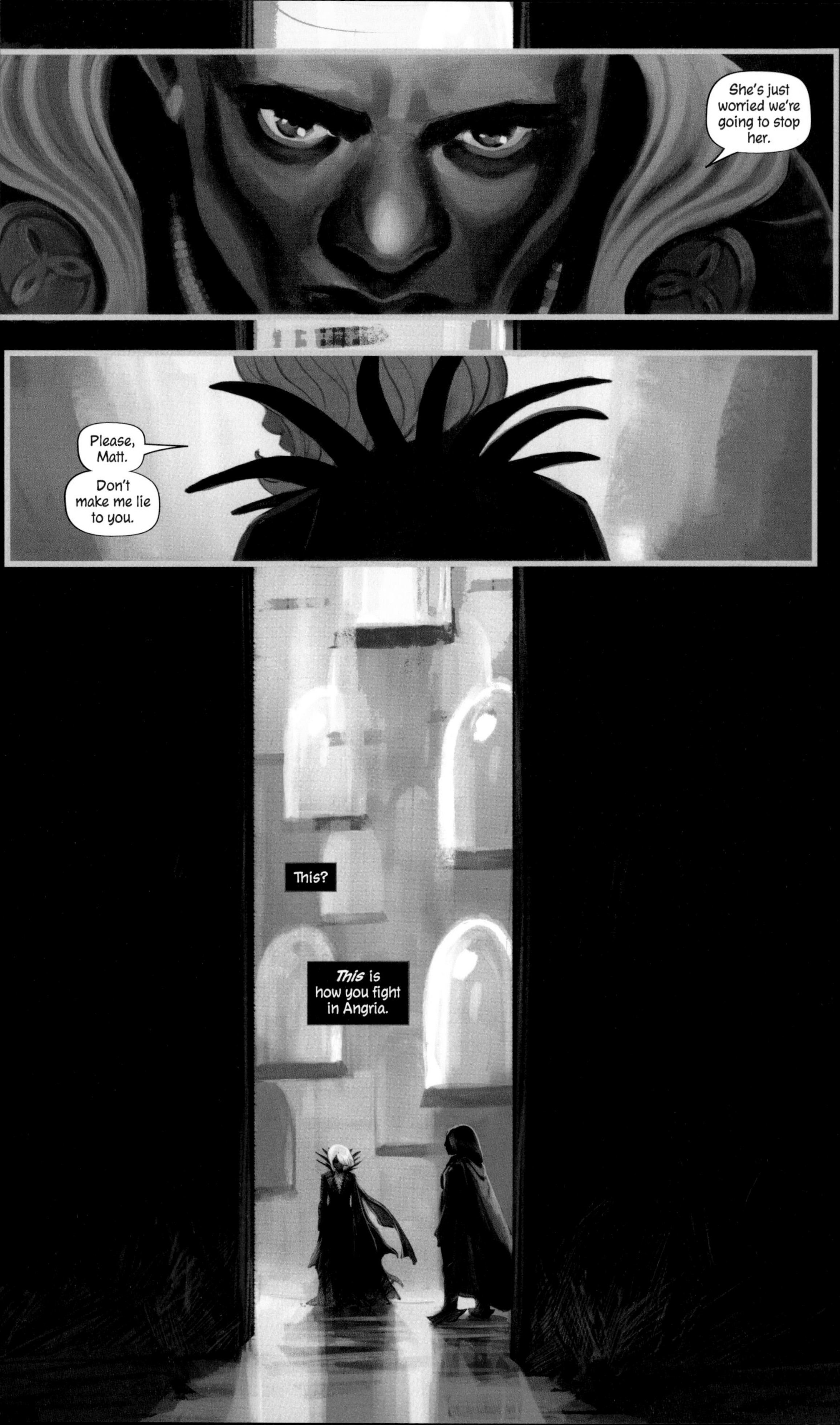

She's just worried we're going to stop her.
Please, Matt.
Don't make me lie to you.
This?
This is how you fight in Angria.

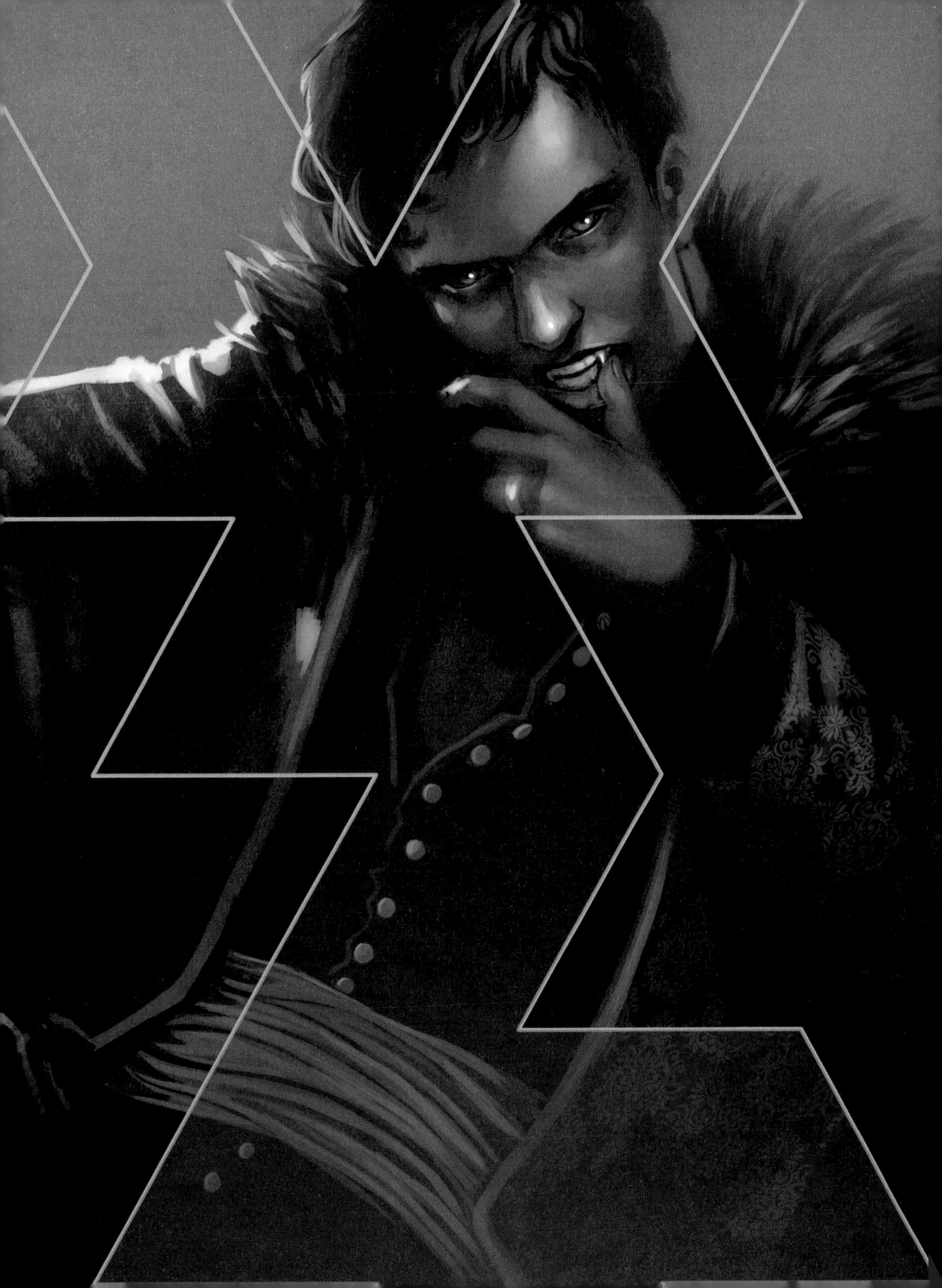

10:
THE X-CARD

"It is better to arm and strengthen your hero, than to disarm and enfeeble your foe."
– *Anne Brontë,*
The Tenant of Wildfell Hall

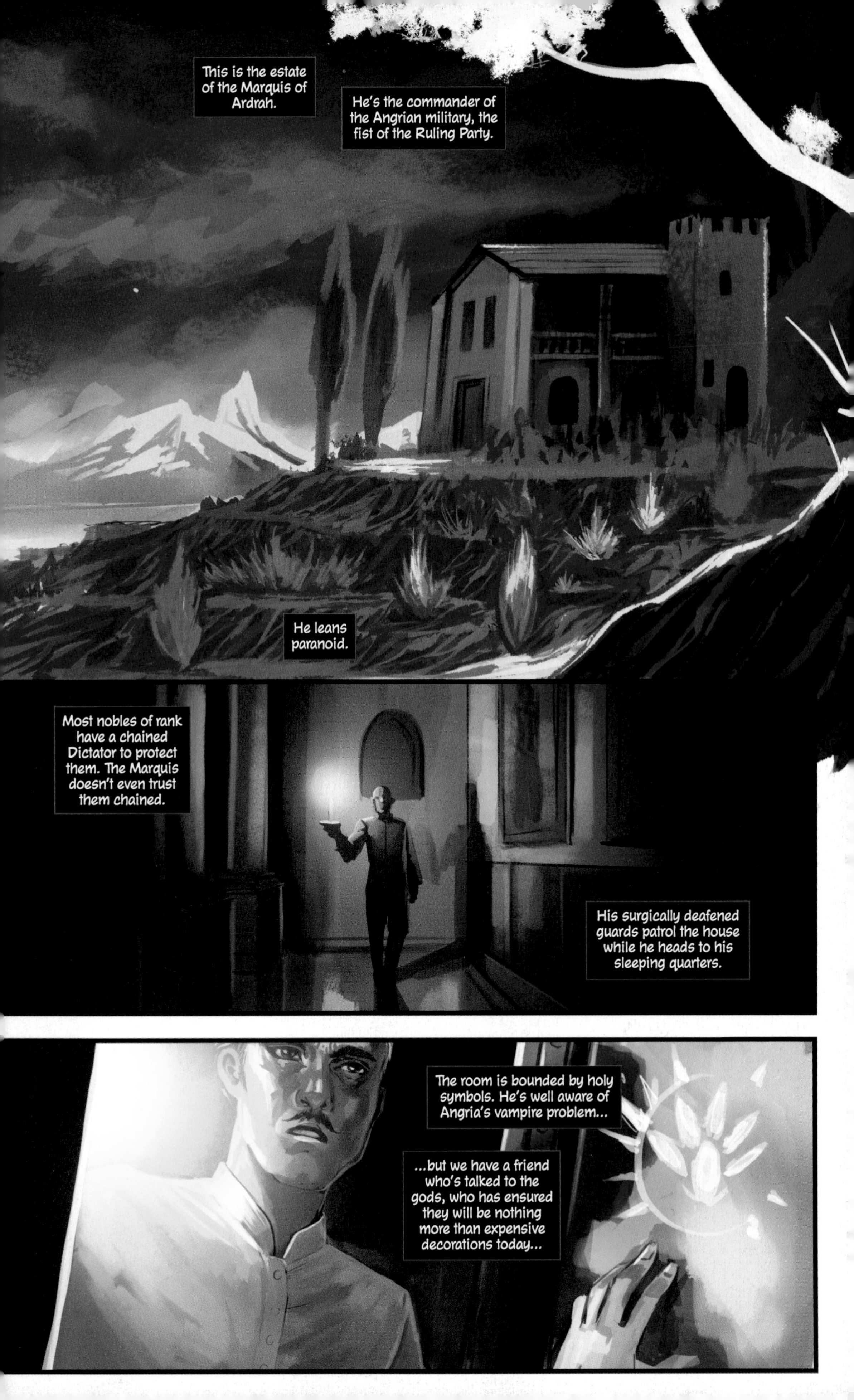
This is the estate of the Marquis of Ardrah.
He's the commander of the Angrian military, the fist of the Ruling Party.
He leans paranoid.
Most nobles of rank have a chained Dictator to protect them. The Marquis doesn't even trust them chained.
His surgically deafened guards patrol the house while he heads to his sleeping quarters.
The room is bounded by holy symbols. He's well aware of Angria's vampire problem...
...but we have a friend who's talked to the gods, who has ensured they will be nothing more than expensive decorations today...

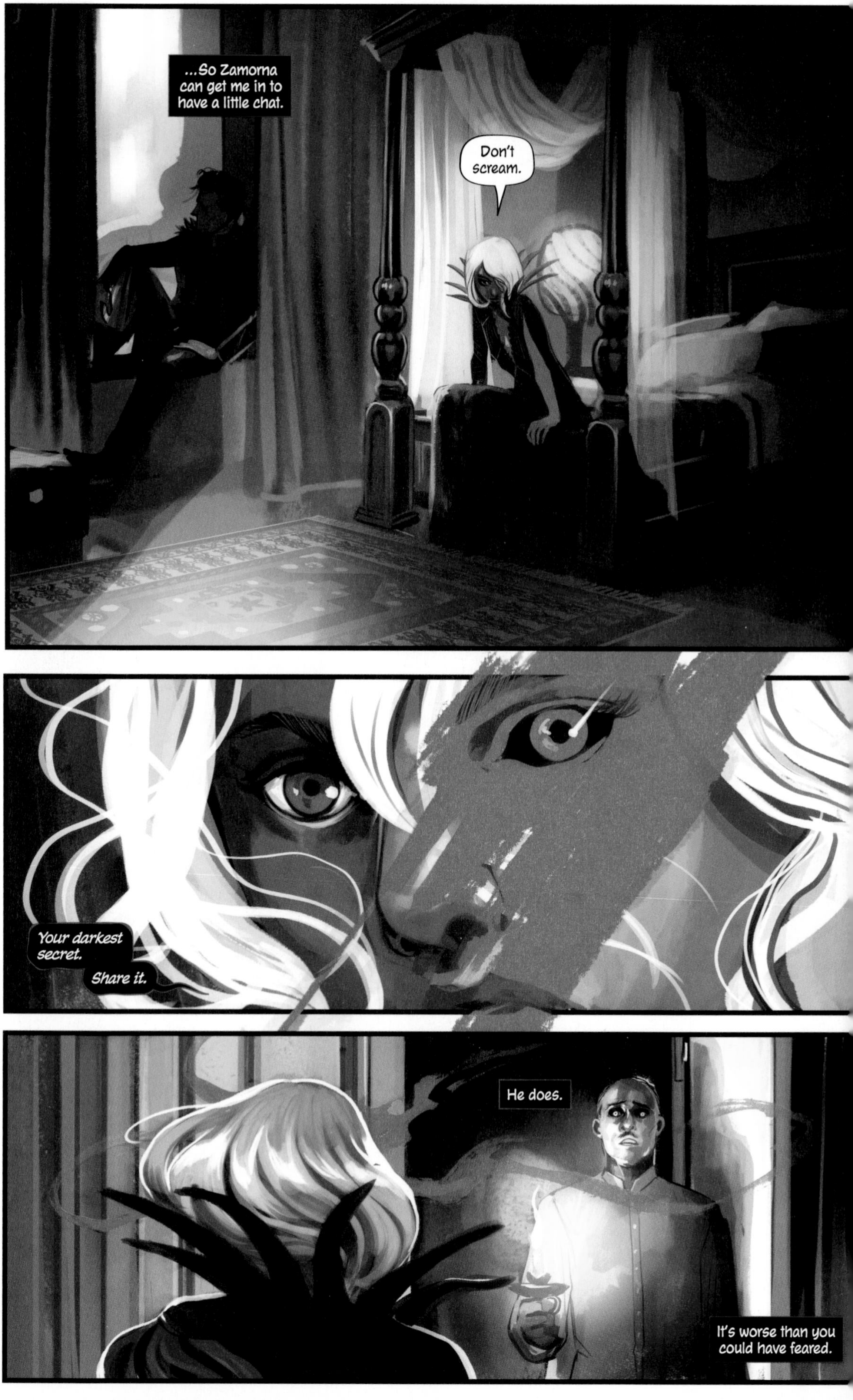
...So Zamorna can get me in to have a little chat.
Don't scream.
Your darkest secret.
Share it.
He does.
It's worse than you could have feared.

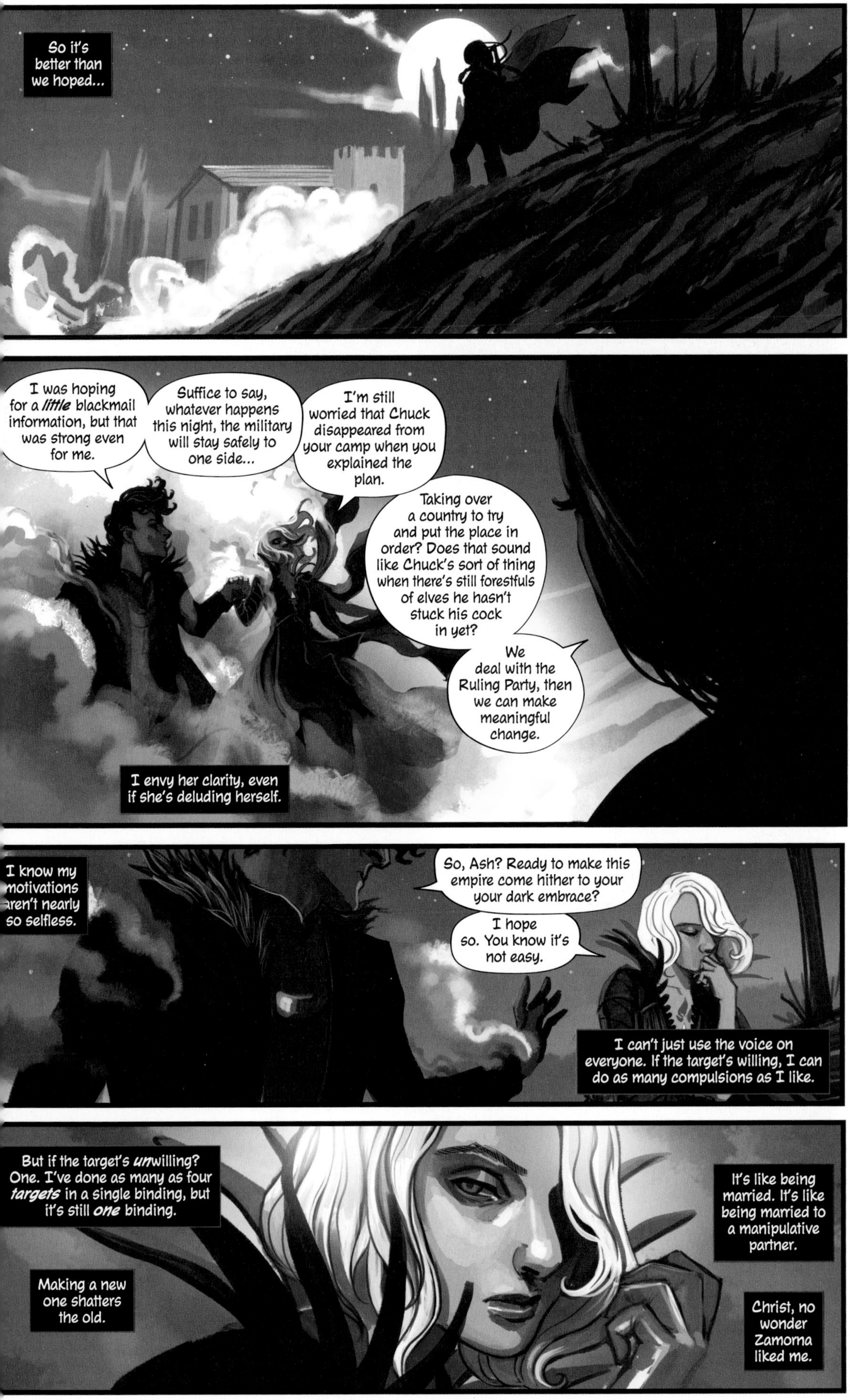
So it's better than we hoped...
I was hoping for a *little* blackmail information, but that was strong even for me.
Suffice to say, whatever happens this night, the military will stay safely to one side...
I'm still worried that Chuck disappeared from your camp when you explained the plan.
Taking over a country to try and put the place in order? Does that sound like Chuck's sort of thing when there's still forestfuls of elves he hasn't stuck his cock in yet?
We deal with the Ruling Party, then we can make meaningful change.
I envy her clarity, even if she's deluding herself.
I know my motivations aren't nearly so selfless.
So, Ash? Ready to make this empire come hither to your your dark embrace?
I hope so. You know it's not easy.
I can't just use the voice on everyone. If the target's willing, I can do as many compulsions as I like.
But if the target's *un*willing? One. I've done as many as four *targets* in a single binding, but it's still *one* binding.
Making a new one shatters the old.
It's like being married. It's like being married to a manipulative partner.
Christ, no wonder Zamorna liked me.

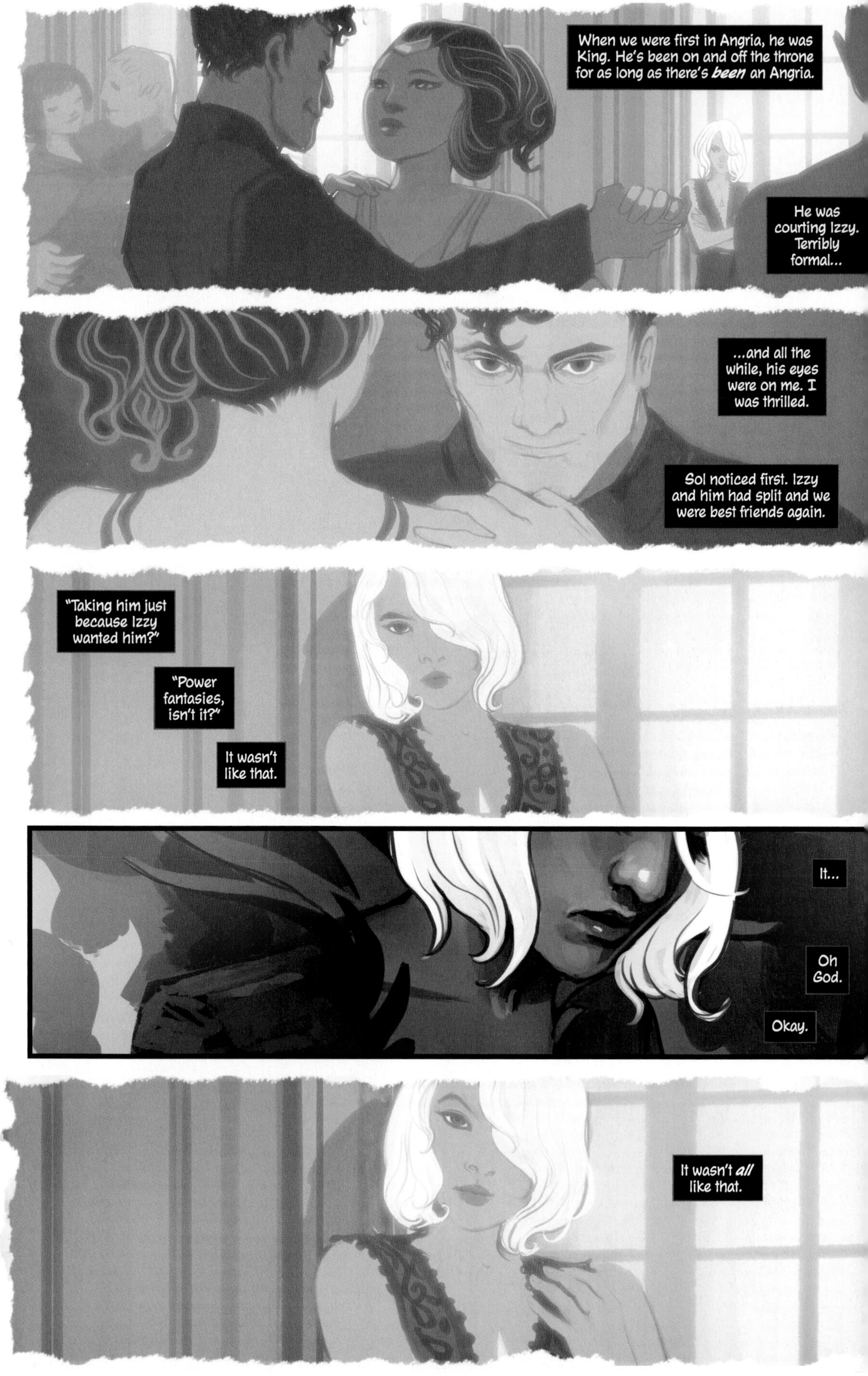
When we were first in Angria, he was King. He's been on and off the throne for as long as there's *been* an Angria.
He was courting Izzy. Terribly formal...
...and all the while, his eyes were on me. I was thrilled.
Sol noticed first. Izzy and him had split and we were best friends again.
"Taking him just because Izzy wanted him?"
"Power fantasies, isn't it?"
It wasn't like that.
It...
Oh God.
Okay.
It wasn't *all* like that.

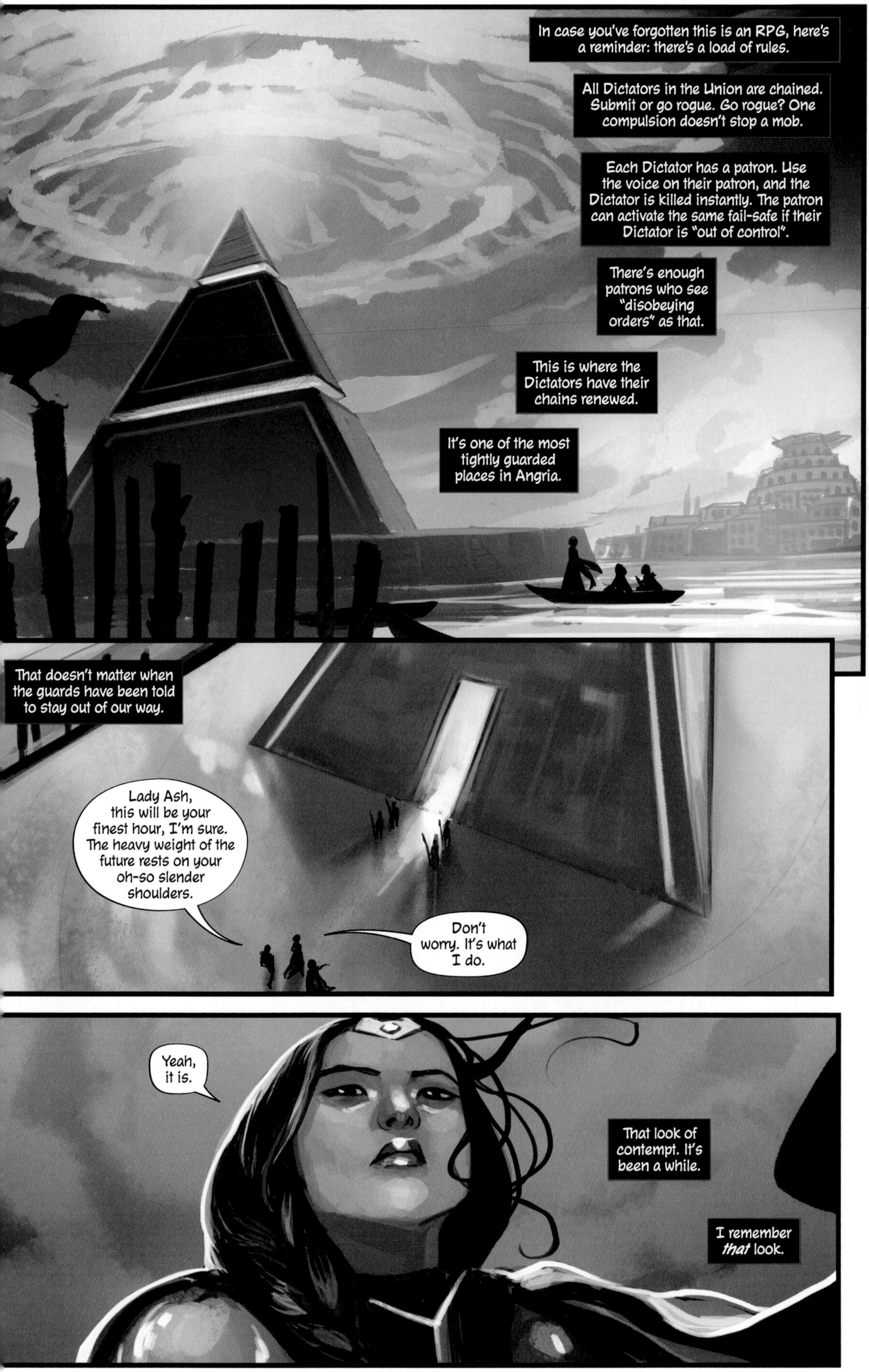
In case you've forgotten this is an RPG, here's a reminder: there's a load of rules.
All Dictators in the Union are chained. Submit or go rogue. Go rogue? One compulsion doesn't stop a mob.
Each Dictator has a patron. Use the voice on their patron, and the Dictator is killed instantly. The patron can activate the same fail-safe if their Dictator is "out of control".
There's enough patrons who see "disobeying orders" as that.
This is where the Dictators have their chains renewed.
It's one of the most tightly guarded places in Angria.
That doesn't matter when the guards have been told to stay out of our way.
Lady Ash, this will be your finest hour, I'm sure. The heavy weight of the future rests on your oh-so slender shoulders.
Don't worry. It's what I do.
Yeah, it is.
That look of contempt. It's been a while.
I remember *that* look.

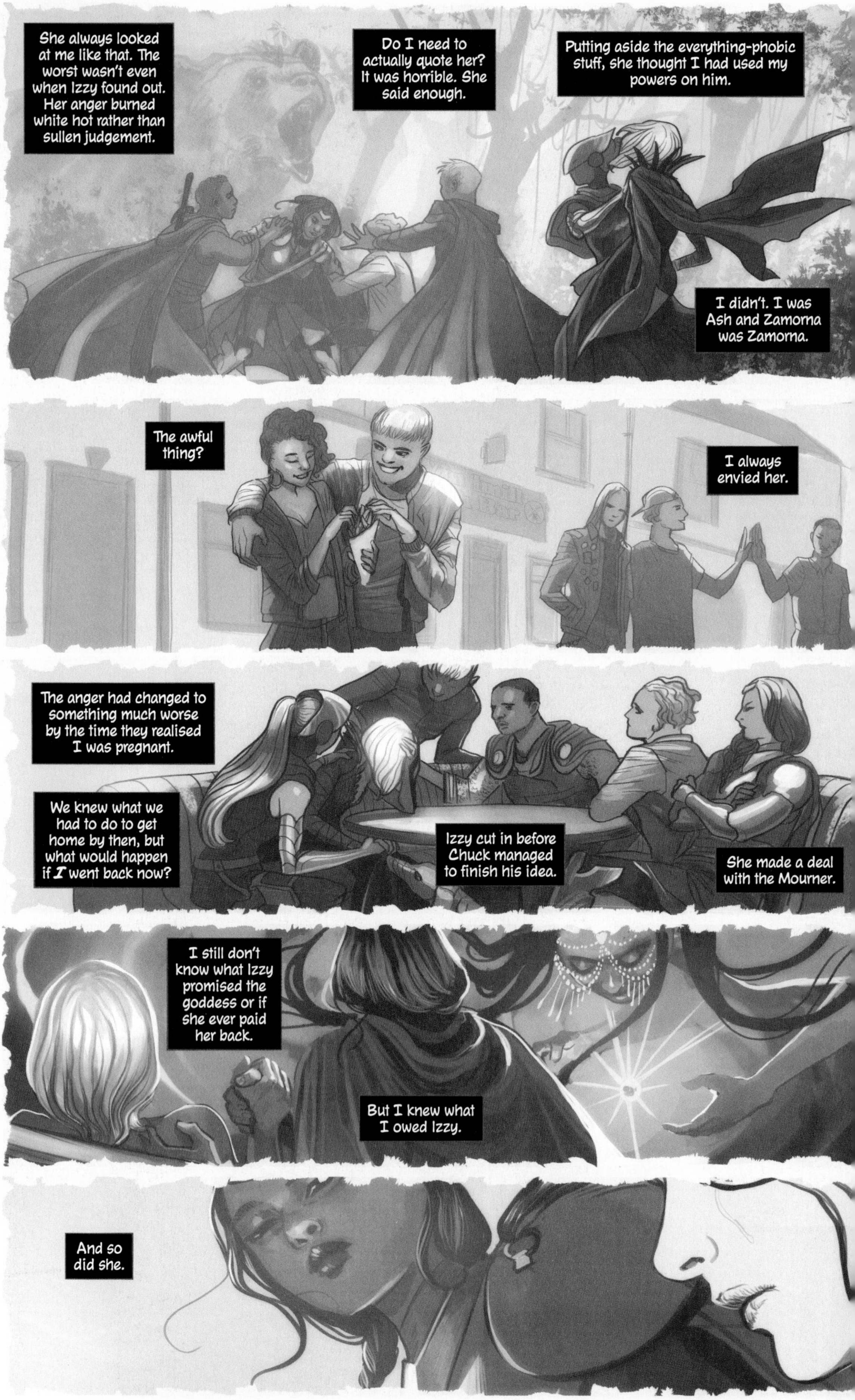
She always looked at me like that. The worst wasn't even when Izzy found out. Her anger burned white hot rather than sullen judgement.
Do I need to actually quote her? It was horrible. She said enough.
Putting aside the everything-phobic stuff, she thought I had used my powers on him.
I didn't. I was Ash and Zamorna was Zamorna.
The awful thing?
I always envied her.
The anger had changed to something much worse by the time they realised I was pregnant.
We knew what we had to do to get home by then, but what would happen if *I* went back now?
Izzy cut in before Chuck managed to finish his idea.
She made a deal with the Mourner.
I still don't know what Izzy promised the goddess or if she ever paid her back.
But I knew what I owed Izzy.
And so did she.

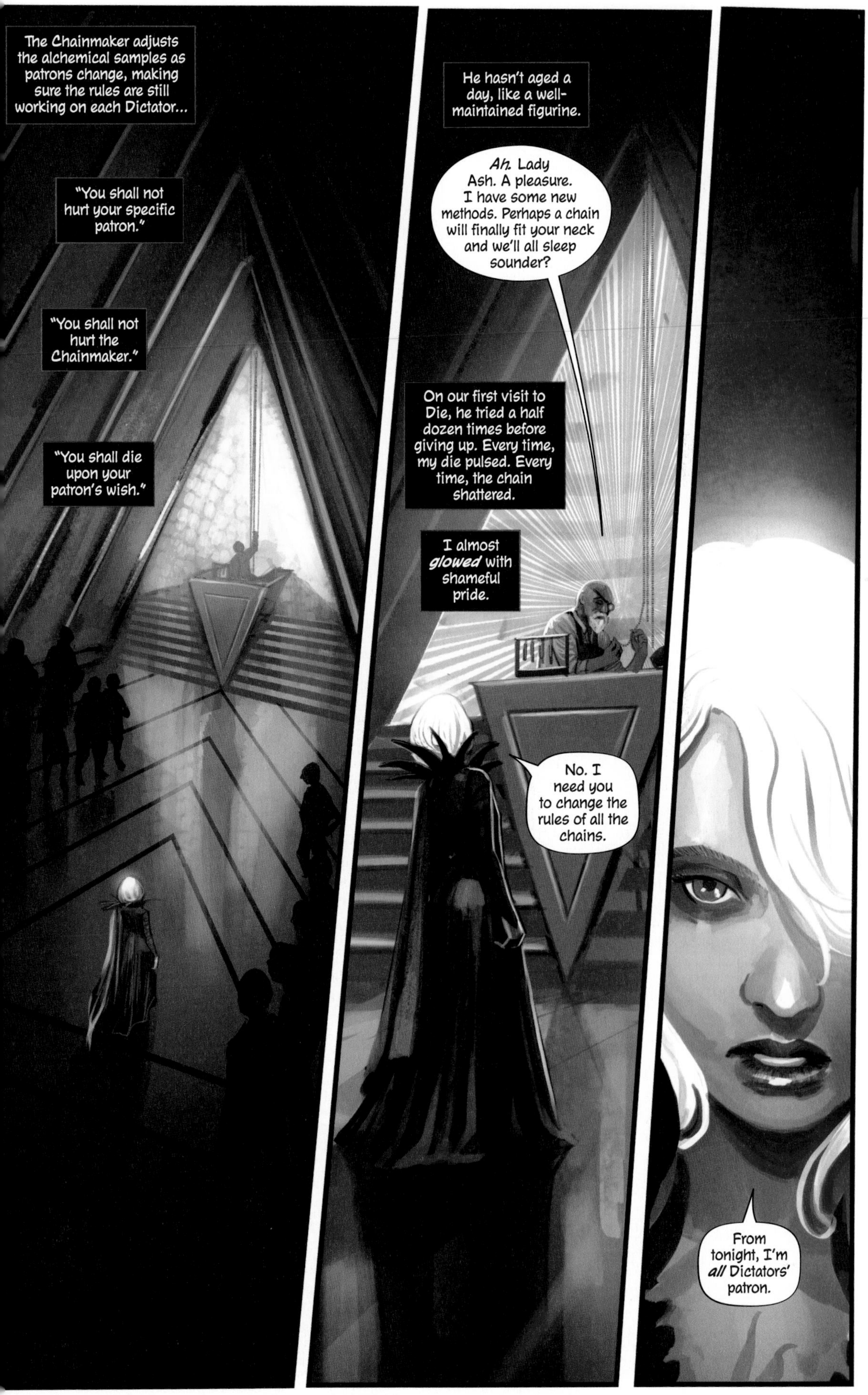
The Chainmaker adjusts the alchemical samples as patrons change, making sure the rules are still working on each Dictator...
"You shall not hurt your specific patron."
"You shall not hurt the Chainmaker."
"You shall die upon your patron's wish."
He hasn't aged a day, like a well-maintained figurine.
Ah. Lady Ash. A pleasure. I have some new methods. Perhaps a chain will finally fit your neck and we'll all sleep sounder?
On our first visit to Die, he tried a half dozen times before giving up. Every time, my die pulsed. Every time, the chain shattered.
I almost *glowed* with shameful pride.
No. I need you to change the rules of all the chains.
From tonight, I'm *all* Dictators' patron.

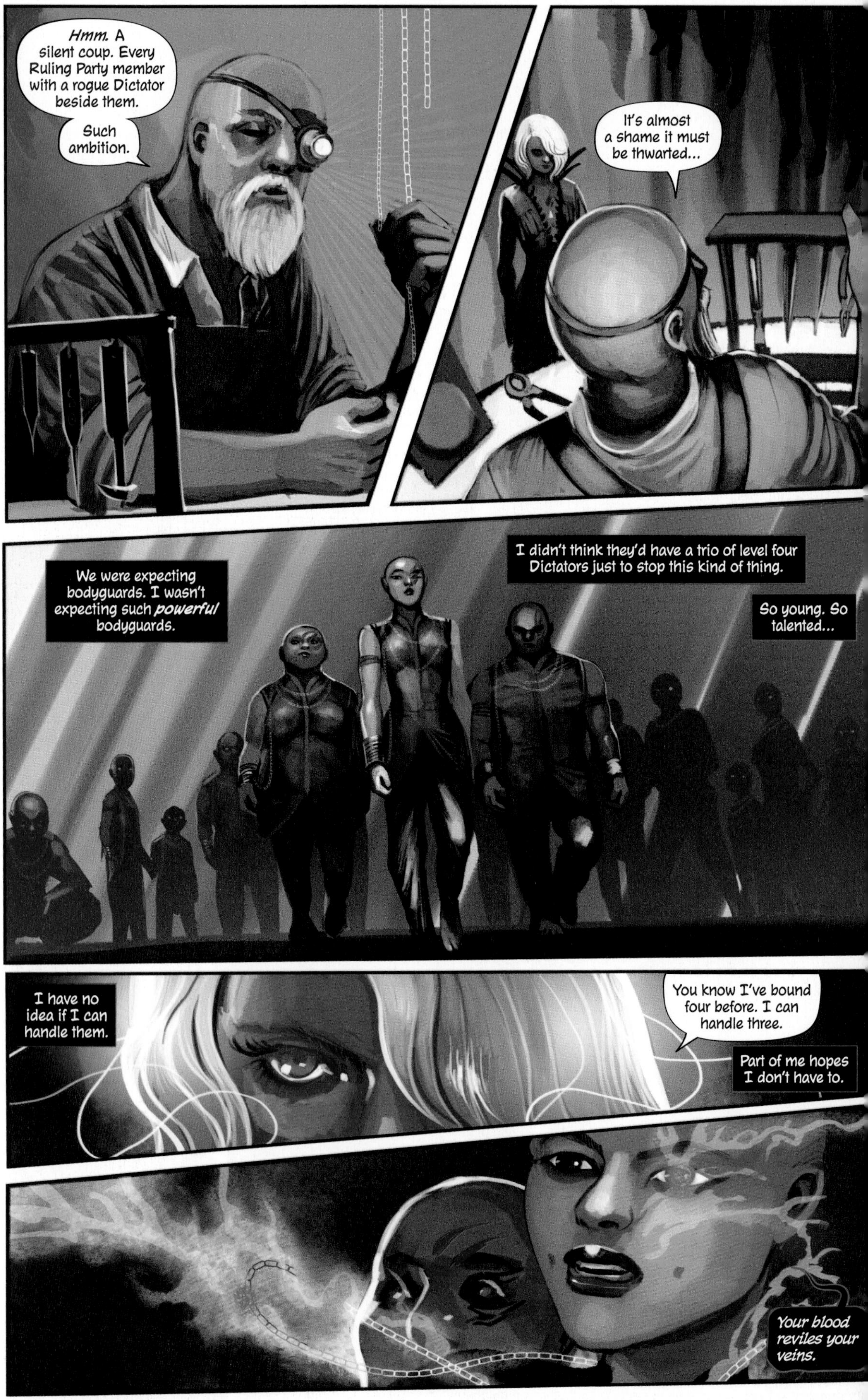
Hmm. A silent coup. Every Ruling Party member with a rogue Dictator beside them.
Such ambition.
It's almost a shame it must be thwarted...
We were expecting bodyguards. I wasn't expecting such *powerful* bodyguards.
I didn't think they'd have a trio of level four Dictators just to stop this kind of thing.
So young. So talented...
I have no idea if I can handle them.
You know I've bound four before. I can handle three.
Part of me hopes I don't have to.
Your blood reviles your veins.

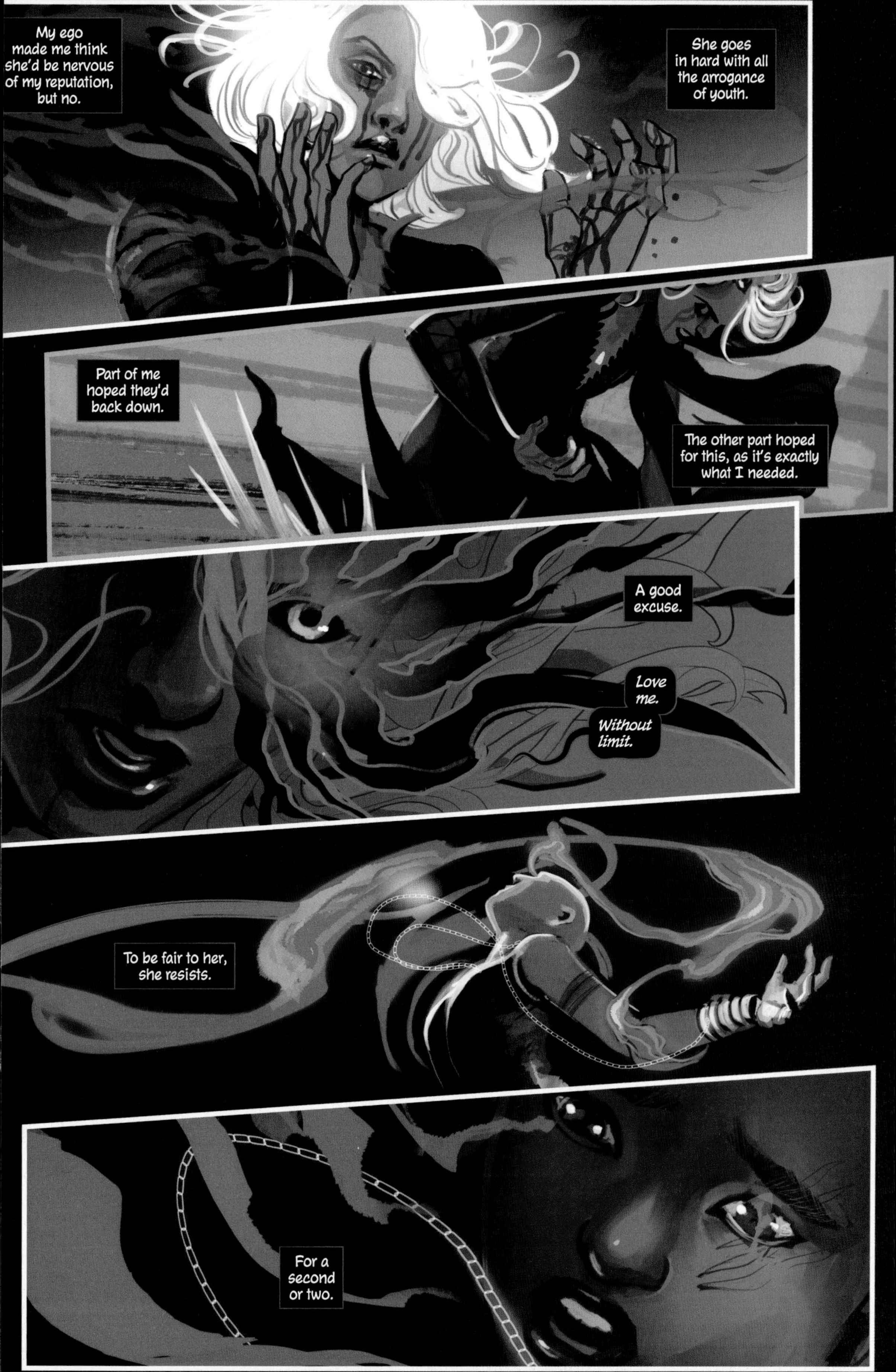
My ego made me think she'd be nervous of my reputation, but no.
She goes in hard with all the arrogance of youth.
Part of me hoped they'd back down.
The other part hoped for this, as it's exactly what I needed.
A good excuse.
Love me.
Without limit.
To be fair to her, she resists.
For a second or two.

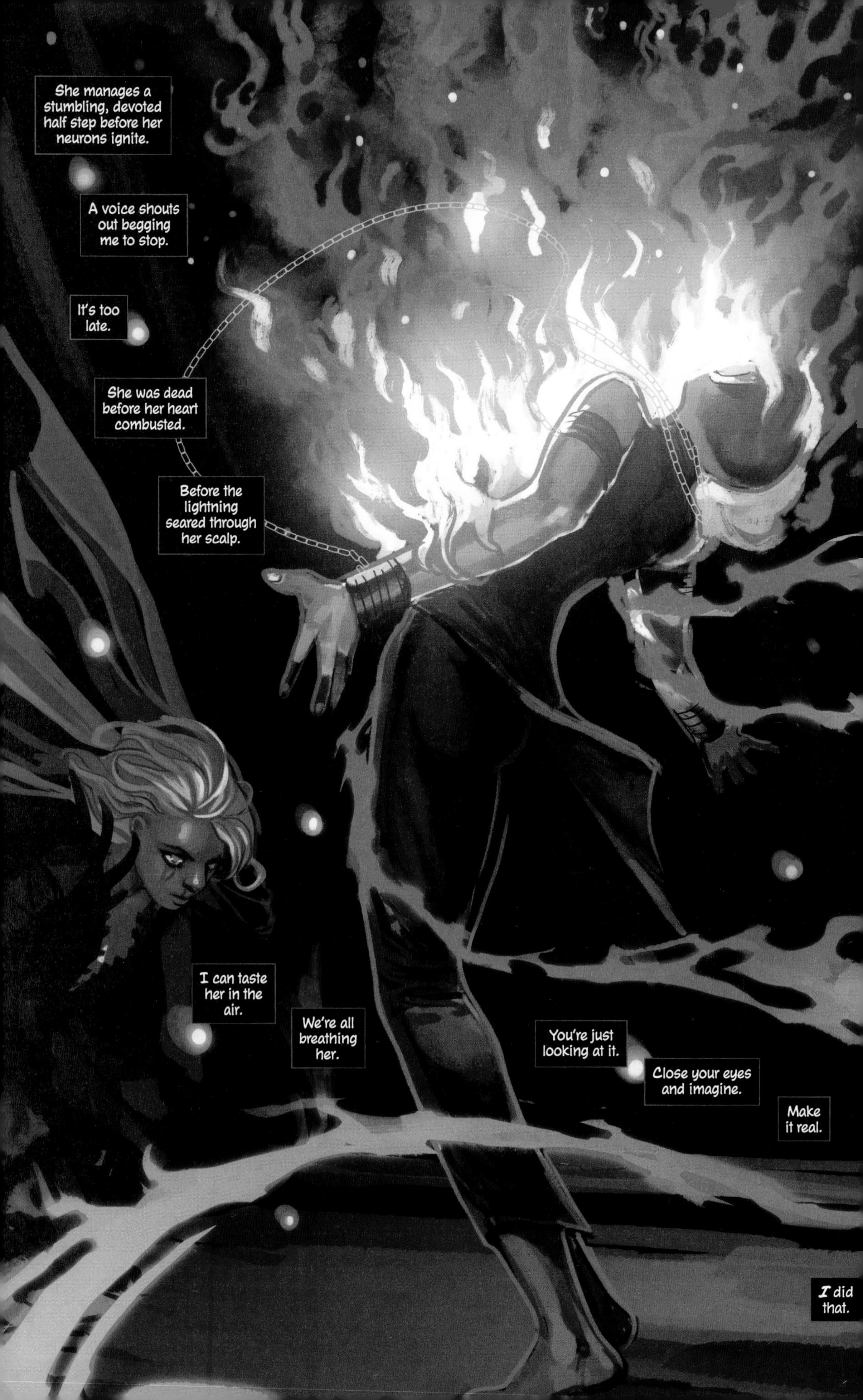

She manages a stumbling, devoted half step before her neurons ignite.
A voice shouts out begging me to stop.
It's too late.
She was dead before her heart combusted.
Before the lightning seared through her scalp.
I can taste her in the air.
We're all breathing her.
You're just looking at it.
Close your eyes and imagine.
Make it real.
I did that.

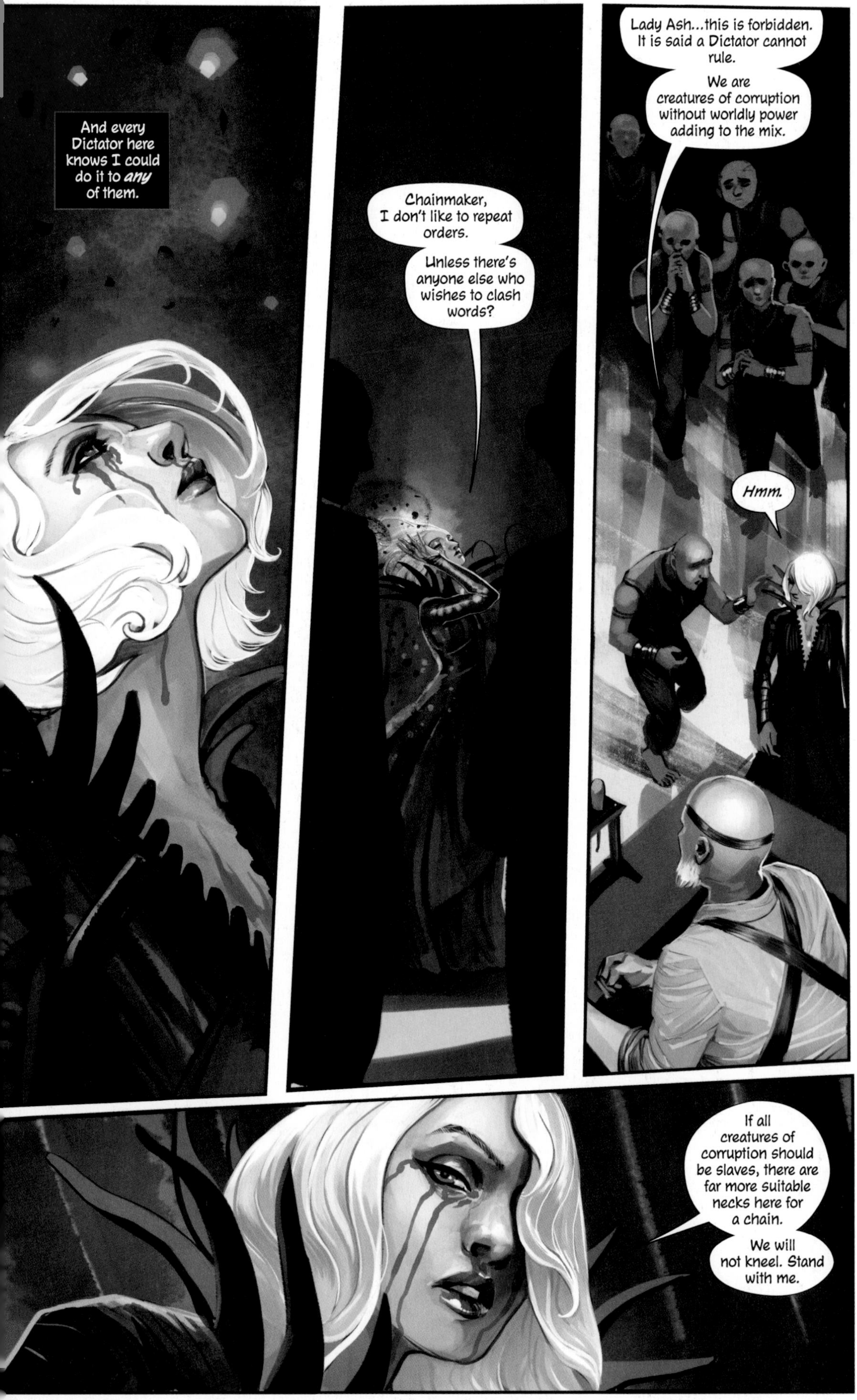
And every Dictator here knows I could do it to *any* of them.
Chainmaker, I don't like to repeat orders.
Unless there's anyone else who wishes to clash words?
Lady Ash...this is forbidden. It is said a Dictator cannot rule.
We are creatures of corruption without worldly power adding to the mix.
Hmm.
If all creatures of corruption should be slaves, there are far more suitable necks here for a chain.
We will not kneel. Stand with me.

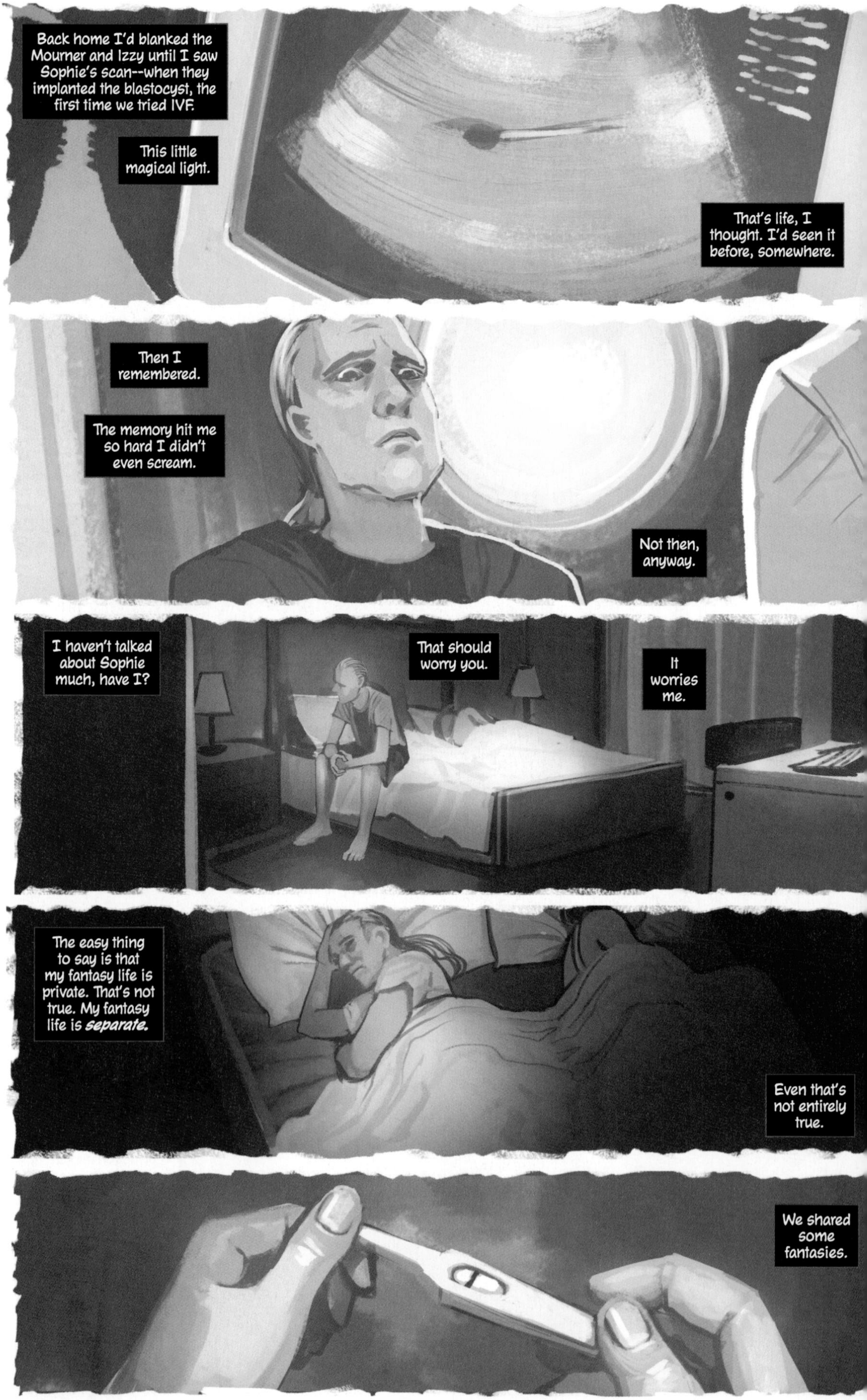
Back home I'd blanked the Mourner and Izzy until I saw Sophie's scan--when they implanted the blastocyst, the first time we tried IVF.
This little magical light.
That's life, I thought. I'd seen it before, somewhere.
Then I remembered.
The memory hit me so hard I didn't even scream.
Not then, anyway.
I haven't talked about Sophie much, have I?
That should worry you.
It worries me.
The easy thing to say is that my fantasy life is private. That's not true. My fantasy life is *separate.*
Even that's not entirely true.
We shared some fantasies.

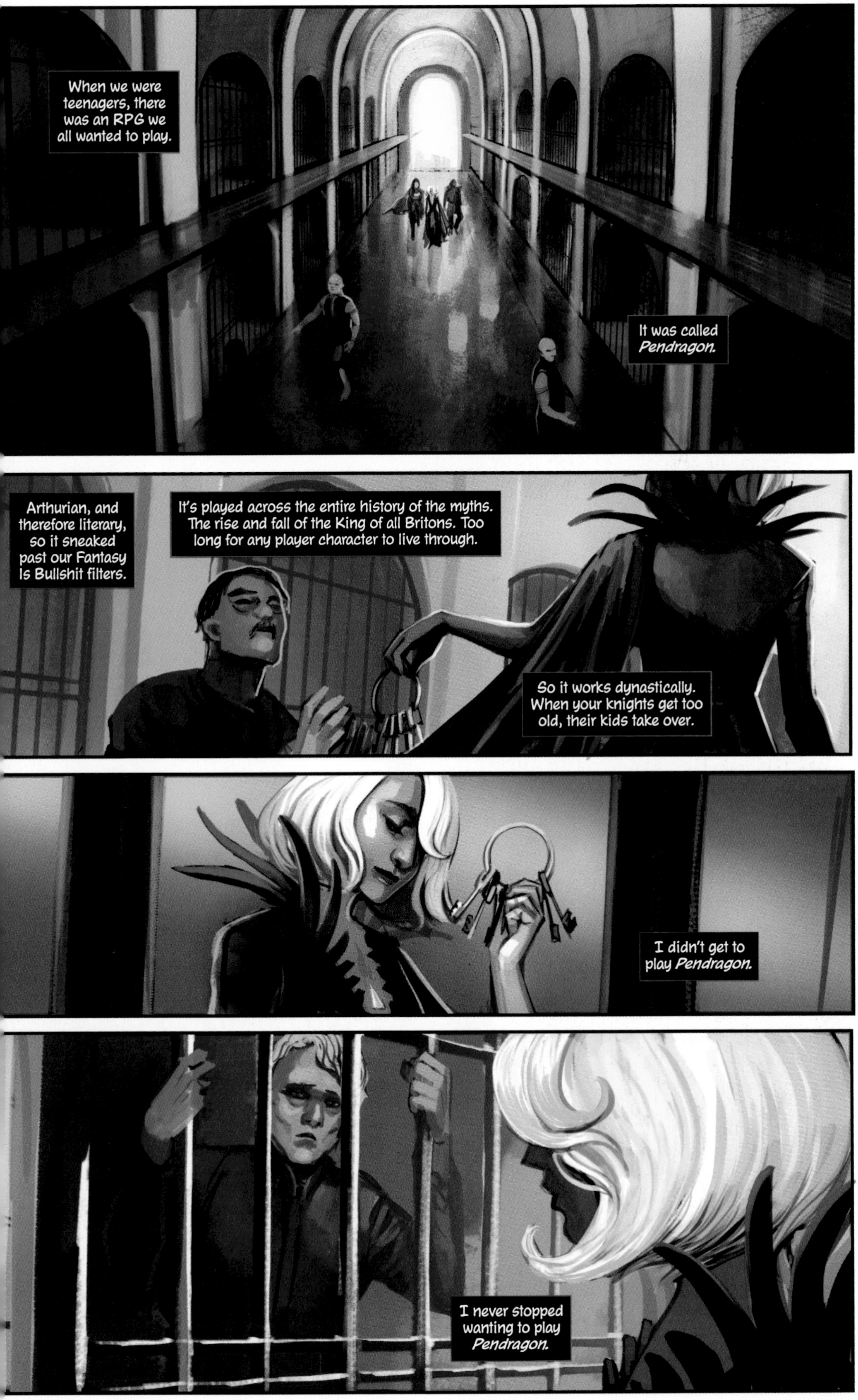
When we were teenagers, there was an RPG we all wanted to play.
It was called *Pendragon.*
Arthurian, and therefore literary, so it sneaked past our Fantasy Is Bullshit filters.
It's played across the entire history of the myths. The rise and fall of the King of all Britons. Too long for any player character to live through.
So it works dynastically. When your knights get too old, their kids take over.
I didn't get to play *Pendragon.*
I never stopped wanting to play *Pendragon.*

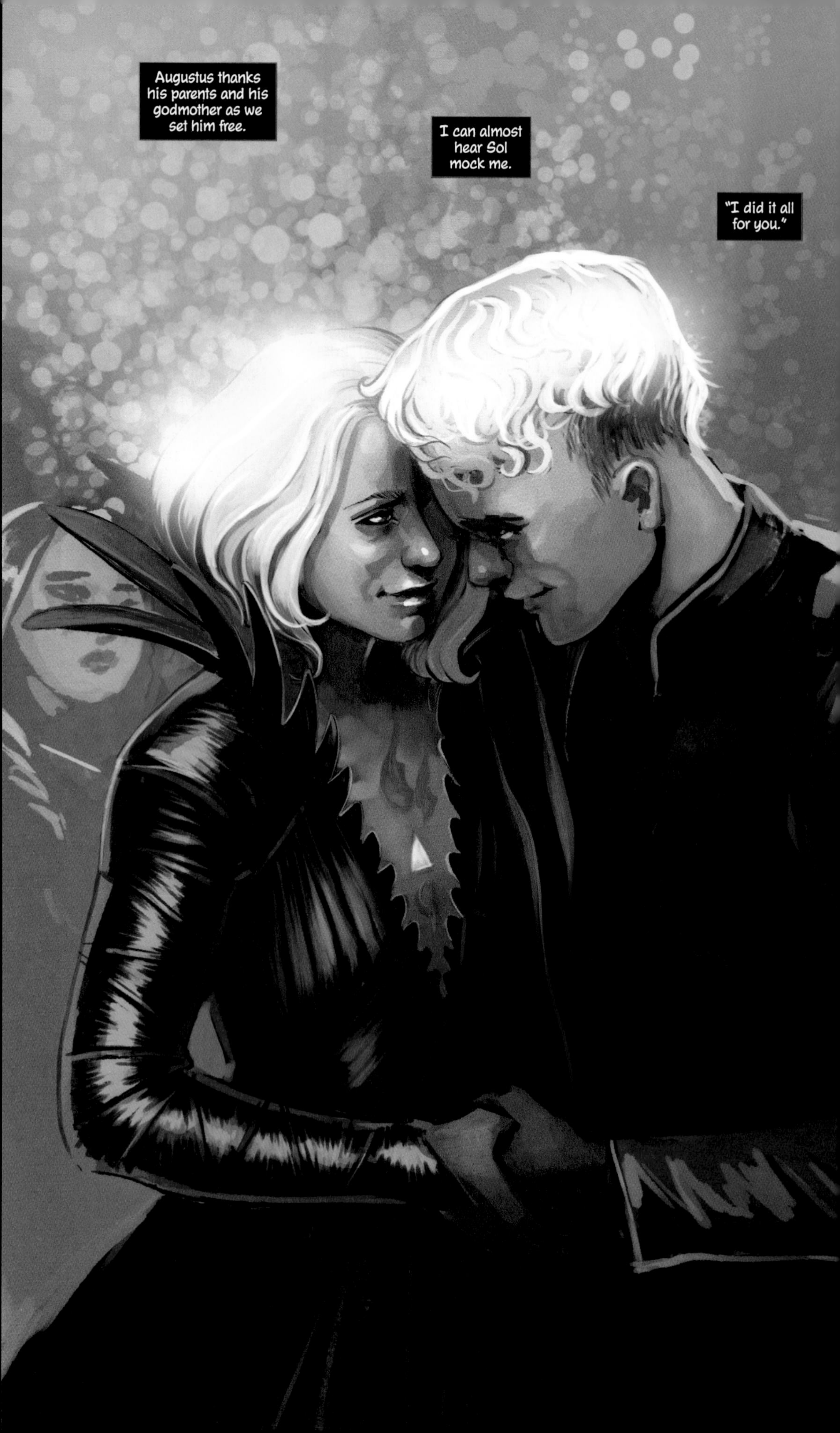
Augustus thanks his parents and his godmother as we set him free.
I can almost hear Sol mock me.
"I did it all for you."

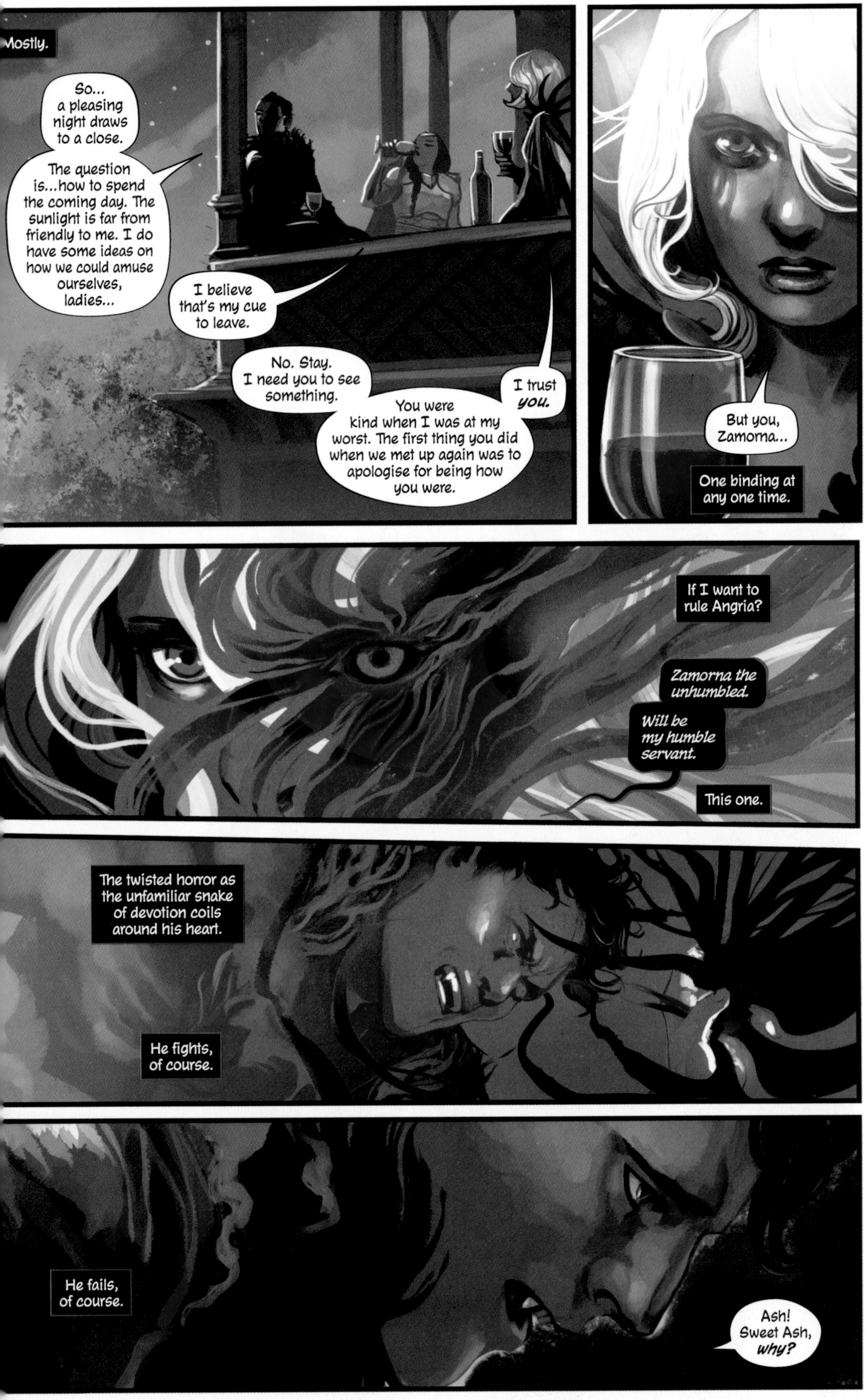
Mostly.
So... a pleasing night draws to a close.
The question is...how to spend the coming day. The sunlight is far from friendly to me. I do have some ideas on how we could amuse ourselves, ladies...
I believe that's my cue to leave.
No. Stay. I need you to see something.
I trust *you.*
You were kind when I was at my worst. The first thing you did when we met up again was to apologise for being how you were.
But you, Zamorna...
One binding at any one time.
If I want to rule Angria?
Zamorna the unhumbled.
Will be my humble servant.
This one.
The twisted horror as the unfamiliar snake of devotion coils around his heart.
He fights, of course.
He fails, of course.
Ash! Sweet Ash, *why?*

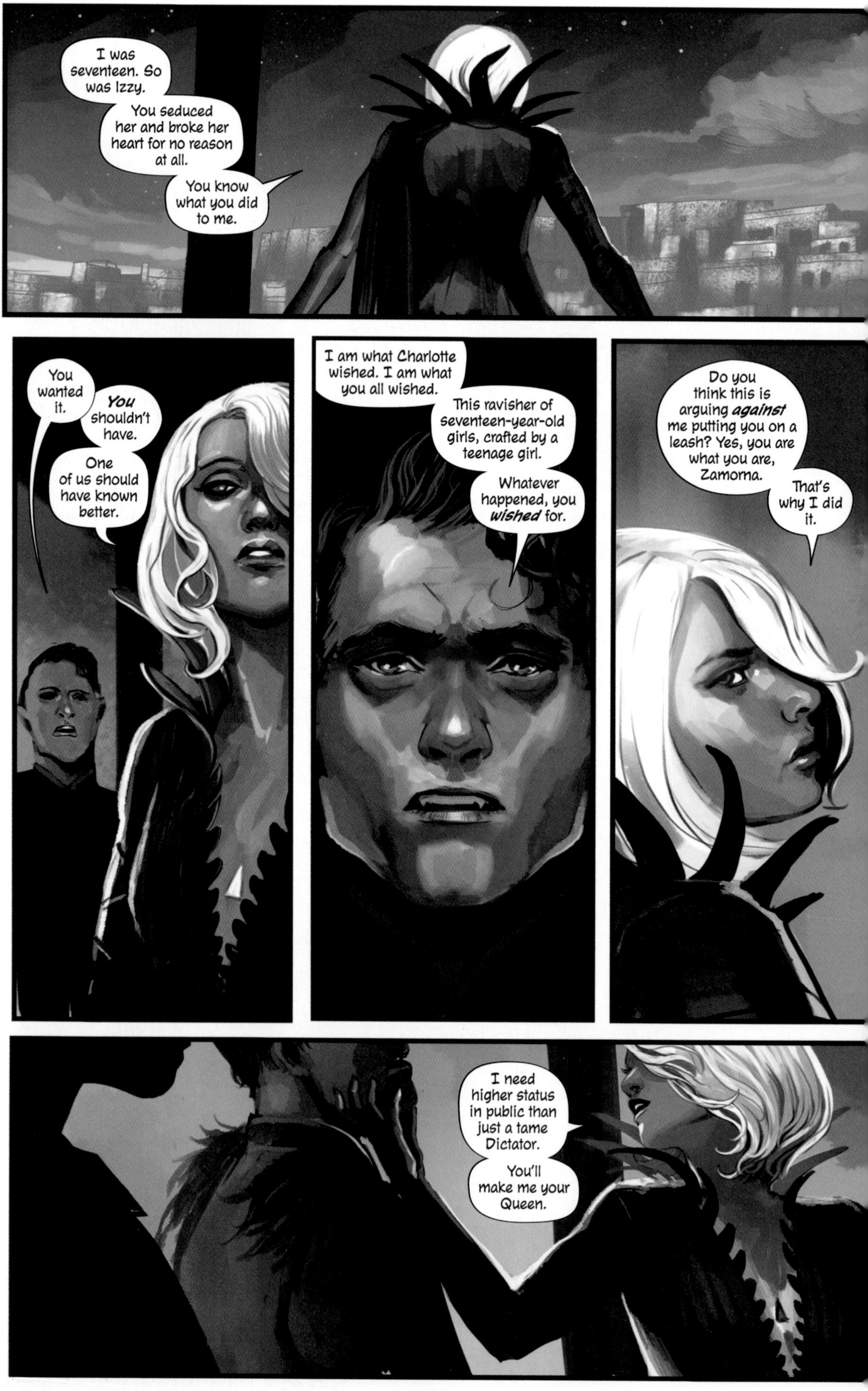
I was seventeen. So was Izzy.
You seduced her and broke her heart for no reason at all.
You know what you did to me.
You wanted it.
You shouldn't have.
One of us should have known better.
I am what Charlotte wished. I am what you all wished.
This ravisher of seventeen-year-old girls, crafted by a teenage girl.
Whatever happened, you *wished* for.
Do you think this is arguing *against* me putting you on a leash? Yes, you are what you are, Zamorna.
That's why I did it.
I need higher status in public than just a tame Dictator.
You'll make me your Queen.

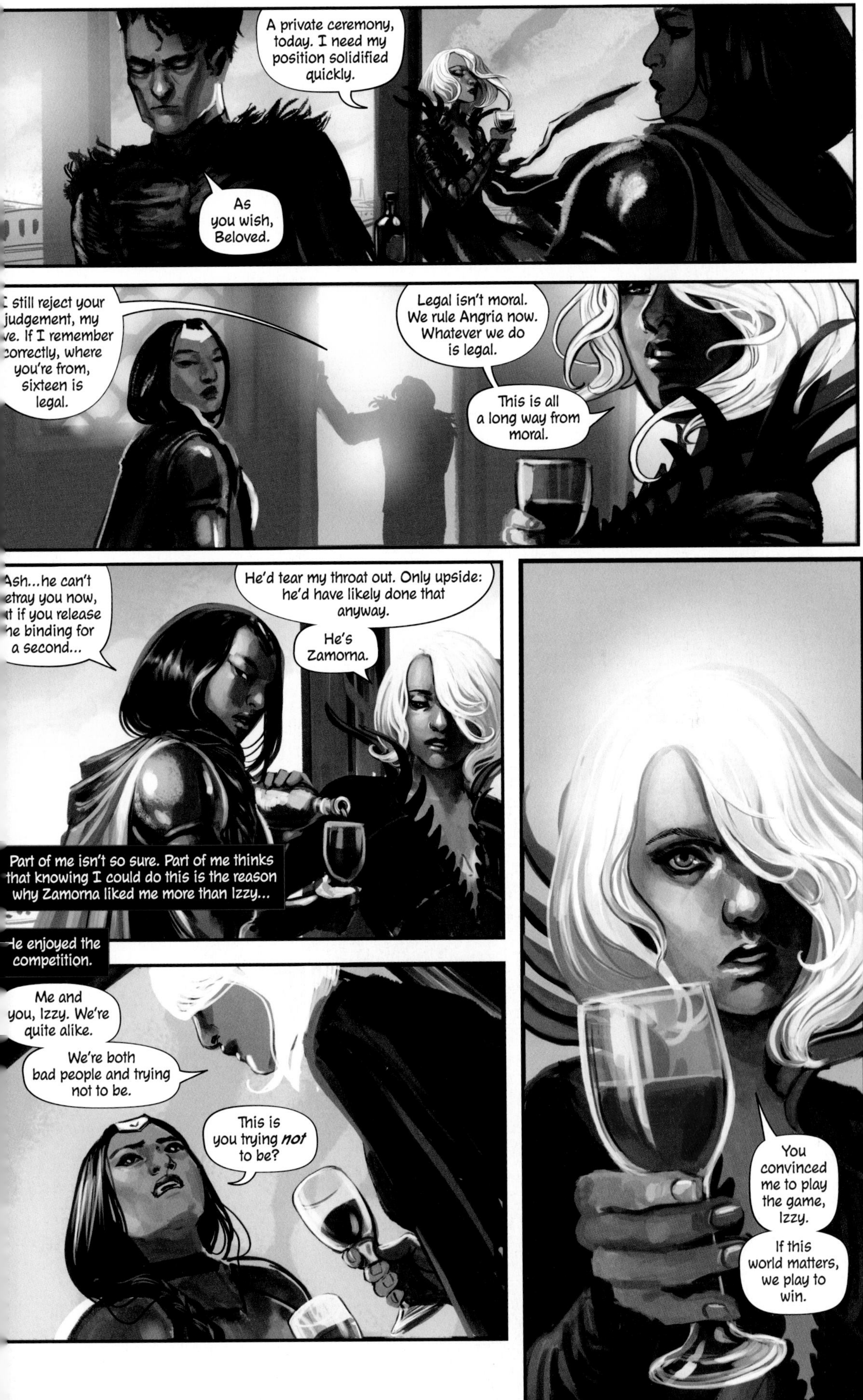
A private ceremony, today. I need my position solidified quickly.
As you wish, Beloved.
still reject your judgement, my ve. If I remember orrectly, where you're from, sixteen is legal.
Legal isn't moral. We rule Angria now. Whatever we do is legal.
This is all a long way from moral.
sh...he can't etray you now, t if you release e binding for a second...
He'd tear my throat out. Only upside: he'd have likely done that anyway.
He's Zamorna.
Part of me isn't so sure. Part of me thinks that knowing I could do this is the reason why Zamorna liked me more than Izzy...
e enjoyed the competition.
Me and you, Izzy. We're quite alike.
We're both bad people and trying not to be.
This is you trying *not* to be?
You convinced me to play the game, Izzy.
If this world matters, we play to win.

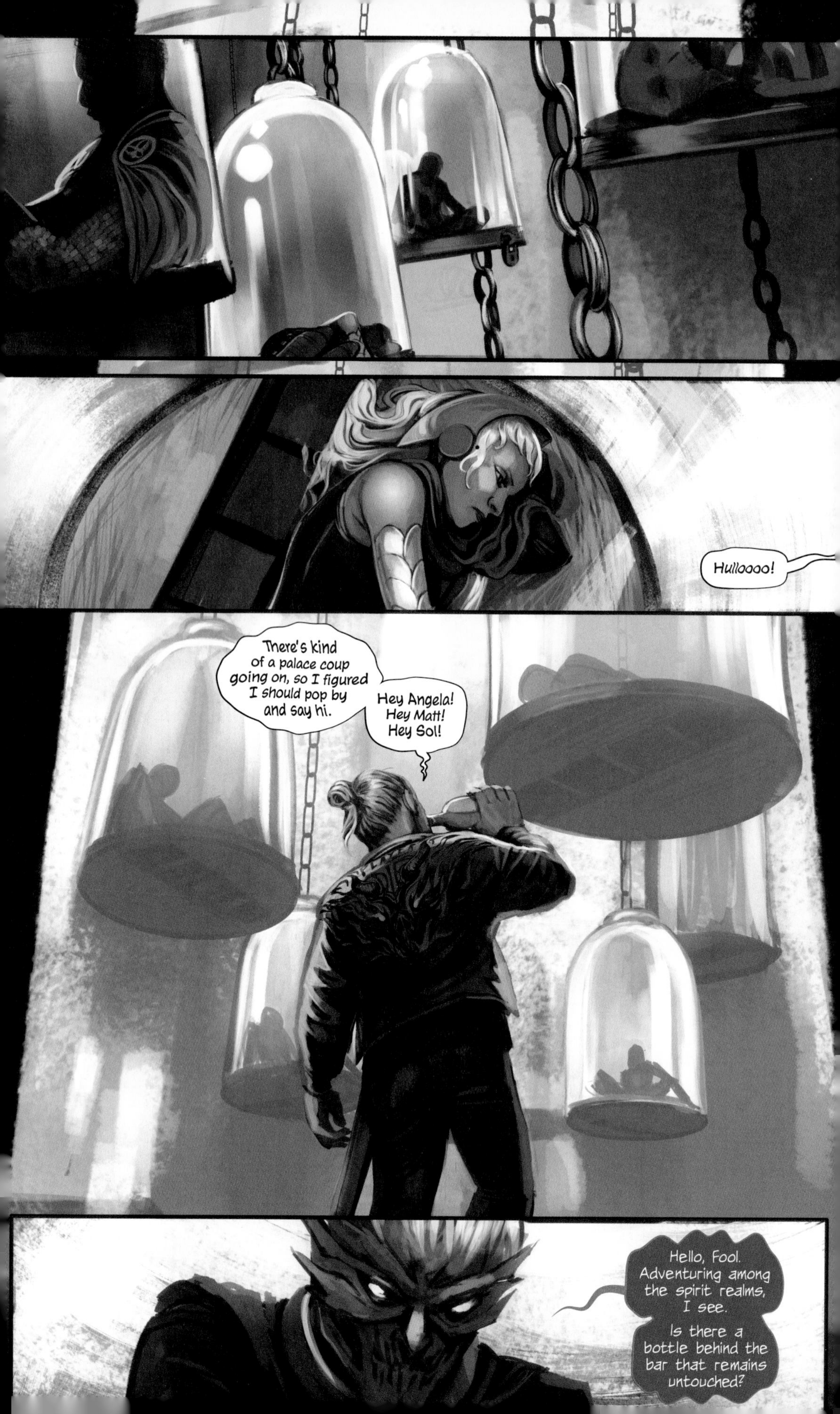
Hulloooo!
There's kind of a palace coup going on, so I figured I should pop by and say hi.
Hey Angela! Hey Matt! Hey Sol!
Hello, Fool. Adventuring among the spirit realms, I see.
Is there a bottle behind the bar that remains untouched?

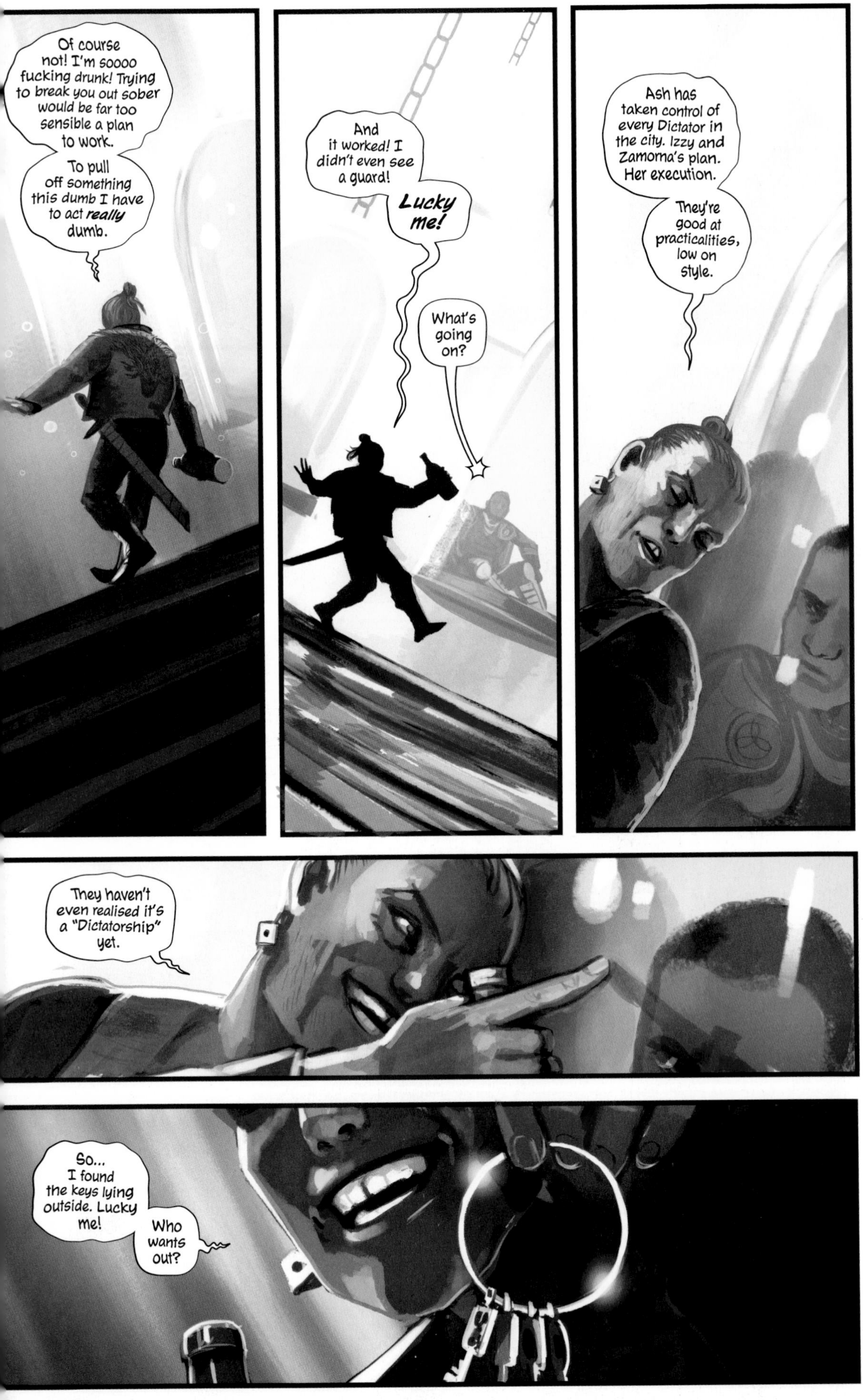
Of course not! I'm soooo fucking drunk! Trying to break you out sober would be far too sensible a plan to work.
To pull off something this dumb I have to act *really* dumb.
And it worked! I didn't even see a guard!
Lucky me!
What's going on?
Ash has taken control of every Dictator in the city. Izzy and Zamorna's plan. Her execution.
They're good at practicalities, low on style.
They haven't even realised it's a "Dictatorship" yet.
So... I found the keys lying outside. Lucky me!
Who wants out?

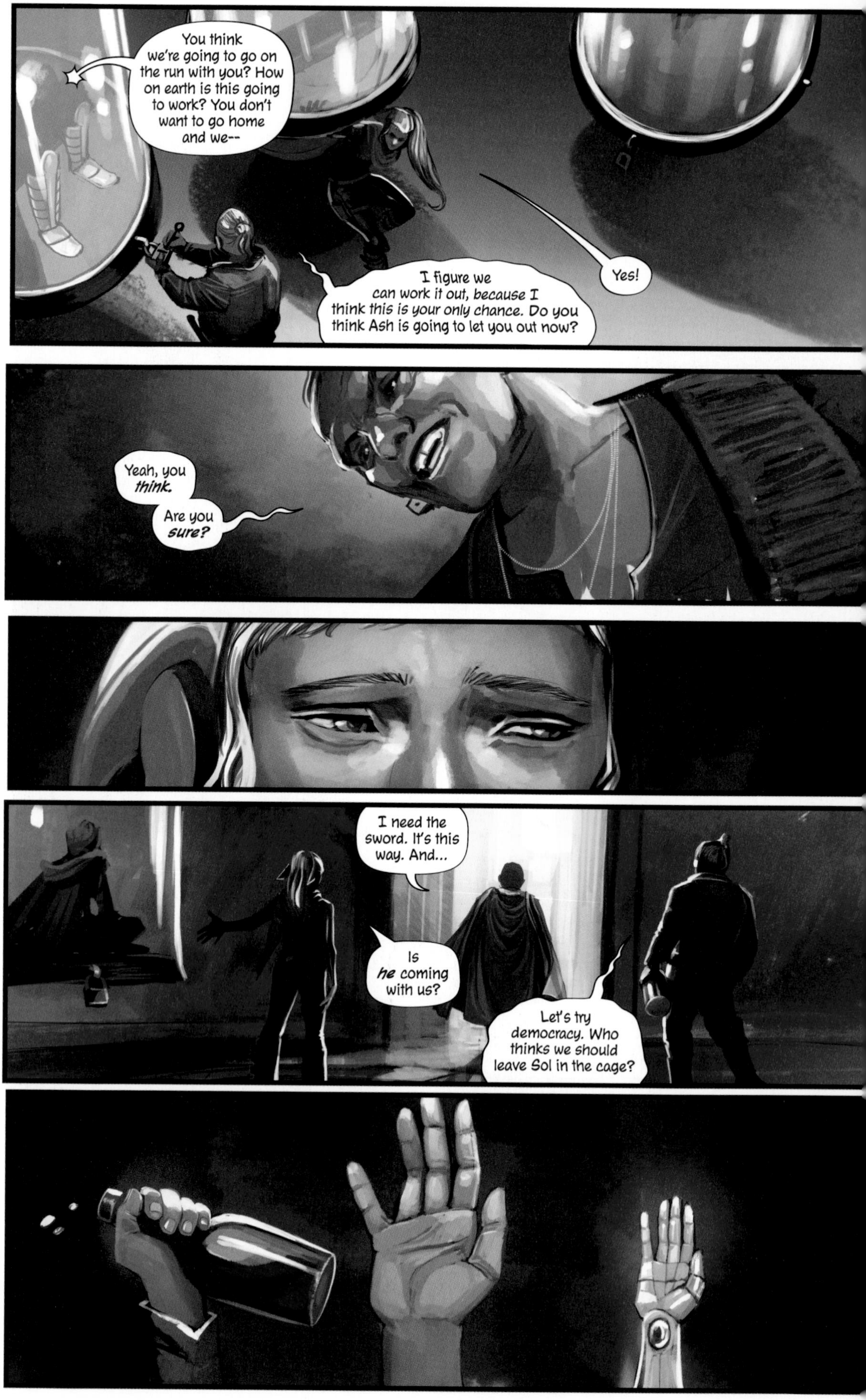
You think we're going to go on the run with you? How on earth is this going to work? You don't want to go home and we--
Yes!
I figure we can work it out, because I think this is your only chance. Do you think Ash is going to let you out now?
Yeah, you *think.*
Are you *sure?*
I need the sword. It's this way. And...
Is *he* coming with us?
Let's try democracy. Who thinks we should leave Sol in the cage?

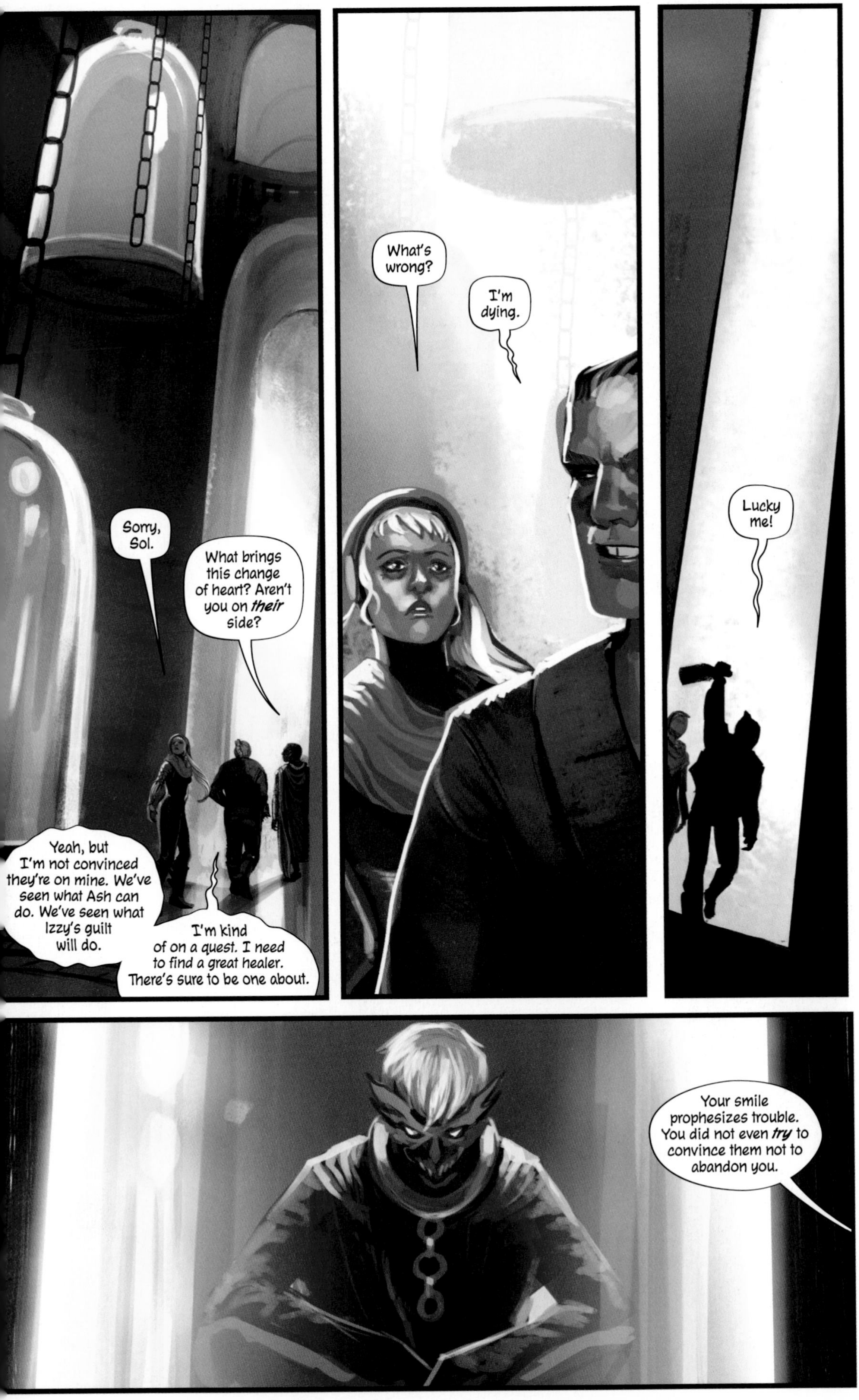
Sorry, Sol.
What brings this change of heart? Aren't you on *their* side?
Yeah, but I'm not convinced they're on mine. We've seen what Ash can do. We've seen what Izzy's guilt will do.
I'm kind of on a quest. I need to find a great healer. There's sure to be one about.
What's wrong?
I'm dying.
Lucky me!
Your smile prophesizes trouble. You did not even *try* to convince them not to abandon you.

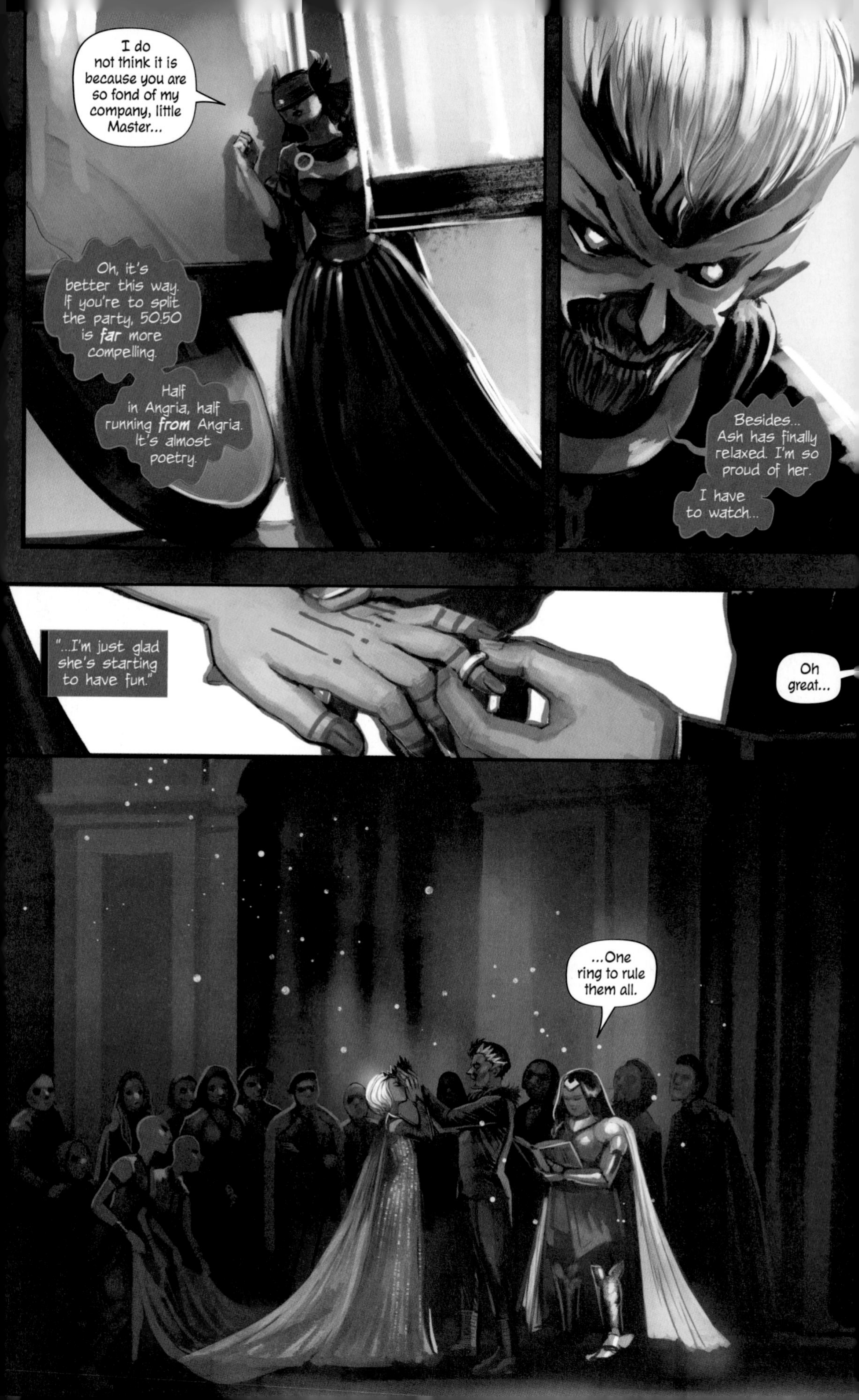
I do not think it is because you are so fond of my company, little Master...
Oh, it's better this way. If you're to split the party, 50:50 is far more compelling.
Half in Angria, half running from Angria. It's almost poetry.
Besides... Ash has finally relaxed. I'm so proud of her.
I have to watch...
"...I'm just glad she's starting to have fun."
Oh great...
...One ring to rule them all.

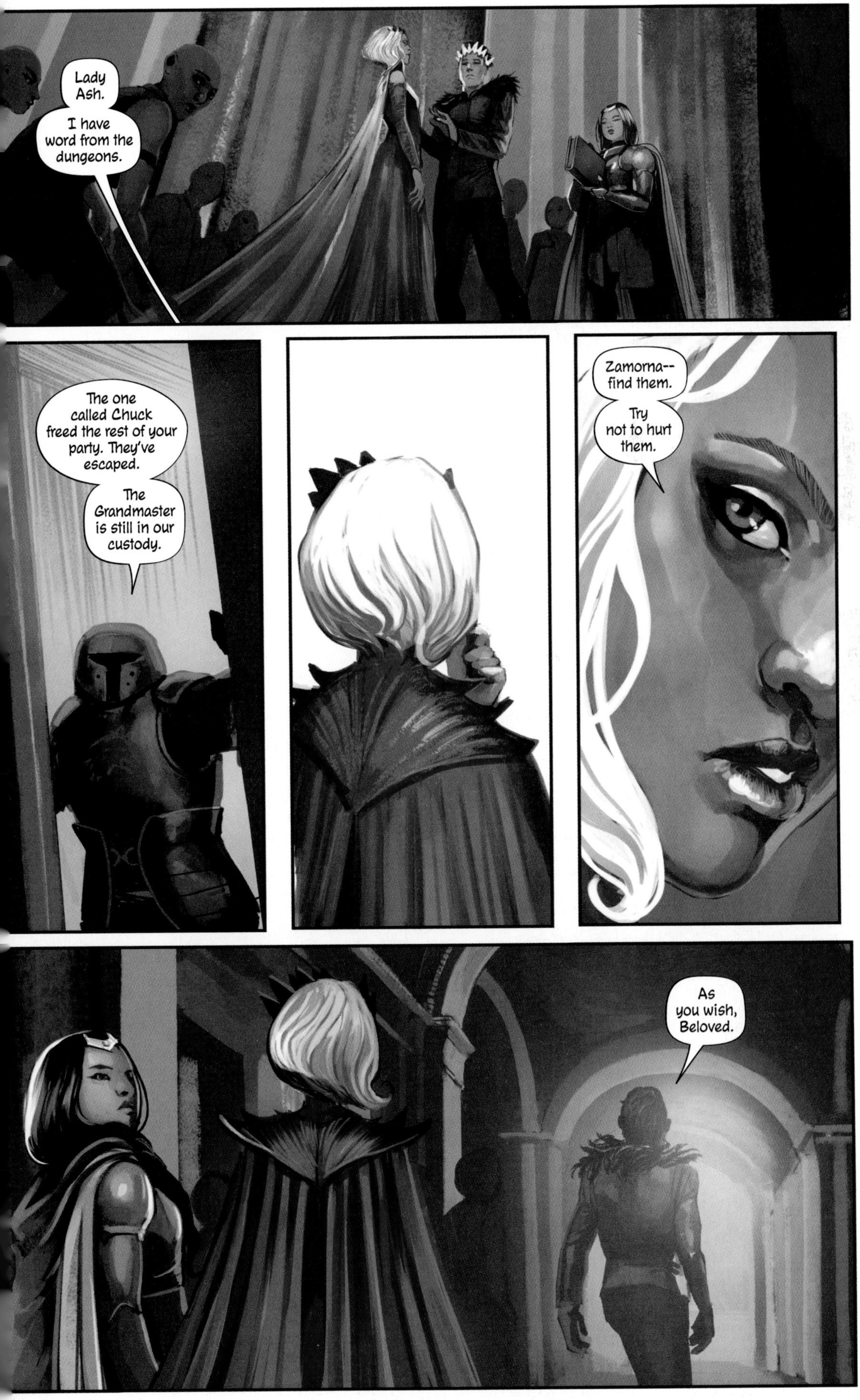
Lady Ash.
I have word from the dungeons.
The one called Chuck freed the rest of your party. They've escaped.
The Grandmaster is still in our custody.
Zamorna-- find them.
Try not to hurt them.
As you wish, Beloved.

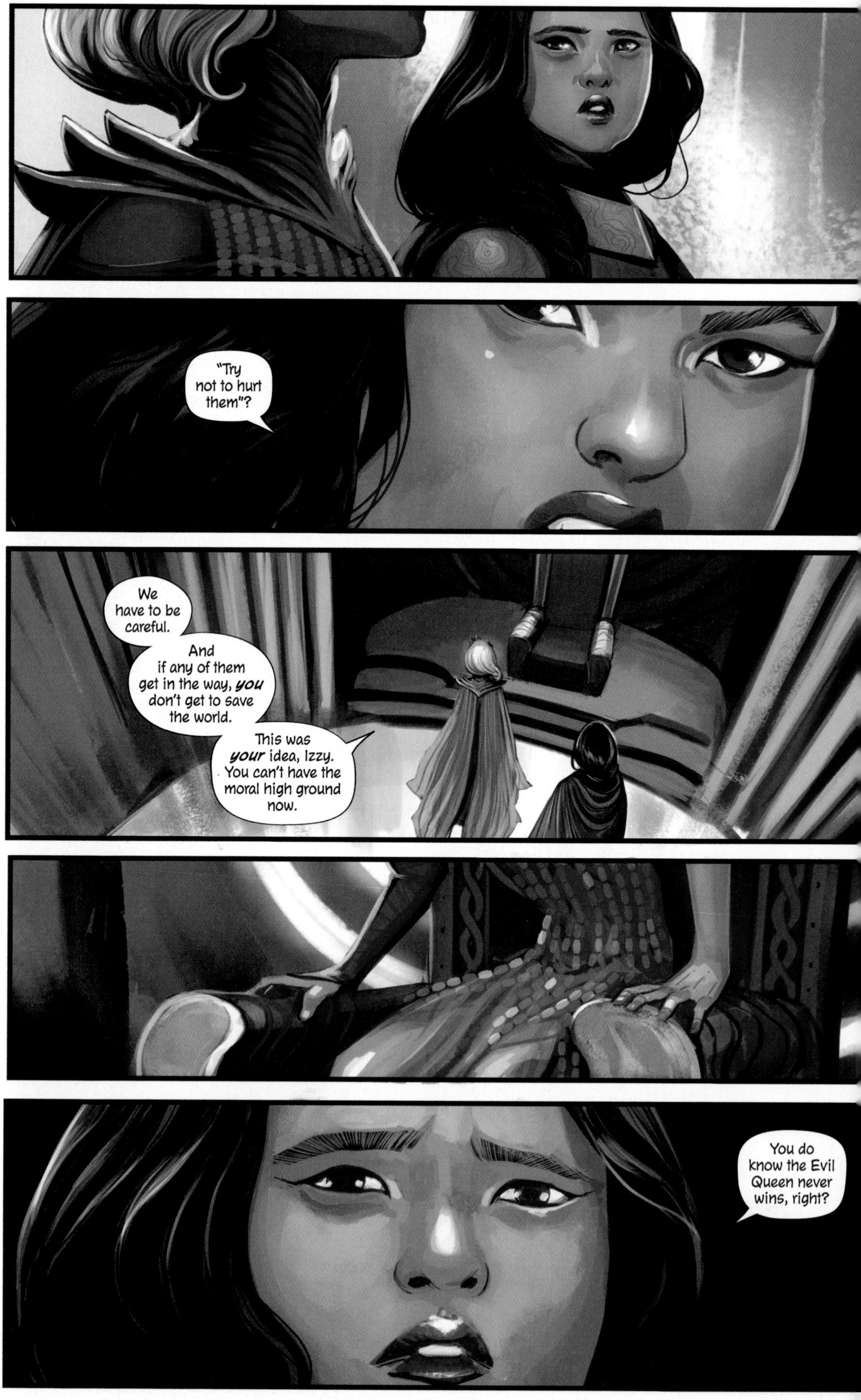
"Try not to hurt them"?
We have to be careful.
And if any of them get in the way, *you* don't get to save the world.
This was *your* idea, Izzy. You can't have the moral high ground now.
You do know the Evil Queen never wins, right?

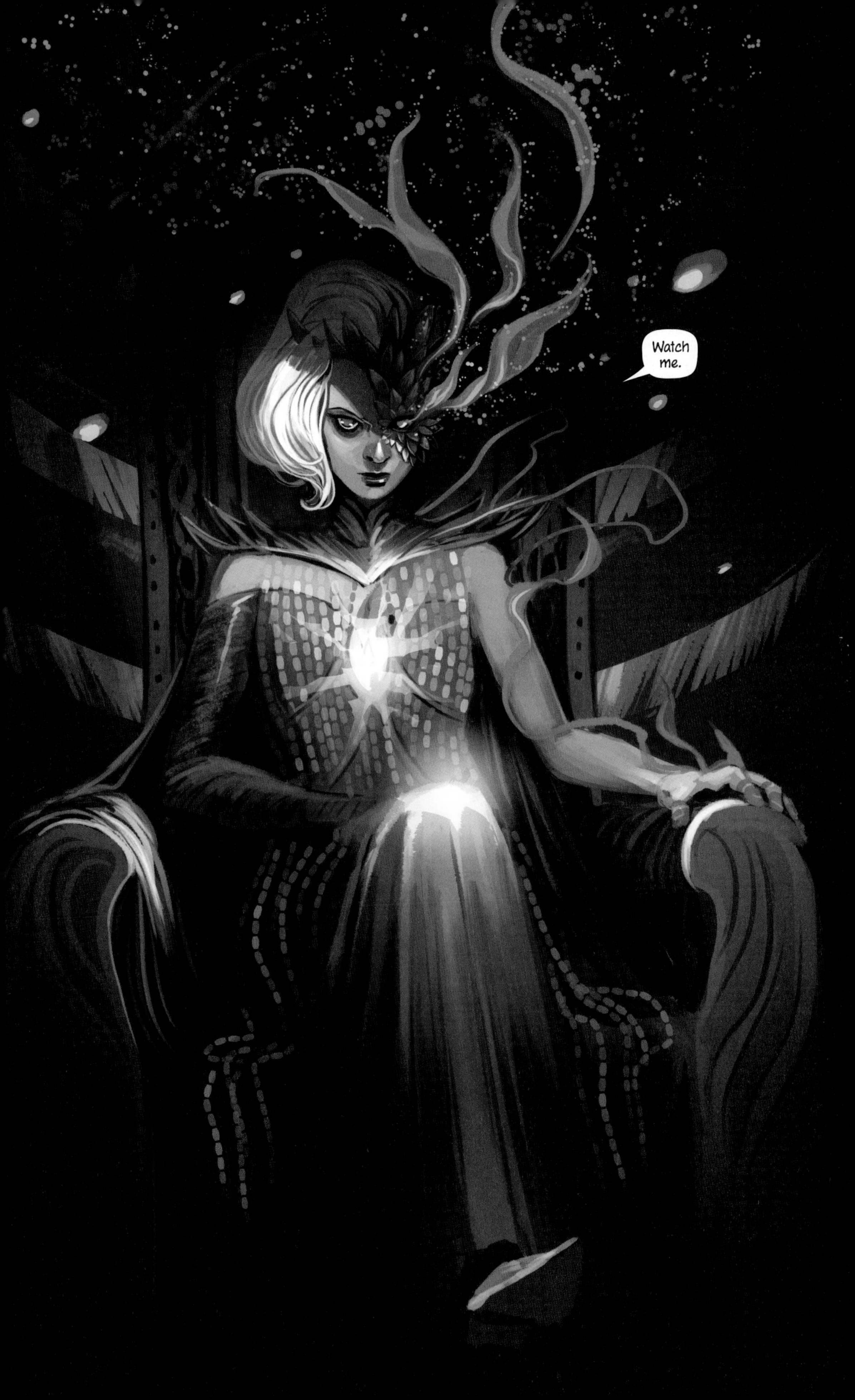
Watch me.

DIE: THE RPG

Turning this whole endeavour into a meta-experience, as part of writing *DIE*, Kieron has been developing a whole RPG. Its beta rules have been released since the first trade dropped, and you can find them here...

www.diecomic.com/rpg

The present rules let you basically recreate your very own version of the first volume. As in, you create a messed up social group, generate some game characters for them, and then drag them into a fantasy world and see if they come home or not. It's designed to take a group of up to six people (including the person running the game) between two and four sessions to play. It's meant to be very flexible and replayable.

When I wrote that last time, it was sort of theoretical. In practice, it's turned out well. There's now an active Discord of folks discussing the game and there's quite a few Actual Play recordings of the game online. The feedback has been worryingly good. This has led to a further release.

As well as some bug fixes and rule tweaks we've also released the Arcana - an additional PDF including lots of other ways to play the game than the basic mode described above. It also includes five folks writing up their experience of running a *DIE* game, which is meant to help people who've never played an RPG get used to the thought process of it. Plus some more essays from Kieron's noggin.

You'll find everything in the link above, including a way to give feedback.

RPG BETA

D
I
E

BASED ON THE COMIC SERIES BY
KIERON GILLEN
AND
STEPHANIE HANS

VARIANT COVERS

Previously to *DIE*, Stephanie was best known as a cover artist. As such, she's entirely thrown herself into commissioning other artists to explore the world she's visualized. The following gallery shows the results of her curation. Kieron just sits and goes "Coo! Pretty."

Peach Momoko
Issue 6 variant

Mathieu Lauffray
Issue 7 variant

Marc Simonetti
Issue 8 variant

Emma Ríos & Miquel Muerto
Issue 9 variant

Anna Dittmann
Issue 10 variant

Justine Frany
Issue 1 cover for Ink Ink

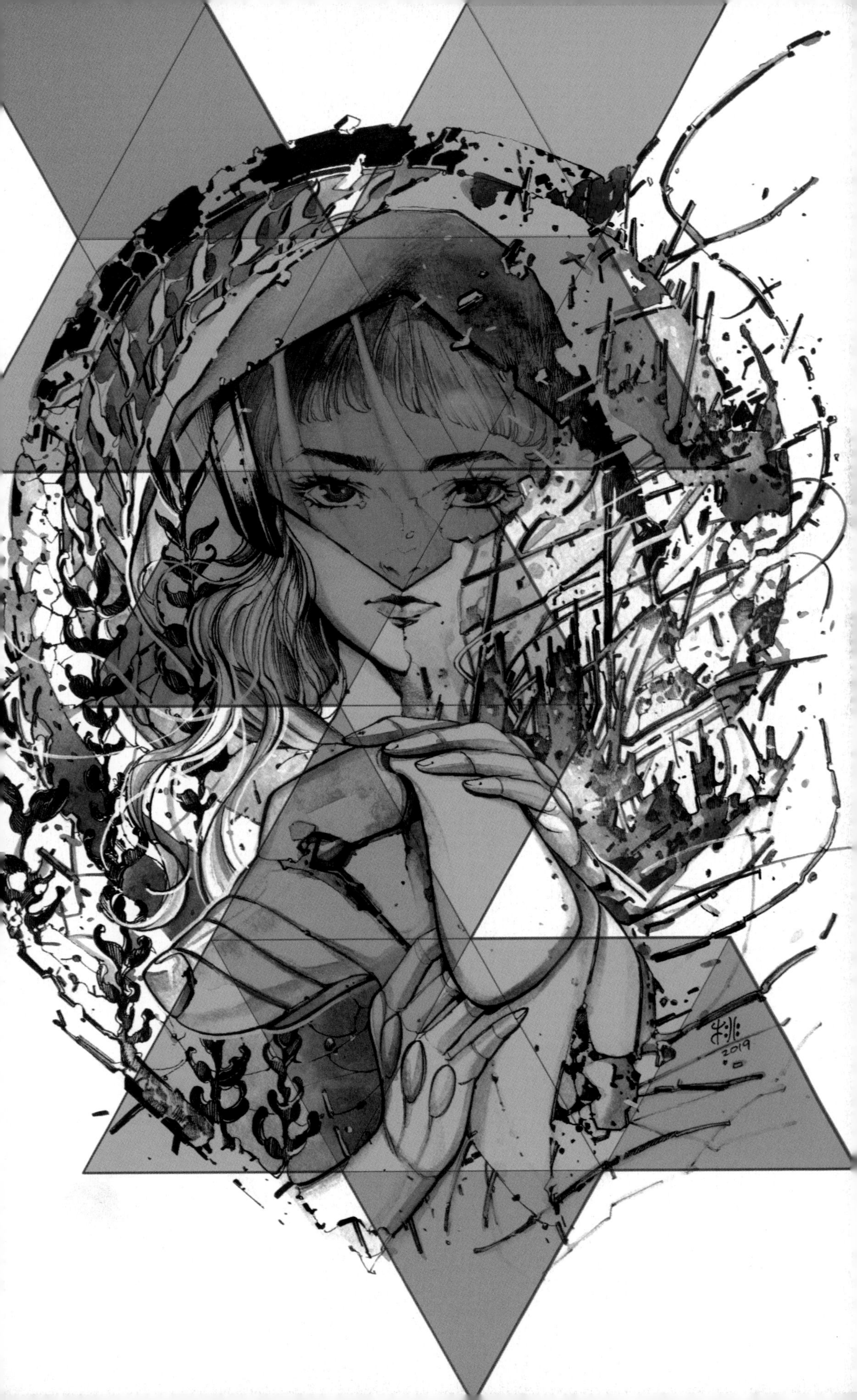

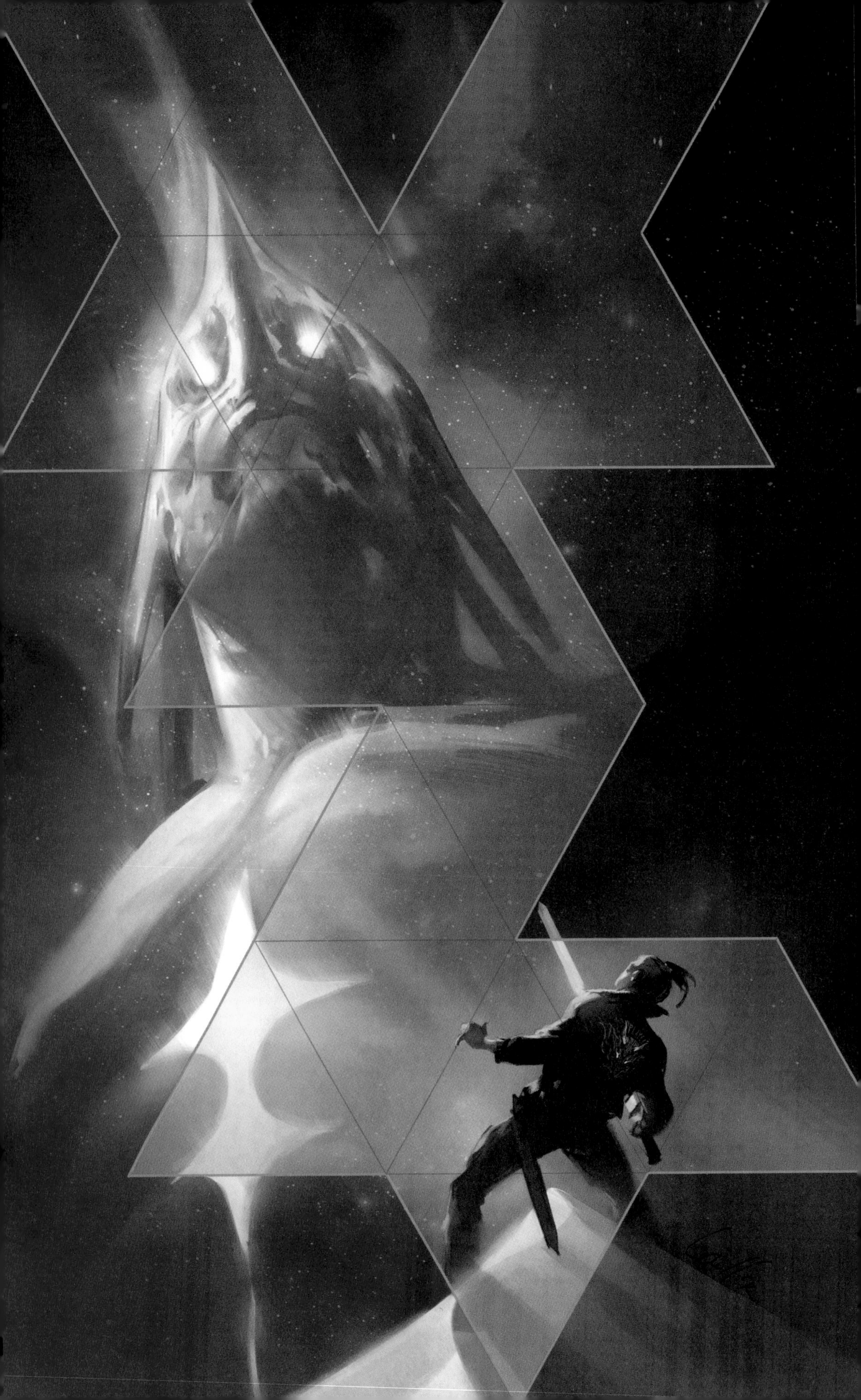

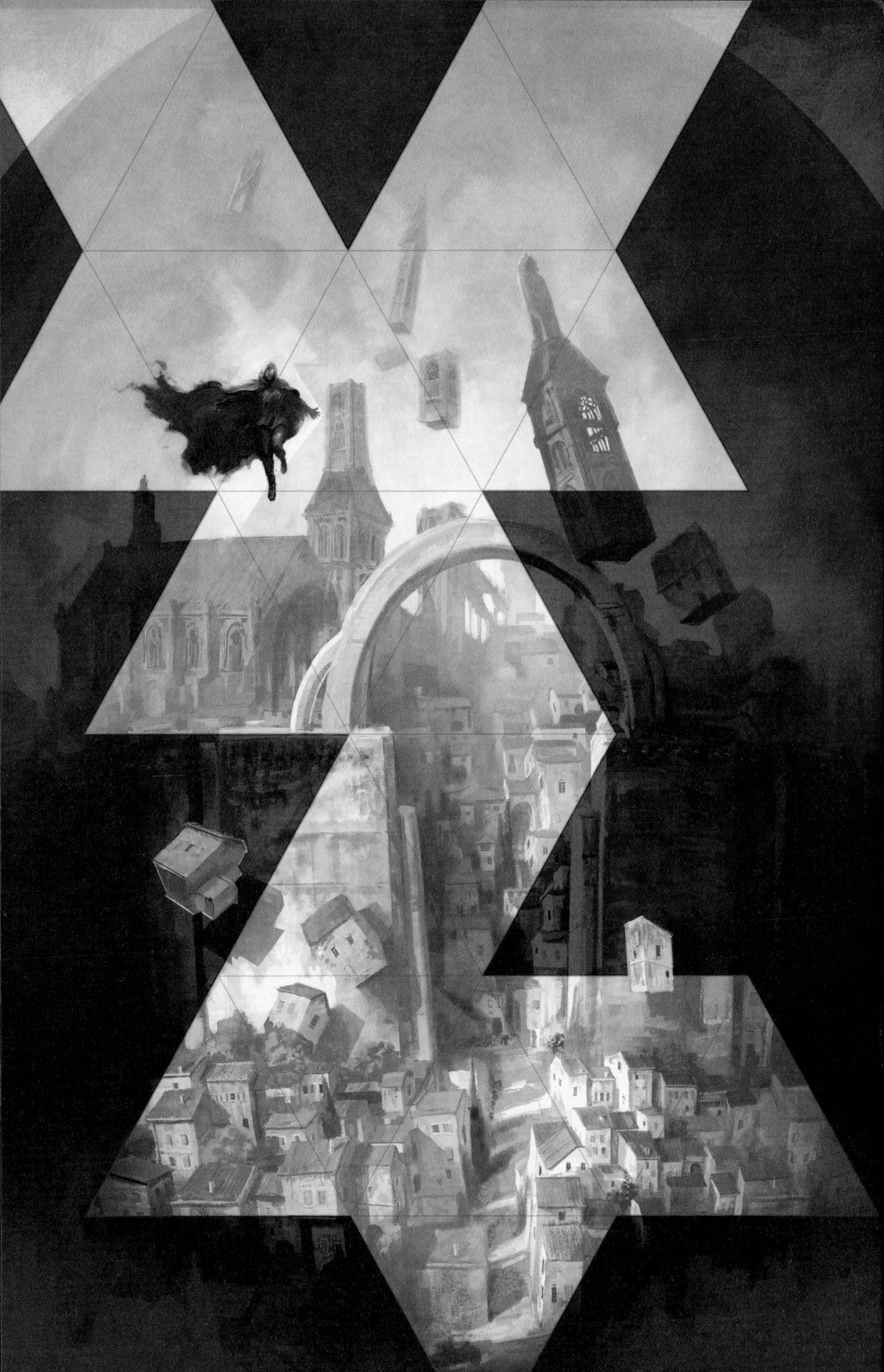

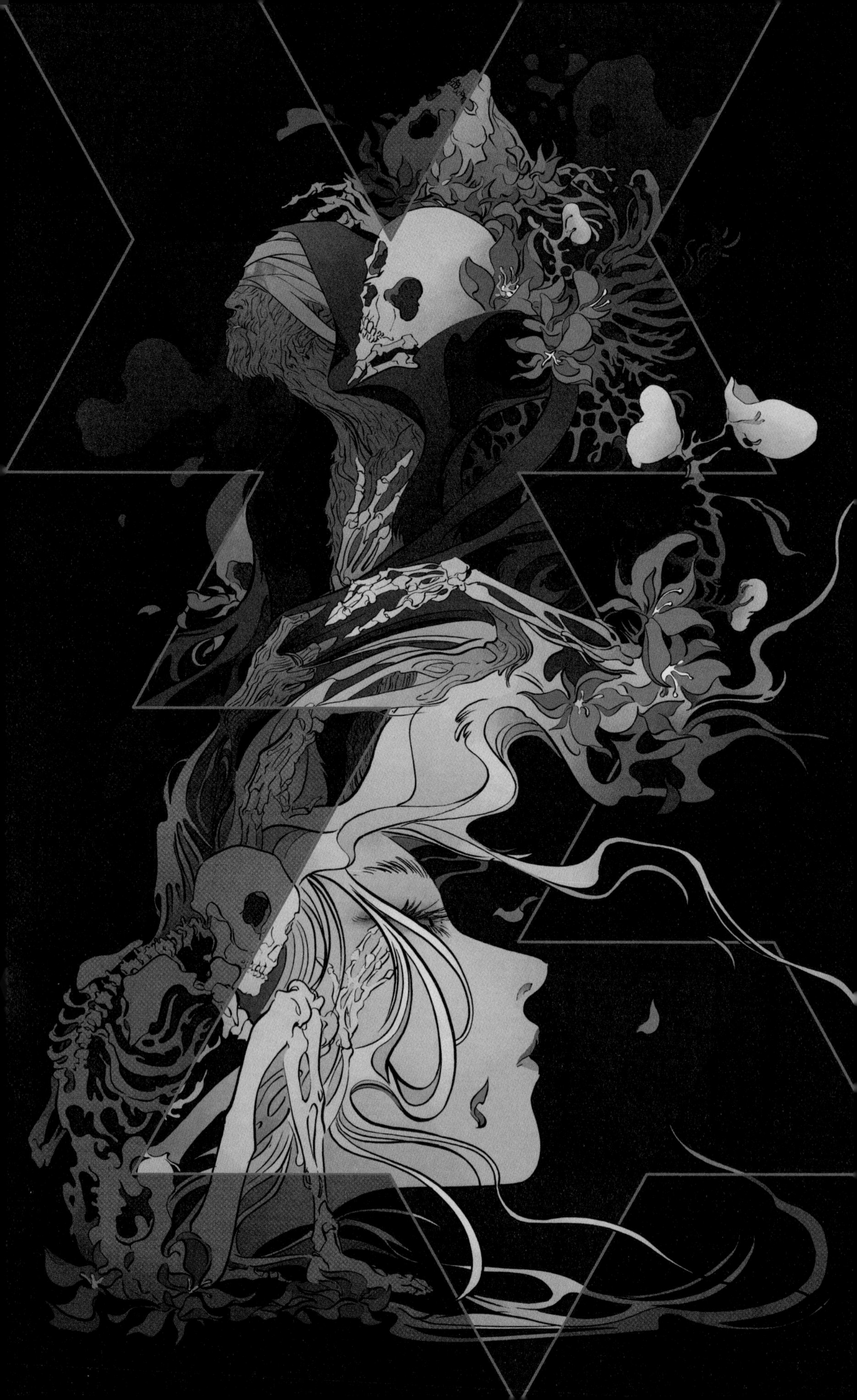

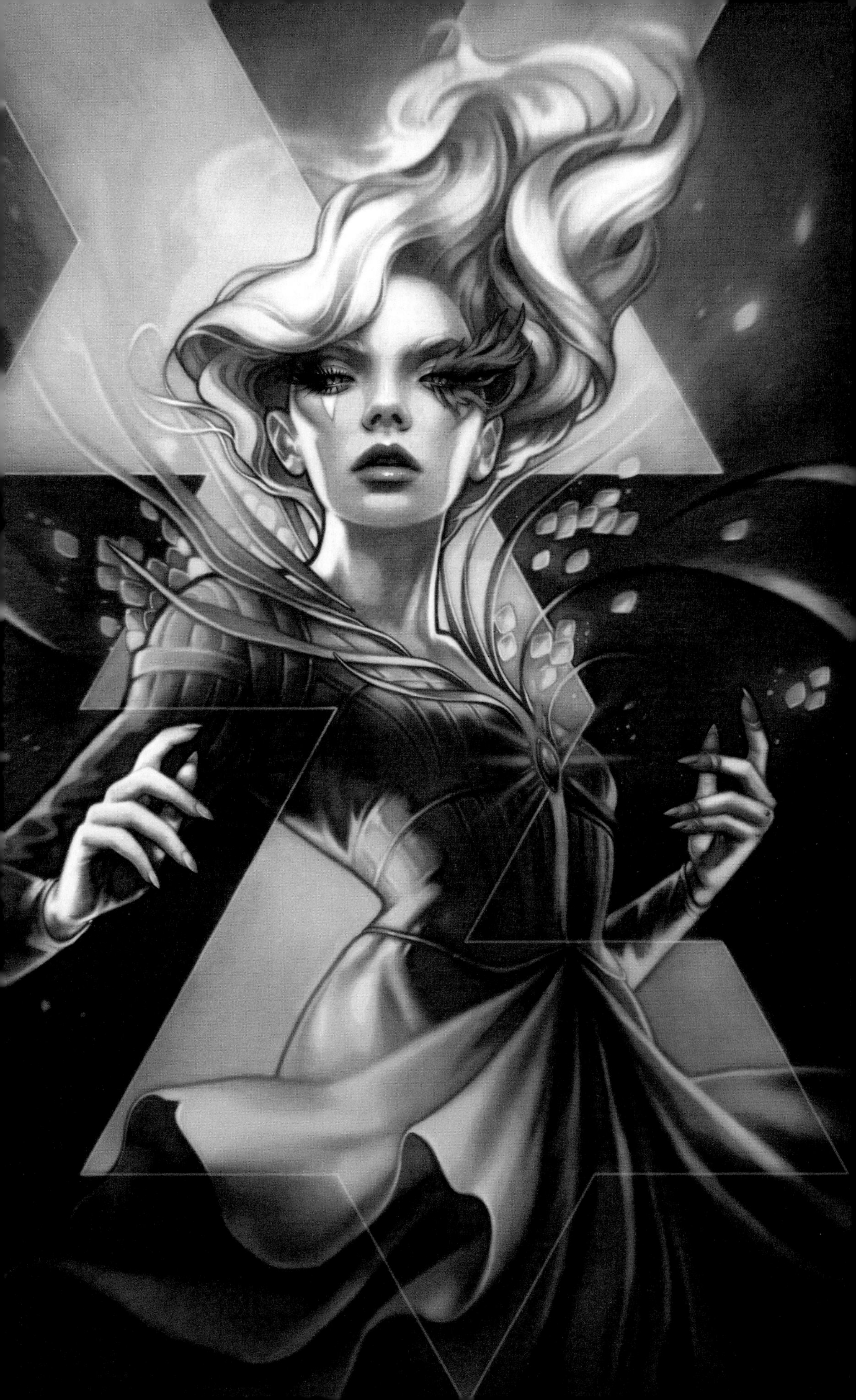

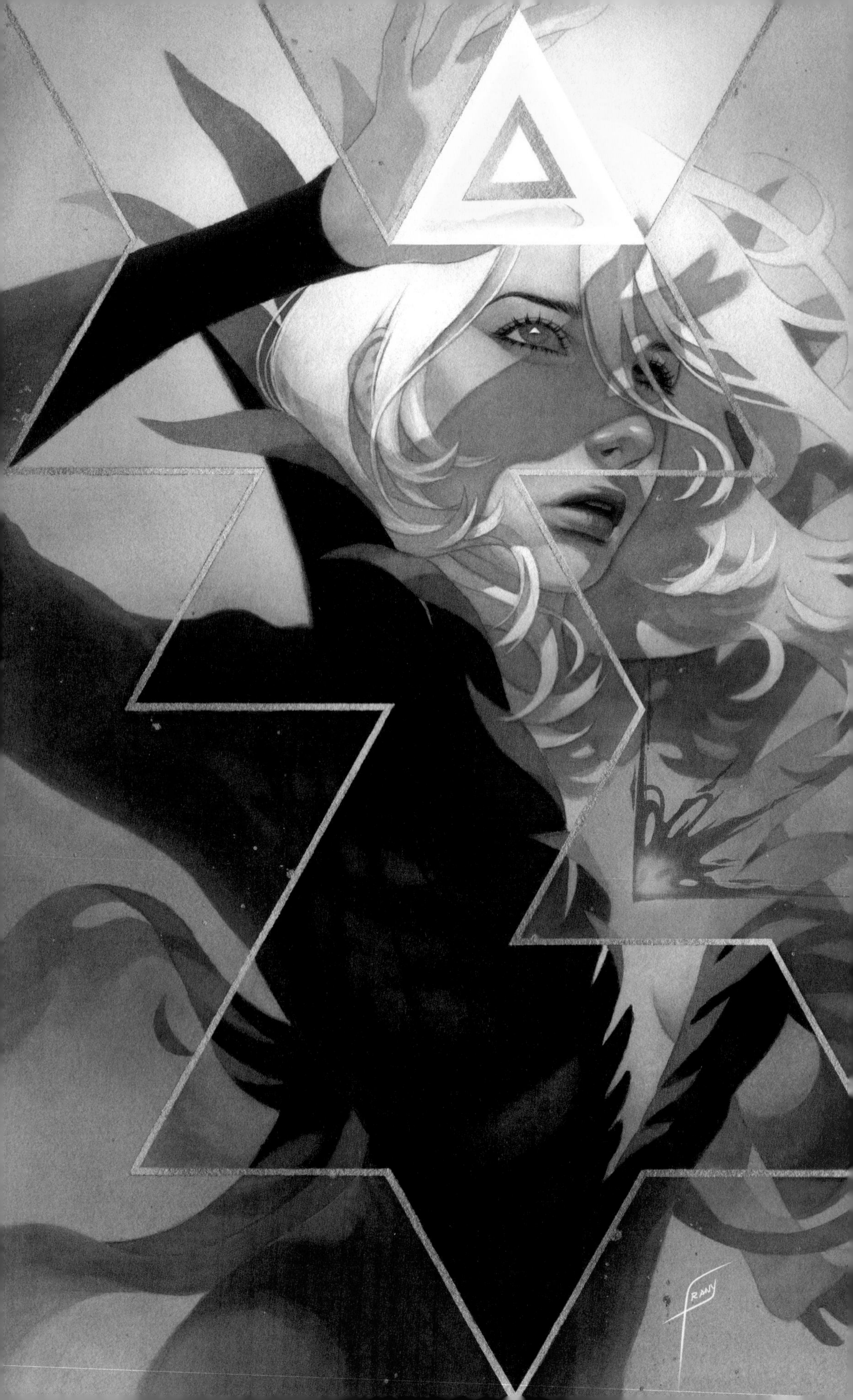

ESSAYS

The single issues of *DIE* have
a variety of backmatter. In the
second arc, with the RPG released,
the space was split between new
experimental rules for the system
and the think pieces which
previously dominated the space.
While rules would be out of place,
the essays are collected here.

BINARY

Welcome back.

I'm worried about this first issue. I said this for every issue of the first arc, so it's not entirely a surprise that I'm feeling it again about this one. But still, it's there. I'm reminded that Matt Fraction had two rules for his *Hawkeye*, which he was very upfront about. If I remember right: "They don't fuck and the dog won't die." Matt has always been a better writer than me.

The issue has two primary influences, one personal and one professional. They're both pretty obvious. I worked as a videogames journalist and critic for fifteen years, and I tried to pay attention. I had to put my cat down last year.

Lemon was found living under a car by a friend. We took her in, and took her to the vet. She didn't have a chip. She did have a heart problem which - as the literature memorably put it - made her "a candidate for sudden death". One day she'd just keel over. One day she did.

We took her to the vet. She was paralysed and in enormous pain. The vet urged us to put her down. We did. It wasn't easy. It isn't easy to write about, and what comes out when you do isn't easy either.

In the first draft of this section, I opened it with something, then instantly deleted it, as it was too cruel to just force it into your mind without warning if you've gone through something similar yourself. That kind of idea must be approached with more kindness. It was "Our cat died last year. We killed it." It's the sort of awful self-lacerating thought that goes through your head, made impossible to easily dismiss because you know it's literally true. It's better that you did it, as the alternative is worse, but it's still true.

Adulthood as that kind of decision. Decisions generally. There's a lot about decisions in life and games both.

It's something a certain generation of game critics thought about a lot. Most key, this is haunted by the famous Sid Meier definition: "a game is a series of interesting decisions". The difference between interesting and meaningful has always fascinated me.

There's some theory in this issue, but a lot more about material reality. In my times interviewing, I got to watch what the industry did to developers. From the off I thought it strange when we mainly talked to them - primarily when a game was about to be released, so they were often visibly exhausted. I felt bad asking questions. I'd have preferred them to have a nap.

This was a long time ago, circa 2000, and while what crunch was was known, the extremes weren't quite so publicly exposed. This was before EA Spouse (yes, google that) and semi-regular exposés of industry practices, followed by public industry decrying of such counter-productive methods before slinking back to something like business as usual. I simplify, but less than you'd hope. There's some companies so tone deaf as to *boast* about how inefficient and brutal their processes are.

The sad thing is that players (generally speaking) don't care. Or don't care enough to actually not buy, which is kind of worse than not caring at all.

I wasn't *planning* on using any of this, of course. With the videogame theme, more elements from that world crept in. With Angela's Neo abilities and the Fair, it'd always be there. The structure of the issue is that of a *Thief* mission (RIP Looking Glass Software) interspersed with a confessional. But, appropriately for a *Thief*-centric issue, it crept up on me. This arc is a process of excavating all these characters. I know them, of course. I knew all the stuff in this story, abstractly. I didn't realise what it meant and why it was relevant to our themes until I started to actually try and turn it into a story. *DIE* is partially about what people are willing to do to other people to get the fantasy they crave. That doesn't just happen in the fantasy worlds.

Honestly, within a week I'm going to go to Stafford to be given an honoury doctorate. Which is both amazing and entirely surprising, but I know there's some videogames graduates in the audience, and I'm not sure a commencement address

which is solely me screaming "BE CAREFUL!" is going to go down well.

I've mentioned a few places to start reading above, but if you want a deeper dive, *Marx at the Arcade* by Jamie Woodcock would be a good bet for a single book. I'm only halfway through the volume, but so far it's an accessible and penetrating look at how the industry works. Or doesn't, if looked through a human filter.

I digress.

You may not think there's much connection between the cathedrals of consumerism that are a modern AAA videogame and small board game design. I'd disagree, and don't have the word count to persuade you otherwise. I suspect I'll come back to it in *DIE*. It's not just the story of the RPG, but how the RPG gave birth to many other things. As I like to say in interviews, what's Twitter other than a game of people pretending to be people they aren't?

A lot surprised me in this issue. Hell, that's the whole of "Split the Party": being surprised at what a deep dive into a character reveals. I don't think any of them are quite as bleak as this one, but your mileage will vary. I think of how *DIE*'s structure is unlike some of my previous work, like *The Wicked + The Divine*, and think of Stephanie's description of me as the Dungeon Master of this world. There is something unusual in the energy of writing the book. I have a conspiracy backstory for the characters (players/ readers) to uncover. I have some sizeable set pieces. But I have six people thrown into the middle of it, and seeing how they respond exactly to the situation is unlike anything I've written before. I've had moments, but not the uncanny sense of peering into a fantastical world.

Given *DIE*'s themes, this is not exactly comforting. **KG**

HACK

Are you aware of *Garth Marenghi's Darkplace*? Cult 00s British comedy about a writer's 1980s hospital-set horror show, framed with 00s-period talking heads. Coiner of memorable phrases such as "I've met writers who use subtext and they're all cowards." Also, too close to home for almost everyone I know in this biz. We're all one bad day away from being Garth Marenghi.

Chuck had his bad days a long time ago, and he's lost in his personal Darkplace.

Hmm. That line may mean today is my bad day and I have become Marenghi, destroyer of words.

I've been surprised how this arc has shaken down. These first two stories are grappling with two different takes on working inside the fantasy industry. The rest aren't - Matt, Izzy and Ash's are something quite different. Finding exactly what the issues are about is very much this arc. When I write an ongoing, the first arc is usually the one which is machine-engineered. It's designed to explain the book. The second arc gives me space to find what the book means

to me. I've taken to describing *DIE* as *Lord of the Rings*, as told solely via conversations in pub toilets. That's not quite true, except for when it is.

We reach the region of Three this time, which is us being cute. I knew I wanted to drop them in the middle of a desert. Where? On the opposite side of Eighteen (the home of Glass Town) is Three. Three, if pronounced with my speech impediment, is Free. It's a free space. The ultimate desert would be a blank region. What's a blank region for? In the world of commercial RPGs, we all know: the expansion pack. Hence, the Expanse. So cute... but also a little sinister. By implication, one day this space will be filled.

This seems a very *DIE* feeling. **KG**

SYSTEMS

I'm something of a control freak. At least part of the magic of role-playing games is that they're out of your control. When you reach for the dice, control is taken away from everyone. That most games don't just exist from a group consensus adds to their reality. Something happened, and no one chose it. That's the reality of the world we live in. We can choose our actions, but not our consequences.

It's something I've tried to cultivate in my thinking around writing *DIE*. Not being random, but things being out of your control, dictated by a system from which novelty emerges. For example, I'm known for doing playlists for my books. *The Wicked + The Divine* one is just shy of 500 songs, each selected for its semiotic load. I tried to work out how the *DIE* playlist would work. I had a couple of false starts. One was period 1991 music - the tactic I used when writing *Rue Britannia* - but the aesthetic didn't match, and *DIE* isn't really *about* 1991 in the way *Rue Britannia* was about 1994-1998. I then tried a *WicDiv* approach, of explicitly just choosing stuff I like which spoke to something in the book. The "like" was the problem. *WicDiv* was about the bangers. *DIE* isn't a banger.

Then the song 'Cherylee' by Gowns came up on shuffle. It's basically four minutes of desolate piano, falling into static, before the vocal lament emerges. It's both bleak, hopeful, odd and just wonderful. I found myself thinking "This is 100% what I want *DIE* to feel like."

I made it into a playlist, and let the algorithm decide what to play when it reached the end. If it suited *DIE*, I added it to the playlist and started again. I seeded the system, but then left it to start making suggestions. Let the machine take care of me. Of course, "take care of" could be meant in the Mafioso sense.

As per usual with my playlists, it comes on when I'm working, and sets me in a "I am working on *DIE*" place. But it's come from somewhere else entirely. Alien mechanics curl around me, and guide (and limit) my choices.

Now, if I was to characterise the classic *D&D* world it would be a "maximalist". As in, anything goes. If you go back to the earliest 1970s days of the hobby, it was even more so - there's many sci-fi notes which have actually been dialled back. Compared to the relative purity of a literary fantasy novel, which tries to create a world with the minimum of moving parts and explore each perfectly, *D&D* will throw in as many kitchen sinks (+3 versus scarabs) as it can.

This isn't a problem. In a world with flying folks, castles wouldn't look like castles do in ours, but we

want castles, so fuck it. This makes archetypal *D&D* actually closer to superheroes than you'd think. Kurt Busiek argued that a core part of superheroes is that you introduce this sense of the fantastic into the modern world, and it basically changes nothing. The point of Spider-Man is that he could swing past your window. If you change the world, you rapidly segue into something that's speculative fiction. Equally, the classical *D&D* games posit that you can introduce huge technological and sociological changes, and still have basically a quasi-medieval world.

If you know RPGs, you're howling exceptions. Just go with me.

Trying to balance the two contrasting elements of RPGs in *DIE* was the battle - one is about 'Anything Can Happen In This Dungeon!' and the other is about what emerges from modelled systems. As in, messy fiction versus pure rules. The former comes in the structuring of the world - *DIE* is a meta world, consisting of twenty realms, each devoted to an influence that went into *D&D*. The messiness becomes the point, and the world politics mirror the elements at war in the genre.

But the rules side is *DIE*'s specific iconography - the paragons, the dice and all that. As such, I try to have as much as possible emerge from a limited set of rules. While the exploration of the 'meanings' of dice is one part, I return time and time again to Robert Plutchik's wheel of emotion (which argued that all emotions were made of eight emotions, differences created by either intensity or mixing them).

If there are knights of each emotion, and they gain power by feeling it... what could each knight be like? I thought it through. The Joy Knights, as shown in this issue, are one of the earliest realisations. A fighter who has to be happy to be effective? That's going to be someone who enjoys fighting... and likely killing, because if they kill and they feel any negative feelings, that's their power gone. So, logically speaking, Knights of Joy are commonly ethical monsters.

If in doubt in the world-building, I tried to reintegrate the wheel. For example, I knew there would be twelve gods - one for each side of the D12. I knew the gods would have to skew to the archetypes required for a pantheon... but archetypes are also traps, clichés with a PhD.

I looked for another limitation, and noticed that there were 24 combinations of two emotions. That's twice as many as I needed. I played with having 24 gods, and then realised that if you took the opposite pairs, you had twelve sets. These were things like 'Shame and Dominance', 'Hope and Unbelief' and 'Love and Remorse'. These tended to be contradictory, which was interesting. I used them as a writing prompt.

I believe the first I made work was 'Delight and Pessimism' - a take on a fate god, but one who knew things were always going to go wrong, and just loved it. Hence, Mistress Woe. If it wasn't her, it was the god of 'Love and Remorse', a fertility/healing god who comes from a place of knowing that all her children will eventually die. The Mourner.

It became a game as much as anything - matching a personality trait to a godly role a pantheon needs. In fact, so much of *DIE* is about making things a game, and knowing that being unable to choose the easy option forces you into novel places. There's also, under it all, a belief that having a system, even if no one else sees it, adds a weight to the world, in the same way the laws of physics keep us grounded in ours. That's the theory, anyway. **KG**

RESEARCH

Yes, when I was down the research hole for this, Los Campesinos' immortal lyric "DON'T READ *JANE EYRE*!" kept coming to mind. I don't think Gareth and company were thinking of the cosmic horror implications though.

We'll have one of these issues in every arc, where we take a major figure in the history of the imagination and explore them. Tolkien was in issue 3. This is different. Tolkien is more obviously connected to the role-playing game than the Brontës - you can assume more knowledge in the readers. In this case, it's more likely people would be unaware of the material, which means we have to be more explicit, as folks need to *know* it.

I include myself in that. I've talked about *Playing at the World* as the history of RPGs which I found the most useful, and this is probably the single biggest thing I found in it. I was already aware of the development of the modern fantasy genre, German wargaming and how various figures straddle the two. I *didn't* know about the Brontës' childhood shared fantasies ("paracosms" to be technical) and how they continued to absorb them throughout their short lives. It's only a small section in the book, but where Peterson describes a teenage Charlotte sitting in the dark, eyes shut, writing stories in tiny text as the only way to satisfactorily immerse herself... well, that was a magical moment. Leaning back, I laughed, happily, in recognition: "Oh god, Charlotte. You are totally my kind of weirdo."

In truth, I hadn't read any of the Brontës before I conceived *DIE*. I'd thrown shapes to 'Wuthering Heights' on dancefloors across the realm, but I don't think that counts. In other words, there was a lot of research - both reading the relevant books, biographies, chunks of the juvenilia, and more. I did a lot of reading with Tolkien, but I knew more of it before I started. This was all new. I had an idea for a story, instantly. This is typical for me: it was true with *The Wicked + The Divine*'s historical issues too. Normally, the delving through the books is about discovering whether the story is viable, and correcting areas where it isn't. The big change from the original conception was how it mirrored the present day cast - I originally thought Charlotte was akin to Sol, being the originator of the whole endeavour. The more I researched, the more I found that Branwell was our Sol. Charlotte, like Ash, desperately wants to give up this dalliance while being enchanted by it. Branwell is all in, for better and worse. Anne and Emily are marginal in the story, but that's an unfortunate side effect of the holes in our sources (i.e. we have far less of their juvenilia). I'm not sure if we'll ever get to the implied war between the four's echoes in *DIE*, but it was a fun thing to hint at.

It was a joy getting to know them. The moment when I tied together the "Rochester as Branwell surrogate" reading, and his particular fate in *Jane Eyre* and how that links to *DIE*'s Sol... well, that's the sort of moment that makes all the work worthwhile.

Er... *Jane Eyre* spoilers.

Then, as with all the things in *DIE*, the strangeness started to creep in.

To choose the smallest thing, "Gondol" is my typo. It slipped into my early notes and stuck, and so *DIE*'s version of the Emily/Anne Gondal has the wrong name. However, I'm far from alone in my mistake. It's all over the place - academic footnotes, articles in the national press, everywhere. And the Brontës' handwriting (and teenage spelling/grammar) is famously abysmal. I kept on wondering whether it *was* meant to be Gondol, and the recurrence of the typo is something trying to reassert itself.

There's also the weird thing with the timing.

I knew I was going to write this issue for about two years. Abstractly, I could have written it at any point for about a year, in terms of just cutting off the research and doing it. As per usual, I left it until the last possible moment.

The Monday of the week I *had* to write this issue, I found myself in Bradford. I realised I was ten miles from the actual Brontë parsonage. I had to be back in London by mid-afternoon, but calculated I could get a taxi there, spend half an hour there, and still make my appointment.

I made the pilgrimage.

For a historical work, this is just useful. Partially it's grounding yourself emotionally in the environment, partially it's just plain factual - you see the details you can't get from sources. You can know things like (say) the kids in the room where they created Angria would be out of sight of their father as he wound the clock on the staircase. You get to see the curious artefacts in the flesh. The tiny books they wrote their stories in are just weird marvels, Charlotte's paintings and drawings...

That Stephanie decided to do the story-within-a-story in traditional inks rather than painted actually seems, to me, to recall the work I was looking at in the parsonage on my visit. Stephanie was joined by Elvire De Cock, who coloured the inks. As people who loved all arts, I found myself thinking the Brontës would approve of their appearance in comics, in form if not content.

So it was useful... but I kept coming back to the strangeness of the timing. The *only* point in the whole year when I was anywhere near the parsonage was the exact day I needed to actually start writing the story.

DIE, once more, feels like an engine turning. Mechanisms moving, ensuring a story is made.

I find this fascinating. I do not always find it comforting. **KG**

SPOTLIGHT

My suspicion of false dichotomies makes me try and avoid those social games where your answer to a single question pretends to meaningfully divide a group into two fundamentally different sorts or people. Am I a Dog Person or a Cat Person? Only if I'm playing a Werewolf or a Tabaxi, mate.

Despite that, some nag at me, and one came to mind when writing this issue. I suspect you can guess someone's aesthetics depending on how they respond to: "Do you like Cersei in *Game of Thrones*?" I'm sure you know my answer.

So, another arc over, a new status quo revealed and our direction set forth. The next arc is the largest scale of any of the books, our War of the Rings with a Godspeed You Black Emperor soundtrack, and we can't wait to show it to you.

Anyway. This issue. It is a lot. On the creative side, I'm aware I've been cramping Stephanie too much in this arc, so I was trying to give as many big moments and splashes as possible. Partially as Stephanie luxuriates in the space, and partially because the climax of the arc needs to feel bigger. There's a general guideline in comic writing that Space Equals Meaning. The emotional size of a panel is increased by the physical size of it. I wanted to lean into that.

I'm also struck by how specifically unusual the collaboration in the book has become. When writing the sequence with the Dictators I gave three options for where to place the pyramid - two researched from various bits of the Angria juvenilia and a third created from scratch. Stephanie could pick whichever she wanted to draw. At the time of writing I don't even know which one she's picked. This is very much not my normal method when writing comics.

Most of all this issue is back to Ash as the lead. I've missed her. This arc was highly character-focused, letting other people step up to the mic. There's a concept in RPGs which maps well to multi-plotted comics - spotlight time. As a GM, you should be aware when a player hasn't done anything in a while, and let them have a chance to step forward. (In passing, one of my fave player attributes is people who actively pass the mic too.)

Anyway - as Ash defined the first arc, this one was about letting the other characters catch up with their spotlight time. Now it's equalised, and we can move to a different mode in the next arc and bounce the spotlight a lot more inside an issue.

And eventually we're going to talk about Sol, yeah?

Talking about spotlights, this is all about the deep dive into the Dictators and some of the big themes for Ash. The issue title is a reference to a safety device for games, where a player taps a card marked with an X to signal their emotional discomfort with what's just happened in a game. The group steps back, and goes a different way. Do google Safety Tools for RPGs as there's lots more, and it's essential. Monte Cook recently released a free guide to consent in gaming, which is a good place to start.

Bar the general theme of consent in the issue, there's also the basic pun of "X-Card". X as Ex. Zamorna is the Ex. He is well and truly played. **KG**

A STORY

I have a story. It is not really a secret but at the same time it is not a story I ever told to anyone. I guess you could call it an origin story.

Here goes...

In June 1998, I went to a party in the woods close to Strasbourg. The weather was sweet, we danced and drank, we made a fire and some of us decided to sleep there.

I woke up at the moment where the night morphs into day, and I remember seeing everything all green around me. The forest was intensely full of life. The green was overwhelming:

intense, beautiful, and my skin was like a radiant reflection of the forest, as was the skin of the people with me. We were 20ish, almost adults, taking our time before letting go of the last moments of our teenage selves. We were young, innocent, and we would live forever.

I took my bicycle, left my friends with a laugh and started to head back, riding alongside the river in the soft light of the sunrise. I saw a hare and a deer. And I remember being so submerged by the beauty of this moment.

A few minuted later, I arrived at the bridge. It was broken. There were tire marks on the road. And a car under the water. And a young man inside.

On this day I learnt something about colours and a thing about tragedy.

Tragedies are the cruellest when they arrive at a beautiful moment. It just feels so incredibly unfair when the universe is so radiant,

full of life and joyous, while at the same time it stabs your heart and crushes your hopes.

In the end this is what I am trying to do when I paint difficult scenes, like the death of a dog. For which I shall never forgive K, let that be said.

The thing I learned about colours, now. Colours talk to each other; they sing in harmony. I almost never use a selection tool or a brush to colour my initial black and white paintings. I prefer to use the gradient tool, trying to emulate this moment where I looked at my friends' faces and their whole bodies and clothes were just a luminous gradient of greens, this perfect moment of my life where I knew I would be eternal.

I now know I am not but this image is in my mind and will certainly go on haunting me as long as I have a mind and a desire to paint.. which is as close to forever as humanly possible I guess. **SH**

FURTHER READING

DIE is one of those books which leans heavily on a larger body of general research. The books which were mentioned in the "Further Reading" list last time are still in use, but here are some key additional things which *DIE* used which may be interesting for those of you wanting to explore a little further.

Tales of Glass Town, Angria and Gondol by the Brontës: the best collection of the Brontë juvenilia that I could find. As well as a broad helping from all the Brontës, it includes an extensive introduction, explanatory notes and a list (with potted bios) of all the characters in the text. This material is what is riffed on wildly for tone and characters.

The Brontës by Juliet Barker: the biography which I drew most of the information on the Brontës' lives from. It was picked via being left on a wall I walked past, at a time

when I was aware that I needed to actually get around to reading a proper Brontë biography. *DIE* is often about following this kind of weird coincidence. This is, of course, how Alice gets lost in Wonderland.

Jane Eyre by Charlotte Brontë and *Wuthering Heights* by Emily Brontë: the two of the Brontës' books whose influence shows most here. The former permeates most of Charlotte's story in this book, and the latter's tone creeps in whenever there's a shadow. Anne is a different creature – I suspect we won't get to her sliver of *DIE* in this story, but if you want to imagine her, imagine her tutting at all this. And rightly so.

Dangerous Games by Joseph P Laycock: this was read much earlier, but I ran out of space in the reading list last time. The subtitle "What the moral panic over role-playing games says about play, religion and Imagined world" says a lot. This digs into the exact nature of conflict between religion and RPGs, and chews over some fascinating stuff.

Shared Fantasy: Role-Playing Games as Social Worlds by Gary Alan Fine: a 1983 piece of research, gathered from observations of gaming groups in the late seventies, and I suspect

the first large piece of serious sociological research on gamers. Its main interest to modern eyes is the portrait of a scene in transition – and especially how bleakly toxic that scene could be to modern eyes. There were some off-hand comments early on which made me want to write to Fine to ask for more information, before the book went and gave the details I was looking for.

Satanic Panic: Pop Cultural Paranoia in the 1980s edited by Kier-la Janisse & Paul Corupe: *DIE* uses satanic panic imagery and ideas in its core concept, but is set considerably after satanic panic's peak. I've only used this lightly, but it's been a useful thing to have.

DIE-Compressed: not a reference for the series, but this podcast dives deep into *DIE*, including reading books around the topic and general discussions. If you don't want to wrestle with this stuff, letting Gen and Drew do the hard work and then listening is a smart move. http://die-compressed.libsyn.com

ALSO BY THE SAME CREATORS

KIERON GILLEN & STEPHANIE HANS:

The Wicked + The Divine #15
Collected in *The Wicked + The Divine* Volume 3

The Wicked + The Divine 1831 #1
Collected in *The Wicked + The Divine* Volume 8

Journey Into Mystery
Collected in two volumes, with Stephanie providing covers and interiors on the final issue

Angela: Asgard's Assassin
with Marguerite Bennett and Phil Jimenez

1602 Witch Hunter Angela
with Marguerite Bennett and more

FOR FURTHER INFORMATION PLEASE VISIT:

www.diecomic.com
For comic and RPG news, new issues and updates

#diecomic
The hashtag for whatever social media you use

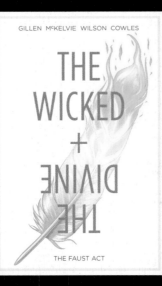

GILLEN McKELVIE WILSON COWLES
THE WICKED + THE DIVINE
THE FAUST ACT

The Wicked + The Divine
Volumes 1-9
With art by Stephanie Hans in Volumes 3 and 8

PHONOGRAM
RUE BRITANNIA
Kieron GILLEN
Jamie McKELVIE

Phonogram
Volumes 1-3

THREE
GILLEN KELLY BELLAIRE COWLES

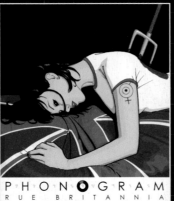

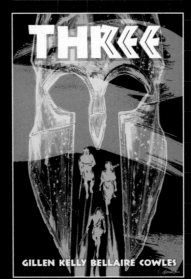

Three
Volume 1

TEAM BIOS

Kieron Gillen is a comic writer based in London, Britain. His previous work includes *The Wicked + The Divine, Phonogram* and *Young Avengers.* He mainly plays low intelligence barbarians or high charisma bards.

Photo: Mauricio de Souza

Stephanie Hans is a comic artist based in Toulouse, France. Her previous work includes issues of *The Wicked + The Divine, Journey Into Mystery* and *Batwoman.* She mainly plays clerics and wizards.

Clayton Cowles is an Eisner Award-nominated letterer, based in Rochester, USA. His credits include everything. He has only played *D&D* once, and was a bard.